A Flowering Tree

A Flowering Tree

And Other Oral Tales
from India

A. K. Ramanujan

EDITED WITH A PREFACE BY

Stuart Blackburn and Alan Dundes

UNIVERSITY OF CALIFORNIA PRESS

Berkeley / Los Angeles / London

University of California Press
Berkeley and Los Angeles, California

University of California Press, Ltd.
London, England

© 1997 by the Regents of the University of California

Some of the tales in this book were published in earlier versions.
Tales 1, 36, 56: "Toward a Counter-System: Women's Tales," in *Gender, Genre, and Power in South Asian Expressive Traditions,* ed. Arjun Appadurai et al. (University of Pennsylvania Press, 1991).
Tales 3, 10, 12, 19, 32: in A. K. Ramanujan, *Folktales from India* (Pantheon, 1991).
Tale 18: "Telling Tales," *Daedalus* 118 (1989): 239–61.
Tale 28: "Hanchi: A Kannada Cinderella," in *Cinderella, A Folklore Casebook,* ed. A. Dundes (Garland, 1982).
Tale 52: "The Prince Who Married His Own Left Half," in *Aspects of India: Essays in Honor of Edward Cameron Dimock,* ed. M. Case and N. G. Barrier (New Delhi: Manohar, 1986).
"A Flowering Tree: A Woman's Tale": in *Syllables of Sky: Studies in South Indian Civilization,* ed. David Shulman (New Delhi: Oxford University Press, 1995).

Library of Congress Cataloging-in-Publication Data

Ramanujan, A. K., 1929–
  A flowering tree and other oral tales from India / A. K. Ramanujan; with a preface by Stuart Blackburn and Alan Dundes.
    p.   cm.
  Includes bibliographical references.
  ISBN 0-520-20398-4 (alk. paper).—ISBN 0-520-20399-2 (pbk.: alk. paper)
  1. Tales—India—Karnataka. 2. Kanarese (Indic people)—Folklore. I. Title.
  GR305.R358   1997
  398.2′0954′87—dc20   95-43422
                                                                  CIP

Printed in the United States of America
9 8 7 6 5 4 3 2 1

Contents

Editors' Preface

Stuart Blackburn and Alan Dundes

"This is my oldest project," wrote A. K. Ramanujan in his unfinished introduction to this collection of oral tales from Kannada, a south Indian language. "In my twenties," he explained "I collected tales from anyone who would tell me one: my mother, servants, aunts, men and women in village families with whom I stayed when I was invited to lecture in local schools, schoolteachers and schoolchildren, carpenters, tailors. I wrote them down by hand and, years later, when I could afford a tape recorder, recorded them. I had no idea what to do with them. I had no thought of writing books. I was just entranced by oral tales. I had read Grimm, Aesop, *Pañcatantra*, Boccaccio, the *Ocean of Story*, and devoured any tale that appeared in any children's magazine. I had no idea I was doing what was called folklore."

A. K. Ramanujan began collecting the tales in this book in the 1950s and continued to collect them until about 1970, by which time he felt he had a representative sample. When he died in 1993, the translations of the tales were complete and he had written notes for many of them; he had also planned to write a brief introduction and a long, interpretive afterword, but neither was completed. Ramanujan's translations and notes appear in the form and sequence in which he left them; his partial list of tellers and collectors and his essay in progress, "A Flow-

ering Tree," are included. As editors we have corrected a few inconsis-
tencies and misspellings in his translations, made minor revisions to his
notes (providing full references and adding others where useful), and
identified tale types and major motifs. We have also provided the bibliography, glossary, and list of tale types. Finally, the sparing use of dia-
critical marks is Ramanujan's.

As both his first project and his final publication, this book spans the
scholarly life of A. K. Ramanujan. He was born in 1929 in Mysore, in
the Kannada-speaking state of Karnataka, where he attended school and
received his B.A. and M.A. in English literature from the University of
Mysore, in 1949 and 1950 respectively. During the 1950s, as a young
college lecturer in several towns across south India, especially in Belgaum, Ramanujan began to collect the tales that appear in this volume.
In 1956 in Bombay he met Edwin Kirkland of the University of Florida,
who encouraged him to send his translations of Kannada tales for publication in the United States (Ramanujan 1956a, 1956b). A few years
later, Ramanujan went to Indiana University to study folklore and linguistics. He received his doctorate in 1963, having already joined the
faculty at the University of Chicago, where he taught for thirty years in
the Department of South Asian Languages and Civilizations and was a
member of the Committee on Social Thought. In those three decades
he inspired a generation of scholars in Indian literature, folklore, and
linguistics, while as a poet, translator, and humanist he reached even
wider audiences. He is the author of eighteen books and many influential essays (see Ramanujan 1996), although his public lectures and in-
formal conversations must also be counted among his many means of
persuasion; one could not speak with him for five minutes without
coming away with five new ideas. No other scholar in the twentieth
century has fostered such a broad understanding of Indian culture
among so many.

His stature was recognized both at home and abroad. In 1976 he
received the Padma Sri, the prestigious cultural award from the Govern-
ment of India, and in 1983 he received a MacArthur Fellowship. In
1990 he was elected to the American Academy of Arts and Sciences.

Toward the end of his life, Ramanujan returned to his "oldest project," the folktale, which in fact he had never put aside. He was interested in all forms of folklore, but as a miniaturist and a student of literature, he was especially drawn to the tale. He read widely and deeply in
folktale scholarship, as his essays on an Indian Cinderella (Ramanujan
1982a) and on Indian versions of the Oedipus story (Ramanujan 1983)

demonstrate. His grasp of the immense corpus of Indian folktales, in their diverse languages, is shown in his masterful foreword to *Folktales of India* (1987) and in his own compilation, *Folktales from India* (1991a). *A Flowering Tree,* offering those tales first collected in the 1950s together with the insights developed over three decades of scholarly inquiry, represents a unique contribution to the study of the folktale in India.

Indian folktales played an influential role in the history of folklore scholarship, supplying nineteenth-century pioneers in the discipline with theories of origins, both Benfey's Buddhist and Müller's mythopoetic (see Dorson 1968). This "Indian School," so-called because it traced the origins of many folklore items to India, arose in part because Sanskrit literature contains the earliest references to some of the best-known stories in the world. The Indian school of folkloristics extended its influence well into the twentieth century because, as one of the mixed blessings of British colonialism, folktales were avidly collected by colonial administrators, missionaries, and their wives. These two strands in the Indian folktale record, Sanskrit story literature and colonial collections, were compared by W. N. Brown in 1919, which might stand as the beginning of the modern study of Indian folktales (Brown 1919). Throughout the twentieth century, tales continued to be collected and analyzed by a similar combination of Indologists and British civil servants, with considerable contributions by Indian and foreign scholars (e.g., Goswami 1960; Islam 1982; Narayan 1989. For bibliographies, see Kirkland 1966; Blackburn and Ramanujan 1986). Research on Indian folktales has also been handsomely assisted by an index of animal tales (Bødker 1957), a motif index (Thompson and Balys 1958), and a tale type index (Thompson and Roberts 1960; see also Jason 1989).

Despite this impressive history of scholarship on Indian folktales—the early theories, later collections, analyses, and indices—several shortcomings are evident. First, the oral performance and social context of Indian folktales are not well researched; second, very few studies analyze multiple versions of a single tale (Troger 1966; Ramanujan 1983; Blackburn 1995); third, careful comparison with international parallels is often neglected; fourth, the emphasis is typically on collection at the expense of meaning; and, fifth, the current tale type and motif indexes are inadequate. Recent and continuing work in Indian languages and European languages has begun to redress these problems, and Ramanujan's scholarship has substantially influenced these efforts whatever the language or continent involved; not only are his books widely read in India, but he personally trained many young folklorists in south India from 1988 to 1991. Although his work did not extend to the first problem listed above, it has contributed to improving the situation in each of the others. Only the work of Verrier Elwin (1902–1964), who collected tribal tales in central India from about 1930 to 1960, bears comparison with that of Ramanujan in that he, too, read widely in folktale scholarship and pursued cultural meanings in the tales; but then Elwin did not know Indian languages as Ramanujan did. Writing a generation later, with the benefit of improved collections and new theory, Ramanujan set a high standard in his scholarship on Indian folktales and stands as a model for others to follow (see Ramanujan 1996).

The genius of his writings on Indian folktales cannot be described in this preface, but a few observations are in order. His knowledge of Indian languages and culture is central, of course, but rarer still is his inventive use of theory (structural, psychoanalytic, and literary). Thematically, one might say that his twin interests were the emotional drama and the cultural patterning of the tale, for these are the focal points of his two sustained analyses (Ramanujan 1982a, 1983). He had a keen interest in the folktale as a genre, yet he always positioned it within wider systems of meaning, such as India's classical literature and devotional poetry. Guiding everything, however, is what we might call Ramanujan's response to the folktale as an aesthetic form. Beyond the motifs and (Proppian) moves, though he attended to these as well, he saw the folktale as a whole, as a fully formed unit.

This coherence he would then break down into formal elements and patterns, such as the multiple meanings of a single word or the hidden structures of repetition or irony. No one reading this book or his other works, for example, will fail to notice his eye for detail, which enabled him, in his own words, to "reanimate" the tale type abstraction. Although motifs might appear to be interchangeable because they occupy the same slot in a plot, they are not identical. The clay mask, which substitutes for the clothes disguise in European Cinderellas, for instance, carries special cultural valences in the Kannada telling. Or, as Ramanujan comments in his essay "A Flowering Tree" (this book), the snake in a male-centered tale is not the same snake as that in a female-centered tale. Concern for the concrete also characterizes his use of theory. He was not interested in grand designs and never reduced a single tale to one conclusion, but he deftly applied theoretical ideas when they actually explained a specific detail in the tale. In this he was like a good storyteller who knows that the imagination loves precision. Perhaps he could be sparing with theories because he understood them so well.

Ramanujan's aesthetic embraced the social as well as the formal; although we pointed out earlier that Ramanujan did not study the social context of tales, this does not mean that he was unconcerned with their social impact. Surely, one of the enduring contributions of his scholarship will be that, with others, he drew attention to the importance of women's tales in Indian folklore and culture generally. Point of view, he said, could so alter the meaning of a tale that the "same" story told by a man and by a woman would be very different. In a widely quoted essay, he showed that women's tales are sometimes "counter-tales," revealing alternative understandings of such key Indic concepts as karma and chastity (Ramanujan 1991b). But one feels that his deepest insights tended toward the personal rather than the cultural, as revealed in the unfinished essay "A Flowering Tree" included here, in which he listens to female voices and leads us into the delicate pain of a young woman's maturation.

The personal depth of "A Flowering Tree" both characterizes this book and separates it from Ramanujan's 1991 collection, which presented "a selection of oral tales from twenty-two languages" in India. Most of those tales were chosen from printed sources, some from the nineteenth century, and from translations of other collectors past and present. In this volume, Ramanujan is more completely in control of the stories because they are all collected from one language, Kannada. One of the four major Dravidian languages of south India, Kannada is spoken by about 35 million speakers, most of whom live in the state of Karnataka. Although less well known than its classical neighbor, Tamil, Kannada has a rich written literature, dating from the ninth century, of mythology, epics (especially Jaina texts), religious poetry, and, more recently, sophisticated novels and plays. Its folk traditions feature a remarkable variety of puppetry, including the life-size shadow puppets in the north, the lively drama of Yakshagana, groups of oral epic singers, and tales. Folktales in Kannada, curiously, have been collected and studied more extensively than tales in any other Indian language (for an overview, see Reddy 1991); dozens of doctoral dissertations have been completed (many published as books) and several thousand tales are now on record, primarily as a result of folklore programs at several universities, the most important being the University of Mysore. It cannot be coincidental that the author of this book was born in that very city.

Strictly speaking, Kannada was not Ramanujan's mother tongue

(Tamil was), but he knew the language intimately; he was born and educated in a Kannada-speaking area, and he used Kannada every day outside his home. Nor did Ramanujan directly collect all of the seventy-seven tales in this book. But he knew them well; he had heard many of them as a boy, had collected many as a young man, and, as a scholar, had discussed many with friends and fellow collectors. He also knew many of these stories on another level because he was a skillful story-teller himself and often recounted them in lectures and conversations.

These are Kannada tales, but they are not only Kannada tales, since many are also told in other Indian languages and in other countries. Separating the Kannada from the Indian from the international content of these tales is beyond the scope of this preface, and we refer the reader to Ramanujan's notes, where he occasionally comments on their over-lapping provenances. Undoubtedly the author would want to qualify any claim that this book represents Karnataka or Kannada tales by pointing out that nearly all the seventy-seven stories were collected in the northern and southern districts of Karnataka; only a few tales come from the western coastal districts, where Tulu and Konkani are spoken, or the mountainous district, where Kodagu is spoken. The tellers, one should add, are disproportionately Brahmin and upper caste. A few of these tales might be characteristic of Kannada ("The Lampstand Woman," for example), but most are known beyond Karnataka. In-deed, these tales might represent Indian tales as well as those collected in any state, since Karnataka, although a "southern state," is quite cen-tral; its northern districts are in contact with Hindi and Marathi, while its southern and eastern areas interact with Tamil, Telugu, and Malaya-lam. Ramanujan would surely point out, too, that while many of these seventy-seven tales are known around the world, no fewer than thirty-two are unrecorded in the international indices. Compare this with Beck's calculation (1986:80) that only 3 percent of the tales in the index of South Asian tales are solely South Asian. Commenting on the inadequate representation of Indian tales in the indices, Ramanujan wrote (in the note to tale No. 10) that "the deficiency of our present tale-type indexes is clearly seen in the absence of all references to mother-in-law tales, a widespread Indian genre. Many of the tales need to be reclassified in Indian terms." In posing these problems concern-ing the linguistic boundaries of tales, their cultural specificity, and their inadequate classification, the author would surely wish this book to stimulate further research.

Interested though he was in these issues, Ramanujan's aesthetic vi-

sion of the folktale always illuminated the tale itself. He often commented, for example, that many Indian tales are "stories about stories."
This was not just a clever concept for him, for he included a section of
these double tales in each chapter of his 1991 book, and he chose both
to begin and to conclude the present work with one of these stories.
Rather it reflects his belief that tales affect those who tell them as much
as those who hear them. As mentioned above, Ramanujan did not seek
the (notoriously elusive) performance context of tales and worked almost exclusively on a textual level. On the other hand, because he listened closely to Kannada tales, letting them tell their own story, he
knew how they lived in their tellings, which is why he so loved the tales
about tales. As the first story in this volume suggests, tale telling is a
form of self-expression so vital that its denial can break up a marriage.
In retelling these Kannada tales, A. K. Ramanujan leaves us a self-portrait. The unsentimental sympathy, the eye for detail, and the laughter
in his translations make this a fitting final book from a brilliant and
generous man.

1. A Story and a Song

A housewife knew a story. She also knew a song. But she kept them to herself, never told anyone the story or sang the song.

Imprisoned within her, the story and the song were feeling choked. They wanted release, wanted to run away. One day, when she was sleeping with her mouth open, the story escaped, fell out of her, took the shape of a pair of shoes and sat outside the house. The song also escaped, took the shape of something like a man's coat, and hung on a peg.

The woman's husband came home, looked at the coat and shoes, and asked her, "Who is visiting?"

"No one," she said.

"But whose coat and shoes are these?"

"I don't know," she replied.

He wasn't satisfied with her answer. He was suspicious. Their conversation was unpleasant. The unpleasantness led to a quarrel. The husband flew into a rage, picked up his blanket, and went to the Monkey God's temple to sleep.

The woman didn't understand what was happening. She lay down alone that night. She asked the same question over and over: "Whose coat and shoes are these?" Baffled and unhappy, she put out the lamp and went to sleep.

All the lamp flames of the town, once they were put out, used to come to the Monkey God's temple and spend the night there, gossiping. On this night, all the lamps of all the houses were represented there—all except one, which came late.

The others asked the latecomer, "Why are you so late tonight?"

"At our house, the couple quarreled late into the night," said the flame.

1

"Why did they quarrel?"

"When the husband wasn't home, a pair of shoes came onto the verandah, and a man's coat somehow got onto a peg. The husband asked her whose they were. The wife said she didn't know. So they quarreled."

"Where did the coat and shoes come from?"

"The lady of our house knows a story and a song. She never tells the story, and has never sung the song to anyone. The story and the song got suffocated inside; so they got out and have turned into a coat and a pair of shoes. They took revenge. The woman doesn't even know."

The husband, lying under his blanket in the temple, heard the lamp's explanation. His suspicions were cleared. When he went home, it was dawn. He asked his wife about her story and her song. But she had forgotten both of them. "What story, what song?" she said.

2. Acacia Trees

The village chief (*gowda*) had four sons and a daughter. The daughter was the youngest child and her name was Putta ("Little One"). All day, everyone lovingly called her, "Putta! Putta!"

Three of the sons were married. The fourth one was still a bachelor. He didn't like any of the girls he saw; they looked at many in faraway places. Finally, one day, he said, "I'll marry my sister who's right here at home," and he was quite obstinate about it.

People said, "You can't do that. Don't try."

But he would not listen to anyone. "If I have to marry, I'll marry only my sister. Otherwise, I won't marry at all," he said.

The family thought, "Let's go along with it and arrange a wedding. Meanwhile, we'll find another girl and make her his bride on the wedding day." They set the date on an auspicious day, collected groceries and things, and prepared themselves for the wedding. But they didn't tell Putta anything about it.

Relatives started arriving. There was no water in the house, not a drop. Everyone was busy with their tasks. No one had a minute to spare. So Putta herself quickly picked up two brass pitchers and went to the canal to fetch water.

There, she saw a woman named Obamma, bathing in the mouth of the canal, sitting in the hollow. When she saw Putta, she called her, "Puttavva, Puttavva, my back is itching. Will you scratch it a little?"

Putta was in a hurry. She said, "Relatives have arrived. The house is full of people, and there's not a drop of water to drink. How can I stop now and scratch your back?"

She had filled her pitchers and started back when Obamma mocked her: "Marrying your own brother, ha! And you're mincing about already. Great way to marry!"

Putta didn't hear her clearly. She asked, "What, what did you say? I didn't hear it right. I'll rub your back, please tell me." And she scratched Obamma's itching back.

Obamma told her, "The elders in your family have decided to get you married to your own elder brother. That's the truth."

Putta carried the full pitchers of water back to her home, put them on the rim of a well, and looked around. There were two acacia trees growing there on either side of the well. She climbed up one of them, and never went into the house. It was getting late and her parents came looking for her. When they saw her perched on the tree, they called out:

> All the areca nuts are getting hard.
> All the betel leaves are getting dry.
> All the relatives are getting up and going home.
> Come down, daughter.

Putta answered:

> This mouth calls you Mother.
> This mouth calls you Father.
> Do you want this mouth to call you Mother-in-law and Father-in-law?
> I'll climb, climb, higher, higher, on this acacia tree.

And she climbed higher.

"What shall we do? We asked her to get down, and she climbed higher," they said, and went home unhappily.

Her three elder brothers came and called out:

> The areca nuts are getting hard.
> The betel leaves are getting dry.
> The relatives are getting up and going home.
> Come down, sister dear.

She replied:

> This mouth calls you Brother.
> Do you want this mouth to call you Brother-in-law?

And she climbed higher.

They went home and her three sisters-in-law came to the tree and called out:

All the areca nuts are hard.
All the betel leaves are dry.
All the relatives are going home.
Come down, dear Sister-in-law.

She answered:

This mouth calls you Sister-in-law,
Do you want this mouth to call you Co-wife?
I'll climb, I'll climb.

All the relatives, some close, some distant, came to the tree and called to her. She gave them all similar replies. Finally, the brother who was going to marry her came there and called out in anger:

All the areca nuts are hard.
All the betel leaves are dry.
All the relatives are going home.
Come down, you!

She replied:

This mouth calls you Brother.
Do you want this mouth to call you Husband?
I'll climb, I'll climb.

And she climbed higher.

Then he thought he would go after her and bring her down; so he too climbed the acacia tree. She jumped to the other acacia that was next to it. He jumped after her, and she leapt back. Thus they leapt back and forth from one tree to another—the brother pursuing, the sister dodging his pursuit.

After several leaps back and forth, she feared she would get caught. She looked down, saw the well between the trees. She thought it would be better to drown and die, and jumped straight into the well. The brother also jumped in and tried to drag her out of the water. The harder he tried, the more she resisted. After hours of struggle, they both drowned, and died in the well.

The people in the house took the bodies out of the well. The relatives said, "We came for the wedding, and look at this irony, we have to stay for the funeral!" They didn't bury the dead right away, but decided to wait till dawn. The daughter appeared in the mother's dream that night and begged of her, "Mother, please don't bury both of us together. Bury him in the mound. Bury me in the field. Please."

Accordingly, the family buried the son in the mound and the daughter in the field.

In time, a sharp spiny bush of thorn grew over the brother's burial place. Over hers grew a great tree of sweet fruit called Bullock's Heart. One of Putta's sisters-in-law walked that way and saw the tree covered with large fruit. She wanted to eat one. But they were only half-ripe. Anyway, she plucked a fine-looking big fruit, took it home, and left it to ripen in an earthen vessel full of *ragi* grain.

Days later, when she put her hand in the vessel to take out some *ragi* to grind, she found the fruit, the Bullock's Heart. It was good and ripe. She laid it aside while she ground the grain. But as she ground the *ragi* into fine flour, her eyes returned to the fruit many times.

"The fruit is so lovely, lovely as a girl. How I wish it were a girl."

No sooner had she said this than the fruit became a girl, sat in her lap, and told her the whole story.

The fruit-turned-girl said, "Look how things are. My brother did evil (*karma*), so a spiny bush grows on his burial ground. I kept my virtue (*dharma*), and a fruit tree grew out of mine. And I'm here."

3. The Adventures of a Disobedient Prince

A king had four wives and four sons, one son by each wife. He had no care in the world, and enjoyed every luxury and pleasure. He had many long titles; twenty-four other kings paid him tribute and his kingdom was truly vast.

One day, as he sat on the swing under the full moon playing love games with his queens, he was struck by a fancy. He summoned his four sons to his presence, and asked the eldest of them, "Son, you are my eldest, the future king of this country. What are your plans?"

He obediently answered, "Father, I'll follow in your illustrious footsteps. I'll try to be a great king like you."

He asked the second son the same question. "Son, what are your plans?"

"Father, I'll be a statesman and help my brother rule the kingdom."

When the third one was asked, he answered, "I'll be a great commander and help my brother rule in peace."

When the fourth son's turn came, he answered differently. "Father, you are the king of kings. Twenty-four kings pay you tribute. I want to be better than you. I'll conquer kingdoms, marry four celestial wives, and build my own city."

"What!" exploded the king. "Do better than me? You beast on two feet! You'll marry celestial wives? And do better than me?"

In his rage, he called his servants and screamed, "Throw him out! Banish him to the jungle at once!"

His mother tried to pacify the old man, but he would not listen to her. So she went in and prepared a bundle of rice for her banished son, and tearfully bade him goodbye.

The youngest son promptly left the palace, went out of the city, and walked straight till he found himself in a forest, where he heard nothing but the roar of tigers and lions on one side and the trumpetings of wild elephants and the grunts of wild pigs on the other. He cautiously climbed a tall tree and spent the night among its branches. At dawn, in the light of day, he came down, bathed in a nearby lake and prayed to the Bull, his family god, to protect him. He then ate from the bundle of rice his mother had given him, and started walking again through the wilderness till night fell. It was dark. He saw a small lamp flickering in the distance, and he made for it, like a bee to a flower. Soon he was standing at the door of a hut. When he called, "Anybody home?" a very old woman came out and took him in. She said, "You must be tired. Wash your feet and rest here tonight."

When she asked him why he was in this jungle, he briefly told her his story, and asked her in turn how she happened to live alone in this forest. She said "My name is Sickle Granny. My story is a long one. Rest now. I'll tell you some other time."

But the young prince was curious and insisted on hearing the story right away. So she told him her story.

"I may not look like it, but I'm the daughter of a great sage. Though he was a sage famous for his austere way of life, one day he went mad with lust and bothered my mother no end. She didn't want to give in to his lust, for that would have cancelled at once all his past history as a sage. She tried to save him from himself. But he wouldn't listen. He took her by force, had his will of her, and satisfied himself. So I was born, ugly as sin. Soon after I was born, he went into that same jungle you just came through, and while he was gathering fruit a tiger attacked him and tore him to pieces, limb from limb. My mother died soon after, and I was orphaned. Because I knew I was very ugly, I stayed on in the forest and never went into town. I just prayed and worshiped every day, and I attained the powers one gets only by such penance (*tapas*). Many marvels have I seen since then. I can tell you more, but it can wait. It's late and you must sleep."

The prince stayed with her and helped graze her cows. The old woman had only one rule for him. "When you take the cows out to pasture, never go towards the north," she had said. He had said, "Yes, I'll remember that," but one day his natural curiosity made him want to see what there was in the north that he shouldn't see. So he drove the herd in that direction. He came upon wonderful sights. He was particularly taken with a beautiful bathing well, built with gold bricks and the steps set in crystal. Green, red, pink, blue, and yellow fish sported in the water. He had hardly sat down under the shade of the *jambu* tree that spread its branches over one side of it when four celestial women appeared, as if from the sky. He hid himself behind the tree and watched them take off their yellow silk *pitambara* saris, jump noisily into the well, and splash each other with the crystalline water, having a great time. On an impulse, the prince picked up one of the saris and fled. The sari belonged to none other than Indra's own daughter. She saw him run off with her sari, so she quickly got out of the water and ran after him, crying out, "O young man, you look like a hero. I'll marry you and no one else. Stop, turn around, and look at me."

Astonished, he stopped, and the celestial woman at once snatched the sari from his hands, changed him into cold stone, and vanished.

When the prince did not return home as usual by evening, the old woman became anxious. Wand and lantern in hand, she set out in search of him to the south, the east, and the west, but she found no trace of him. She guessed that he must have gone to the forbidden north, and when she went in search of him there she found him lying on the ground, a piece of rock. She struck it with her wand, and he returned to life, standing up in his own body. They hurried home to safety and she scolded him.

"Didn't I tell you never to go north? By 'never' I meant 'never.' "

"Yes, Granny, you did tell me. But I knew somehow that's where my life would be fulfilled. So I couldn't resist it, I went. In fact, I want to go there again."

"All right, go if you must. But take some precautions. Don't take the cows with you. And don't be beguiled by those celestial wenches, their looks and sweet words. This time, when you pick up the sari, run straight home. I'll be waiting for you, and I'll take care of the rest."

He followed her instructions. Next day, he ate his morning meal early and went back to the place of the beautiful well and hid himself under the *jambu* tree. This day, too, the women arrived and unwrapped their saris before his unbelieving eyes. He gazed on them, his eyes moving from head to toe. What shapes, what complexions! Kohl-streaked eyes, faces like the moon, cascades of black hair flowing down to their buttocks, round breasts like perfect melons, and all of them young and virginal. They dived into the water, leaving their saris and pearls on the dry ground. The prince leapt out of his hiding place, quickly snatched the same sari he had taken the previous day, and ran. Its celestial owner ran out of the water and followed him, weeping and calling to him. But he was not deceived. He ran straight to the hut and handed the heavenly sari to the old woman, who changed him at once into a small baby and put him in a cradle. She pretended to rock him to sleep and lull him with lullabies. With her magic, she had also placed the sari inside the baby's thigh and sewn it up without a seam showing. A few moments later, the celestial woman arrived at her door, panting, and asked her, "Did anyone come this way? A young man?"

"A young man? No, no one has come this way. I've been here for hours," said the old woman.

"He may be hiding here somewhere."

"Before you do anything, dear, you must hide your shame. It's not a good idea to go around naked. Take this cotton piece. This is no way to be."

After a few minutes of this pretense and teasing, the old woman said to her, "I know where your sari is. You can have it back if you agree to marry him."

The celestial woman agreed. The old woman changed the prince back to his original form. They were married right there, in that hut, with the old woman as the wedding priest.

They lived there for a few days and one day took leave of the old woman and moved on. He had yet to win three more wives for himself, hadn't he?

The prince and his celestial bride talked to each other endlessly on their journey and soon found themselves at the gates of a city. The townspeople were struck by their beauty; they thought he was like Lord Krishna and she like his consort Rukmini, the very dwelling-place of all that is lovely. A boy in the street who was eating a piece of jaggery was so entranced watching them that he began to bite into his fist. A woodcutter missed his stroke and axed his own leg. People forgot themselves in looking at these splendid newcomers.

The prince rented a small house and found a job with the local king. A few days later, when the prince and his wife were sitting on a swing, gently swaying, two of the king's servants came there to give him his month's pay. They were so dumbstruck by his wife's beauty that they ran back to the king and, as soon as they found the words, stammered: "Your Highness, we've found you a most fitting prize in that new man's house. It's his wife. She looks so fantastic that she doesn't seem to be a mortal woman."

The king lost his reason and fell into a fantasy. The more vividly they described her the more he wanted her all for himself.

When the young man went to the court the next day as usual, he found that the king was absent. He inquired where he was, and was told that the king was sick with a pain in the stomach. So he hurried to the king's quarters in the palace and greeted him, "Victory to the king!" The king's voice was feeble.

"I'm glad to see you. You're like a long-lost brother. I'm dying of an ulcer in the stomach. The only cure, my doctors tell me, is the poison of the snake Karkotaka. Who can get it for me?"

The prince did not see through the old man's guile. He volunteered and promised to get it if it would save the king's life. He went home, thinking of how he should go about getting the poison of Karkotaka, the most deadly of serpents. He sat down lost in thought, forgetting even to eat. His wife roused him from his deep reverie by asking him what was troubling him. He told her about the king's illness and the remedy. She had a way.

"Go to the north beyond Jambu Peak, and you'll reach the Seshadri hills in a few miles. On those hills, under a *tamala* tree, you'll find a snake mound. I'll give you a letter; throw it in its hole and wait," she said, and gave him a letter to take.

He ate his dinner and slept happily, woke up early next morning, and set out on his quest. On his way, he noticed a *bharani* worm writhing miserably in a spider's web on the twigs of a tree. He carefully released the worm from the filaments and saved its life. Then he walked on till he reached the snake mound and slipped his wife's letter in the hole. Soon he heard noises from within. Several serpents came out to carry him magically into the netherworld, and set him before the King of Snakes, who was intently reading the letter, which said:

O Snake King of the Netherworld, this is a letter from Indra's daughter, who is like one of your own daughters. The bearer of this letter is my husband. As I am rather lonely in the earth-world, please get your daughter married to this fine man, and send her with him. The two of us will be happy together, I assure you. Please grant his request, about which he will tell you.

Yours, etc.

The Snake King liked his looks and proceeded to arrange a wedding with his daughter right away. Then he arranged for the newlyweds' journey. His personal retinue went with them to ensure their safe conduct till they had crossed Jambu Mountain. The prince was also given a sealed vial of Karkotaka's venom. When they reached his home by evening, the two women, who were old friends, were ecstatic to see each other and gave each other many hugs.

The next day the prince took the vial of deadly venom to the king, who asked his servants to open it carefully in the palace courtyard. Even as they opened it a little, the tamarind tree in the yard began to smolder, caught fire, and became a heap of ashes. The king asked them to take it far away and bury it deep.

So the king's first ruse didn't succeed. The young man didn't get killed or lost; he managed to get the deadliest venom of all. The king was now even a little afraid of the young man.

A month later, on a holiday, the king's servants brought him his monthly pay at home as they had done before. This time they saw two beautiful women instead of one sporting with him, and they hurried back to the king with their drooling descriptions. The king was beside himself with desire for the young man's fabulous wives. He sent for the prince again and said he had another of his terrible headaches, for which the cure would be a crocodile's bile. Would the brave young man bring it for him?

The prince went home, lost in thought. Both his wives asked him in unison, "Lord and husband of our souls, what is ailing you?" And he told them what his king wanted from him. Where could he go for a crocodile's bile? For his wives, that seemed like nothing extraordinary. They both sat down at once, wrote letters, and asked him to throw them in the great ocean.

He felt confident again, ate and slept well that night, and set out early the next morning in the direction his wives told him to go. On the way, a young crocodile was stranded on dry land and was growing feebler by the hour. He carried it tenderly to the river, where it revived at once, finding its element. The grateful animal said, "O mortal, you saved my life. If you are ever in need, think of me," and glided into the depths.

He reached the seashore and as soon as he threw the letters into the waves, four crocodiles appeared and carried him safely to the presence of the King of All The Seas, who, after reading the letters, eagerly offered his daughter to him with a dower of the ocean's best diamonds and, of course, a supply of the best crocodile bile.

When he returned home, the three unearthly beauties were happy together. Next day, when he brought the king the crocodile bile he had asked for, the king's heart sank. He knew his plans had failed again.

The next month when the servants brought him his pay, they were dazzled by the sight of three celestial damsels laughing mischievously with the prince on the swing after a sumptuous meal together. They rushed back to the king as they had done before and told him what they had seen—three women who were out of this world, beautiful beyond compare. The women's charms had made them eloquent. The king went almost mad with desire.

So he summoned the young prince again next day and praised him: "You are really a hero. You obviously can do anything. Do you think you can go to Indra's heaven and find out how my father, mother, and brothers are doing? Only you can bring me such news."

"As you wish, my king," said the prince, who then went home to consult his wives.

All three of them sat up all night and wrote letters—five hundred of them. He took the whole sackful of them, went to the king, and asked him to get ready a deep pit of fire for him. When the pit was filled with firewood and lit, he leapt into the flames. At once, the god of fire, who was waiting for him, transported him to his world, read the celestial women's letters addressed to him and other gods, and offered his own shining daughter in marriage to him. Then he sent him back to the earth. On his way back home, the prince had casually noticed a stream of water running towards an anthill, and he had stopped to divert the stream away from the ants. He slept well that night surrounded by four loving women.

Next morning, he took a letter to his king and another to the minister who was giving him advice. The letter to the king read as follows:

Dear son,
Your messenger brought us all the news about you and made us very

happy. We are comfortable here without a care. We eat, drink, and dress like gods. Why don't you come and see us here? You can stay with us forever. You can come the same way your messenger came. Really, there is no other way. Come soon. We will be waiting eagerly for your visit.

Yours, etc.

The king and his wicked minister were excited by these letters. They were filled with the desire to go bodily to heaven. The king ordered a great fire built before sunrise. The news spread and the whole town was ready to jump in. Everyone wanted to go to heaven and see their dead relatives. But the prince said, "Good people, be patient. Let Our Royal Highness and the Honorable Minister go first." The king and the minister, resplendently dressed, entered the fire with their entire family and entourage, and were burned to ashes before everyone's eyes. The prince sent the townspeople home with the words, "Look, the wicked king and his villainous minister are dead, as you can see. This fire won't take you to heaven. It will only burn you. Go home now, and live your lives well."

When he went into the king's palace, in the king's chamber he found the name of a brahmin on a piece of paper. He at once searched for the brahmin, found him in a little hut, and crowned him king, though the brahmin protested.

"I'm a poor man and I like it that way. What do I need a kingdom for? You rule it yourself."

But the prince persuaded him. "No, this is all yours. You can give me shelter when I come here next."

Then he left town with his four wives for the forest, where, with their help, he cleared a large space, built a great new city, and lived there happily for a while.

Meanwhile, his father had fallen on bad times, lost his kingdom and wealth. He had become so poor that he was cutting and selling wood for a living. The whole royal family roamed from place to place in search of a pittance and, one day, arrived in the new city. The prince saw them from his balcony as they were walking in the street down below. He brought them home and gave them every comfort and luxury.

One day soon after, before going on a hunt with his three elder brothers, he gave his first wife's sari to his mother for safekeeping, with strict warnings not to let it out of her sight and not to give it to anyone. At that time, the daughters-in-law were bathing. The first wife somehow found out about the sari and asked her mother-in-law, most sweetly, "Mother, let me see that new yellow silk *pitambara* sari. It's beautiful. Give it to me. Let me wear it today."

The mother-in-law replied, "No, no, I can't. My son has asked me not to give it to anyone."

"What, not even to me?" said the first wife in a hurt tone. Then she used her wiles, spoke beguilingly, and won over the somewhat simple old woman. She wheedled the sari out of her, and before anyone could say a word, the four celestial women quickly wrapped themselves in it and flew straight to heaven. That very moment, the great new city that was their creation also vanished, and nothing was left but the primeval jungle in its place.

The old mother began to cry helplessly. The prince and his brothers, who were out hunting, seemed suddenly caught in an unknown fastness in the jungle, as if it had thickened around them before they knew it. The brothers asked him, "What's happening?" He knew. "It's all our mother's doing," he said. They slashed all about them with their swords, somehow extricated themselves from the tangle of bushes and creepers, and came to where the mother was sitting distraught and in tears. The young prince brought them all to the kingdom now ruled by the brahmin, who was very happy to receive them.

Then he went in search of his errant wives.

The celestial wives spent a while in the world of the gods, but soon began to miss their husband. They remembered his pranks with longing. So they decided to come down to the earth, found him wandering aimlessly, and offered to take him with them to their world.

"Meet my father," said the first wife, Indra's daughter, "and you will be able to bring us all back with his permission. You kidnapped me then and didn't get his permission."

"Why not? I will come and meet your father and get his permission. Let's go," he said, and they transported him at once to the world of the gods by changing him into a fish in a vessel of water for the duration of the journey. And once they were in the upper world, they vanished, abandoning him in a strange place. "Women!" he muttered to himself, and started asking around for Indra's capital. He was soon taken there. Everyone was amazed at the presence of a live earthling. It was not long before he was in the presence of Indra, who heard his tale and said, playfully, "If you want these girls, you'll have to prove yourself worthy of them. You must perform four tasks that I shall set you. If you succeed, I'll marry them all to you once more."

Indra scattered a basket of tiny sesame seeds in a vast field and said,

"There! Pick them all in three hours and you can have the Fire God's daughter back."

The prince was baffled at first and thought hard. Suddenly he remembered the ants he had saved from being washed away. As soon as he remembered them, a whole swarm of them appeared and, according to his wish, picked out every sesame seed scattered in the field and left them in a neat heap. Thus he won back one wife, his youngest.

Indra then threw his signet ring into a deep well that looked bottomless, and asked him to retrieve it. In a flash, the prince remembered the frog, which darted into the well at his bidding. [The hero's previous encounter with this frog was apparently omitted by the storyteller.— Eds.] But he returned almost at once, looking mortally afraid because there was a coil of snakes guarding the bottom. He then summoned his young tadpole son and took him down into the well, where he threw him to the snakes, which came up to eat the tadpole. The old frog dived in and leapt up with Indra's ring. Thus the prince won back the princess of the water world.

"Now," said Indra, taking the prince to a plantain tree, "I want you to cut this tree in three pieces with one stroke. You'll then get back the Snake Princess."

The young prince at once thought of the crocodile he had saved on his way to the sea. The reptile appeared even as he thought of it, saluted him, and asked what he wanted done.

"Do you see this plantain tree? I want it cut in three pieces with one stroke of your sharp tail."

Before he had even finished saying this, the tree lay before him in three neat pieces. He had won the snake princess as well. Now Indra set him his last test. With his magic, he made his daughter's three friends look exactly like his own daughter, and said, "Tell me who is your first wife."

The prince was completely at a loss. He was faced with four lookalikes. He could not tell them apart, though he looked at them closely. Suddenly he remembered the *bharani* worm, which arrived from nowhere, now a winged insect, touched the sari-end of Indra's daughter, and flew in circles around her head. At once, the prince said, "There, that's my first wife!" and seized her hand. He had won her, too.

The gods were amazed at the way the humble animals of the earth-world had come to the help of this mortal man. Indra, who had hugely enjoyed the fun of it all, arranged a heavenly wedding ceremony for the young people and got them married according to celestial customs.

The prince descended to the earth with all four wives and went straight to his father's kingdom and original capital, which were now in the hands of foreign kings. He conquered them and all the minor kings around them, became king of the old kingdom, and brought back his parents and brothers to the capital.

One day, under the light of the full moon, as he sat on the palace swing with his four queens, he remembered another such day. He asked for his father, and when he arrived, the son said to him, "Father, did I do what I said I once would do?"

To which, the father replied, "Yes, son, you did. If one has sons, one must have sons like you."

4. Bride for a Dead Man

A king and his queen had no children, though they were getting on in years. Half their life was already over. So the king decided he would pray to get an heir for his kingdom. He began his penances by standing in the middle of a tank on a twelve-yard stone, with another such stone on his head. He stood there like that for twelve whole years and prayed to Siva.

Siva said, "I'm burdened by this man's devotion. His twelve years weigh on me. The stone on his head weighs on me. So I'll go down and give him the child he wants."

He came down from Kailasa, his mountain, to where the king stood steadfastly in the water.

"Come out of the tank," Siva said. "I'll give you a child."

"I'll come out only when you grant me the boon. Not till then."

"All right, I give you my word," said Siva, "but I'll not give you the boon here. I'll come to your house and grant your wish." And he promised to visit the king, and sealed his promise by putting his hand in the king's hand.

"Go home now and I'll come tomorrow," Siva said, and the king ended his penance, came out of the water, and went home to tell his wife.

"Siva has given me his word. He'll come here tomorrow and give us children. Wash and wipe the whole palace, bathe, and offer worship. You must be ready tomorrow morning. Also, get five *uttatti* fruit."

But his wife wouldn't believe him. He insisted, "No, no, it's true. Siva will come here himself. You'll see."

Next morning came very fast, and Siva did descend from the sky. As he walked towards the palace, he looked at himself, alms-bag on his shoulder, a cane in his fist, a trident slung on his back. "How can I go into the world looking like this?" he thought, changed into a holy man, and went begging from shop to shop before he reached the palace. The shopkeepers were devout and gave the holy man diamonds and pearls as gifts, but he wouldn't touch them. He said, "What shall I do with these stones? If you wish, give me the fat of a flea and the fat of a bedbug. I'd like that."

"Where shall we go for the fat of fleas and bedbugs?" the bewildered shopkeepers asked.

Meanwhile, Siva was dancing, leaping into the sky. He swayed like a peacock. But he would take nothing and asked only for the fat of fleas and bedbugs, which they couldn't get. So he went hopping through the market all the way to the palace.

The king and queen were waiting. They washed his feet and fell at his feet. He gave the queen two betelnuts from his waist band and said, "This is for you. I know you want a child. What would you like? A smart son who'll live only twelve years or an idiot who'll live to be a hundred?"

She said, "What shall I do with an idiot son? He has to rule this kingdom. Give me a smart son for twelve years."

"Think well. He'll live only for twelve years, not a day longer. Once you've chosen, nothing can change it later. Think again."

"I know what I want," she said. "A smart son. Give him to me. I can't wait."

So Siva granted her a smart son who would live only for twelve years. The queen's periods stopped, her pregnancy made her fuller by the day, and, exactly nine months and nine days later, she gave birth to a boy. Siva had decreed that a tiger would bring him his death on his twelfth birthday. The astrologers who could read such things also said so and warned his parents.

As a growing boy, he went out to play ball in town. The girls who were going to the river to fetch water said, "You're the king's son. What's the matter with you? Playing ball with the ordinary town boys! As the prince of the kingdom, you've got to go to the forest and hunt lions, tigers, and such. Then you'll be a real prince."

So he went straight home, threw away the ball, and said to his mother, "Why didn't anybody tell me what princes do? I'm going to hunt lions and tigers in the forest."

The mother was panic-stricken. She remembered the prophecy. "My boy, you're only twelve. Don't think of hunting and wild animals. Don't you have playmates? We'll find you some."

But he was obstinate and wouldn't listen. He called for the servants, the stable boys, and prepared himself for a hunt. The mother said, "At least wait till I look at the omens."

She went out to look for good omens, but all she saw were oil sellers, people carrying pickaxes and spades—bad omens. She came home and tried to stop the boy.

"I see only bad omens everywhere. Don't go, my son. You can go tomorrow," she pleaded.

She wept, she even fell at his feet and held on to them. But he wouldn't hear any of it. He had already taken a step outside the threshold.

"See, Mother, I've already stepped outside. No real prince will take back his step and retreat inside. By your blessings, I'll come home safely. You'll see," he said, touched her feet, and left for the forest, this twelve-year-old boy. His mother's brother, his uncle, followed and joined him in the hunt.

The hunt was a fierce success. They brought down many tigers, lions, and gryphons, stood proudly on their carcasses, and loaded them in cart after cart to send them home. When the distraught mother saw these carts coming into the palace yard, filled with wild animals ripped apart by her son's arrows, her heart revived. The cartmen said, "The prince has sent all these so that Your Highness may see and stop worrying about him. More are coming."

"O Siva," she said, relieved and happy. "That's truly my son. He has killed so many tigers and lions in one hunt, his very first. They said a tiger would kill him. They were afraid even of a tiger in a picture, and removed all tiger pictures from the palace. How ridiculous!"

While she was exclaiming like this ecstatically, the prince had finished his hunt and was returning home. On the way, it occurred to him to stop at their family god's temple and offer worship after his first adventure. As soon as he spoke of this plan, his uncle hurried before him. There were many pictures of tigers on the temple walls, and he knew that he could never stop his rash nephew from doing what he wanted. So he spattered the pictures with mud, and asked servants to hold curtains on either side of the prince as he entered the temple.

"Don't look around and dillydally. Go straight to the god's image, bow before it, and then let's go home. It's late," said the uncle.

But did he listen? He prostrated himself before the god and as he turned back he saw the curtains. Impatiently, he tore them down, saying, "What's all this curtain-holding? Are you afraid I'll die? I've killed seven tigers today, remember?"

As he tore down the curtains, he saw tigers, tigers, tigers all around. They opened their mouths wide and rose from the pictures on the walls. When he saw their red tongues coming towards him, he became dizzy, fell into a swoon, and died on the spot.

His uncle cried and cried all the way, as he brought the body home.

"O Siva, I brought him safely till this point and yet couldn't save him. My sister bore him in her old age, after so much trouble. Now he's dead. What shall I do?"

The mother heard it all and ran out weeping.

"O Siva, you still took him as you said you would. After killing real tigers, he was killed by a tiger in a picture, just as they said. I wanted to see him married. Even now, I will. We'll not bury him till we find a bride for him," she said in her grief.

And even as they were preparing the bier and the chariot for the last procession of the dead boy, she sent a cartload of gold hitched to a camel with messengers: they had to find a bride, whatever the price.

The cartload went from street to street and from town to neighboring town, loudly announcing the search for a bride for the dead prince. The messengers finally met with a brahmin who had a twelve-year-old daughter named Chennavva. The poverty of the family was harsh beyond words. They said to the poor man, "Give us your daughter. We'll unload the gold here."

He agreed and gave them his daughter. At once her mother began to weep. She brought out a little oil in a cup, some turmeric, took her daughter in and gave her a ritual oil-bath, crying all the while, "O Daughter, widowhood is not for you. How can it be? You're only twelve years old."

Then she dressed her up in fresh clothes, put auspicious marks of turmeric and vermilion on her forehead, and blessed her, saying, "May you be like Savitri. May you keep your husband." And she sent her with the royal messengers.

Galloping, they took her to the palace, where she was married in a proper ceremony to the dead boy. As in any wedding, they put auspicious marks of turmeric and vermilion on the bride's face, threw grains of rice, and tied the wedding thread round her neck.

When it was time to lift the dead body and take it away, they wanted her to stay behind. But she refused to stay behind. Firmly, she said,

"I'm going with my husband. Bury me with him. What's the point of living without him?"

So she sat next to the body and was carried with it. As they reached the burial grounds, a great rainstorm descended on them. It seemed as if more water fell than the earth could hold. Everyone ran and found shelter from the wind and the rain. The dead body was left alone, and Chennavva held on to it. The night was dark, the place was a dismal burial ground, and she was alone with the body.

"What shall I do? This is my lot," she said. She had sweated and her body was caked with mud. She sat down and scraped it, added more mud to it, then molded the image of Siva's Bull with it. She installed it in front of her, sang songs, and worshiped the image with flowers she picked off the dead body. As she sang and worshiped, the mud image of the Bull was filled with life. He got up, snorted, and walked about. He said, "Chennavva, your devotion is great. I'd like to do something for you."

And he went to heaven and pleaded with Siva, "Lord, you must give back Chennavva's husband his life. You must give back her marriage to her. You must."

"Dear Bull," said Siva, "you're quite taken with that Chennavva, aren't you? We can't give back life like that. Wait, let's send her a tiger and let's see what she does."

So he sent a tiger to Chennavva. She at once stood with her back to her husband's bier and, stretching out both her hands, prayed to the tiger, "Don't eat him. Eat me."

Which pleased the tiger too. He said, "We'll send you Siva himself. You're too good for us."

The tiger went to Siva and pleaded: "O Siva, you must give back Chennavva's husband his life."

Then he sent lions, gryphons; he even sent she-demons, but she wasn't afraid of any of them. She guarded her husband's body and offered her own. When they all came back pleading her cause, Siva decided he would go down himself and see what she was like. He picked up his alms-bag and his cane and stood before her asking for alms. "What can I give this beggar, sitting here in the burial ground?" she thought, then took down the only precious thing she had on her, her wedding thread with its golden pendant (*tali*), and put it in his alms-bag.

"What's this, you've given me your wedding *tali*? Don't you have anything else to give?" said Siva, astonished.

She said, "No, Sir. That's all I have. What else can I have, sitting here in the burial ground?"

Siva was touched. He tied the *tali* back on her neck, breathed life into her husband's body, and went back to heaven. The young prince woke up as if from a long sleep. The happy couple talked all night till it dawned silver in the morning. They had much to talk about.

The people from the palace were worried all night about the body and the twelve-year-old girl they had left with it in the rainstorm. They came running as soon as the storm passed and it was light. They found the two of them talking. When they heard what had happened, they marveled at Chennavva, the power of her virtue, and how she had brought a dead man to life. His parents, summoned there by then, placed a coconut in the grave that had been dug and closed it up. The bride and bridegroom were carried back in palanquins to the palace and a whole new wedding was arranged.

When the time came for the bride to give the ritual offerings of *bagina* to her relatives, Chennavva said, "No one took my *bagina* earlier. I'm not going to give it to anyone now. I'll give it to the river goddess, Ganges," and took it to the river.

When the wedding took place the first time, no one had received her or her bridal gifts as they should have. Everyone in the town had shut their doors on her. Why should she give it now to anyone?

"I married a dead husband and no one thought of me then. Now I'm married to a live one, I'll give *bagina* to the goddess and take gifts from her," she said, and offered them to the river goddess. Then she came back, completed the wedding ceremony, and lived happily with her husband and her in-laws.

5. A Brother, a Sister, and a Snake

A raja had a son and a daughter. His queen died before her time and the raja married another woman. The second woman didn't like her stepchildren. She even wanted to kill them. So she put a baby snake in a spouted cup (*gindi*) studded with pearls, filled it with water, and gave it to the girl to drink. The innocent girl drank it all up. The baby snake entered her stomach and grew inside her as she herself grew up. When her belly began to swell noticeably, the queen got the ear of the king, accused the young girl of being pregnant, slandered the children, and had them cast into the jungle.

While the young boy and girl were wandering in the forest, eating leaves and fruit, a kindly ogre's eye fell on them. He took them home and settled them there. He turned over the management of his entire household to them. Years passed.

He had buffaloes in his yard. One day the sister milked a buffalo, put the milk pot on the hot stove, and went to sleep. When the milk boiled over and the whole house was filled with the sweet smell of scalded milk, the snake in her stomach was enticed by it. It came out, went straight to the boiling milk, drank it and died. Now that the snake had come out, the sister slept even better. The brother saw the snake and cut it to pieces, threw it in the next room, and locked the door. He forbade his sister to open the door of that room.

One day, when her brother was not around, she got inquisitive and opened the door. To her astonishment, she saw a big green jasmine bush in full blossom. She gathered the flowers and made a lovely garland. When her brother came home, she affectionately tried to put it around his neck. When the brother saw the flowers he knew at once what had happened. He begged her not to put the garland round his neck. But she wouldn't listen; she was stubborn. Then, seeing no way out, he gave her three pebbles and said to her, "If you must throw that garland around my neck, take these three pebbles first. If something terrible happens to me, throw those pebbles on me."

She said, "All right, I'll do as you say, but I must put this garland round your neck. I made it for you," and put the garland around his neck. At once, he turned into a snake, and began to slither away. She was shocked at the result of her action, and followed it everywhere, till it glided into a snake hole in the forest floor. She sat there waiting for him to come out.

Her father, the raja, came there on one of his hunting trips. He saw this beautiful girl, didn't recognize her, fell in love with her, and asked her to go home with him. She told him of her brother's plight. The king at once called his snake charmer, who played his flute, enticed the snake out of the hole, and caught it. They all went to the king's palace, with the snake in a basket. In the palace, she remembered what her brother had said about the three pebbles and threw them on the snake. The snake vanished, and in its stead stood her brother.

The king now insisted that she marry him. She and her brother knew by now that he was their own father. She said that they should decide on their marriage in the open court. Then she asked for a pearl-studded spouted cup (*gindi*), and got one.

In the assembled court, the young woman placed the pearl-studded *gindi* in front of her and began her story. As she began, "Once there was a king. . . ," and went on, the *gindi* listened and nodded. She told it everything, all about her stepmother who gave her the baby snake to swallow, how they were banished to the forest, how her brother had changed into a snake, and all the rest. The *gindi* nodded at every pause. It didn't take long for the king to see that the young man and woman were his own lost children. He threw out his wicked queen and lived happily with his children.

6. A Buffalo Without Bones

In a certain town, there were three brothers. They had a sister who had been given in marriage to a man from another town. The brothers were also married and each had a son. Their sister had a daughter. In the course of time, the eldest brother grew old and was about to die. His son, who was by now a young man, came to him and asked, "*Appa,* what did you do for me?"

The father said, "What have I not done for you? I'm leaving you lands, orchards, fields, wealth, sheep and cattle. The house is full of gold and silver. What else do you want?"

The son replied, "I'm not asking for wealth and property. You didn't get me married while you were still able to do so."

The father shook his head in agreement. "Oho, that's true, that's true. But never mind. My sister has a daughter whom you can marry according to our custom. She is a fine girl and very beautiful. Wait for a few days and go talk to your aunt. Ask her to give you her daughter in marriage. Tell her I said so."

Having said this, he breathed his last. The son buried him in the proper manner and mourned him for a long time.

The second brother also grew old and it was time for him to die. His son too came and asked him, "Father, what did you do for me?"

The father said, "What haven't I done for you? I'm leaving you plenty!"

"That's not what I'm talking about. You didn't get me married while you were still strong and able."

"That's quite true. I should have and I didn't. But no matter. Your aunt's daughter is a fine girl and very beautiful. When you're ready, go and ask your aunt's permission and marry her daughter."

Hardly had he finished saying what he did when his life left him. The son dutifully buried him according to the proper rites and mourned him for a long time.

When it was time for the third brother to die, he too told his son that he should marry his aunt's daughter, and then died.

One fine day, the three sons of the three brothers dressed themselves up in their best clothes, put on their best jewelry, and arrived at their aunt's house. She gave them water for their hands and feet, asked them to sit on the cot, and inquired why they had come and what they would like. Then the eldest nephew said, "When my father died, he told me that I should marry your daughter. So I've come to ask for her hand."

The other two brothers' sons also said the same thing.

The aunt was quite bewildered. "What shall I do?" she cried in distress. She even sat for a while with her head in her hands. Her husband came there and soon found out what the matter was.

"By god, this is difficult. We have only one daughter and here you are, three eligible young men ready to marry her. Whom shall we give her to?" he said, and thought of a way out. He called each of them and gave each a hundred rupees (which was a lot of money in those days), and said, "Dear boys, use this money to buy what you consider the best thing this money can buy. The person who brings the very best thing will get my daughter, for he would be the smartest of the three. Let's see what you bring. Go now."

Off the three cousins went with the money, looking for the best thing it could buy. They traveled hundreds of miles through many regions and arrived in a strange city. There, in the marketplace, a man was offering a mirror for sale. The eldest of the three cousins was taken with the mirror and asked for the price. The man said, "A hundred rupees."

"Why a hundred rupees for this mirror? What's so special about it?" asked the cousin.

The man replied, "This is no ordinary looking glass in which you look at your face. If you stand in a high place, utter a spell (*mantra*), and look into this mirror, you can see everything that's happening in the world."

"Aha, this indeed is the best thing in the world," said the cousin, and bought it at once for a hundred rupees.

The second cousin was also wandering in the same town, wondering what he should buy, when he saw a merchant with a weird-looking chariot. The cousin asked him the price and was told it would cost him a hundred rupees.

"Why a hundred rupees for this old piece of junk?"

"Because it is no ordinary chariot. If you sit in it and utter a spell, it will carry you anywhere in the world, this chariot will."

"If that's so, I'll buy it," said the second cousin, and bought it at once.

The third cousin thought, "My cousins have already bought their things; one has a mirror, another a chariot. What shall I buy that's better than theirs?" As he roamed the streets, he came across a man with a stick in his hand. The stick looked unusual. It too cost a hundred rupees. The young man asked him, "Why should a mere stick cost a hundred? It isn't made of gold!"

The man explained: "This is better than gold. If a man dies of snake-bite, scorpionbite, or even plague, this stick can bring him back to life. Rub some *kasturi*-musk into asses' milk, dip this stick in it, and put it in the dead man's mouth, and he will sit up alive."

So the youngest of the three cousins bought the stick. When the three of them were returning home, each thought he alone had made the best purchase.

On the way, the eldest said, "It's more than a year since we left our aunt and uncle. Who knows what has happened during this year? Well, I've this mirror in which you can see everything that's going on in the world. Let's look and see."

Then he went up a hill, uttered a spell, and looked into the mirror. His aunt and uncle were all right, but their daughter whom all three had wanted to marry was dead. A black scorpion had bitten her to death. Relatives had gathered, placed her dead body on a bamboo stretcher, and were about to take it to the graveyard to bury it. When the three cousins were worrying about what to do and how to get there, the second cousin said, "Why do you worry? I've this chariot. Get into it."

All three of them climbed into it and he uttered a spell. It carried them hundreds of miles in no time and landed them in their aunt's place. Just as relatives were lifting the dead girl on to their shoulders to take her to the burial grounds, the third cousin stopped them, asked for some *kasturi* and some asses' milk, rubbed the *kasturi* in the milk, dipped the stick in it and let a few drops fall on the dead girl's lips. At once, she sat up, stretching and yawning, asking everyone how long she had been asleep and what the crowd was all about.

Now the youngest cousin told his aunt, "I brought her to life. So you should let me marry her."

The second cousin said, "We were hundreds of miles away. But for my chariot, how could we have come here in time? So I deserve the bride."

The eldest one said angrily, "Aha, so what if this fellow had a magic stick which brought her to life, and so what if this other fellow had a chariot to bring us here? What would we have done if we hadn't known our dear aunt's daughter was already dead? That's why my mirror is the best. I'm the one who's going to marry her. Arrange the wedding."

So the three of them fought with each other, each thinking that he was the rightful suitor for the dead girl now come alive. The case went to the village councils and to court after court of appeal, but no one could decide who was right. At one of these places where they were arguing with each other, a wise old man held their hands and asked them to tell him what the dispute was.

All three showed him their magic objects and told him about the aunt's daughter. The old man listened to them carefully and asked them to wait while he went and talked to their aunt and her daughter. When he came to their house, he found the two women wringing their hands in great distress over the three suitors. "How can I marry three men?" cried the girl. The old man quieted them and told the young woman, "Think about what I'm going to say. There's a buffalo with no bones: one without hands milks it, and one without a mouth drinks the milk. Think about this." Then he left as he had come.

It was evening. The three quarreling cousins came there, still arguing. The daughter poured some warm milk in a bowl and asked all three to drink it. All three of them asked, almost in chorus, "How can we drink milk from the same bowl?"

She said, "You are like fathers to me, all three of you. Have you ever heard of fathers marrying daughters? You gave me life. So I can't marry you. Each of you will have to find someone else to marry."

So they went their ways, and married suitably elsewhere, and found happiness.

What's the meaning of the old man's saying? "A buffalo without bones; one without hands milks it, and one without a mouth drinks it": the rain cloud is a buffalo without bones, the wind is the one without hands that milks it, and the earth is the one without a mouth that drinks the milk of the cloud. The rain, the wind, the earth, the three together give us life; they are like parents. These three cousins together gave the girl life and so were like her parents. That's why she wouldn't marry them. She married someone else, a nice handsome man, and found happiness.

7. Cannibal Sister

An oil seller's wife had several children. Her seventh one turned out to be a monster. At birth it looked hideous, terrifying. Its eyes were set in the crown of its head. All day, it would play and cry like other babies. But at dead of night it would change into a horrible demon. It would roam in the dark, eat the townspeople one by one, come back at dawn, and sleep in the cradle like a baby. In a few days, the town was full of the news of a son gone, a father's bloody remains in the alley, a daughter who had disappeared. Nobody knew what had happened to the missing persons.

One day a brother of the demon woke up at night for some reason and he saw the baby change into a monster right before his eyes. Then, when it went out he followed it and saw it eat a couple of people and return quietly to the cradle as a baby.

Next day, he talked to his parents and relatives in secret. "This is no baby. It's an ogress. I've seen it eat people, with my own eyes. Let's leave the house and go far away," he said.

But they didn't believe what he said.

"Look at it," they said, "that's a harmless baby. You should get your head examined."

He replied, "If you don't want to go, I will," and mounted his horse and left town.

In a few days, the demoness had devoured the townspeople and then went after the family. Having finished them, it waited to snare and eat anyone who visited the town.

The brother meanwhile went galloping through strange cities till he came to one where he heard of a contest. There was a crater outside the town and any one who was able to leap across it on a horse would receive a reward and a bride. As soon as he heard this, he egged his horse on and, in one jump, cleared the crater. So he won the reward and married into that town. He settled down there and prepared himself for what he had to do.

First, he captured a tiger cub and a lion cub and reared them carefully. He taught them various tricks; he even taught them to understand human language. Soon they grew into big powerful animals, and he was ready to go back to his hometown. Before he left, he told his wife, "I have to go visit my parents and brothers. Don't worry about me. If these pets of mine, this tiger and this lion, cry and make unhappy growling noises, that means I'm in danger. Untie them at once and set them free."

When he rode his horse into his hometown, he couldn't believe his eyes: it was a ghost town. He couldn't recognize it. The demoness sat on the threshold of their old house in the form of a woman. She called to him sweetly, "O Brother, I was waiting for you. Tie your horse in the stable. Come in and eat."

Though he was terrified and shook in his bones, he managed to say, "All right," and went into the kitchen. She sat him down and gave him something to eat. While he was eating, she went out, became a demon, broke his horse's leg and ate it. She called out, "Brother, Brother, do horses in your part of the country have only three legs?"

He had seen it all from the kitchen window.

"Yes, yes, Sister. Only three legs," he answered, not knowing what else to say.

She ate another leg and asked, "Brother, Brother, do horses in your country have only two legs?"

He answered, "Yes, yes, only two legs."

Then she finished the fourth leg and asked, "Brother, Brother do horses in your part of the country have no legs at all?"

He answered, "No, not even one."

When she was eating the horse's chin, he jumped out of the window and started to run. By this time, she had eaten the whole horse. She came in looking for him, found he was gone, saw the open window, and jumped out to pursue him. He ran up a tree. She began to climb after him, growling at the branches.

Meanwhile, at home, his tiger and lion had become restless and they were straining at the leash. They howled and growled. His wife quickly untied them and let them go free. They came galloping to where their master was. They attacked the monster as she was getting close to her brother and tore her limb from limb.

Now he could go home in peace and live with his wife and pets.

They are there and we are here.

8. Chain Tale

A man gave up the world and became a *sanyasi*. All he had was a thin loincloth to hide his shame and to control his sexual desire.

But every night his sleep was disturbed by a mouse who gnawed at his loincloth. So he acquired a cat and brought it up. The cat needed milk. So he found a generous man who gave him a cow. After all, someone had to milk the cow and take care of it. So he needed a woman. Once he found the woman, he felt like marrying her, and did.

So he didn't need the loincloth anymore.

9. Another Chain Tale: What an Ant Can Do

An ant lived on a small hillock with its young, in a hole close to a tank. One day, a baby ant was playing outside when it slipped and fell plunk! into the water. It called for its mother, *"Ayyo, Amma! Amma!"* The mother ant came out of the hole and saw its young one struggling in the water. She looked this way and that, crying, "Who'll save my baby?" A frog was hopping about close by. The ant went to him and asked him to help.

"Brother Frog, Brother Frog, my baby has fallen into the water. Take him out and save him, please. Won't you, please?"

The frog wouldn't do anything of the kind. "What do I care if your baby falls in the water?" he said.

"Is that all you can say? Wait till I get you. You'll be sorry," said the ant, and ran till she found a snake in a snake hole.

The mother ant went to the mouth of the snake hole and called out, "Brother Snake, Brother Snake!"

The snake peeked out of the hole and said, "Who's there?"

"It's Mother Ant. My baby is drowning and that frog refuses to help me. Just go and eat up that frog in one gulp!"

"What do I care if the frog doesn't help you? I'm not hungry just now," said the snake sleepily.

"Is that what you say? Wait till I get you. You'll be sorry," said the ant and ran farther till she found the snake charmer's hut.

The ant talked to the snake charmer. "Brother Snake Charmer, there's a bad snake in the snake hole. He won't help me. Go and catch him, pull out his fangs, and put him in your basket."

But the snake charmer was in no mood to get up. "What do I care if a snake doesn't help you? I don't need any snakes now. I won't pick up even a worm," he said.

"Is that all you can say?" said the angry ant. "Wait till I get you. You'll be sorry."

As she ran, her eye fell on a rat hole in a wall. She called out to the rat. "Brother Rat, Brother Rat! That snake charmer refuses to help me. Will you go and gnaw a hole in his basket and let his snake escape?"

"What do I care if the snake charmer won't help you? I can't do anything now," said the rat.

"Is that what you say? Wait till I get you. You'll be sorry," said the ant and ran on till she saw a cat sitting outside a house.

"Brother Cat, Brother Cat, that rat out there refuses to help me. Will you go catch him, eat him, and crunch his bones?" The cat was resting after a meal, licking his whiskers.

"What do I care if a rat won't help you? I'm not hungry now. Don't bother me," he said.

"Is that what you say? Wait till I get you. You'll be sorry," said the ant and ran till she found a dog.

"Brother Dog, Brother Dog, that lazy cat refuses to help me. Will you chase him out of town?"

"What do I care if a cat won't help you? I can't do anything about it," said the dog.

"Is that all you can say? Wait till I get you. You'll be sorry," said the ant.

In one corner of the verandah of that house stood a stick. The ant went up to it and called softly, "Brother Stick, Brother Stick!"

As he soon as he heard this, the stick said, "Whom shall I beat? Whom shall I beat?"

"That dog won't help me. Beat him," said the ant.

The stick said, "Take hold of me at one end and throw me at the dog."

But how could a little ant lift the stick?

So she went to the little boy Putta who was reading a little book and asked him, "Brother Putta, Brother Putta, will you please take that stick and beat that dog?"

"O, I can't. Go away. I have to study," said Putta.

The mother ant was very angry by now.

"That bold stick who doesn't even have hands and legs is willing to help. But all of you fellows who have hands and legs are unwilling to help me. You too, Putta, don't want to help. Is this what the world is coming to? Wait till I get you. You'll be sorry," she said and climbed on to his thigh and stung him hard. Putta cried, "*Ayyo,* let me go, let me go. I'll help you!"

"Then pick up that stick and throw it at the dog!"

Putta got up and threw the stick at the dog. The dog whined in fear and groveled.

"Don't hit me! What do you want me to do?"

The ant gave orders: "Chase that cat!"

The dog barked and ran after the cat. The scared cat mewed and mewed, "Meow, Meow, what do you want me to do?"

The ant said, "Go get the rat!"

As the cat went after him, the rat squealed, "*Chiev, Chiev,* what do you want me to do?"

"Go make a hole in the snake charmer's basket."

The snake charmer was fast asleep. The rat gnawed a hole in the basket with his teeth. The snake inside came crawling out, happy that he was suddenly free. The ant stood in his way.

"Brother Snake, I'm the one who freed you from that basket. You'll have to help me, or else I'll sting the snake charmer and wake him up. He'll catch you and put you in the basket again."

"What do you want me to do?" asked the snake.

"I want you to gobble up a frog near that tank. I'll show you."

The hungry snake eagerly moved towards the frog.

The frog saw the snake coming and cried, "What shall I do, what shall I do?"

The ant was ready with her orders: "Jump into the water and bring my baby safely to the shore."

The frog dived glunk! into the water, asked the baby ant to climb on his back, and brought it back to its mother, who was very happy now. She sent the frog and the snake their separate ways, and took her young baby safely to the hole.

There was a snake in the snake hole, wasn't there? A snake who wouldn't help the ant? The ant hadn't forgotten him. She had a plot worked out to punish him.

The snake charmer was quite unhappy when he woke up from his nap to find that there was a hole in his basket and his snake had escaped through it. The ant went to him and said, "I know you're worrying about how to get a new snake. I'll show you one nearby. It's sleeping in a snake hole. Bring your gourd flute (*pungi*) and you can catch it."

The snake charmer went with the ant to the hole and played his *pungi* flute. The snake was charmed by the music, forgot himself, and came out swaying his hood. The snake charmer captured him, pulled out his fangs, and shut him up in a strong new basket. And he was very grateful to the mother ant.

A mere ant did all these things.

10. The Clever Daughter-in-law

A mother-in-law was a terrible tyrant. She gave her daughter-in-law no freedom. She saw to it that the young woman did all the housework, cleaned the cow shed, and carried water from the well. By this time it would already be evening. Mother and son would then eat by themselves, and give the daughter-in-law leftovers and stale rice. If the young woman so much as breathed a complaint, the mother-in-law would pick up the broomstick and rain blows on her head. If she wept, the old woman would let loose a barrage of abuse: "You slut, you hussy, you want to wash away our house in your tears and bring bad luck, you daughter of a whore," and so on. The son was meek and kept his mouth shut.

In their backyard, a snake gourd plant grew and thrived; long gourds swung from it. Everyone's mouth watered when they saw the gourds. In season, the mother-in-law would make a big potful of delicious snake gourd *talada*. She and her son would eat most of it and give the daughter-in-law some leavings. Once, after several days of this semistarvation, the young woman was seized with a craving to eat a full meal of the delicious snake gourd *talada*.

One day, the daughter-in-law came home with her garbage basket and called her mother-in-law in a hurry.

"Why are you howling like a vixen? What's the matter with you?" shrieked the mother-in-law.

"I ran into Big Auntie's husband. He says Auntie isn't well and wants to see you. She is seriously ill and holding on to her life only to see you, he said. He wanted me to tell you that."

"*Ayyo*, my sister is dying. O Sister, what happened to you?" cried the mother-in-law, beating her breast. "Come in now, I'm sautéeing the *talada*. You take care of it. I'll go and see my sister," she said, and left the house.

The daughter-in-law was quite excited. She made some more *talada*. She cooked all sorts of other dishes and served her husband a big meal.

Then she poured all the *talada* into a big vessel, carried it on her waist, and went out as if she were going to get water for the house. She went straight to Goddess Kali's temple, entered it, and closed the door behind her. There was no one there. She sat there and ate an entire potful of *talada*. The Goddess, who was looking at all this, was astonished by the speed of her eating and the quantity she consumed. In her amazement, she put her right hand on her mouth. The daughter-in-law didn't notice any of this but continued to eat to her heart's content. When she was done, she belched a big belch of utter satisfaction, picked up the empty vessel, and went to the pond to wash it.

When she came home with a pot of water, the main door of her house was closed. Her mother-in-law had returned. She tapped on the door, which was soon opened by her angry mother-in-law. Sparks were flying from her eyes. She had a stick in her hand, and blows fell on the young woman's back and waist till she fell to the ground crying pitifully. "You daughter of a whore, how long have you waited to cheat me like this? You've gobbled up a pot full of *talada* like a buffalo, you dirty slut!" screamed the woman and rained some more blows. When the husband came home, he too joined in the punishment.

Meanwhile, the whole town was buzzing with the news that the Kali image in the temple now had its hand on its mouth. People from other towns also came to see this miracle, and everyone had their own interpretation. Everyone was scared that this was a bad sign. Something terrible was going to happen to the village, they thought, and shuddered. Worship and rituals were performed all over the village.

"Someone has polluted the Goddess. That's why she has shut her mouth with her hand. She is angry. There won't be any rain. No children will be born in this village anymore," they said and were terror-stricken. They arranged festivals and sacrificed goats. But nothing seemed to please the Goddess. So the village elders sent the town crier through the area to announce a big reward to anyone who would make the Goddess remove her hand from her mouth. No one came forward.

The daughter-in-law watched all this and came to her mother-in-law one day and said, "Mother-in-law, tell the elders we'll get the Goddess to remove her hand from her mouth. I know how to do it."

The mother-in-law was furious at first. "Look at your mug! She wants me to lose face in the village. She wants to act big as if she is a holy woman. What no one could do, she says she'll do. Fat chance!" she sneered. But the daughter-in-law persisted and finally convinced her that she knew something no one else knew.

On the appointed day, she took with her the broomstick and the garbage basket full of rubbish and went to the temple. She shut everyone out and closed the door behind her. She put down the basket in front of the Black Goddess and, brandishing her broomstick, challenged Kali: "You jealous female! What's it to you if I ate my snake gourd *talada*? Why do your eyes burn? If you'd only asked me, I'd have given you some. May your face burn, may your cheeks swell and explode, may your eyes sink and go blind! Will you take your hand off your mouth now or shall I beat you with my tamarind broomstick! Now!"

There was no answer. The daughter-in-law was now furious and looked like Kali the Black Goddess herself. She went up to the image and gave Kali's face several whacks with her broomstick. Kali whimpered and cried, "*Ayyo!*" She removed her hand from her mouth and the image now looked as it had always looked. "That's better!" muttered the daughter-in-law, picked up her basket and broom, and came home with the news that she had managed to get Kali to remove her hand from her mouth.

The whole village was agog with the news. Everyone ran to the temple to see for themselves and they couldn't believe their own eyes. They praised the daughter-in-law as the greatest of chaste wives (*pativrata*) whose virtue had given her miraculous powers. They gave her a big reward and many gifts.

Now the mother-in-law was terrified by this incident. She felt that her daughter-in-law had strange powers and would take revenge against her for all the terrible things she had done all these years. The young woman knew some kind of magic, and who knows what she will do?

On a dark New Moon day, in the dead of night, mother and son whispered to each other. She said to him, "Son, this one frightened even Kali the Mother Goddess and made her take her hand off her mouth. She won't let us go unharmed. We have beaten her, starved her, given her every kind of trouble. She'll take revenge. She'll finish us off. What shall we do?"

"I can't think of anything. You tell me," said the cowardly son.

She said, "She's now asleep. We'll gather her up in her mat, take her to the fields, and burn her in the pit there. I'll get you a beautiful new bride."

"All right, let's do it right now," said he, and they both gagged her quickly and rolled her in her bedclothes and mat. She knew that they were going to do something awful to her but she mustered courage and lay still. They carried her to the pit in the field outside the village and hid her behind the bush while they went looking for twigs and firewood. As soon as they left, she rolled around and loosened the mat around her. She slid out of it, pulled at the string around her hands and tore it, took the gag from her mouth, and found a log nearby, which she wrapped in her bedclothes and mat. Then she walked a little distance, climbed a banyan tree, and hid herself in its branches.

Mother and son came hurrying back, spread twigs and branches all around the bundle in the mat, put logs over it, and lighted it. They covered it with dry straw. It burned with leaping flames as they watched it burn and burn. When the knots in the fuel crackled and burst, they said, "The bones, the bones are splitting." When the log inside caught fire, its knot cracked in the flames and went off like a gunshot. They were satisfied that the skull had now exploded as it does in a cremation. It was dawn and they went home.

The daughter-in-law crouched in the branches. That night, four robbers came there to sit under the tree, to divide up the loot among themselves. They had just broken into a rich man's mansion and plundered jewelry, gold, and cash. As they sat down, they saw a fire burning at some distance. So one of them climbed the tree to see if anyone was near the fire. He came right up to the branch where the daughter-in-law was perched. When he saw someone sitting there, he said softly, "Who's there?" She boldly put out her hand, gently shut his mouth, and whispered, "Ssh, not so loud. I'm a celestial. I'm looking for a good handsome man. I'll marry you and make you rich beyond your dreams. Just be quiet!"

The robber couldn't believe what was happening to him. He thought he had reached heaven and seen the Great White Elephant descend from the sky. He held her hand and said, "Are you for real?" She said, "Hmm." Then she slowly pulled out her little satchel of betel leaf and betel nut, gave him some, and put some into her own mouth. He came closer to kiss her. She turned away, saying, "Look, we're not married yet. But you can put your betel leaf into my mouth with your tongue. When I've eaten from your mouth, I'll be as good as your wedded wife. All right?"

He was beside himself with joy. He put out his tongue with the chewed betel leaf on it and brought it close to her mouth. She at once closed her teeth on his tongue powerfully and bit it off. Screaming with unbearable pain, he lost his grip and fell down. The robbers below ran helter-skelter in panic. The man who had fallen had lost his tongue and could only babble and blabber and spit blood, making noises like "*Da da dadadada . . .*" as he too ran after his companions. His noises scared them even more and they fled faster, with him squealing behind them.

When dawn came, the daughter-in-law cautiously climbed down the tree and saw to her amazement lots of gold, jewelry, and money! She quickly bundled them all up and went straight home. When she tapped on the door, calling out, "Mother-in-law, Mother-in-law, please open the door!" the mother-in-law opened the door hesitantly, her face blanched with fear. There, in front of her, was her smiling daughter-in-law. The mother-in-law fainted at the sight. The daughter-in-law carried her into the hall, sprinkled cool water on her face, and revived her. Her son just stood there, not knowing what to think.

When she came to and opened her eyes, the mother-in-law asked her, "How did you . . . ? How is it you are . . . ?"

The daughter-in-law briskly replied, "After you cremated me, messengers from Yama, the god of death, took me to Him. His eyes were shooting flames like our Kali, our village goddess. As soon as He saw me, He said, 'Send this one back. Her mother-in-law is a sinner. Bring *her* here and put the Iron Crow to work on her, to tear her to pieces with its beak. Dip her in cauldrons of boiling oil.' He ranted on like that about you. I fell at His feet and begged Him, 'Don't do this to my mother-in-law. She is really a very fine woman. Give me whatever punishment you wish. Please spare my mother-in-law.' He was pleased, even smiled and said, 'You can go now. We'll do as you say. But if your mother-in-law ever gives you any trouble, we'll drag her here. My messengers will always be watching.' Then He gave me all this gold and jewelry and money and sent me home. People say bad things about the god of death. But He was so good to me."

The mother-in-law embraced her daughter-in-law with fear and trembling in her heart.

"*Ayyo*, you're really the angel of this house. You've saved me from the jaws of death's messengers. From now on, I'll do as you say. Just forgive everything I've done to you. Will you, my darling daughter-in-law?" she said, touching the daughter-in-law's chin tenderly.

The daughter-in-law was now the boss in the house. Her mother-in-law and her husband followed her wishes and everyone was happy.

11. A Couple of Misers

A miserly man married a miserly woman and they had a little son. They were such misers that they wouldn't eat a betel nut; they would carefully suck on one and wipe it and put it away. They ate meals only because they needed to eat to keep alive. Still they complained and asked God why he had to make a stomach that they had to fill every day so many times.

They had a secret grain pit in the gods' room, and their life's ambition was to fill it with money by the time their little son grew up. The wife bitched about the size of the cucumbers in their backyard: if only they could have been twice the size, the family could have dined on them for two more days. When her husband asked her to wear the one or two pieces of jewelry she had received at her wedding, she would say, "Are you crazy? If I wear them, I'll wear them out. Who's the loser then? You and me!" The husband would beam at his wife's wisdom.

For years, no guest had ever entered their house for a drink of water or a morsel of food. One rainy season, the couple had shut all the doors when suddenly they heard someone banging on their door. The husband opened it and in came a holy man, grumbling, "What a terrible rain, what a terrible rain!" As soon as he came in, he shut the door behind him and praised them.

"You are such good people. I'd have caught cold in that rain and died. You took me in and saved my life."

As he had come in like a wet dog, he wet the whole house with his drippings. The wife said, "That's all very well. You've dripped water all over the house."

The husband chimed in, "What shall we do if the house gets too damp and the walls crumble?"

The holy man was not worried. He said, "No such thing will happen. After all, a holy man like me is in this house. Why don't you bring some cow dung and wipe the floor with all this water and make it clean and nice?"

The husband couldn't bear this man's intrusion. "We don't yet know why Your Holiness is here," he said, quite bluntly.

The man said, "What does a holy man do in his devotees' house? It's very hard these days to find real devotees like yourselves. You're two in a thousand. Because of the likes of you, holy men survive in this world. Well, anyway it's time for dinner. You could give me some dinner.

Then, you can spread a mat. I'll lie on it and be gone in the morning. Anyway, good generous people like you are very rare. I'd rather get a glimpse of your sweet faces than go on a pilgrimage to Kashi."

He didn't seem to wait for any yes or no from them. The couple stood there with their mouths open. He didn't notice them at all. He took off most of his wet clothes, wrung them out then and there, and hung them up to dry on the peg. He even took the dry shirt and dhoti of the host from the clothesline, put them on, and sat on a chair without a word of apology. He asked the bewildered host to sit down on the other chair, and asked the woman, "Will you finish cooking soon?" The husband sat down where he stood, his mouth still open. His wife went in to cook.

She had some leftover rice from the afternoon. She felt that wouldn't be enough and made some more. She meant to serve the leftovers to the guest and the fresh hot rice to her husband. But she was too flustered to do so, and actually served her husband the leftovers and the guest the fresh rice. The holy man relished everything he ate and asked for more chutney and more ghee and more everything. She couldn't help serving him whatever he asked for, to the great astonishment of her husband, who knew her very well. The guest talked ceaselessly through the meal and even afterwards as he relaxed in his chair and praised her cooking fulsomely.

"What a wonderful cook you are! It was like ambrosia. The spices, the proportions! Others may bring the whole spice bazaar to the kitchen but can't cook one good curry."

The wife ate the small scraps of food left over from this hearty meal, and came out of the kitchen, somewhat exhausted. The holy man addressed them both with great satisfaction.

"Look, as I said, we don't get devotees like you every day. I'm very pleased with your hospitality. I'll give you three wishes. Ask what you want."

Now the faces of the miser and his wife blossomed. The man came and fell at the guest's feet and said, "Sir, please, may whatever I touch turn into a heap of silver rupees."

The holy man asked him first to let go of his legs, and when he had done so, said, "Done."

The husband put his hands out and touched a couple of things around him, and they fell down in a clanging heap of rupees. His joy knew no bounds. He jumped up and down, touching everything he could see, turning things into heaps of rupees.

The wife now fell at the holy man's feet, and thinking of the cucumbers in her backyard, said, "*Swami,* may whatever I touch grow as long as a yard."

The holy man quickly said, "Let go of the legs first," released himself, and then said, "So be it."

Whatever she touched grew at once as long as a yard. She went into the kitchen and touched the hot chilies. They became a yard long. She touched the cucumbers. They too grew a yard long. She touched whatever she fancied and made them all long.

Right at that moment, her little son was wakened by all this noise and began to cry. The mother ran in happily and touched his nose, saying, "My rajah!" And his nose at once grew long, a yard long. She screamed, horrified by her son's bizarre looks. When the husband ran in, the child was howling, unable to bear the weight of his nose on his face. "O my poor son," said the man and picked up the child, who at once crumbled into a heap of rupees. Then the husband and wife realized their blunder. They ran weeping to the holy man, who carefully kept his distance, and they begged of him, "Please, give us the third wish at once."

"Tell me what you want."

"We want everything to be as it was. Please see to it that our first two wishes are cancelled."

The holy man said, "So be it."

The child began to play in the cradle as before. The chilies and cucumbers shrank back to their normal size. The heaps of rupees vanished, and things returned to their original shapes. When the man and the woman turned around, the holy man was nowhere to be seen. They said, "Look, that was God himself, come down to teach us a lesson."

From that day on, they gave up their miserly ways and lived happily.

12. The Dead Prince and the Talking Doll

The king had a daughter. One daughter, but no sons. Now and then a beggar would come to the palace. He was strange, for every time he begged, he would say, "You'll get a dead man for a husband. Give me some alms." The girl used to wonder: "Why does he say such weird things to me?" And she would silently give him alms and go in. The holy man (*bava*), this beggar man, came to the door every day for twelve years. And he said every day, "You'll get a dead man for a husband."

One day the king was standing on the balcony and heard him say, "You'll get a dead man for a husband, give me some alms." The king came down and asked his daughter, "What's this talk, daughter?"

She replied, "This *bava* comes every day and says, 'You'll get a dead man for a husband. Give me some alms.' Then I give him something. He has been saying it for twelve years, ever since I was a little girl."

The king was disturbed when he heard this. He was afraid the prophecy would come true. He didn't wish his only daughter to have a dead man for a husband. He said, unhappily, "It's no good staying in this kingdom. Let's leave and spend our time in travels." And he got his servants to pack everything, and left the place with his entire family.

Around that time, the prince of the neighboring kingdom fell mysteriously ill and died. But his body looked as if he had only fallen asleep. Astrologers said he would return to life after twelve years. So, they didn't bury him; instead of burying him, his father the king built a bungalow outside the town, laid his son's body in it, mortared and whitewashed the house on all sides, and left the body there, fully clothed and adorned. The father locked the main door and left a written message on it. The message said, "One day a chaste woman who has made offerings to the gods for her husband will come here. Only she can enter the place. When she touches the door, it will open. It will open to no one else."

It was soon after this sad event that the first king arrived there with his wife and daughter and his entourage. They were all hungry and began to cook a meal for themselves. The king's daughter went for a walk and saw the locked door. The lock was of exquisite design and gleamed from a distance.

She went near and held it in her hand. As soon as she touched it, it sprang open, and the door opened. She went in. The door closed and locked itself behind her. Ahead of her were twelve doors, one behind another; they all opened at her touch, and each closed behind her as she went through them.

Right in the heart of the house she found a dead man on a cot. He looked as if he was fast asleep. Before she could wonder about what was happening to her, how doors opened before her and shut behind her, she was in the presence of the dead man.

His family had left provisions for twelve years in the house: vessels, dishes, clothes, grains, spices. The princess saw all these things around her.

She remembered the holy beggar's words, and thought, "I didn't escape it: his words are coming true." She unveiled the face of the body. It was dead as dead could be, but calm as a face in deep slumber. "Well, what's to be done? It looks as if I am imprisoned here with this dead man. Let's do something," she said, and started massaging his legs.

For almost twelve years she tended and massaged his body. She would wake up in the morning in the locked house with twelve locked doors, and where could she go? She bathed and cooked, kept house and looked after the dead body, and thought about all the things that had happened to her.

Meanwhile, in the forest, the mother had said, "The food is all ready, where's our girl gone?" Her father had walked outside and called her. She was nowhere to be seen. But they could hear her cries from inside the house. They had called out, "Daughter, why are you in there? Come out!"

She had answered from within, and told her father what had happened.

"I touched the locks, and they fell open. As soon as I came in, they locked themselves shut. I am alone here."

"What is in there?"

"A dead man is lying here. Nothing else."

"My girl, your luck has caught up with you. What the *bava* said is coming true. The locks can't be opened."

They had tried to enter the house from the sides and from behind, but it was as if it was sealed. They had tried and tried and finally said, "What else can we do? We'll go, and leave you to work out your fate." They left sorrowfully. Time passed, and they grew old.

Inside the locked house, night and day the princess massaged the dead man's legs, took ritual baths and worshiped the gods at the right times, made offerings for her husband. Around the tenth year, an acrobat's daughter came that way. She looked all around the house, tried the doors, and at last climbed onto the roof.

The princess was lonely. She was dying to see another human face. "If there's a chink in the house, I could pull in at least a child. If only I could have a girl for a companion!" she thought. Just then, she saw a young woman looking through a window.

"Hey, girl! Will you come inside?"

"Yes," said the acrobat girl.

"Do you have any father or mother? If you do, don't try to come in. You can't get out. If you don't have parents, come inside."

"Oh no, I've nobody."

She pulled the girl in through the window. The acrobat girl was agile. She twisted and contorted her body and got in. The princess was happy; she had company now. With a companion inside, time went fast. Two more years rolled by.

The prince's twelve years were coming to an end. The time for his life to stir again was near.

One day, when the king's daughter was taking her bath, she heard the omen-bird speak from the branch in the window. It said, "The twelve years are coming to an end. If someone would pluck the leaves of this tree, grind them and press them in a silver cup, and pour the juice into the man's mouth, he will come to life again."

The king's daughter heard it. At once she plucked some leaves and pressed the juice out into a silver cup. Just when she was about to take it to the dead man's lips, it occurred to her that she had not bathed yet. She should finish her bath, purify herself, offer worship to the Lord Siva properly and then give the juice to the prince. So she put down the cup and went back to bathe and offer worship.

The acrobat girl asked her, "What's this stuff in the cup? Why is it here?"

The princess told her about the bird's message and what the cup contained. As soon as she heard all this, the acrobat girl thought this was her chance. While the princess sat in worship, the acrobat girl parted the dead prince's lips and poured the juice from the silver cup. As the liquid went in, he woke up as if he had only been asleep. Exclaiming, "Siva, Siva," he sat up straight. He saw the woman next to him and asked, "Who are you?"

She said, "Your wife."

He was grateful to her. They became husband and wife while the princess sat inside, long absorbed in prayer, the woman who had served him for twelve long years.

When she came out, she heard the two of them whispering intimacies to each other. "O Siva, I did penance for twelve years, and it has turned out like this. Obviously, happiness is not my lot," she thought. She began to work as their servant while the prince and the acrobat woman sat back and enjoyed themselves.

Yet, after all, she was a princess, born to a queen. The other girl was only an acrobat's daughter. The prince began to see the difference between them in manners and speech. He began to suspect something was wrong. So later that day, he said to both of them, "I'm going out for a hunt and then I'll go to the city. Tell me what you want."

The acrobat girl, who had been longing for her kind of gypsy food, asked for all sorts of greens and dry flat bread to eat. He was disgusted. A woman should ask for saris and silk and blouses, but this one asks for wretched dry bread! Then he told the acrobat girl to ask the other woman in the house what she would like. The princess answered, "I don't want anything much. Just tell the master what I'd really like is a talking doll."

"This one is strange, too. All she wants is a talking doll," he thought.

After a good hunt in the jungle, he brought the acrobat girl the evil-smelling greens and leaves and dry bread from some gypsies, and for the princess a talking doll. The acrobat girl was overjoyed at the sight of the rough food; now she began to thrive and get color in her cheeks.

That night, after everyone had eaten and gone to bed, the talking doll suddenly began to speak and said, "Tell me a story."

The princess asked, "What story can I tell you? My own life has become quite a story."

"Then tell me your life's story," insisted the doll.

So the princess told the doll her entire story, as I've told you so far. Just like that.

The doll nodded and said, "Hmm, hmm," as the princess told her tale. The prince lying awake in the other room heard it all. Finally she said, "I left the silver cup there, on that ledge, and that woman gave the juice to the prince before I got back from my prayers. Now she's the wife, I'm the servant. That's the way it turned out." And she ended the story.

As he heard the story from where he lay in the next room, the prince felt his anger mounting. When the story came to an end, he took a switch and lashed at the acrobat girl sleeping next to him, and drove her out of the house.

"You're not my wife, you're an acrobat wench! Get out of my sight!" he screamed.

Then he went in and consoled the princess who had served him lovingly for twelve years; and they talked happily to each other all night.

In the world outside, his father and mother had counted up the days and years. They knew the twelve years were over and were anxious to see what had happened to their son. They came, and all the town came with them. They found the doors unlocked, and found in the heart of the house the couple, prince and princess, whispering loving words to each other.

Gratefully, the father-in-law and mother-in-law fell at the feet of their young daughter-in-law and said, "By your good work in many past lives, and your prayers in this one, our son came back to life. He looks as fresh as if he had just woken up from a long night's sleep. It's all your doing."

They took them to their palace and celebrated the wedding with great pomp and many processions. For the grand occasion, they sent for the bride's parents, who had grown weak and old. Their eyes had become like cottonseed, and they were ready to lie down in the earth. But their spirits revived at the good news, and they too hurried to the reunion at their daughter's wedding.

13. A Dog's Daughters

A king had many wives but no children. So he went to a sage and asked for help. The sage gave him a magic mango and asked him to give it to his queens, which he did. The queens happily sat on the balcony, cut up the mango, shared the sweet flesh among themselves, and threw away the seed and the peel. A poor dog that lived under the balcony ate the peel and the seed. All the queens soon got pregnant, and so did the dog. The whole palace looked after the queens and fussed over them till they gave birth. When they went into labor and actually gave birth, alas, they gave birth to puppies, every one of them. But the poor dog whom nobody cared for somehow took longer than usual, and gave birth to two beautiful girls.

When the queens and their servants tried to take away the babies, the dog picked them up and ran away into the nearby forest. She hid them in a stone cave and brought them up. She would go into town, and when the housewives weren't looking, would steal food and clothing for her babies. They grew up to be two lovely young women.

One day, two young men went hunting in the forest and happened to sit outside the cave to rest. They heard something stirring in the cave, looked in, and found two lovely young women. The dog had gone somewhere. They fell in love with the women at once and wanted to take them home and marry them. They and their servants carried them away on horses.

The older sister, who was now called Big Honni, was quite happy to get away from the forest. The younger sister, who was now called Little Honni, was quite unhappy to leave her mother behind and to go away without telling her. So she tore pieces of her sari and left a trail behind her.

The dog was frantic when she came back to the cave and found that her children were gone. She looked everywhere till she found the trail and the smell of her daughter's sari, followed it till she reached the house of Little Honni, who was delighted to see her mother, took her in, gave her a warm bath, and looked after her. But she told no one who the dog really was.

A few days later, the dog wanted to see Big Honni, the older sister, and went to her house. Big Honni didn't want anyone to know she was born to a dog. She muttered to herself, "Look at this bitch, she has come all this way to ruin my life. Everybody will say, Big Honni is a dog's daughter, the bitch!" Then she took a stick and beat the dog till it died. She asked the servants to throw the carcass in the garbage heap.

Three days later, Little Honni came to Big Honni's house and asked her, "Mother came to see you. Where is she?"

Big Honni replied, "She came here to ruin our lives. Everyone will know we are a dog's daughters. So I beat her and threw her in the garbage heap."

Little Honni ran to the garbage heap, picked up the dog's body, carried it home, washed it and wiped it clean, put it in a box and kept it in her bedroom without telling anyone about it. After a few days, her husband, who was watching her taking extra care about a box, asked her what was in it. She said, "Something my mother sent me."

He was curious. He wanted it opened at once. She made excuses. She knew her secret would be out. Finally, her heart beating violently with the fear of discovery, she opened the box. She was astonished, and so was everyone else, when she found there not a dog's rotting body but a bar of pure gold.

The husband was intrigued. "You've made such a secret of your family. You've never taken me to meet them. They must be fabulously rich to send you a bar of gold as a gift. I want to meet them, and right away," he said.

As he would take no excuses from her, she had to obey and set out on a journey. She didn't know where to go. They all went to the forest where the couple had originally met. She led the party a long way, aimlessly, through trees and bushes. What could she do? Everyone was wearied by the journey and didn't quite know what was happening or where they were going. One day, in her despair, she said to her husband, "I'm going out to do Number One," and took a walk, looking for some way to kill herself. She found a snake hole and plunged her hand deep into it, praying that the snake inside it would bite her. But the snake did not bite her. Instead, when she took her hand out, it came out and said to her, "I'm grateful to you. You've done me a good turn."

She didn't understand. She said, "What good turn? I put my hand in so that you could bite me and put an end to my troubles."

"When you put your hand into my hole, it touched this ripe boil on my head and broke it. It put an end to my pain. I've been suffering from it for months. But then why did you put your hand in it? What's your sorrow?" asked the snake.

Little Honni told him her story. The snake shook its head and said, "It's my turn. I'll help you. Go north from here for a mile or so. You'll see a big house. You'll find every kind of comfort and luxury there. That will be your mother's house. When you leave after a week, on your return journey make sure to turn back and look. Then everything will be all right."

She was very happy. She roused her party and they all rode north till they found a beautiful palatial house, with gardens, servants, and every kind of luxury. The snake was waiting for them in the form of a rich man and introduced himself as Little Honni's maternal uncle. Her mother was there too in human form. Little Honni's husband was overjoyed and greatly impressed by his wife's aristocratic "family."

After a few days, they took leave of the mother and the uncle, who loaded them with gold and gifts. A few miles into their return journey, she remembered to look back. She and her entire party were aghast at what they saw. The palatial house they had left behind was going up in flames, and as they watched it, it burned and burned till it was a heap of smoking ashes. They went home in utter bewilderment and grief. But Little Honni was secretly happy that she would never have to go through the ordeal of taking her husband to her "mother's house" again.

When they got home, Big Honni wanted to know where they had been and how her little sister got all the gifts. Little Honni told her everything, beginning with the death of the dog, the bar of gold, her husband insisting on seeing her mother's house, the snake in the forest, the palace he created for her, everything down to the last detail.

Big Honni went home in a hurry. She found a street dog, got it killed, and put the carcass in a box. In a few days it began to rot and stink. Her husband asked her what it was and why she kept it in her bedroom. She said, "It's a gift from my mother's house."

"Your mother's house? Where is it? You've always been secretive about it. Where's your mother? Let's go visit her. I understand your sister just visited her and came back with a lot of gold. Let's go," said her husband.

They too set out on a journey. When they had ridden a long way into the forest, she too said, "I want to go do Number One," and went in search of a snake hole. When she found it, she thrust her hand into it. There was an angry snake in the hole, and it stung her to death.

14. A Dog's Story

A king had two sons named Alakanna and Malakanna. When Alakanna, the older brother, grew up to be a handsome strong young man, the family looked for a beautiful young bride for him and arranged a gala wedding. A few years passed and Alakanna had to go to a distant place to fight a war. He bade tearful goodbyes to his father, mother, and wife. He called his younger brother specially, and said to him, "Look, I have to go to war. I'll be back as soon as I can. Look after things here while I'm gone."

And then he went. But he couldn't get back soon. His wife, beautiful, young, and alone, grew restless when her husband didn't come back for months. Meanwhile, Malakanna, the younger brother, was growing up strong and tall. His parents wanted to get him married too, but they decided to wait till the elder brother got back home. Malakanna was a wrestler, worked out twice a day, and drank ten pots of milk a day. His sister-in-law's eye fell on this handsome young fellow, who seemed to grow handsomer by the day. She began to think, "How shall I grab him? What kind of net will trap him in?" She sent her maids a few times to get him to come and see her, but he didn't respond.

One day he and his friends were playing ball in the yard. During the game, he kicked the ball rather hard and it rose in the air and landed in his sister-in-law's backyard. One of the boys ran up to her door and asked her for the ball. She said, "Send me the fellow who kicked the ball here, and I'll give it to him."

So Malakanna ran up to her door and asked his sister-in-law to give him the ball. She asked him to come in and, without any warning, proceeded to kiss him and hug him.

"O Sister-in-law, Sister-in-law, what are you doing?" he cried, trying to ward off her advances.

She said, "Nothing really. I want you, that's all. Come in and satisfy me, or else . . ."

"What kind of talk is this? A sister-in-law is like a mother. Sleeping with you would be like sleeping with my mother. How can you think such dirty thoughts?"

"I don't care what you say. Will you do as I say, or shall I call everyone in and tell them that you tried to seduce me?" she said.

He saw what she was like and knew he couldn't stay there one minute longer. He left the ball where it lay, and before she could raise her voice he jumped over the back wall and ran from the place. She said to herself, "How far can he go, where will he escape? Let's see," and sent for the local magician. The maid went into town and brought the magician (*bawa*) to her room.

"Look here, *Bawa*, take as much money as you want, a cartload if you want. See to it that Malakanna surrenders to me," she begged of him. A cartload of cash was no small temptation for the magician. What did he care? He asked the maid to bring him a bunch of jasmine flowers and a thorn. He placed a spell on both of them and said to the sister-in-law, "Wear this bunch of jasmine in your hair. Before the flower fades, the young fellow will be in your hands. When he comes, everything will be fine if he yields to you; if he does not, grab him and stick this thorn deep into his forehead. He will change into a dog and lick your feet. Take these," he said, and went on his way.

The woman had no reason to wait anymore. She went in, took a bath, applied talcum and attar to her face, wrapped herself in her best sari, combed her hair down, and wore the bunch of jasmine in her braid, and waited for him. "He'll come now, he'll come now," she muttered to herself, and looked at the door every other minute.

Meanwhile, as Malakanna walked with his friends, his nose picked up the scent of jasmine. None of his friends could smell it, but it hit his nostrils like something not of this earth. After all, he was a full-blooded young man, and as it hit him, the scent of jasmine went to his head.

"What woman could be wearing such fantastic jasmine?" he thought. "If the scent itself is so wonderful, how much more wonderful should the woman wearing such flowers be?" His head was in a swirl. Wherever the scent wafted, he followed. He didn't have any idea where he was going. Caught in the haze of that fragrance, he came straight to his sister-in-law's house. "Got you, young fellow!" thought the woman, and, as soon as he came in, asked the maid to bolt the doors. He was aware of nothing that was happening around him. He went straight to her bedroom, where she sat waiting, with the jasmine in her hair. But he took one look at her face and saw that it was his sister-in-law! That woke him up from his trance at once. "What am I doing?" he cried, and tried to flee the place. But how could he escape? The doors were bolted. "Come here, my love," said the woman, with her arms open, as he started stepping backwards.

"Come now, you've no choice. If you don't do as I say, I'm not responsible for what happens next," she threatened.

"Come what may, I won't go to bed with you," he said firmly.

"Do you mean it? Is that your last word?"

"Yes."

"Think carefully. It's not easy to know the nature of a woman, a horse, or a river. Think about it."

He didn't yield an inch. She cajoled, cooed, and threatened, but he wouldn't have anything to do with her. Then she and her maid grabbed him and stuck the thorn deep into his forehead. At once the young man ceased to be a man and became a whimpering dog, wagging his tail, licking her feet. She laughed at him as he groveled and licked her hands and feet, maybe in the hope that she would turn him back into a human being. But she wasn't going to do anything of the sort. She pointed to the dog again and again and shook with laughter. The maid fixed a collar around the dog's neck and tied him up in a corner.

After all, the brother who had gone to war had to return one day, and Alakanna did return. His army had won and he was a victor. As soon as he entered the house, he fell at the feet of his father and mother and received their blessings. His next question was about his brother: "Where is Malakanna, where has he gone on the day of my return?" People around him said, "Nobody knows where he's gone. He has a way of going off like that for days. We haven't seen him for eight or ten days."

"Eight or ten days?" The brother was worried.

Maybe he has gone hunting, he explained to himself. Still he continued asking questions. He asked Malakanna's friends where he might be. They didn't know. They too had begun to wonder. When he came home to see his wife, he was still deep in thought. She gave him water for his hands and feet, talked to him sweetly. But he was troubled. She showed displeasure.

"You've come back a victor. You're seeing me after so long. Why are you looking so miserable?"

"I'm troubled about Malakanna. Where could he have gone?"

By this time, the dog in the corner was straining at the leash, whining and barking. He knew his brother had come back, but how could Alakanna know about it? He said, "What's the matter with that dog? Anyway, where did you get it?"

"O, that dog. My mother's family sent it to me. Forget about the dog. Come in, let's eat," she urged him.

Then she served him a big meal and slowly said to him as he was eating, "That brother of yours, he was after me the moment you left. He tried to seduce me. I was safe only because my maid was here."

And so on, she told him a story, adding lurid colors to it. The brother couldn't but believe her. "That's why he's gone out of town. He was afraid I'd beat him up. God, whom can you trust if you can't trust your own kid brother?" he thought, and felt very hurt and angry.

When the meal was over, he came out of the room and sat outside. According to custom, his wife then went to eat her dinner. The dog, which had now been tied outside the house, began to get very agitated, pulled at the chain, barked, and whimpered. "I don't know whether they have fed him or not, poor thing," he said, and went up to the dog, unhooked him from the chain, and carried him to where he was sitting. He put him on his lap, teased him, and played with him. The dog was beside himself, licked him, and sniffed him all over, wagging his tail violently to and fro. Alakanna also loved the dog and petted him a lot. As he rubbed him and massaged his body playfully, his hand went to the dog's head and felt the thorn in the middle of his forehead. It was deeply embedded. "Poor thing, that's why it has been crying like this!" he said to himself, and pulled the thorn out of the dog's forehead. What can I tell you? At once, the dog turned into Malakanna! And he embraced his brother tightly, calling him *Anna, Anna.* Alakanna didn't understand what was happening to him. Malakanna told him the real story about his sister-in-law with tears in his eyes.

"Is that what happened? Wait," said the older brother, and called his wife and her maid, as he took out his whip. They came and saw no dog but Malakanna, alive and well, standing tall. Alakanna brandished the whip in his hand.

"Will you now tell me the truth or shall I whip you all the way to the marketplace?" he shouted.

The two women fell at his feet and whined and whimpered and begged forgiveness. He lashed out with his whip and raised weals on their backs. He called them whores and bitches and other such names, slashed their breasts and buttocks, and threw them out of the house. Then he found himself a new bride and found another for his brother, married again, and lived happily.

15. Dolls

In a certain town there lived a couple. The husband would bring home a bushel of fish every day. His wife would eat up all the middles of the fish and leave him only fish heads and fish tails. She did this every day.

What did he do? He had a sister in town. He went to her house one day and said, "Sister, every day I bring home a bushel of fish. When I come to eat, the fish have only heads and tails, no middles. What shall I do?"

His sister told him, "If that's the case, Brother, go to the carpenter, and ask him to make three dolls for you. Place one doll next to the cooking fire. Place another with the pots and pans. Put the third one in the niche in the wall. After you've done that, bring home as usual your bushel of fish and then leave. Let's see what happens."

He did exactly what his sister told him to do. He went to the carpenter and got three dolls made. He placed one near the cooking fire, a second one among the pots, and another in the wall niche. And he brought in his daily bushel of fish, gave it to his wife, and went out as usual.

She cooked the fish in a hurry, and was going to pick up a platter when the doll among the pots piped up and asked, "Why a platter?"

The doll in the wall answered, "To eat like a thief."

The doll near the cooking fire added, "Without her husband!"

She gasped, "They talk, and like that!"

She was scared of the dolls and rushed out of the house, and didn't get back till her husband came home. When he came home, she fed him, and then ate her own dinner. The fish were whole, as whole as when they were brought.

Her husband said nothing. He finished his meal, and went to his sister's house. He said to her, "Sister, I did as you told me to. Today, all the fish were whole."

16. Double Double

A very poor couple lived in a small hut. They lived by gathering firewood and selling it. One day, the husband felt like eating millet *dosés* (pancakes). But he had no millet at home. So he thought he would go to the hills, pray to God, and ask him for a small measure of millet. So he went to the hills, performed penances, and God was very pleased. He appeared to the man and asked, "What do you want?"

"I want just a small measure of millet. I don't want anything else."

"Sure, go home and you'll find a measure of millet."

Just then, the man thought he could ask for more.

"God, God, could you please double it for me?"

"Sure, go home and your millet will double itself."

When he went home, he found his measuring vessel full of millet. He gave it to his wife and said, "Grind it and make a *dosé* for me."

She took it and poured it into a winnowing fan. The millet doubled itself. She put it in the mouth of the grinding stone. As she ground it, the millet doubled itself. When she gathered the flour in the winnowing fan, the flour doubled itself.

She mixed it in butter and started frying the *dosé* in a frying pan. When she finished making one, she found she had made two. She could never stop. She had many many *dosés* on her platter.

The husband was beside himself with joy and took one pancake in his hand. He found he really had two. When he put one in his mouth, he found he had still another. As he chewed on them, he had another in his mouth, even as he had one in his hand. He ate and ate till he swelled and burst.

Four men came to carry his dead body on their shoulders to the burial ground. As soon as they buried him, they found they had another body on their shoulders. When they passed it on to another four men, they had still another body appear on their shoulders. The more bodies they buried, the more they had, till every foursome in town had a body to carry.

God saw the confusion. He saved them by taking back his boon and making everything as it was before.

17. Dumma and Dummi

A dwarf couple named Dumma and Dummi lived in a town. He loved *holigi,* a sweet pancake with goodies for filling. So he asked his wife, "Dummi, Dummi, I feel like eating *holigi*s, will you make some?"

Dummi said, "*Ayyo,* it's nothing. Get me lentils and jaggery. I'll make it in a trice."

So Dumma brought lentils, jaggery, and wheat. Dummi said to him, "Look, you brought everything except firewood for the stove."

So Dumma went to the hillside and started cutting wood. A tiger came out of the hill and said to him, "Why are you cutting my wood? I'll break your bones and eat you up."

Dumma said, "Mister, don't eat me. I'll give you a *holigi* too." The tiger said, "All right then."

Dumma came home with the firewood and Dummi started making *holigi*s. Even as she made them he ate them and ate them. Dummi got only what was left in her hand at the end. Just as she put the last piece in her mouth, the tiger came to their door and said, "Dumma, Dumma, you didn't give me a *holigi*," and stood on the threshold. Dumma began to shake with fear.

Dummi said to him, "*Ayyo,* you're a man. Why are you shaking so much? Make a hole in that pumpkin and we can both hide in it."

So they both hid in the pumpkin and found it very snug. But Dumma had eaten many many *holigi*s. His tummy was full of gas and he had to fart.

"Dummi, Dummi I've got to fart. What shall I do?" he asked helplessly.

"Fart then, fart!" she said.

Dumma let go and farted a big one. The pumpkin exploded with a terrifying DUBB! sound. The tiger was terrified and fled for his life, crying *Ayyo! Ayyoo!*

18. Dwarfs

A he-dwarf and a she-dwarf lived together. When the dwarf went to dig holes in a field, the she-dwarf brought him food. She lowered her basket and called him, "Midget, midget, come eat!"

When he heard her call him midget, the dwarf went after her to cut her to pieces. She ran. But he followed till he caught her and cut her to pieces. He buried the pieces in the earth, and a black gram (*togari*) plant sprouted there. The *togari* plant grew tall; its pods dried and rattled in the wind. One day, when the dwarf was walking that way, he heard the *togari* plant rattle its pods and say, "Midget, midget, *gulak gulak!*"

So he cut the plant and gave it, leaf, pods, and all, to the buffalo. The buffalo ate it and mooed, "Midget, midget, *booynkbooynk!*"

He killed the buffalo and gave its meat to the dog, which began to bark, "Midget, midget, *owk owk!*"

In a fury, he cut up the dog and threw it in the river. The river said, as it flowed over the stones, "Midget, midget, *dadak dadak!*"

So he took his long knife and went into the river to cut it to pieces and drowned in it. Thus the he-dwarf and the she-dwarf came to a bad end. But you are here and alive. Sleep now.

19. A Flowering Tree

In a certain town, the king had two daughters and a son. The older daughter was married.

In the same town, there lived an old woman with her two daughters. She did menial jobs to feed and clothe and bring up her children. When the girls reached puberty, the younger sister said one day, "Sister, I've been thinking of something. It's hard on mother to work all day for our sakes. I want to help her. I will turn myself into a flowering tree. You can take the flowers and sell them for good money."

Amazed, the older sister asked, "How will you turn into a flowering tree?"

"I'll explain later. You first sweep and wash the entire house. Then take a bath, go to the well, and bring two pitchers full of water," said the younger sister.

The older sister listened to her carefully, swept and wiped and cleaned, took a bath, and brought two pitchers of water without touching them with her fingernails.

Right in front of their house stood a tall tree. The sister swept and wiped the ground under it too. Both girls then went there, and the younger one said, "Sister, I'll sit under this tree and meditate. Then you pour the water from this pitcher all over my body. I'll turn into a flowering tree. Then you pluck as many flowers as you want, but do it without breaking a sprout or tearing a leaf. When you're done, pour the water from the other pitcher over me, and I'll become a person again."

The younger sister sat down and thought of the Lord. The older one poured water from the first pitcher all over her sister. At once, her sister changed into a beautiful tree that seemed to have a flower next to every leaf. The older sister plucked the flowers carefully, without hurting a stalk or sprout or leaf. After she had enough to fill a basket or two, she emptied the second pitcher of water over the tree—and the tree became a human being again, and the younger sister stood in its place. She shook the water from her hair and stood up. They both gathered the flowers in baskets and brought them home. The flowers had a wonderful fragrance. They wove them into garlands.

"Where shall I sell them?" asked the elder sister.

"Sister, why not take all of them to the king's palace? They will pay well. Mother is always doing such awful jobs for our sake. Let's pile up some money and surprise her," said the younger one.

So the older sister took the basketful of garlands before the king's palace and hawked her wares, crying, "Flowers, flowers, who wants flowers?"

The princess looked out and said, "Mother, Mother, the flowers smell wonderful. Buy me some".

"All right, call the flower girl," said the queen. They both looked at the flowers, and they were lovely. The queen asked, "How much do you want for these?"

"We are poor people, give us whatever you wish," said the older sister. They gave her a handful of coins and bought all the garlands.

When the older sister came home with the money, the younger one said, "Sister, Sister, don't tell mother. Hide it. Don't tell anyone."

They sold flowers like this for five days, and they had five handfuls of coins.

"Shall we show these to Mother?" asked one.

"No, no, she'll get angry and beat us," said the other. The two girls were eager to make money.

One day the king's son saw the flowers. They smelled wonderful. He had never seen such flowers anywhere. "What flowers are these? Where do they grow, on what kind of tree? Who brings them to the palace?" he wondered. He watched the girl who brought the flowers; one day he followed her home to the old woman's house, but he couldn't find a single flowering tree anywhere. He was quite intrigued. On his way home he tired himself out thinking, "Where on earth do they get such flowers?"

Early the next morning, while it was still dark, the king's son went and hid himself in the tall tree in front of the old woman's house. That day too, the girls swept and washed the space under the tree. As usual, the younger girl became the flowering tree, and after the older one had gently plucked all the flowers, the tree became the young woman again. The prince saw all this happen before his very eyes.

He came straight home, and lay on his bed, face down. His father and mother came to find out what the matter was. He didn't speak a word. The minister's son, his friend, came and asked him, "What happened? Did anyone say anything that hurt you? What do you want? You can tell me."

Then the prince told him, bit by bit, about the girl turning into a flowering tree. "Is that all?" asked the minister's son, and reported it all to the king. The king called the minister, and sent for the old woman. She arrived, shaking with fear. She was dressed in old clothes and stood near the door. After much persuasion, she sat down. The king calmed her, and softly asked her, "You have two girls at your place. Will you give us one?"

The old woman's fear got worse. "How does the king know about my daughters?" she thought. She found her voice with difficulty and stammered: "All right, master. For a poor woman like me, giving a daughter is not as great a thing as your asking for one, is it?"

The king at once offered her betel leaf and betel nut (*tambula*) ceremonially on a silver platter, as a symbolic offer of betrothal. She was afraid to touch it. But the king forced it on her and sent her home.

Back home, she picked up a broom and beat her daughters. She scolded them: "You bitches, where have you been? The king is asking after you. Where did you go?"

The poor girls didn't understand what was happening. They stood there crying, "*Amma,* why are you beating us? Why are you scolding us?"

"Who else can I beat? Where did you go? How did the king hear about you?"

The old woman raged on. The terrified girls slowly confessed to what they had been doing—told her how the younger girl would turn into a flowering tree, how they would sell the flowers, and hoard the money, hoping to surprise their mother. They showed her their five handfuls of coins.

"How can you do such things, with an elder like me sitting in the house? What's all this talk about human beings becoming trees? Who's ever heard of it? Telling lies, too. Show me how you become a tree."

She screamed and beat them some more. Finally, to pacify her, the younger sister had to demonstrate it all. She became a tree and then returned to her normal human self, right before her mother's eyes.

Next day, the king's men came to the old woman's house and asked her to appear before the king. The old woman went and said, "Your Highness, what do you want of me?"

The king answered, "Tell us when we should set the date for the wedding."

"What can I say, Your Highness? We'll do as you wish," the old woman said, secretly glad by now.

The wedding arrangements began. The family made ritual designs on the wedding floor as large as the sky, and built a canopied ceremonial tent (*pandal*) as large as the earth. All the relatives arrived. At an auspicious moment, the girl who knew how to become a flowering tree was given in marriage to the prince.

After the nuptial ceremony, the families left the couple alone together in a separate house. But he was aloof, and so was she. Two nights passed. "Let him talk to me," thought she. "Let her begin," thought he. So both groom and bride were silent.

On the third night, the girl wondered, "He hasn't uttered a word, why did he marry me?" She asked him aloud, "Is it for this bliss you married me?"

He answered roughly, "I'll talk to you only if you do what I ask."

"Won't I do as my husband bids me? Tell me what you want."

"You know how to turn into a flowering tree, don't you? Let me see you do it. We can then sleep on flowers and cover ourselves with them. That would be lovely," he said.

"My lord, I'm not a demon, I'm not a goddess. I'm an ordinary mortal like everyone else. Can a human being ever become a tree?" she said very humbly.

"I don't like all this lying and cheating. I saw you the other day becoming a beautiful tree. I saw you with my own eyes. If you don't become a tree for me, for whom will you do that?" he chided her.

The bride wiped a tear from her eyes with the end of her sari, and said, "Don't be angry with me. If you insist so much, I'll do as you say. Bring two pitchers of water."

He brought them. She uttered chants over them. Meanwhile, he shut all the doors and all the windows. She said, "Remember, pluck all the flowers you want, but take care not to break a twig or tear a leaf."

Then she instructed him on how and when to pour the water, while she sat in the middle of the room, meditating on God. The prince poured one pitcherful of water over her. She turned into a flowering tree. The fragrance of the flowers filled the house. He plucked all the flowers he wanted and then sprinkled water from the second pitcher all over the tree. It became his bride again. She shook her tresses and stood up smiling.

They spread the flowers, covered themselves with them, and went to bed. They did this again and again for several days. Every morning the couple threw out all the withered flowers from their window. The heap of flowers lay there like a hill.

The king's younger daughter saw the heap of withered flowers one day and said to the queen, "Look, Mother, Brother and Sister-in-law wear and throw away a whole lot of flowers. The flowers they've thrown away are piled up like a hill. And they haven't given me even one."

The queen consoled her: "Don't be upset. We'll get them to give you some."

One day the prince had gone out somewhere. Then the king's daughter (who had meanwhile spied and discovered the secret of the flowers) called all her friends and said, "Let's go to the swings in the *surahonne* orchard. We'll take my sister-in-law; she'll turn into a flowering tree. If you all come, I'll give you flowers that smell wonderful."

Then she asked her mother's permission. The queen said, "Of course, do go. Who will say no to such things?"

The daughter then said, "But I can't go alone. Send Sister-in-law."

"Then get your brother's permission and take her."

The prince came there just then and his sister asked him, "Brother, Brother! We're all going to the *surahonne* orchard to play on the swings. Send Sister-in-law."

"It's not my wish that's important. Everything depends on Mother," he answered.

So she went back to the queen and complained, "Mother, if I ask Brother, he sends me to you. But you don't really want to send her. So you are giving me excuses. Is your daughter-in-law more important than your daughter?"

The queen rebuked her, saying, "Don't be rude. All right, take your sister-in-law with you. Take care of her and bring her back safely by evening."

Reluctantly, the queen sent her daughter-in-law with the girls.

Everyone went to the *surahonne* orchard. They tied their swings to a big tree. Everyone was playing on the swings merrily. Abruptly, the king's daughter stopped all the games, brought everyone down from the swings, and accosted her brother's wife.

"Sister-in-law, you can become a flowering tree, can't you? Look, no one here has any flowers for their hair."

The sister-in-law replied angrily, "Who told you such nonsense? Am I not another human being like you? Don't talk such crazy stuff."

The king's daughter taunted her, "Oho, I know all about you. My friends have no flowers to wear. I ask my sister-in-law to become a tree and give us some flowers, and look how coy she acts. You don't want to become a tree for us. Do you do that only for your lovers?"

"*Che*, you're awful. My coming here was a mistake," said the sister-in-law sadly, and she agreed to become a tree.

She sent for two pitchers of water, uttered chants over them, instructed the girls on how and when to pour the water, and sat down to meditate. The silly girls didn't listen carefully. They poured the water on her indifferently, here and there. She turned into a tree, but only half a tree.

It was already evening, and it began to rain, with thunder and lightning. In their greed to get the flowers, they tore up the sprouts and broke the branches. They were in a hurry to get home. So they poured the second pitcher of water at random and ran away. When the princess changed from a tree to a person again, she had no hands and feet. She had only half a body. She was a wounded carcass.

Somehow in that flurry of rainwater, she crawled and floated into a gutter. There she got stuck in a turning, a long way off from home.

Next morning, seven or eight cotton wagons were coming that way and a driver spotted a half-human thing groaning in the gutter. The first cart driver said, "See what that noise is about."

The second one said, "Hey, let's get going. It may be the wind, or it may be some ghost, who knows?"

But the last cart driver stopped his cart and took a look. There lay a shapeless mass, a body. Only the face was a beautiful woman's face. She wasn't wearing a thing.

"*Ayyo*, some poor woman," he said in sorrow, and threw his turban cloth over her, and carried her to his cart, paying no heed to the dirty banter of his fellows. Soon they came to a town. They stopped their carts there and lowered this "thing" onto a ruined pavilion. Before they drove on, the cart driver said, "Somebody may find you and feed you. You will survive." Then they drove on.

When the king's daughter came home alone, the queen asked her, "Where's your sister-in-law? What will your brother say?"

The girl answered casually, "Who knows? Didn't we all find our own way home? Who knows where she went?"

The queen panicked and tried to get the facts out of the girl. "*Ayyo!* You can't say such things. Your brother will be angry. Tell me what happened."

The girl said whatever came to her head. The queen found out nothing. She had a suspicion that her daughter had done something foolish. After waiting several hours, the prince talked to his mother.

"*Amma, Amma.*"

"What is it, son?"

"What has happened to my wife? She went to the orchard to play on the swings, and never came back."

"O Rama, I thought she was in your bedroom all this time. Now you're asking me!"

"Oh, something terrible has happened to her," thought the prince. He went and lay down in grief. Five days passed, six days passed, fifteen days passed, but there was no news of his wife. They couldn't find her anywhere.

"Did the stupid girls push her into a tank? Did they throw her into a well? My sister never liked her. What did the foolish girls do?" He asked his parents, also the servants. What could they say? They, too, were worried and full of fear. In disgust and despair, he changed into an ascetic's long robe and went out into the world. He just walked and walked, not caring where he went.

Meanwhile, the girl who was now a "thing" somehow reached the town into which her husband's elder sister had been given in marriage. Every time the palace servants and maids passed that way to fetch water, they used to see her. They would say to each other, "She glows like a king's daughter." Then one of them couldn't stand it any longer and decided to tell the queen.

"*Amma, Amma,* she looks very much like your younger brother's wife. Look through the seeing-glass and see for yourself."

The queen looked and the face did seem strangely familiar. One of the maids suggested, "*Amma,* can I bring her to the palace. Shall I?"

The queen pooh-poohed the idea: "We'll have to serve her and feed her. Forget it."

Again the next day the maids mumbled and moaned, "She's very lovely. She'll be like a lamp in the palace. Can't we bring her here?"

"All right, all right, bring her if you wish. But you'll have to take care of her without neglecting palace work," ordered the queen.

They agreed and brought the "thing" to the palace. They bathed her in oils, dressed her well, and sat her down at the palace door. Every day they applied medicines to her wounds and made her well. But they could not make her whole. She had only half a body.

Now the prince wandered through many lands and ended up outside the gate of his sister's palace. He looked like a crazy man. His beard and whiskers were wild. When the maids were fetching and carrying water they saw him, then went back to the queen in the palace and said, "*Amma,* someone is sitting outside the gate, and he looks very much like your brother. Look through the seeing-glass and see."

Grumbling indifferently, the queen went to the terrace and looked through the seeing-glass. She was surprised. "Yes, he does look remarkably like my brother. What's happened to him? Has he become a wandering ascetic? Impossible," she thought.

She sent her maids down to bring him in. They said to him, "The queen wants to see you."

He brushed them aside. "Why would she want to see me?" he growled.

"No, sir, she really wants to see you, please come," they insisted and finally persuaded him to come in. The queen took a good look at him and knew it was really her brother.

She ordered the palace servants to heat up whole vats of oil and great vessels of steaming water for his baths. She served him and nursed him, for she knew he was her brother. She served new kinds of dinner each day, and brought him new styles of clothing. But whatever she did, he didn't speak a word to his elder sister. He didn't even ask, "Who are you? Where am I?" By this time, they both knew they were brother and sister.

The queen wondered, "Why doesn't he talk to me though I treat him so royally? What could be the reason? Could it be some witch's or demon's magic?"

After some days, she started sending one or another of her beautiful maids into his bedroom every night. She sent seven maids in seven days. The maids held his hands and caressed his body and tried to rouse him from his stupor. But he didn't say a word or do a thing.

Finally the servant maids got together and dressed up the "thing" that sat at the palace door. With the permission of the disgusted queen, they left "It" on his bed. He neither looked up nor said anything. But this night, "It" pressed and massaged his legs with its stump of an arm. "It" moaned strangely. He got up once and looked at "It." "It" was sitting at his feet. He stared at "It" for a few moments and then realized "It" was really his lost wife. Then he asked her what had happened. She who had had no language all these months suddenly broke into words. She told him whose daughter she was, whose wife, and what had happened to her.

"What shall we do now?" he asked.

"Nothing much. We can only try. Bring two pitchers of water, without touching them with your fingernails," she replied.

That night he brought her two pitchers of water without anyone's knowledge. She uttered chants over them and instructed him: "Pour the water from this pitcher over me, I'll become a tree. Wherever there is a broken branch, set it right. Wherever a leaf is torn, put it together. Then pour the water of the second pitcher."

Then she sat down and meditated.

He poured the water on her from the first pitcher. She became a tree. But the branches had been broken, the leaves had been torn. He carefully set each one right and bound them up and gently poured water from the second pitcher all over the tree.

Now she became a whole human being again. She stood up, shaking the water from her hair, and fell at her husband's feet.

Then she went and woke up the queen, her sister-in-law, and touched her feet also. She told the astonished queen the whole story. The queen wept and embraced her. Then she treated the couple to all kinds of princely food and service, and had them sit in the hall like bride and bridegroom for a ritual celebration called *hasé*. She kept them in her palace for several weeks and then sent them home to her father's palace with cartloads of gifts.

The king was overjoyed at the return of his long-lost son and daughter-in-law. He met them at the city gates, then took them home on an elephant howdah in a grand ceremonial procession through the city streets. In the palace, they told the king and the queen everything that had happened. Then the king had seven barrels of burning lime poured into a great pit and threw his youngest daughter into it. All the people who saw it said to themselves, "After all, every wrong has its punishment."

20. Flute of Joy, Flute of Sorrow

A loving couple had a son after many years. But before the boy reached the age of three or four years, his mother died. The father didn't know what to do. Should he marry again? If he didn't, who would look after the boy? He thought a lot about it, and then married a second wife, who did look after his son very well for a while—till she got pregnant and gave birth to a son of her own.

As her own son grew bigger, she began to send her stepson to the fields to graze their cattle. They had seven cows, and the boy used to herd all seven to the grassy fields. The stepmother would send him with the previous evening's cold rice, spiced up a little. He would take it with him to the fields, eat some of it, and give some to the cows. When he felt lonely, he cried by himself. At home, his stepmother would fondly feed her own son cream of wheat and sugar and melted butter. But somehow he never grew strong, looked thin as a finger, whereas the other boy who went crying every day to the fields with the seven cows seemed to thrive on his hardships. This was because the cows were pleased that the boy shared his food with them, stale though it was. They talked among themselves and began to give him milk, all seven of them. As a result, they had little milk left in their udders when they came home in the evening. The woman watched them and the boy suspiciously for many days. She thought, "I feed my own son nothing but cream of wheat, sugar, and melted butter, but he looks thin as a finger. But this fellow is getting fat on stale rice and hot pepper." She resented her stepson, didn't want him around. She even thought she should get him killed.

So, one day, she tied a black cloth around her head, covered herself with a sheet, and took to bed. When the husband came home that evening, he tried to get her up, but she wouldn't get out of bed.

"What's the matter?" he asked. "Tell me," he pleaded.

"I'll stay in this house only if you do as I ask you. Otherwise I'll leave and go to my mother's," she said.

"All right, tell me what you want."

"Kill that son of yours and bring me his blood. If you put his blood on my brow, I'll get up," she said.

Shocked though he was, not knowing what else to do, he picked up his axe and went to the field in search of the boy. From a great distance, the seven cows saw the man coming towards the field, axe in hand. They surrounded the boy and began grazing all around him. When the man came close and got ready to axe the boy, all seven cows attacked him and tossed him into the air with their horns. One cow took the boy on her back, made him sit between her great big horns, and carried him to a faraway hill. The other six followed.

The man knew he had to take blood to his wife. Or else she wouldn't get up from her bed. So he killed a sparrow, took its blood, and smeared her forehead with it. Then she got up.

The cows nursed the boy as if he were their own child. They gave him a flute of joy and a flute of sorrow, and said to him, "If you are in any trouble, if you are hungry, if you need anything, play on the flute of sorrow. We will come at once, give you milk, and take care of your needs. But if you are happy, play on the flute of joy. Then we will know our son is well."

Then they left him seated among the branches of a large shady banyan tree. Whenever he was hungry, he would play on the flute of sorrow and all seven cows would appear at once, feed him milk from their udders, and disappear. When he was happy, he played the flute of joy. They would hear the joyous notes and know their son was happy and they would be content.

Days and months went by like this. One day, the neighboring king's daughter came to the hill to answer nature's call. Thinking to wash the little brass water pot she carried, she came to the well under the banyan tree. As the princess scrubbed the pot, the boy happened to scratch his head, sitting high among the branches. His hair shone, like filaments of gold. A golden hair fell on the princess's hand. She looked around to see where it had come from. She saw nothing around her. Then she looked up and saw him, wild and handsome, among the branches. She decided at once that she would marry him.

As soon as she went home, she tied a piece of cloth round her neck and took to bed. Her father tried to get her out of bed, but she wouldn't get up. She was his only daughter. He had no sons. He had brought her up tenderly.

"I'll bring you whatever you want. Why are you lying like this? Please get up. Tell me now what you want," he pleaded.

She said, "Outside this town, there's a big banyan tree. A young man is sitting on it. Bring him and get me married to him. If you promise to do so, I'll get up."

"Is that all?" asked the king, and sent five or six of his palace servants to bring the young fellow down.

The king's men came to the tree and asked him to come down. He didn't. So they started climbing the tree. He took up the flute of sorrow and played on it. At once, all seven cows gave up their grazing. They said, "Our son is in trouble." They came leaping and running from nowhere, pitchforked the king's servants, and scattered them helter-skelter. They were happy to see that their son who had been frightened at first was now amused. They gave him some milk and went back to where they came from.

The servants fled to the king and told him what had happened. "That's weird," he said, and went there himself with twenty or thirty men. The young man saw him coming from a distance and sounded his flute of sorrow. The cows knew that their son was in trouble again and came running. They found quite a little army of men at the foot of the tree. All seven cows assaulted and stabbed them with their horns, tossed them aside, and dispersed them. The king's men ran for their lives.

The princess was disappointed. She refused to get up.

In that place, there was a crow called Bronze Beak Crow. He was a very clever crow. They called in the crow and told him their problem.

"Whenever that pretty boy is in trouble or hungry, he plays a flute and summons his guardians, the cows. They are fierce. You must surprise him then, grab it from him, and bring it here," they instructed.

But just when the crow flew over to the banyan tree, he was playing the flute of joy. Thinking that this was the flute they wanted, the crow swooped down, plucked it from his hands, and flew away. He then played on the flute of sorrow. The cows came, gave him another flute of joy, and left him happy.

Bronze Beak Crow came again and sat above him on the tree. The young fellow looked up once and saw the wily crow, ready to rob him again of a flute. As he quickly reached for the flute of sorrow, the crow swooped down and snatched it away from his hands.

Now he had only one flute. Even when he was in distress, all he could play was the flute of joy, because that was all he had. The cows would hear the happy notes all day and think, "Our son is well." The king came with his retinue soon after, brought him down from his perch, took him home in a procession, and got him married to his daughter. And she was happy.

But he was sad. His thoughts were with his seven cows. He wanted to bring them home, but the people at the palace were afraid he would slip away, and wouldn't let him out of their sight. Many days passed.

The seven cows wondered why their son had not played either of his flutes. "We have not heard from him. Something has happened to him. Let's go and see," they said and went to the banyan tree. He was missing, and nowhere to be found. They mooed and mooed, cried "Baa, baa" over and over, and died there, broken-hearted.

After a long time and many attempts, the sad young man was able to talk to the princess and to the king and persuade them to go with him to the forest. When he came to his banyan tree, he saw at once that the cows had died. That was so long ago, only their bones lay there. He picked seven pebbles, chanted a prayer, and threw a pebble at the leg bone of each cow.

Hardly had the pebbles struck them than they rose again as full-bodied cows. They scrambled up, crying "Baa, baa," and licked him all over as if he were a long-lost calf. Then he herded them home as he had done many times before, in times long gone. In the palace, the cows were looked after royally as if they were seven queens. In time, he and the princess inherited the kingdom and reigned happily.

21. Fools

In a certain town lived a fool and his wife who was also a fool. They had grown worse in their folly by fighting daily about the question of who was the better fool. Their neighbors were quite tired of their noisy fights. One day, when their fight was at its noisiest, a clever man arrived in town, and it didn't take him long to discover the cause of their fights. He knew right away that advice would not be of any use. So he cornered the fool and told him, "Go and see the world. See how many kinds of fools there are in the world. What's the point of fighting like this?" And he sent him out to see the variety of folly in the world.

So the fool wandered long and far till he came to a town where everyone was an idiot. The houses were filled with darkness even at midday. So they were trying to gather sunlight in baskets and carry it into the houses. The fool watched them and laughingly asked them, "What are you doing?"

They said, "Don't you see? We're trying to bring light into our houses. So we're filling up these baskets with sunlight. But our houses are still dark."

"O, that's easy. If you pay me a fee, I'll fill your houses with light."

They were delighted and gave him a hefty fee. He went into each house and opened all the windows and skylights. Where they didn't have any, he axed the walls and made big holes. Light poured into the rooms. The people of the town were amazed.

Then he wandered on till he saw a house where grass grew on the terraced roof where a little sand had collected. The woman of the house wanted her buffalo to eat the grass. So she was trying to get the buffalo to climb to the top of the house. The fool asked her, "What are you trying to do?"

"O, my son's buffalo is hungry. I want to let it graze on the terrace. But the buffalo is stupid. Even though I beat him, he won't climb onto the roof. What shall I do?"

"For a fee, I'd be happy to graze him," he offered.

"Take it, here," said the woman, giving him some money.

He at once asked for a ladder, climbed onto the terrace, cut some of the grass, and threw it in front of the buffalo, who happily began to chew on it.

Right then, he heard people making a rumpus in another lane. The fool went there to see what was happening. Several wrestlers and weight lifters were engaged in the task of taking a huge piece of timber into a house. The door was too narrow for it and they couldn't get the piece past it. When the fool arrived there, the big fellows were getting ready to break down the door and the surrounding wall. He offered to help, for a decent fee, of course. They were happy to get any help. He made them cut the piece of timber in quarters and carry it in.

When he looked at all these fools who were much worse than he, good sense dawned on him.

"My wife and I are such smart people—not like these dolts!" he thought.

So he returned home and began to live like other people.

22. A Jackal King

A jackal roamed in the rain all day looking for food. He didn't find any, and it got dark. He sneaked into town and entered a washerman's house. He ate whatever he could put his snout to, and as he ran in a hurry he fell into the washerman's indigo vat. He tried to get out of it, but he couldn't. He struggled till morning, when a clever idea occurred to him. He lay in the vat motionless, his legs stiff, as if dead. The washerman came to dip his clothes in the vat and found what looked like a dead animal in it. "Didn't God give this wretched animal any eyes to see where he was going?" he grumbled, and he picked up the jackal in disgust and threw it on the rocks outside town. The jackal waited till he disappeared and then got up and ran. Once he found himself in a safe place, he looked at himself only to find that he was stained a strange blue all over. He couldn't recognize himself. How would other animals recognize him? Maybe he could work this to his advantage and become the king of the forest, he thought. He was after all a jackal. Nobody had to teach him tricks.

He called a meeting of all the jackals and addressed them: "O jackals all, the goddess of this forest appeared to me yesterday and poured ambrosia all over me and blessed me. She said, 'From now on, my son, you are the king of this forest,' and she appointed me king. If you don't believe me, just look at my body. So, from today on, you are my subjects and I am your king. Don't you ever forget it!"

They looked at him in amazement. His body was indeed colored an astonishing blue. The jackals thought, "Maybe this is all true. Why else would he be blessed with this unearthly color?" They asked him, "Your Highness, what's your name?"

How could he say just "Jackal"? Was he an idiot? He said instead, "Jackal Tackal Lackal Raja."

They, poor things, couldn't remember such a long name. They simply hurrahed: "Long live our raja! Victory to our maharaja! *Jai!*"

From that day, the jackal made the other jackals serve him. Soon the other animals also shouted *Jai!* and became his subjects. Even powerful animals like lions and tigers submitted to his rule, impressed by the color of his body. Whenever he went anywhere, he had to ride the elephant. He had to have the lion to his right, the tiger to the left, and packs of jackals behind him and in front of him. Who wouldn't grow vain with such power and royalty? He no longer cared for his own kind. He wouldn't let a fellow-jackal anywhere near him. All the despised jackals slunk away from him.

One day, a wise old jackal said to them, "Don't worry about him, fellows. His time is up. If he was born one of us and now acts too big to be friends with us, it means his downfall is near. The tiger and the lion fear him only because they don't know he's a jackal. If they find out who he is, they won't wait a minute. They'll tear him to pieces. All these days, I thought, 'After all, he's one of us. He is rising in life. Let him enjoy it.' But now he has turned against us, what does it matter if he lives or dies? When he comes to this evening's assembly, surround him and set up a big howl. Howl for all you are worth. The rest is God's will." The jackals agreed.

The court assembled that evening. King Jackal Tackal Lackal arrived in style with his retinue and sat on his throne. As if in great jubilation, all the jackals raised their voices and howled and howled. King Jackal forgot himself and joined them in their howls. He was in his element—he howled louder than the rest.

The tiger and the lion, at first taken aback, soon realized that this was only a common jackal who had become king by deceiving them, the imposter! They pounced on him at once and tore him to pieces.

That's why wise people say: "You can't change what you are born with. A dog is a dog even when it sits in a palanquin."

23. For Love of Kadabu

A man went to his mother-in-law's, in a nearby village, to enjoy the royal treatment a son-in-law usually gets. The mother-in-law lovingly made *kadabu* (sweet puffs) for him. He loved them, but he felt too shy to eat as many as he would have liked. His mother-in-law placed a platter full of them in front of him, but all he could manage to do was shyly nibble on one or two. But he was thinking all through the meal that he would hurry home, ask his wife to make a lot of these delicious things, and eat them and eat them to his heart's content. He didn't know what they were called, but by careful inquiries he found out that *kadabu* was the name of the delicacy, and he memorized it. *Kadabu, kadabu, kadabu,* he muttered to himself all the way home. Unfortunately, on his way, maybe because his attention was not on the road, he slipped and fell. In the shock of the fall, he forgot to say *kadabu,* and began to say *badaku, badaku.*

When he reached home, he quickly washed his hands and feet, and called his wife in a hurry.

"Look here, you must make some *badaku*s for me."

"What's *badaku*? I have never heard of it."

"Don't you know what *badaku* is? Everyone knows what it is."

"No, I don't. *Badaku* sounds funny. *Badaku, badaku!*" she teased him.

He was balked, vexed, and soon he got very angry. He grabbed a stick that lay in a corner and beat her. Then he slapped her cheeks and boxed her ears. His wife, who had never seen him like this before, ran out of the house weeping aloud and sought the help of a neighbor, an elderly lady, who said to her, "He has no business beating you. I'll come and talk to him. Maybe he's drunk or something."

The lady brought the young woman back to her house and rebuked the husband roundly. "Have you any sense in your head? You've beaten up the poor girl so badly. Look at her, her cheeks have puffed up like a *kadabu!*"

"O, O," he cried in recognition, jumping up. "That's it, that's it. *Kadabu, kadabu,* that's what I want."

It was then that it dawned on his wife that all this fuss was for a *kadabu.*

"Why didn't you tell me so in the first place? *Badaku, badaku!*" she screamed at him, and went to work on making *kadabu*s.

She made three big luscious *kadabu*s. She liked them too, as much as he did. So they fought over who should have two. Neither wanted one and a half, so they made a pact. They would both go lie down in the front room, without making a sound. Even if a mosquito bit them or a fly sat on their nose, they would not move a muscle or make any noise. Whoever moved or spoke first would be the loser and get only one *kadabu;* the silent one would get the other two.

So they both left the precious *kadabu*s behind in the kitchen and lay down silently in the front room. Evening came, night fell, and soon it was the next day.

In the morning, the nosy neighbors noticed no movement in the house. They worried about the couple not waking up as usual. They wondered what had happened to them. They waited a while, then cautiously pushed the front door open. They found the couple on the floor, their eyes closed, unmoving, lying there as if dead. Someone said, "They are dead, poor things." "The bodies are hardly cold," said another. But the husband and wife moved not a muscle. So the neighbors proceeded to carry them out to the cremation grounds.

There they piled dry cow dung cakes on the bodies and lighted the funeral pyre. The fire touched the wife's hair first, and she screamed, "*Ayyo,* I don't want to burn!"

At once the husband started up in triumph, shouting, "There! You lost. I'm the winner. One for you and two for me!"

The neighbors were scared out of their wits to see the dead come alive, and they fled the place.

The couple shook themselves loose, went home arguing all the way, and ate the *kadabu*s, which had gone quite cold by now.

24. A Girl in a Picture

In Simhala country, one Vikrama was the king—young, unmarried, a smart ruler of his people. One day a diamond merchant came to him and reported: "Your Majesty, every full-moon day a flowering tree rises out of the ocean. A beautiful woman lies luxuriously on a golden cot under that tree. She enjoys the ocean breeze for a half hour or so, and then the tree, the cot, and the woman sink and go under the surface. What could be the meaning of it?"

That full-moon day, he went with the merchant to the center of the ocean. By midnight, as he watched the moonlit waters, a tree in full flower rose from the sea, just as the merchant had said. Under it was a golden cot. On it a celestial beauty lay luxuriously, served by maids.

The beauty of it all went to the king's head. He felt he was going crazy. He stood there gaping at the scene. About half an hour later, the tree began to sink in the ocean. The young king was no coward. He loved adventure. So he jumped into the waves and grabbed a branch of the disappearing tree, which took him at once into a nether world of Nagas. The girl he had seen earlier was there, still on her couch, served by her maids. When their eyes met, they were both thrilled. The girl sent a maid to bring him closer to her. As the maid took him by the hand, he asked her who this celestial beauty was. She explained, "She is a god's daughter. She has taken a vow that she would marry only someone who had the courage to risk his life and come here all by himself. Here, you've arrived. She's yours to marry."

He married her and lived in ecstasy with that divine female. A wish-fulfilling tree gave them whatever they desired. He had a goddess for wife. What else did he need?

One day she came to him and showed him a girl's picture and said, "My king, my love, enjoy whatever you want in this world of mine, but don't ever covet the girl in this picture. That's the only thing you've got to do without."

The king said, "That's easy. I've everything."

One day when he was alone in his palace, his eye fell on the picture. He was curious. He passed his fingers over the girl in the picture. At once she came alive and kicked him hard on the chest. Before he could even blink his eyes, he was in his palace in Simhala country.

From that moment on, he could find no pleasure in anything in his palace or his kingdom, and renounced it all to become a wandering *sanyasi*.

25. The Glass Pillar

It was the business of a singer of holy and moral tales to recite good stories and make people moral. Once he proclaimed, "Good men all, listen. Above all, do not go after women, do not fornicate. Do you know what happens to fornicators? There's a big glass pillar in hell. They heat it till it's red-hot and they make the sinners go through a hole no bigger than a needle. Beware!"

The audience was very impressed and said, "True, true," shook their heads, admired his skill with words, and gave him ten *pice* instead of the usual one *pice*. His favorite harlot was also in the audience. She found the talk about the glass pillar in hell quite terrifying.

The singer finished his day's recitation and, after he had made sure everyone was safely home in bed, went secretly to the harlot's house. He knocked on the door. Without opening the door, the harlot said, "*Ayyo*, why did you come? You yourself said: there is a red-hot pillar in hell, and sinners will be sent through a hole no bigger than a needle. Aren't you scared?"

"O, you innocent, don't fear. Millions of people have gone through that hole. So it's become enlarged, so large indeed that even elephants and camels can pass through it without any harm. Come, open the door!" he said.

26. A Golden Sparrow

One morning, a poor old woman was washing the small yard in front of her door so that she could draw a *rangoli* design on it. While she was smearing the floor with cow dung paste to prepare the ground for the design, a thorn entered her palm. The hand began to swell. She showed it to everyone. "Look how it's swollen!" she said to everyone she met.

Some people said, "Foment it." Some others said, "Prick it with another thorn." Others suggested medicines, herbs. Each person had his or her own remedy. But the old woman did nothing. The hand got worse. She felt a throbbing, a movement, a crackling like *chutu chutu*. When she looked at her hand, the painful swelling broke. It burst with a big sound, and out came a sparrow. Before she could say, "*Ayyo*, a sparrow!" it chirped and hopped all over the house, laying golden eggs wherever it perched. The old woman was delighted. She put them away carefully, and sold an egg at a time and lived on the money. Soon, she pulled down her ramshackle hut and built a fine gold-plated house in its place. She began to wear good clothes, bought nice knickknacks, and got new pots and pans.

The woman next door asked her one day, "Old woman, you didn't have a thing. How did you suddenly get all this?"

"How can I tell you? I was smearing cow dung in the yard one day and a thorn went into my hand. My hand got swollen. Everyone told me what to do. Everyone had a different remedy. I did nothing. Finally, it burst and, do you know? a sparrow came out of it. It chirped and hopped all over the house and laid real golden eggs," she said.

The neighbor thought she could do the same thing. So she gathered some cow dung. She made sure it had a thorn in it. She saw to it that a thorn went into her palm.

"Ha, I've a thorn in the right place. It'll swell by tomorrow," she said, and waited happily. But it didn't. She got worried. Several days later it did become painful and swollen. She too showed it to everyone, like the old woman, and they all advised her the same way. All she was worried about was the sparrow that would come out of it. But there was no sign of any sparrow. In a week, it got worse. The whole hand was swollen. She writhed in agony. Finally it burst. She expected a sparrow. But all she saw was blood and pus. She waited another day for the sparrow. Then another. In a few days the hand began to rot with gangrene. When she showed it to the doctor, he said the hand would have to be cut off.

27. The Greatest Thing

A devotee spent all his time thinking of God. Not a day passed that he didn't bathe and offer worship to his family gods. One day a mendicant gave him a doll and asked him to worship it. The man asked him, "Is this the greatest thing in the world?"

The mendicant said, "I think so. But if you find anything greater, worship *that*."

So he brought the doll home and started offering it worship. As part of his offering, he would place a banana, peeled and sliced, in front of the doll. Every day a mouse would come and eat the banana. He was very happy to see that the banana was gone every morning and thought that god was personally eating his offerings. So he continued to offer bananas. One day he caught sight of the mouse eating the banana.

"Ah, I didn't realize it. This mouse is greater than that god. He's the real god," he said, and started worshiping the mouse. One day a cat stalked the mouse, killed it, and ate it. "O, so a cat is greater than a mouse," he said, and started to worship the cat. He lighted oil lamps and had beautiful ceremonies for the cat. This went on for a while. Meantime his little son acquired a dog, which jumped on the cat one day. The scared cat fled for dear life.

"Ah, the dog is so much greater," he said and transferred his worship to the dog. One day the dog went into the kitchen and put its snout into a fresh pot of cooked rice and lentils and ate it up. His wife caught it in the act and thrashed it with a stick till its back broke.

Now he knew that his wife was greater than even the dog. So he started worshiping her. Yet he wanted his meals on time every day. When, one day, she was late with them, he got very angry. As she was bringing his plate, he grabbed a stick and beat her.

He stopped smack in the middle of this incident, for he realized that he himself was greater than his wife. And while he was preparing himself to worship himself, he realized that his stomach was what he truly worked for. Everything he ate went into his stomach, and so he began to worship it. What he did next, we don't know.

28. Hanchi

An old woman had two children, a son and a daughter. The girl had golden hair, but the brother had not been struck by it till, one day, when both of them were grown up and the girl was a lovely young woman with hair of gold, he happened to see it as if for the first time and at once fell in love with her.

He went to his mother and begged her to give his sister in marriage to him. The poor old woman was shocked and knew at once that disaster was ahead. But she hid her feelings and sent him to the nearby town to bring rice and flour and lentils for the wedding. As soon as he left the house, she went to her daughter and said to her, "Daughter, the time has come for you to leave me. You're as good as dead to me after this day. You're too beautiful to live here in safety. You have hair of gold; no one can look at it without desire. So I shall get a mask made for you; it will hide your face and save you from future danger."

Then she ran to the potter and gave him a gold vessel and bought a clay mask to fit her daughter's face. That very night she sent away her daughter with the parting words, "Never remove the mask from your face till your situation is better." When her daughter was gone, the poor woman poisoned herself in her grief. The son came home next day, found his sister gone, and his mother dead. Searching for them everywhere, he went mad, and became a wandering madman.

The girl with the clay mask wandered from place to place as long as her mother's bundle of bread and rice lasted. She changed her name to Hanchi (*hanchu* means a clay tile). She would stop by wayside brooks, untie her bundle of bread, and eat at noon and by moonlight. At last she came to a place very far from her hometown and struck up acquaintance with an old woman who gave her food and shelter. One day the old woman came home and said that a nearby *saukar* (rich man) needed a servantmaid, and that she had arranged to send Hanchi to his place. Hanchi agreed and went to the big house to work there as a servantmaid. She was an expert cook, and no one could equal her in making dishes of sweet rice.

One day, the *saukar* wished to arrange a banquet in his orchard and ordered Hanchi to make her special dishes of sweet rice. That day, everyone in the household went to the orchard for a grand meal—everyone, that is, except Hanchi and a younger son of the *saukar*, who had gone out somewhere. Hanchi thought she was alone, so she heated water for an oil-bath. She wished to finish her bath before they all returned. She took off her mask, undid her splendid golden hair, applied oil all over her parched body, and started bathing. Meanwhile the young man who had gone out came back home, and shouted for the maid. Hanchi did not hear him in the bathhouse. Impatiently, he went in search of her, heard noises, and peeped in the bathhouse, and saw her in all her beauty. He was still young. He sneaked away before she saw him; but he fell deeply in love with the glowing beauty of her body and the glory that was her hair and decided at once to make her his wife.

As soon as his mother returned from the orchard he took her aside and told her of his desire. She was quite puzzled by her son's fascination with a black-faced servantmaid. She asked him not to make a fool of himself over a dark lowborn wench, and promised to get him a really good-looking bride from a rich family if he would wait a little. But he would not hear of it. He was stubborn and they had a heated argument at the end of which he dragged his mother to Hanchi, put his hand to the girl's face, snatched off her mask, and dashed it to the ground. There stood Hanchi in all her natural loveliness, crowned by her splendid tresses of gold. The mother was struck dumb by this extraordinary beauty, and found her son's infatuation quite understandable. Moreover, she had always liked the modest good-natured Hanchi. She took the bashful Hanchi with her to an inner chamber and asked the young woman a few questions, listened to her strange story, and liked her all the better for it. At the first auspicious moment, Hanchi was married to the young man.

The newlyweds were happy as doves, but their happiness didn't last long. For there was a holy man whom everyone called Guruswami in the *saukar*'s house. He was the rich man's chief counselor. He had a reputation for secret lore and black arts of many kinds. This man had been casting lecherous glances at Hanchi and wanted her for himself. When Hanchi's mother-in-law told him one day of her eagerness to see a grandson by Hanchi, he had his plan ready. He told her that he could make Hanchi conceive with the help of his magic arts, and asked her to send Hanchi to him with some plantains, almonds, betel leaves, and nuts, which he would use in his magical rites.

On an auspicious day, Guruswami summoned Hanchi. He had before him all the fruits and nuts over which he had chanted his magical formulae. If she ate them, his love magic would work on her, and she would be irresistibly drawn to him. When she visited him, he was chant-ing secret spells and praying that Hanchi should become his. Hanchi was a clever girl and knew all about these wicked magicians. When he gave her a plantain, she secretly dropped the enchanted fruit into a trough and ate another that she had brought with her. Guruswami went to his room, trusting that his magic would draw her to him and bring her into his waiting arms. While he lay waiting for her, a she-buffalo ate the enchanted plantain in the trough and fell in love with Guruswami. She was in heat and came running to Guruswami's cham-ber and butted at his door with her horns. Thinking that Hanchi had come, he hastily opened the door and was badly mauled by the amo-rous buffalo.

But he did not give up. On several days he asked Hanchi's gullible mother-in-law to send Hanchi to him for certain rites. When she came, he gave her enchanted almonds, betel leaves, and nuts. But clever Han-chi played the same old trick on him and ate the harmless almonds, leaves, and nuts, which she had carefully brought with her. She palmed away Guruswami's gifts and put them into measures and bowls on her way back to her quarters. As Guruswami lay waiting for her in his bed-room that night, the measures and vessels came rolling towards his room and knocked on his door. He hastily opened his door for the long-awaited Hanchi, but, instead of her caresses, received hard blows from inanimate vessels that were irresistibly drawn to him. After the third visit, she threw the magic nuts at a broomstick that stood in a corner. When Guruswami opened the door and received a thorny broomstick into his greedy arms, he accepted failure. He changed his tactics.

He went to his old friend, Hanchi's father-in-law, and suggested that they should have another of his famous picnics in the garden. The old man agreed. As before, Hanchi prepared her fine dishes of sweet rice and, like a good daughter-in-law, stayed back to look after the house while everyone was away.

When everyone was at the orchard picnic, Guruswami found an ex-cuse to go back home. He told everyone he had left something behind, and hurried home. On the way, he collected pieces of men's clothing like coats and turbans. Then, while Hanchi was in the kitchen, he stole into her room and planted a man's coat and turban there and threw bits of chewed betel and smoked stubs of cheroot under the bed and on the floor.

After planting all this false evidence in Hanchi's room, he ran breathlessly to the garden where the family was enjoying itself and cried, "Your daughter-in-law is a whore! I surprised her with a lover. She has forgotten the dignity of her family, her womanhood. This is sinful. It will bring misfortune to the whole clan! The slut!"

At these shocking words from their trusted family friend, all of them ran to the house. With righteous indignation, Guruswami showed them the hidden clothing and the telltale cheroot stubs and betel pieces as unquestionable evidence of Hanchi's adultery. Hanchi was as surprised as the rest of them, but her protests were just not heard. She accused Guruswami himself of being a bad man, and told them of his black magic, but they all got so angry that they beat her till she had blue welts. When she found that everyone was against her, she became silent and gave herself over to her fate. They shut her up in a room and starved her for three days, but they got no confession out of her. Her stubborn silence put her husband and his father into fits of rage. Then Guruswami, finding that his plot was prospering, suggested, "All this will not work with this wretched woman. We must punish her properly for her sin. Put her into a big box and give the box to me. I will have it thrown into the river. You are too good to this sinner. We must punish her as she deserves!"

Anger and shame had made them blind. They listened to him. She was dragged out, shut up in a box, and handed over to Guruswami. He had it carried out of the house, happy that his plot had succeeded.

Then he had to think of a way to get rid of the servants. He asked them to carry the box to an old woman's house outside town and to leave it there till morning, as the river was still a long way off. The old woman was no other than Hanchi's good friend who had helped her to get a job and settle in the town. Guruswami told the old woman that there were ferocious mad dogs in the box; he was taking them to the river to drown them next day. He asked her to be very very careful with it, not to meddle with it or open it lest the dogs should be let loose. When he left her, he had scared her more than he intended to. He promised that he would soon come back to take the dangerous dogs away.

After he left, the old woman heard peculiar noises coming from the box. At first, she thought it was the dogs. But then she heard her own name being called out. Hanchi in the box had recognized her old friend's voice and was calling for help. The old woman cautiously pried open the lid and found, to her great astonishment, Hanchi crouching inside the box! She helped the miserable girl out of her prison and gave her food and drink. Hanchi had eaten nothing for days and she was ravenous. Hanchi told her all about her misfortunes and the villain Guruswami's plot to get her. The old woman listened carefully, and her mother wit soon found a way out. She hid Hanchi in an inner room, went into town, and found someone who was about to get rid of a mad dog. She had it muzzled, brought home, and locked up in the box. She had taken care to loosen the muzzle before she locked up the dog.

Guruswami was back very soon. He was eager to taste his new power over Hanchi. He came perfumed and singing. When he examined the locks, the old woman assured him in a frightened voice that she was too scared even to touch the box. He asked her now to leave him alone in the room for his evening prayers.

He closed the door carefully and bolted it from the inside. And calling Hanchi's name lovingly, he threw open the lid of the box. His heart leaped to his mouth when he saw a hideous dog, foaming at the mouth, which sprang upon him and mangled him horribly with its bites. He cursed his own wickedness and cried that he was served right by all-seeing God, who had transformed a woman into a dog. Full of remorse, he called for mercy as he sank down under the dog's teeth. Neighbors, drawn by the cries of the wretched man, soon gathered and killed the dog. But they could not save Guruswami. He had been fatally bitten by the dog and infected with rabies.

Hanchi's husband and his family were shocked by what happened to their friend Guruswami. Months later, the old woman invited them to her house. The good woman could not rest until she had seen justice done to Hanchi. When Hanchi's in-laws came, the old woman served them a scrumptious meal, wonderful dishes of sweet rice, which no one but Hanchi could have prepared. Everyone who tasted it was reminded of her and felt sad. They naturally asked who this excellent cook, who had equaled Hanchi, was. Instead of a reply, the old woman presented Hanchi herself in flesh and blood. They were amazed and could not believe their own eyes. They had believed Hanchi was dead and gone, drowned beyond return in the river. Guruswami had got rid of her for them, and the poor fellow had gone mysteriously mad soon after. The old woman cleared up the mystery of Hanchi's reappearance by telling them the true story about her and the villain Guruswami.

They were full of remorse for what they had done to Hanchi and were ashamed that they had been taken in by such a viper as Guruswami. They cursed him at length and asked Hanchi to pardon them.

Hanchi's good days had begun. Her luck had turned and brought her every kind of happiness from that day.

29. The Horse Gram Man

A farmer was short of money. So he went to the fair in the nearby town to sell a load of horse gram. He sat at the fair till evening, but no one bought his gram. When he started home with his load, night fell. So he stopped in a temple outside a village and lay down. He had eaten nothing since morning and he was unhappy that he couldn't sell his horse gram. So he tossed about sleeplessly.

Now the local *gowda* and his lover used to keep a tryst every night at the deserted temple. As usual, she came there in a pretty sari, with fresh-cooked food for her *gowda*. The horse gram man was lying there. It was dark. She thought he was the *gowda*, woke him up, asked him to make no noise, and quietly fed him the wonderful meal she had brought. Then silently she joined him and they made love. When it was all over, she quickly got up and left. The horse gram man now had his belly full and also had had his pleasure. He fell asleep happily. The *gowda* came a bit later and groped around. When the horse gram man spoke up, the *gowda* realized that this was not a woman but a stranger. So he asked the man to get up and go sleep on the verandah. Then he waited for his woman, who never turned up. He walked up and down restlessly and he too went to the verandah.

When he saw the man sleeping there, he felt like sleeping with the man. So he gently woke up the man and told him what he wanted. The horse gram man said, "All right, but you must go first." What could the *gowda* do? His need was great. "All right, you do it first," he said, bent down, and bared his bottom to the horse gram man, who did it to him. Now it was the *gowda*'s turn. But the horse gram man raised his voice and said, "No, no, this won't do. If you insist, I'll call out and make a scene. I haven't sold a grain of horse gram all day, and there's all this bother at night." The *gowda* was a village elder, an important man, a much-respected man. If people heard about this, he would lose face. So he pacified the horse gram man and said, "All right, then, forget this ever happened. Go and sleep in our house. Don't make a scene, please." Then he called a servant who was fast asleep on a stone platform nearby and sent the horse gram man with him.

The horse gram man came to the *gowda*'s house and lay down comfortably in a front room on the *gowda*'s bed. He couldn't sleep. He moved his hands around and found three bells tied to ropes near the bed. Curious, he rang one.

Now the *gowda* had three wives. He used to summon them by ringing one of these three bells. As the horse gram man had rung the biggest bell of the three, the *gowda*'s eldest wife came to his bed. She massaged his hands and feet, slept with him, and when she was ready to leave, she whispered, "*Gowda,* get me a nice new yellow silk sari." The horse gram man said gruffly, "Go away. I've not sold a grain of horse gram all day and you want a yellow silk sari. Would a measure of horse gram buy you a silk sari? Yellow silk sari! Go, go now!" She knew at once that this was not her *gowda*. In shock, she quietly returned to her bed.

The man rang the second bell. The *gowda*'s second wife came, slept with him, and begged him, "*Gowda,* get me a nice nose ring." "Hey, go now!" said the horse gram man. "I haven't sold a grain of horse gram all day. Would a measure of horse gram buy you a nose ring? Go, go." She knew this was not her husband. If she made any noise, others would know what she had done. So she slipped away quietly.

Then he rang the third bell, a small one. The *gowda*'s youngest wife came to his bed, slept with him, and insisted, "*Gowda,* get me some jewelry." He said, "Go away. I haven't sold a grain of horse gram all day. Would a measure of horse gram buy you a jewel? Go now!" She too knew now that she had made a terrible mistake and quietly left the room. The horse gram man got up quite early, picked up his horse gram, and left for his village, leaving no trace behind him.

The *gowda* returned home in the morning. When he went for his bath, all three wives attended to him. One massaged his head, another scrubbed his back, the third poured warm water. Just then, he had to fart. He said, "Damn it, it's all that horse gram man's doing!"

His wives thought, "*Ayyo,* the *gowda* knows what we did last night!" They began to quarrel and said, "Not me, *Akka* the eldest went first!" "No, not me, she the junior one went first!" "No, not me, her!"

The *gowda* now realized what had happened. The horse gram man had had everyone, him and all his women. Marveling at the man's powers, he got out of the bathhouse.

30. Hucca

Hucca ("Crazy") was the last of three brothers. Whatever his real name, the nickname Hucca stuck to him because he *was* crazy. He didn't mind being called that. He was a simpleton and didn't know how to keep secrets or tell lies. Actually, certain mischievous people in town would tell him scandalous things when they wanted the whole town to know. They would tell him in great secrecy, "Hucca, don't tell this to anyone. Remember?" And Hucca would tell everyone and his brother the very secret in a loud whisper, ending with, "Remember, don't tell this to anyone."

His parents died and left behind a great deal of wealth. The two elder brothers, who were married, divided up the property between them and thought Hucca wouldn't mind living with one of them. But he made a row.

"I'm also my father's son. Give me a portion of the property!" he screamed.

The brothers said, "All right, then, what do you want?"

Decisions were a problem for Hucca. After much shilly-shallying he said, "Give me a bull."

The brothers had an old good-for-nothing bull. They happily gave it to him. Now Hucca believed he was on his own, even though he lived and ate with his brothers. He began to spend time with his beloved bull in a backyard shed. He would massage it, groom it, graze it, walk it to the river, and wash it. He would nurse it and tend it like a baby. He would talk to it all day. If the bull shook its head, flapped its ears to ward off flies, or shook its tail, he would read meanings into it and talk about it. If it was hungry and licked his face, he would beam and tell every passerby, "A jewel, this bull. Look how loving it is!"

He named it Prince of Bulls. He would worry about it like a mother and say all day, "Our Prince didn't drink enough water today. . . . He didn't move his tail at all. . . . He didn't bellow like every day. . . . Something's wrong, I'm sure."

The old bull didn't understand a word he said. Once Hucca held its tail and twisted it, saying, "My prince, why aren't you moving your tail?" And the bull kicked him for all it was worth. Hucca lost interest in the animal at once.

When, one day, he heard that his brothers had sold two of their cows because they needed money, Hucca thought that he could sell his bull too. He set out at once for the town nearby. It was not even the day of the fair. His bull was a doddering old animal. Who would want it? For days, he would stand in the sun with his bull till evening and then drag it home.

On one of these trips, he heard a dry summer tree creak and rustle in the wind. Grk! Grk! it seemed to say.

Hucca listened attentively.

"O tree sir, are you talking to me?"

"Grk! Grk!"

"You want to know how much I want for my bull?"

"Grk! Grk!" said the tree.

"Look, it's a fine bull. I can't sell it for less than twenty-five rupees."

"Grk! Grk!"

"You want it? All right, you can have it, if you give me the money."

"Grk! Grk!"

"Tomorrow? You'll have the money tomorrow?"

"Grk! Grk!"

"All right. Who's born with money in hand? I'll come and collect it tomorrow," said Hucca, who tied the bull to the tree and went home.

As they sat down to dinner, the brothers asked him, "What happened to your bull, Hucca?"

"I sold it."

"For how much?"

"Twenty-five rupees."

Our brother is smart, they thought, he has sold the old good-for-nothing for twenty-five.

"Where's the money?"

"He said he'd give it to me tomorrow," said Hucca. They thought, "Maybe he has really sold it."

Next morning, Hucca went back to the tree. The bull wasn't there. Some butchers had found it unattended and driven it home.

Hucca said to the tree, "Tree, Tree, give me my money."

Today too the old tree made its "Grk! Grk!" sounds.

"What? What did you say? Tomorrow? You mustn't let me down tomorrow. You shouldn't say, 'Tomorrow and the day after.' It isn't good business, see? It's all right this once. I won't stand for it tomorrow," said Hucca firmly and went home.

When the brothers asked him again about the money, he said, "He didn't have it in hand today. Tomorrow, he said. Positive."

"But tell us to whom you sold it," insisted the brothers.

"Remember the old tree on the road? I sold the bull to that tree."

"When will you learn?" despaired the brothers. But Hucca explained.

"Poor fellow, he wanted the bull very much. He pleaded and pleaded till my heart melted. So I gave it to him. But if he doesn't give me the money tomorrow, I'll teach him a lesson. Just wait and see."

They didn't pursue the matter. They were saved the trouble of burying an old decrepit bull. Good riddance, they said to themselves.

Next day Hucca went to the tree, axe in hand.

"Will you give me my twenty-five rupees today?"

"Grk! Grk!" went the tree.

"I won't have your Grk! Grk! anymore. You give me my twenty-five or you'll have to get twenty-five strokes of my axe. What do you say?"

"Grk! Grk!"

Hucca was furious. He began to swing his axe into the trunk of the tree, counting "One, two, three. . . ." It was a dry old tree. Before he axed it eight or ten times, it broke and fell with a great crash.

Some robbers had used the bole of the old tree to hide their loot of silver and gold. When it crashed, all of it spilled out of the old tree's belly. "That's my boy!" said Hucca and bundled up as much of it as he could and ran home to his brothers, who had just sat down to a meal. He poured it all onto their dinner plates.

The brothers were amazed and thrilled at the same time at the sight of such dazzling treasure.

"Hucca, where, where did you get this?" they stammered.

"I told you, didn't I, that I sold my bull to that tree. It didn't give me rupees, but it gave me gold and silver instead. It still has a lot more in its stomach," said Hucca.

"Then let's go!" said they, and ran with him to the place. Sure enough, just as Hucca had said, there was a heap of silver and gold, vessels, coins, and jewelry. They scraped it clean, tied it in bundles, and gave a small one to Hucca to carry.

"Hucca, you must keep this a secret. Don't tell people about our finding gold and silver, do you hear?" they warned Hucca, who said, "No, I won't."

But, as the three brothers were hurrying home, they ran into the village priest, who was returning from out of town. He, of course, asked the brothers, "What are you carrying on your heads? Seems heavy." The eldest brother said, "O nothing, really. The usual millet and things."

Hucca corrected him at once. "Brother, how can you lie even to our priest? Look, sir, we are carrying real gold and silver. Lots and lots of it. You can see if you wish."

And he untied a bundle and showed him the fabulous treasure. The priest slobbered at the mouth at what he saw. "Yes, yes, real gold, real silver!" he spluttered as he began to transfer handfuls into his own satchel. Hucca wouldn't stand for this liberty and flew into a rage. Crying "*Bhappare!* you greedy Brahmin!" he struck the crown of the poor man's shaven head with the staff in his hand. The priest collapsed and died on the spot, with the name of Lord Hari on his lips.

The brothers felt wretched at this turn of events, scolded Hucca, and hastily threw the dead body in a nearby pit before they left. But they took care to return that very night without Hucca's knowledge, removed the body, and buried it elsewhere. They also threw a dead he-goat in the pit. After a couple of days, the villagers started gossiping and inquiring about the missing priest. When Hucca heard of it, he said, "O yes. I know. I hit him with this staff. He died on the spot, poor fellow, and we threw him into a pit. I can show you."

The villagers said, "Where? Where is the body?"

"I'll show you," said Hucca, and took them to the pit by the roadside and got down into it himself. He shouted from below, "Didn't our priest have a beard?"

"Yes, he did," they said.

"Didn't our priest have two curved horns on his head?"

The people were puzzled. So they went into the pit to examine the body, only to find a dead goat's carcass.

"This Hucca is a moron and we are even greater morons for following him here," they muttered to themselves and left, feeling utterly foolish.

From then on, whenever Hucca told people that the old tree gave him and his brothers gold and silver, no one believed him. They only laughed at him.

31. The Husband's Shadow

A merchant had a pretty wife. One day, she was standing at her doorstep braiding her hair, and the king happened to see her. His mind was filled with desire for her. He asked his servants who she was and found that she was the merchant's wife. He went back to his palace, secretly summoned a crone who was an expert go-between, gave her a hundred rupees in a closed fist, and promised her more if she would entice the merchant's wife to sleep with him. She soon made friends with the merchant's wife and won her heart. She came back to the king and told him, "She's waiting for you. She wants you to go to her house right now."

The king was ecstatic. He perfumed himself all over with attar and fragrant oils, dressed himself up, entered her backyard, and appeared at her windows. Just as she was about to unlatch the back door for him, her husband appeared at the front door and called out to her. She turned around and opened the door for her husband. Her husband was now in the house, and her paramour was waiting in the backyard. She wondered how she could tell her paramour that this was not a good time, and thought of a way. She filled a winnowing fan with wheat and started grinding it in her quern, singing a song:

Round and round you circle me.
Someone is waiting ready to get you.
If you come in, you'll die for me.
And I'm already dying for you.

The king heard the song, understood the situation, and returned to his palace. But the merchant at home was suspicious. He said, "Look here, woman. You seem to be fornicating in my absence. Was a lover waiting outside? Were you singing to warn him that your husband was home?" And, in his jealous anger, he kicked her.

She said, "*Ayyo*, why would I cheat on you? You're my man made of gold. Talk to me after you've understood the meaning of my song."

"Then tell me, what does it mean?"

"A fisherman went to the pond to catch fish. He had baited his hook with an earthworm and thrown his line in the water. A fish came around to swallow the bait when the worm said to the fish the following: You swim round and round to eat me. But there's a man waiting to eat you. If you eat me, you'll die. I'm already half-dead for fear you'll eat me. That's what the worm said to the fish. I sang it to see whether you would get it. Do you get it now?"

The merchant admired his wife's intelligence and was very pleased with her. He praised her all day and was happy.

The king waited in the palace wondering when she would send word to him. The day did come when the merchant had to go out of town on business. Being still suspicious, he appointed a man to guard over his wife, but the man was a nitwit. As soon as her husband was safely out of sight, she sent for the king. He came to her in a hurry and spent time with her. After he left, the nitwit asked her, "Who is that man who came and went just now?"

She said, "Oh, that is my husband's shadow."

"What is a shadow?" he asked.

"A shadow is what you see in a mirror. Look for yourself," she said. He looked into a mirror and said, "Oh, that, I know that."

On another day, when the king and the merchant's wife were sleeping together, the merchant returned from his travels and banged on the door. The king got up in a hurry, jumped the backyard fence, and vanished. When she then opened the door for him, her husband was full of suspicions. He called the nitwit and questioned him.

"Did anyone come here when I was gone?"

"No, sir. Only your shadow came and slept with the mistress. No one else."

"My shadow? What do you mean by 'shadow'?"

"Come here, sir," said the nitwit, and took him to the mirror. He showed his master his shadow and said, "Look there, that's the shadow I mean."

The merchant laughed. His doubts about his wife were cleared. "Oh, that shadow? It's all right if that shadow comes to see my wife. You don't have to stop him," he said.

Now his wife could sleep with her lover whenever the merchant was away. The nitwit didn't ever report it again.

32. In the Kingdom of Foolishness

In the kingdom of foolishness, both the king and the minister were idiots. They didn't want to run things like other kings. So they decided to change night into day and day into night. They ordered that everyone should be awake at night, till their fields and run their businesses only after dark; and they should all go to bed as soon as the sun came up. If anyone disobeyed, they would be punished with death. The people did as they were told for fear of death. The king and the minister were delighted at the success of their project.

Once a guru and a disciple arrived in the city. It was a beautiful city, it was broad daylight, but there was no one about. Everyone was asleep, not a mouse stirring. Even the cattle had been taught to sleep. The two strangers were amazed by what they saw around them, wandered about town till evening, when suddenly the whole town woke up and went about its daily business.

The two men were hungry. Now the shops were open, they went to buy some groceries. To their astonishment, they found that everything cost the same, a single *duddu*—whether they bought a measure of rice or a bunch of bananas, it cost a *duddu*. The guru and his disciple were delighted. They had never heard of anything like this. They could buy all the food they wanted for a rupee.

When they had cooked and eaten, the guru realized that this was a kingdom of fools and it wouldn't be a good idea for them to stay there. "This is no place for us. Let's go," he said to his disciple. But the disciple didn't want to leave the place. Everything was cheap here. All he wanted was good cheap food. The guru said, "They are all fools. This won't last very long and one can't tell what they'll do to you next."

But the disciple wouldn't listen to the guru's wisdom. He wanted to stay. The guru finally gave up and said, "Do what you want. I'm going," and left. The disciple stayed on, ate his fill every day, bananas and ghee and rice and wheat, and grew fat as a streetside sacred bull.

One bright day, a thief broke into a rich merchant's house. He had made a hole in the wall, sneaked in, and as he was carrying out his loot, the wall of the old house collapsed on his head and killed him on the spot. His brother ran to the king and complained: "Your Highness, when my brother was pursuing his ancient trade, a wall fell on him and killed him. This merchant is to blame. He should have built a good strong wall. You must punish the wrongdoer and compensate the family for this injustice."

The king said, "Justice will be done. Don't worry," and at once summoned the owner of the house.

When the merchant arrived, the king asked him questions. "What's your name?"

"Such and such, Your Highness."

"Were you at home when the dead man burgled your house?"

"Yes, my lord. He broke in and the wall was weak. It fell on him."

"The accused pleads guilty. Your wall killed this man's brother. You have murdered a man. We have to punish you."

"Lord," said the helpless merchant. "I didn't put up the wall. It's really the fault of the man who built the wall. He didn't build it right. You should punish him."

"Who is that?"

"My lord, this wall was built in my father's time. I know the man. He's an old man now. He lives nearby."

The king sent out messengers to bring in the bricklayer who had built the wall. They brought him tied hand and foot.

"You there, did you build this man's wall in his father's time?"

"Yes, my lord, I did."

"What kind of a wall is this that you built? It has fallen on a poor man and killed him. You've murdered him. We have to punish you by death."

Before the king could order the execution, the poor bricklayer pleaded, "Please listen to me before you give your orders. It's true I built this wall and it was no good. But that was because my mind was not on it. I remember very well a harlot who was going up and down that street all day with her anklets jingling and I couldn't keep my eyes or my mind on the wall I was building. You must get that harlot. I know where she lives."

"You're right. The case deepens. We must look into it. It is not easy to judge such complicated cases. Let's get that harlot wherever she is."

The harlot, now an old woman, came trembling to the court.

"Did you walk up and down that street many years ago while this poor man was building a wall? Did you see them?"

"Yes, my lord. I remember it very well."

"So you did walk up and down, with your anklets jingling. You were young and you tempted him. So he built a bad wall. It has fallen on a poor burglar and killed him. You've killed an innocent man. You'll have to be punished."

She thought for a minute and said, "My lord, wait. I know now why I was walking up and down that street. I had given some gold to the goldsmith to make some jewelry for me. He was a lazy scoundrel. He made so many excuses, said he would give it now and he would give it then and so on all day. He made me walk up and down to his house a dozen times. That was when this bricklayer fellow saw me. It's not my fault, my lord, it's that damned goldsmith's."

"Poor thing, she's absolutely right," thought the king, weighing the evidence. "We've got the real culprit at last. Get the goldsmith wherever he is hiding. At once!"

The king's bailiffs searched for the goldsmith, who was hiding in a corner of his shop. When he heard the accusation against him, he had his own story to tell.

"My lord," he said, "I'm a poor goldsmith. It's true I made this harlot woman come many times to my door. I gave her excuses because I couldn't finish making her jewelry before I finished the rich merchant's orders. They had a wedding coming, and they wouldn't wait. You know how impatient rich men are!"

"Who is this rich merchant who kept you from finishing this poor woman's jewelry, made her walk up and down, which distracted this bricklayer, which made a mess of his wall, which has now fallen on an innocent man and killed him? Can you name him?"

The goldsmith named the merchant and he was none other than the original owner of the house where the wall had fallen. Now justice had come full circle, thought the king, back to the merchant. When he was rudely summoned back to the court, he arrived crying, "It's not me but my father who ordered the jewelry! He's dead! I'm innocent!"

But the king consulted his minister and ruled decisively: "It's true your father is the true murderer. He's dead, but somebody must be punished in his place. You've inherited everything from that criminal father of yours, his riches as well as his sins. I knew at once, even when I first set eyes on you, that you were at the root of this horrible crime. You must die."

And he ordered a new stake to be made ready for the execution. As the servants sharpened the stake and got it ready for the final impaling of the criminal, it occurred to the minister that the rich merchant was somehow too thin to be properly executed by the stake. He appealed to the king's common sense. The king too worried about it.

"What shall we do?" he said, when suddenly it struck him that all they needed to do was to get a man fat enough to fit the stake. The servants were immediately all over town looking for a man who would fit the stake, and their eyes fell on the disciple who had fattened himself for months on bananas and rice and wheat and ghee.

"What have I done wrong? I'm innocent. I'm a *sanyasi!*" he cried.

"That may be true. But it's the royal decree that we should find a man fat enough to fit the stake," they said, and carried him to the place of execution.

The disciple remembered his wise guru's words: "This is a city of fools. You don't know what they will do next." While he was waiting for death, he prayed to his guru in his heart, asking him to hear his cry wherever he was. The guru saw everything in a vision; he had magic powers, he could see far, and he could see the future as he could see the present and the past. He arrived at once to save his disciple, who had got himself into a scrape again through love of food.

As soon as he arrived, he scolded the disciple, told him something in a whisper, then went to the king and addressed him: "O wisest of kings, who is greater? The guru or the disciple?"

"Of course the guru. No doubt about it. Why do you ask?"

"Then put me to the stake first. Put my disciple to death after me."

When the disciple heard this, he caught on and began to clamor: "Me first! You brought me here first! Put me to death first, not him!"

The guru and the disciple now got into a fight about who should go first. The king was puzzled by this behavior. He asked the guru, "Why do you want to die? We chose him because we needed a fat man for the stake."

"You shouldn't ask me such questions. Put me to death first."

"Why? There's some mystery here. As a wise man you must make me understand."

"Will you promise to put me to death if I tell you?" asked the guru. The king gave him his solemn word. The guru took him aside, out of the servants' earshot, and whispered to him, "Do you know why we want to die right now, the two of us? We've been all over the world, but we've never found a city like this or a king like you. That stake is the stake of the god of justice. It's new, it has never had a criminal on it. Whoever dies on it first will be reborn as the king of this country. And whoever goes next will be the future minister of this country. We're sick of living the ascetic life. It would be nice to enjoy ourselves as king and minister for a while. Now keep your word, my lord, and put us to death. Me first, remember."

The king was now thrown into deep thought. He didn't want to lose the kingdom to someone else in the next round of life. He needed time. So he ordered the execution postponed to the next day and talked in secret with his minister. "It's not right for us to give over the kingdom to others in the next life. Let's go up the stake ourselves and we'll be reborn as king and minister again. Holy men do not tell lies," he said, and the minister agreed.

So he told the executioners, "We'll send the criminals tonight. When the first man comes to you, put him to death first. Then do the same to the second man. Those are orders. Don't make any mistakes."

That night, they went secretly to the prison, released the guru and disciple, disguised themselves as the two, and, as arranged beforehand with their loyal servants, were taken to the stake and promptly executed.

When the bodies were taken down to be thrown to crows and vultures, the people panicked. They saw before them the dead bodies of the king and the minister. The city was in confusion.

All night they mourned and discussed the future of the kingdom. Some people suddenly thought of the guru and the disciple and caught up with them as they were preparing to leave town unnoticed. "We people need a king and a minister," said someone. Others agreed. They begged of the guru and the disciple to be their king and their minister. It didn't take many arguments to persuade the disciple, but it took long to persuade the guru. They finally agreed to rule the kingdom of the foolish king and the silly minister on the condition that they would change all the old laws. From then on, night would again be night and day would again be day, and you could get nothing for a *duddu*. It became like any other place.

33. In Search of a Dream

A king had three sons, two of whom were idiots. The youngest son was a smart fellow and the king was very fond of him. He had even decided to pass the kingdom on to him.

One night, the king had a weird dream. In it, he saw a beautiful garden and, in the middle of it, a silver tree with emerald leaves and a ruby fruit. From its branches hung a golden swing. On it perched an emerald parrot, singing and swinging gently. In the dream, the king had a serpent-jewel in his hand with which he struck the bird, and the whole garden vanished at once.

The king wanted to see in real waking life what he had seen in his dream. So he called his three sons, described the dream to them, and said, "If any of you can show me what I saw in that dream, this kingdom will be his." All three agreed to try, and the king made all the necessary arrangements for their journeys. The two older brothers headed in one direction and the youngest took the opposite direction.

The two older brothers journeyed for five days and got bored. The road was rocky, the forests scary, the towns tempting. So they stopped in a nice place, spent time there enjoying themselves till all their money was gone, and went home to tell their father they couldn't find the garden or the bird of his dream.

Meanwhile, the youngest son found an old woman who asked him to stay with her. He behaved himself and was a good boy for three days.

When he was sure that the old woman liked him a lot, he told her what he was after. She knew all about it already, and told him, "If you walk to the north of this town, you'll find a marble fortress. Inside its walls is a garden. It's very hard to get to it. But I'll tell you how to get in. First, look for a large peepul tree. You'll see a snake hole under it. A giant serpent lives there. Every night it comes out of its hole, takes out the divine serpent-jewel from its forehead, puts it down under the tree, and looks for food by the light of the jewel. If you can somehow get that jewel, its light will show you the way into the garden, where you'll find four princesses. At night one of them becomes the silver tree, another becomes the emerald leaves, the third the ruby fruit. The fourth changes into a golden swing. If you show them the jewel in your hand, they will all become yours. You spoke of an emerald parrot. I know nothing about it. But I've an elder sister in the next town. Go and ask her. She may know something about it."

The young prince saluted her gratefully and traveled northwards for three whole days till he found the marble fortress. Its gates were shut. He waited till night fell and the gates opened by themselves. He went in and was soon in front of an enormous peepul tree. Sure enough, there was a snake hole under it. He climbed the tree, hid among the branches, and waited for the snake. It was a long fearsome creature when it came out. It chose a spot, shook out the jewel from its forehead, which lighted up the ground all around it. While it foraged for food in that circle of light, the prince came down with handfuls of leaves he had plucked and deftly covered the jewel with them. The light was gone and the snake looked all over in the dark for its jewel for a long time, getting more and more frustrated. Finally, in utter rage, it struck its hood again and again on a rock nearby and died a bloody mess.

The prince quickly picked up the jewel and by its light he could now see a beautiful garden in front of him. As he entered it, he could see the silver tree, the emerald leaves, the ruby fruit, and the golden swing. As soon as he pointed the jewel towards them, all of them vanished and in their place stood four princesses, each one lovelier than the other. Each said to the other that she would marry this young man. But he asked them to stay where they were till he had finished the next task, and promised to come back for them in a few days.

The prince now went in search of the emerald bird. He went to the next town, where again he earned the goodwill of an old woman by being a very good boy for three days. Once he was sure that the old

woman liked him enough, he asked her if she had any sisters and brothers. She said, "Yes, I've a younger sister in another town." Then he told
her how he had met her sister, and how she had helped him, and how
he was now looking for the emerald parrot. The old woman knew all
about it and told him: "On the other shore of the seven seas, you'll find
a lake. A large lotus grows in it. A princess plays on the lotus leaf all day
and changes into an emerald parrot by night."

"How do I get there?" asked the prince.

"You already have the means. Worship the snake-jewel with real devotion, and a *garuda*-bird will appear. It will take you beyond the seven
seas."

The prince did as he was told, and a giant *garuda* promptly appeared, took him on his back, flew over the seven seas, and landed him
near a lake. He looked for a large lotus and there it was, in front of him.
Under it was an even larger lotus pad, on which the sweetest-looking
princess of all was fast asleep. When he pointed the shining serpent-
jewel at her face, she woke up with a start, looked long at the prince
standing in front of her, and suddenly bent her head, overcome with
shyness. He asked her, without any ceremony whatever, "Will you
marry me?"

She moved her head in consent.

Then the two of them sat on the *garuda* and flew over the seven
seas. The giant bird left them safely in the second old woman's house
and took leave. The old woman blessed them and showed them the way
back. Then they entered the marble fortress, and the four princesses he
had left behind were delighted to see the fifth one. He told them his
father's dream, and they said, "All five of us are sisters. A wicked demon
kidnapped our eldest sister and kept her in a lake beyond the seven seas.
At night, he slept under water in the lake. He was sure no mortal would
ever come there, but you are braver than all: you went and released our
sister from that bondage. We'll never leave you. Marry us."

"But what shall I do if my father asks me to make his dream come
true? He wants to see again in broad daylight whatever he saw at night
in his dream," he said.

They had an answer. "Stand all five of us in a row and with one
stroke cut off our heads. We'll change into all the things your father
saw in his dream. If you strike the parrot with the snake-jewel, we'll
return to our human forms. That's all."

Delighted that his task had been accomplished, he took them to the
first old woman, who blessed them all. But she had one wish. She

wanted to live with her elder sister. The prince at once took out the jewel and offered worship to it. At once, the *garuda* arrived and took the old woman to her sister.

The prince now traveled on with his bevy of princesses and reached home. His father said, "I asked you to make my dream come true. Instead you've gone and got yourself all these women." The prince asked the five princesses to stand in a row and, to everyone's horror, took out his sword and with one stroke cut off all their heads. At once, miraculously, the king's dream was reenacted right before his eyes: the silver tree, the emerald leaves, the ruby fruit, the golden swing, and the emerald parrot.

The prince now struck the parrot with the jewel, and the princesses reappeared in their original forms. The king was ecstatic. He arranged a splendid wedding with the five princesses for his youngest son and gave him the kingdom. The young man was a good ruler and made everyone happy, including his two dim-witted brothers.

34. King and Peasant

A peasant and his wife were very poor. They had little to eat and very little to wear. They labored somewhere or other every day so that they could have some gruel. Such was their miserable life.

One day the king and the queen were traveling through the countryside in their two-horse coach when they saw the poor peasant couple laboring in the hot sun without even a piece of cloth on their backs. The king said to the queen, "Look at those poor people. Their life is such a struggle, it's hard to watch them. God seems to be blind to their misery."

The queen replied, "God has nothing to do with these people's plight. The woman of the house is no good. So all their labor is wasted. Even if they work day and night, they won't escape poverty."

"How come?" asked the king.

The queen said, "I'll wager with you. Let me manage this peasant's house for six months. Let the peasant's wife go and live in the palace in my place and manage it for six months. You'll see the difference for yourself."

And so they exchanged places. The king took the peasant's wife to the palace with him, called all his servants and ordered that they should treat her with respect, do everything she asked them to do, and serve her just as they did the queen.

Meanwhile, the queen entered the peasant's house. It was so dirty that she gagged looking at it. Garbage, sticks and stones, unwashed pots, unswept floors, and a pile of ashes in the stove. The queen set about at once to clean up the place. She swept it, washed it, drew *rangoli* designs on the floor, cleaned all the pots, burned incense for the gods, insisted that the peasant bathe and wear a fresh loincloth every day, and said to him, "*Appa*, look here. You must go into town every day and work there. You must bring home whatever you earn and give it to me. You must never come home with an empty hand. If you can't get work on some days, you must still pick up something, at least a stick from the road, and bring it home."

Accordingly, he would go out every day and work for daily wages somewhere or other and bring home whatever he earned to the queen. After the day's expenses, she would save the pennies, put them away in a secret pot, and with that money she began to furnish the place in modest ways. The peasant ate well and soon began to look rounded and well-cared-for.

In the palace, the peasant woman quarreled with all the servants, scolded them any way she pleased, and threw about jewelry and clothes everywhere till whatever was there today wasn't there tomorrow. Precious things were lost every day. The queen's quarters were now covered with dust, garbage wet and dry, and dirty linen. The king saw that the palace was in a shambles and getting worse by the hour. He waited anxiously for the end of the six-month period.

One day, the peasant couldn't find any work though he tried everywhere. Frustrated, he turned towards home in the late afternoon. A dead snake lay on the road. He remembered at once the queen's words that he should never come home empty-handed but bring whatever he found by the roadside. So he picked up the limp cold snake and took it to the queen. She consoled him, saying, "No matter. You did well," and she threw the dead snake on the thatched roof. Then she gave the peasant water for his hands and feet and served him food. Meanwhile, a *garuda*-bird was flying overhead with a fabulous necklace of rubies and pearls in its beak; it had picked up the necklace in the palace, maybe out of the garbage. But, now, when its eagle eyes fell on the snake on the peasant's roof, it swooped down to snatch it up, dropped the necklace while doing so, and whirled away into the sky. The queen heard the clatter, went out, and saw the necklace. She called out to the peasant, who clambered onto the roof and brought down the necklace. She asked him to take it at once to the market street and sell it at the jeweler's for a good price. He did as he was told, received a fabulous price, and brought back a bagful of money. She used it to buy him a new house and some land, furnishings, cattle and buffaloes, and arranged it all so that he would never want for anything. By this time, six months had come to an end.

The king couldn't wait to get the queen back. He rode to the peasant's village and pleaded with his queen, "You must hurry back. We live in chaos. We have lost so much already. I can't bear it anymore."

He was amazed at the prosperity of the peasant. The queen explained, "Now you know. The woman in the house is like Lakshmi, the goddess of good fortune. Even in the poorest household, if she is tidy and manages with care and looks after the welfare of the man who works, Lakshmi will seek out that house and dwell in it. Otherwise, you know very well what misery follows."

With these words, she installed the peasant's wife back in her place, gave her lots of advice, and went home to her palace to clear the garbage there and set it up for the good life again.

35. Kutlavva

In a town just like ours, there lived a brahmin couple. They had plenty of money, but they had no children. They made long pilgrimages, made vows to many gods, and finally one of the gods was pleased with them. So they had a daughter. They distributed sugar to the whole town and named her Kutlavva. They doted on her and proudly saw her grow up to be a pretty young woman. Then they bought her splendid saris and costly jewelry and got her married. Maybe the gods didn't like anyone to be loved so much. Kutlavva suddenly took to bed and died one day. The whole town mourned her death with her parents. They took the body to the burning ghat and cremated her.

Just as they were slowly getting reconciled to their loss, a stranger came one day to town with a bundle of firewood for sale. He hawked it all through the hot afternoon, but no one would buy it from him. Quite disgusted with his lot, he set down his load and sat leaning against the brahmin's house. The brahmin's wife came out, saw him sitting there, and asked him, "Where do you come from?"

"O, don't ask me, lady. I come straight from the burning ghat and I'm going back there," he said, weary of life.

The poor woman remembered that they had taken her daughter to the burning ghat when she died. So she asked him, "O, you come from the burning ghat? That's Kutlavva's place. Do you see our Kutlavva there? How is she doing?"

"She's doing very well. My house and her house are right next to each other."

The brahmin's wife was filled with joy. She looked for her husband to give him the good news, but he wasn't home. She bustled about, went into her room, gathered together all the jewels she had kept for Kutlavva, put them into a box, and brought it to the stranger.

"Look here, good man, we had got a lot of jewelry made for our daughter at the time of her wedding. Here it is. Can you take it and give it to her?"

"Gladly," said the man. He took the jewelry box and walked away, leaving behind his bundle of firewood.

Soon after, her husband came home riding his horse. His wife couldn't wait to tell him the happy news: "Do you know, a man came from the burning ghat today. I asked him how Kutlavva was and he said she was fine. So I gave him all her jewelry and asked him to give it to her."

The brahmin struck his forehead in despair at what his simple wife had done. He mounted his horse again, asked which way the stranger had gone, and followed him. He rode out of town and through the fields.

Meanwhile, the man had hidden the box somewhere and was standing on a mound, pretending to shoo some sparrows off a tree. The brahmin stopped in front of him and asked him, "Did you see a man go this way with a box in his hands?"

The man said, "Yes, yes, he went right into that sugarcane field. If you go quickly, you can catch him."

How can a horse go through a sugarcane field? So the brahmin said, "Do me a favor. Please look after this horse while I go chase after that thief."

Then he left the horse in the stranger's hands and ran into the sugarcane field. The blades of the sugarcane grass slashed his face and hands and drew blood. He searched everywhere in the field but couldn't find the thief.

When he came out, his horse too had vanished. So had the man who was chasing sparrows. Then the brahmin knew he too had been taken. The thief had taken the jewelry from his wife and the horse from him.

When he came home downcast, his wife asked him, "Where's your horse?"

The brahmin replied, "Well, I sent the horse also to Kutlavva."

36. The Lampstand Woman

A king had an only daughter. He had brought her up lovingly. He had spread three great loads of flowers for her to lie on and covered her in three more, as they say. He was looking for a proper bridegroom for her.

In another city, another king had a son and a daughter. He was looking for a proper bride for his son.

A groom for the princess. A bride for the prince. The search was on. Both the kings' parties set out, pictures in hand. On the way, they came to a river, which was flowing rather full and fast, and it was evening already. "Let the river calm down a bit. We can go on at sunrise," they said, and pitched tents on either side of the river for the night.

It was morning. When they came to the river to wash their faces, both parties met. This one said, "We need a bridegroom." That one said, "We need a bride." They exchanged pictures, looked them over, and both parties liked them. The bride's party said, "We spread three great big measures of flowers for our girl to lie on and cover her in three more. That shows how tenderly we've brought up our girl. If anybody promises us that they'll look after her better than that, we'll give the girl to that house."

To that, the boy's party replied, "If you spread three great measures of flowers for her, we'll spread six." They made an agreement right there.

When they were getting the town ready for the wedding, the rain god gave them a sprinkle, the wind god dusted and swept the floors. They put up wedding canopies large as the sky, drew sacred designs on the wedding floor as wide as the earth, and celebrated the wedding. It was rich, it was splendid. And soon after, the princess came to her husband's palace.

The couple were happy. They spent their time happily—between a spread of six great measures of flowers and a cover of six more.

Just when everything was fine, Mother Fate appeared in the princess's dream, and said, "You've all this wealth. No one has as much. But who's going to eat the three great measures of bran and husk?" So saying, she took away all the jasmine, and spread green thorn instead. The girl, who used to sleep on jasmines, now had to sleep on thorns. Every day Mother Fate would come, change the flowers, make her bed a bed of thorns, and disappear. No one could see this except the princess. The princess suffered daily. She suffered and suffered, got thinner and thinner till she was as thin as a little finger. She didn't tell anyone about Mother Fate's comings and goings or about the bed of thorns she spread every night. "My fate written on my brow is like this. Nobody can understand what's happening to me," she said to herself, and pined away.

The husband wondered why his wife was getting thinner by the day. Once he asked: "You eat very well. We look after you here better than they do at your mother's house. Yet you're pining away, you're getting thin as a reed. What's the matter?" The father-in-law, the mother-in-law, and the servantmaids all asked her the same question. "When Mother Fate herself is giving me the kind of trouble that no one should ever suffer, what's the use of telling it to ordinary humans? It's better to die," she thought, and asked for a crater of fire. She insisted on it.

She was stubborn. What could they do? They did what she asked. They robed her in a new sari. They put turmeric and vermilion on her face. They decked her hair in jasmine. They piled up sandalwood logs for the pyre, sat her down in the middle of it, and set fire to it. Then a most astonishing thing happened. Out of nowhere, a great wind sprang up, picked her out of the burning log fire, raised her unseen by others' eyes into the sky, and left her in a forest.

"O god, I wanted to die in the crater of fire, and even that wasn't possible," she said, in utter sorrow.

When the wind died down, she looked around. She was in a forest. There was a cave nearby. "Let a lion or tiger eat me, I can die at least that way," she thought, and entered the cave. But there was no lion or tiger in there. There were three great measures of bran and husk heaped up, and on the ground were a pestle and a pot. She wondered if this was what Mother Fate meant when she had asked in her dream: "Who's going to eat three great measures of bran and husk?"

What could she do? She pounded the bran each day, made it into a kind of flour, and lived on it. Three or four years went by this way. All the stock of bran and husk disappeared.

One day she said to herself, "Look here, it's three or four years since I've seen a human face. Let's at least go and look." She came out of the cave, and climbed the hill. Down below, woodcutters were splitting wood. She thought, "If I follow these people, I can get to a town somewhere," and came down. The woodcutters bundled their firewood and started walking towards a nearby market town like Bangalore. As they walked on, she walked behind them, without being seen.

As the men walked, the sun set in the woods. They stayed the night under a tree. She hid herself behind a bush. Then she saw a tiger coming towards her. "At least this tiger will eat me up; let it," she thought, and lay still. The tiger came near. But he just sniffed at her and moved on. She felt miserable, and she moaned aloud, "Even tigers don't want to eat me." The woodcutters heard her words.

They got up and looked around. They saw a tiger walking away from where she was. They were stunned, terrified. When they could find words, they came close and talked to her. They said, "You must be a woman of great virtue. Because of you, the tiger spared us too. But you are crying! What's your trouble? Why do you cry?"

She begged of them: "I've no troubles. Just get me to somebody's house. I'll work there. It's enough if they give me a mouthful of food and a twist of cloth. Please do that much, and earn merit for yourself."

They said, "All right," and took her with them.

Nearby was a town, like Bangalore. The woodcutters went to the big house where they regularly delivered firewood, and talked to the mistress there. "Please take in this poor woman as a servant here," they said. She said, "All right," and took her in. The woodcutters went their way. She started work in the big house, doing whatever they asked her to do.

One day the mistress's little son threw a tantrum. The mistress said to her, "Take this child out. Show him the palace. Quiet him down." So she carried him out, and as she was showing him this and that to distract him, a peacock pecked at the child's necklace, took it in its beak, and swallowed it. She came running to the mistress and told her what had happened. The mistress didn't believe her.

She screamed at her, "You thief, you shaven widow, you're lying! You've hidden it somewhere. Go, bring it at once, or else I'll make you!"

The poor woman didn't know what to do. She cried piteously. "No, no, I swear by god. It's that bird, that peacock, it swallowed the necklace," she said.

They didn't listen to her. The mistress said, "This is a tough customer. She won't budge for small punishments. We'll have to give her the big one."

And she proceeded to punish her most cruelly. She had her beaten first, then had her head shaved clean and naked; asked the servants to place a patty of cow dung on it, and put an oil lamp on it; and herself lighted the wick.

She was given household chores all day. At night she had to carry the lamp on her head and go wherever they asked her to go. Everyone called her Lamp Woman, Lamp Woman. Time passed this way.

One day, the mistress's elder brother came there. He was the Lamp Woman's husband. But he didn't know anything. He came to his younger sister's house, dined there, and sat down to chew betel leaf and betel nut. The mistress sent the Lamp Woman to light the place where he was sitting, enjoying his quid of betel leaf.

She knew at once that this man was her husband. She swallowed her sorrow and stood there, with the lamp on her head. Though he looked at the Lamp Woman, he didn't recognize her. She had changed so much. He believed that his wife had perished in the fire. He thought this was some shaven-headed servantwoman getting punished for some wrong she had done. Without even looking at her, he asked her, "Lamp Woman, tell me a story."

"What story do I know, master? I don't know any story."

"You must tell me some story. Any kind will do."

"Master, shall I tell you one about what's to come yet or what's gone before?"

"Who can see what's to come? Tell us about what's gone before."

"It's a story of terrible hardships."

"Go ahead."

The Lamp Woman told him about the palace where she was born, how she got married, slept between cartloads of flowers, how Mother Fate appeared every night in her dream and tormented her on a bed of thorns, how she thought she could escape it all by dying on a pyre of sandalwood, how the wind miraculously carried her to a forest, and how she lived there on a meal of bran and husk; how she came with the woodcutters to this place and entered domestic service; how the peacock swallowed the necklace when she was consoling the child; how she was called a thief and made to look like a shaven widow; and how she was condemned now to walk about as a Lampstand Woman. All this she told the prince, in utter sorrow. As he heard the story, he listened to her voice and began to see who she was. He recognized that this was his long-lost wife. He took down the lamp from her head and lovingly hugged and caressed her. He scolded his younger sister and brother-in-law for punishing his wife so cruelly. They fell at his feet and asked forgiveness—but he put his wife on his horse and left at once for his own town.

Everyone was very happy to see that the princess hadn't really perished in the fire.

37. The Magician and His Disciple

A childless king did penance (*tapas*) and prayed to Siva. By His grace, he had two sons. The king and queen fondly doted on these children of their late years. Enemy kings took advantage of his being very old and his children being very young. They laid siege to his kingdom. The king could not withstand the attack. Vanquished, he left the palace with his wife and children while it was still honorable to do so. He went to a faraway kingdom and lived there as a beggar. The hardships of his life did not bother him, but he did worry about his children. They were already seven and eight, and he was anxious about their education. One day he went to a learned guru and pleaded with him: "You must take my children under your wing and give them a proper education. I am poor. I cannot offer you money. But I can give you one of my children as repayment."

The guru agreed and kept the children with him. The old king returned to his beggar's life.

The guru was good to the boys. He sent the older boy to graze cows and taught him little skills like counting. The younger boy was very smart. When the guru showed him one thing, he learned ten things. He learned the eighteen mythologies, the six sciences, and the four Vedas. Besides, he became expert in the arts of magic—sorcery, legerdemain, especially in metempsychosis, the subtle art of entering other bodies. Very soon he was better than his guru.

One day the younger son sat in a corner and looked into the far distance with his inner eye to see what his parents were doing. He was grieved by their hardships. His heart melted for them. They had not one but two sons. Yet their old age was empty; they had nothing but trouble. He also learned about his father's promise. As repayment for his sons' education, his father was going to give away one of them. But the clever guru had taught his elder brother only to be a cowherd, and had educated only him, the younger of the two. There must be some trick, some treachery in this arrangement.

The young man got up, thinking, "If I don't do something about this right now, my parents will lose me and die in poverty." He changed at once into a bird, flew to his parents' place, and changed back into himself before he entered their hut. As their son touched their feet respectfully, the old king and queen were full of joy. They touched his hair, fondled his face, held his hand, and blessed him.

"Son, what brought you here? Is everything well? Tell us," they asked.

The son said, "Father, ever since you left us in the care of our guru, my brother and I have done everything to please him. The guru has taught me everything, but he has neglected my brother. He sends him out everyday with the cows. I know you've promised to give one of us to him. When the time comes, offer to give the guru my brother and ask for me. He will tell you all sorts of things—how wonderful my brother is, how much smarter and better educated he is. But you must be stubborn, insist that you want only the younger boy. I'll take care of the rest. I came here only to tell you this."

Then he touched their feet again, changed into a bird, and flew away.

His old father waited for the right day, chose an auspicious hour, and went to the guru. When the guru learned of the father's visit, he dressed the older brother in silk, brought him to the school room, made him sit in front as if he were a top-ranking Number One student, and spread big books in front of him. In his conversation, he named him several times. As for the younger brother, he was dressed in rags and made to sit with the stupidest pupils. When the old father arrived, the guru showed him both his sons and said, "Look, of your two sons, the older boy is brilliant. He learns everything before you even mention it. He has become a great scholar. But the younger fellow listens to nothing I say. Nothing enters his head. He doesn't want to do anything. He grazes cattle. You can have one of these two. Tell me which one you want."

The old king remembered what his young son had told him when he came as a bird. He replied, "Wise sir, you've taught at least one of them some good sense. You've taken a lot of trouble over them. That's a great thing. Whatever happens to me now, you shouldn't be harmed or cheated. So I'll give you the smart fellow, the older brother. You keep him. I'll take the stupid one. The older fellow is too smart for us; when he sees how poor we are, he'll leave us one day in search of better things. The younger fellow will adjust to our poverty better."

The guru thought, "I gave him a finger. He took the whole hand." In spite of all his persuasions, the old king insisted on taking the younger son, and finally did so.

When they reached home, the son was hungry and wanted food. As the father had spent all day in travel, he had not gone out that day to beg. So there was no food at home. The parents told him how they lived, showed him how little they had. That night they all drank water and went to bed.

Early next morning, the son heard a town crier beat his tom-tom and make an announcement: "A reward, a reward for anyone who will bring a rooster to fight the palace rooster!"

The young man woke up his father at once and said, "Father, let's make some money. I'll become a rooster. Take me to the palace and sell me for a thousand rupees."

And he changed into a big fat rooster. Somewhat fearfully, the father held the rooster under his arm and took it to the palace. The local king was thrilled with it. He gave the old man a thousand rupees as a reward and also a new turban as a special gift. The servants brought an iron coop and covered the rooster with it. As soon as they disappeared, the rooster turned into a bandicoot, burrowed a hole in the ground, and returned to his parents as their beloved prince.

That evening the palace was ready for the cockfight. When they picked up the iron coop, the cock was gone. There was only a big rat hole in the ground. The servants ran to the king and told him that a bandicoot had eaten up the rooster. He couldn't believe it, so he too came and looked. In his dismay, he said: "It's a shame that in such a solid palace as ours there are bandicoots and rats that make burrows. I'm ashamed to live in such a palace. Break it down and build a stronger palace!"

Work began that very day.

The thousand rupees the parents got for the rooster didn't last very long. "What next?" asked the old man. The son said, "Father, in this town there's a merchant named Ratnakara. He fancies horses. I'll change into a rare breed of horse. You can sell it to him for a thousand rupees."

Then he changed into a rare breed of horse called *Pancakalyani*, "the breed of five virtues." The old king took the horse to the merchant

Ratnakara. The merchant looked at it and knew at once what a splendid horse it was. He said, "This looks like a valuable horse. But we must get its quality, the condition of its teeth and the whorls on its body, examined by experts."

Then he sent for the guru who had taught him much about horses. The guru came down and carefully examined the horse's mouth and teeth and every inch of its body all the way down to the tip of its tail. It didn't take him long to discover that the horse was no other than his own pupil, who was now playing tricks on people. He was still hurting from having to give him up. He knew he had been outwitted then by his own prize pupil. He felt he couldn't let it happen again. He couldn't let the young fellow get too strong and do his master in. So he made plans to destroy him. He told the merchant, "O surely, this is a rare breed. No doubt about it. But there are things wrong with its quality, the whorls aren't right. The science of horses says that only a *sanyasi* can ride it safely. So I'll buy it. Why don't you give me a gift of a thousand rupees? Giving a brahmin such a gift will earn you merit."

The merchant Ratnakara gave him the money. The guru gave the bewildered old king the thousand rupees and bought the horse.

Then the guru mounted the horse and rode it roughshod. He rode it into pits and craters, onto boulders and craggy places, till the horse was dying of fatigue and thirst, and then he took it to a creek with a tiny trickle of water. The pupil who was the horse knew his guru's treacherous plans and made his own calculations. As soon as he touched water, he changed into a fish and glided away in the water. The guru saw what was happening and at once called his disciples. He asked them to pour poison into the water. They ran to the hermitage to get the poison.

The prince, who was now a fish, knew he would be killed if he stayed in the water. He looked around. He saw an untouchable whetting his knife, getting ready to cut up a dead buffalo. The prince quickly left his fish form and entered the carcass of the dead buffalo. When the untouchable turned around, he saw the dead buffalo get up and walk away. He started running, panic-stricken, screaming that a demon had entered the dead beast. The watchful guru knew at once that this was another of his star pupil's tricks. He stopped the untouchable and told him, "Look here. If you run like this, this demon buffalo will destroy you. You must kill it now. I'll help you."

They quickly captured the fleeing animal and forcibly tied it to a tree. The guru told the untouchable, "Strike now with your knife."

The prince didn't know what to do and was about to give up when he saw a many-colored parrot lying dead in the bole of that very tree. Just as the untouchable was swinging his knife at him, the prince entered the parrot's body and flew up into the sky. The guru took the form of a brahmany-kite and gave him chase. But after all, the pupil was young, the guru was old. Though the kite had large wings, he couldn't move them fast enough. The parrot flew farther and farther away. As he flew over a palace, he saw a princess on the terrace, shaking out and drying her long hair in the sunshine after a bath. She was exquisitely beautiful. The parrot flew down and perched right on the back of her hand. She was amazed. Who wouldn't be glad if a lovely parrot came all on its own and perched on one's hand? She caressed it, kissed it, talked to it. She was beside herself with delight when she found that the parrot could also talk.

When the kite saw her take the bird in, he knew his enemy had eluded him. He was downcast, but he flew on, hatching new plots.

The princess loved the many-colored parrot and took great care of it, never letting it out of her sight. She would bathe, eat, and sleep in the company of the parrot in the cage. After several days, the prince who was now a parrot waited one night till the princess was asleep and came out of the cage. He changed into his human form, gently undressed the princess, fondled her all over, and returned to the cage as a parrot.

In the morning, when the princess woke up, her sari was in disarray. Her body still remembered the touch of a man. Was it a dream, or had someone come into her bedroom? All the doors of her chamber were shut. The sentinels outside were still there. Not even a fly could have come in past the wakeful sentinels and the bustling maids. Who could have entered her bedroom and done these things to her? If he (she was sure it was a man) came once, he would come again. She would catch him next time, she decided, and settled her disheveled clothes.

That night she didn't play long with the parrot. She went to bed early and lay there pretending to be asleep. At midnight, the parrot came out of the cage and turned into a prince. He came to her bed and started doing what he had done the previous night. The princess got up suddenly, caught his hands, and asked him, "Who the devil are you? How did you get here? You were a parrot. How did you become a man?"

The prince, caught in the act, had to tell her the truth. He told her his whole life. He confessed: "It's true what I did was wrong. But I couldn't control myself when I saw you lying there in all your beauty. You must become mine. Or else, I'll be heartbroken."

As he blurted out his love, the princess too loved him.

"Who in the world has your looks, your magical powers? You are my husband from this moment. I'll help you in any way I can," she promised.

The prince used his magical inner eye again and learned of his guru's plots even as he sat there on her bed. Then he said to her, "Princess, tomorrow my guru will come to this palace in the guise of an acrobat. He wants to kill me. He will please your father with his marvelous acrobatic feats and ask for a reward. When your father offers him gold and silver, he'll refuse it and ask for the parrot in the princess's bedroom. Your father will send maids to get the parrot. You must refuse. He will send maids again and again, many times. Then you get into a rage and break the neck of the parrot in front of them all. But my guru will not stop there. He'll ask for the necklace of pearls round your neck. At that point, you tear off the pearl necklace and throw it down. I'll do the rest."

After this talk, he made love to the princess most tenderly, and went back to the cage as a parrot.

Next day, just as the prince had foretold, the guru did come in the guise of an acrobat. He showed the king and the court various kinds of fabulous tricks. They all shouted happily, "Great! Terrific!" The delighted king held out to him a handful of gold coins. But the acrobat would have none of it. He said, "Your Highness, your daughter has a many-colored parrot. That's what I'd like to have. Give it to me if you wish. I want nothing else."

The king sent maids to the balcony, where the princess sat watching. She refused to yield the parrot two or three times. When the king insisted, she came down, threw a tantrum, and twisted the parrot's neck, killing it then and there.

The acrobat now asked for the pearl necklace that had appeared magically around her neck. In her rage, she pulled it off and spilled the pearls on the court floor. The pearls turned into little worms. The acrobat ran towards them, quickly changed into a hen, and began to peck at them and devour them. At once the prince, who was now the worms on the floor, abruptly changed into a tomcat, leaped on the hen, and held it by its neck.

The guru cried out from within the hen, "*Ayyo*, I'm defeated. I surrender. Let me go now. Remember, you were once my disciple."

The disciple screamed from within the cat, "No, you're full of lies. I'm going to kill you this time, so that you won't bother me or anyone else again."

All the people who were standing around were astonished at the turn of events. Cats and hens talking like human beings! Can such things be?

The king, who had recovered his poise sooner than others, raised his voice: "Who are you? What's with all these shapes?" he asked.

The hen squeaked, "Ask the cat."

The cat explained, beginning with, "This is my guru. I was his disciple," and went on to tell the whole story: how his father had lost his kingdom, how he had sent his two sons to the guru, how the guru had tried to cheat his father, how he had himself escaped all the villainous plots, right up to the present moment. The king heard the story and said, "A guru shouldn't be killed. Let him go. He will not bother you anymore."

The prince was now confident of his powers. He could counter whatever the guru did, escape every snare. So he showed mercy and let the guru go. Both of them gave up their animal forms, as cat and hen, and became human again.

The king married his daughter to the young prince and gave him half his kingdom as dowry. The prince brought home to the palace his elder brother from the guru's place, and sent palanquins to his parents, who had seen life at its worst, a king and a queen who had lived as beggars. He waged war against his father's old enemies and won back his father's kingdom for him.

Everyone was happy. Even the guru.

38. A Minister's Word

A king had a fine minister who had the habit of saying, "That's good, very good. God did well." He would say this in the best of times and in the worst of times.

The kingdom was attacked once by its neighbors, and so the king had to go to war. He fought well and won the war, but in the fray an enemy sword slashed at him and he lost his little finger. He felt a little sorry for himself and showed it to the minister, saying, "Look what happened. I lost my little finger in battle."

The minister promptly replied, as usual, "Good, very good. God did very well."

The king was furious at this insensitive reply and banished the minister as unfit to help him govern the country. The minister said, "Good, very good. God did well," and accepted exile as if he were going home.

A few weeks later, the king went to the hills on a hunting trip. He pursued a deer deep into the woods, leaving his soldiers far behind. Night fell and it grew dark. So he tied his horse to a tree and slept in the fork of its big branches.

Now bandits lived in the forest of the foothills. They heard the neighing of a horse, came to the tree, found and captured the king in the branches. Shouting great hurrahs, they brought him down. All through that season they had been looking for a man of royal blood to sacrifice to their goddess, and as luck would have it, here was one who fell into their hands. They tied him up, covered him with flowers, and carried him to the temple. The king was alone among a whole host of them. When the day dawned, and the right hour came, the sacrificer raised his long sword to cut off his head and offer it to the Dark Goddess, Kali: a king's head, the rarest of offerings. In that breathless moment, the chief bandit cried out, "Stop, stop. This sacrifice is no good. Look, this man may be a king, but he is imperfect. He has lost his little finger. What we need is a man with all his limbs intact."

The crowd was greatly disappointed. They carried him away in disgust and threw him near the hut of a sage in the woods, who happened to be no other than the banished minister himself. In the morning light, the king and the minister recognized each other. The king gratefully embraced him and said, "What you said was right, though I didn't see it then. My little finger saved me. It was good. God did well. But I've one question. Did God do well by you? You were unjustly banished and you had to suffer hardships in these woods."

"That too was good, very good. God did well by me too. If I'd been your minister, I'd have been hunting with you. Those bandits would have let you go and sacrificed me instead. Remember, I happen to have all my limbs intact," said the minister, wiggling his little finger.

39. Monkey Business

A monkey lived in a forest. Once, as he leapt from tree to tree, a splinter broke in his tail. He was sitting on a branch howling in pain and nursing his tail when he saw a barber walking that way. He called the man closer and begged of him: "Brother Barber, Brother

Barber, a thorn or something is hurting my tail. Please take it out with your razor, bless you."

When the barber was taking out the splinter, which was in a tricky place, the whole tail broke off with a snap. The monkey began to cry in a loud voice, "Give me my tail back! My tail, my tail!"

The barber didn't know what to do. So he said, "Take my razor instead of your tail."

The monkey took the barber's razor and began to walk. On his way, he saw a potter patting clay and turning a pot. The monkey said, "Take this razor," and gave it to him. The potter took it and put it to one of the pots to cut an edge, but the razor broke in his hand. The monkey set up a howl: "You broke my razor! My razor, my razor!"

So the potter gave him a pot in exchange for the razor.

The monkey was walking along with the pot when he saw a farmer watering cucumber plants with his bare hands. So the monkey gave the pot to the farmer. Before he could water two cucumbers with it, the pot slipped from his hands and shattered. The monkey wailed again, "Give me back my pot! My pot, my pot!"

The farmer gave him a cucumber in exchange.

Next the monkey met a peasant who was eating dry bread. So the monkey gave him the cucumber. But as soon as he finished eating it with his bread, the monkey howled, "My cucumber! Give me back my cucumber!"

The peasant, the good man, didn't want any trouble. So he gave the monkey his old ox.

The monkey now rode the ox till he saw some acrobats carrying bamboo poles and drums and things on their heads. The monkey said to them, "Why do you want to carry all that stuff on your heads? Put it all on this ox's back."

The acrobats were glad to load the ox with everything they had and walk next to it swinging their hands. The ox was very old and could not really bear the burden. He soon sank to the ground and fell down dead. The monkey jumped up and down and cried, "My ox, my ox! Give me back my ox!"

The acrobats couldn't stand this monkey business and gave him his big drum.

The monkey beat his drum and began to sing:

Out went the tail,
   in came the razor, *dum dum!*

Out went the razor,
   in came the pot, *dum dum!*
Out went the pot,
   in came the cuke, *dum dum!*
Out went the cuke,
   in came the ox, *dum dum!*
Out went the ox,
   in came the drum, *dum dum!*
Out went the tail,
   in came the drum, the drum, the drum,
dum dum dum! dum dum dum!

40. The Mother Who Married Her Own Son

Brahma had a daughter. She came of age and stayed at home. Brahma and his wife used to go out every day to create the world and all the things in it. One day the daughter asked: "*Appa,* where do you go every day?"

"Daughter dear, I go out to create the world and people. Then I write their future on their foreheads."

"What do you write, *Appa?*"

"Child, you won't understand if I tell you. I write whatever is their fate."

"Then what is my fate?"

Brahma thought for a while. Should he tell her, or shouldn't he? But the daughter was insistent. She asked him the same question again and again. Brahma yielded at last. He looked at her forehead and said, "Daughter dear, I've written that you will marry your own son, the son of your womb." Then he went out to work.

Brahma's daughter was horrified, angry. "Can there be such injustice?" she thought. "If I'm here, what *Appa* has written will come true," she argued with herself. Then, without telling anyone, she left home and came down to earth. She went to the seven hills and shut herself up in a deserted cave. There she lived in exile, on fruit and vegetables.

One day she was thirsty. She went down the slope of the hill and looked for water. A bull had urinated in a rock pool. Brahma's daughter didn't realize what it was. Thinking it was ordinary water, she drank it, found it a bit salty, and came back to the cave. Because she had drunk a bull's urine, she became pregnant. Months later, she gave birth to a male child.

She was panic-stricken. Her father's word had come true. In her anger, she threw her baby son on a rock, closed her eyes, and pounded him with another rock. She tore off the end piece of her sari, wrapped the baby in it, and threw him down the hillside.

A childless cowherd was grazing his cows in the valley. His eyes lighted on a baby wrapped in a piece of cloth. The baby was badly bruised and crushed in places. The head was bloody. But he was still alive. The cowherd took him home, nursed him, and looked after him. He and his wife, long childless, loved the foundling child and brought him up. He grew up to be a robust young fellow.

Living in the hills for years, Brahma's daughter began to get bored. Fruits and nuts were getting scarce. She came down the hill slopes. She was hungry. She saw a house and went into it for food. The family asked who she was and where she came from. Hearing that she had no one in the world and nowhere to go, they asked her, "Would you like to stay with us?" She felt that it would be nicer to stay in one place with people than to roam here and there. So she agreed to stay. The couple in the house had once found a son at the foot of the hill; now they were delighted to find a girl at their door. They thought, "Here we have a daughter," and treated her as one. The boy and girl lived well together as sister and brother. Unwittingly, Brahma's daughter had joined her own son.

The foster-son came of age. His parents thought of getting him married. They asked him what his wishes were. He said, "*Appa*, my marriage can wait. Get Sister married first."

The parents had reared them both lovingly, and wanted good marriages for both. They said, "It doesn't matter who gets married first. Whoever gets a good match should marry first. Don't you agree?"

The young man agreed, and so did the young woman.

The parents went to the elders and the astrologers. Wherever they went they had trouble with their son's horoscope. They could find no suitable brides for him. Astrologers said, "The horoscope says that he is destined to marry a girl who lives in his own house." What could they do? They came home and told the son about what the astrologers said. He was furious.

"I've called her 'Sister, Sister,' all my life. I've grown up with her. How can I marry her? I'll go to some other town and ask other experts. Give me fifty rupees," he said.

He took the money and went with an older man to the big town to consult astrologers. There too they gave him the same message as before. Downcast, his face drawn, the son came home.

"I'll never marry," he said, and sat down, dejected.

The father and mother were full of worries now. "We have one son. Even this son, we heard him crying in the woods and we found him. We want to see him married before death shuts our eyelids. But he says he'll never get married. What shall we do?"

Then they brought a council of elders from seven villages to talk to their son. The elders counseled: "Look here, you were found in the woods. Your poor parents picked you up because they had no children of their own. This girl too, like you, came from somewhere else and joined this family. How can the two of you be brother and sister? Did you come out of the same womb, or what? We would have agreed that you were brother and sister if you had the same mother. That isn't the case, is it? The astrologers and all the signs say that you two should marry. Would God accept it if we went against the signs? Come now, give your consent to the marriage. Accept this girl, marry her, be happy. Make your parents happy."

The young man bowed to the elders' wishes. The girl too, who had been saying "No! Never!" all this while, was persuaded by all sorts of ruses. Then the wedding took place. Without their knowledge, mother and son had married each other. And it was a good match. They were harmonious and happy as husband and wife. She soon gave birth to a son.

One day, Brahma's daughter was combing her husband's hair, and looking for lice. She noticed that his scalp was full of scars and scabs of old wounds. She thought dimly of something. She asked him, "Why is your head like this?"

"I don't know. It's always been that way," he said.

Just then, their foster-father happened to come in and hear their conversation. He told them the whole story of how he had found the baby in the valley. He even went in and brought out the piece of sari that the baby had been wrapped in.

As soon as she saw the end piece of the sari, Brahma's daughter remembered everything. She recognized the sari as her own. She was convinced that her husband was no other than her son. "*Appa*'s word came true at last!" she cried, beating her breasts in despair.

"I married my own son, a son born from my own womb! How could I? How could I?" she said over and over, and hanged herself with her own sari twisted into a rope, and died.

41. Muddanna

In a certain town there lived a rich man named Mud-danna with his wife and his only son. For one reason or another, they went through a bad time, all their riches slipped away, and they became poor. The wife had to go begging from door to door and bring home some food every day. One day she got tired of it and said to her husband and her son, "I've been begging food for you two while you sit at home and eat. Why don't the two of you harness our two bullocks and till the little bit of land we still have?"

Muddanna thought it was a good idea, harnessed his two bullocks named Rama and Lakshmana, and went to till the field. He worked till noon, when God came down to see him in the guise of an old beggar with a begging bowl and a stick and asked for alms. Muddanna looked at him and thought to himself sadly, "What can I give? My garden is dried up. If I'd tilled last year and grown something, I could have given this beggar something now. I must at least beg and get something for him."

Just as he was leaving the field, his wife met him with three balls of cooked flour that she had collected from begging in town. She asked them all to sit under the shady tree, which they did. Just when his wife was about to distribute the food she had brought, Muddanna said, "You take half a ball, I'll take the other half. Let our son and this *swami* take one each."

When they finished eating, the *swami* said, "*Avva*, I need some water."

The wife said, "This place is dry. There's not a drop of water anywhere nearby. What shall we do?"

The *swami* said, "I'll tell you where to go. Go a little distance in this direction till you find a patch of sand. Dig in it a little. You'll find a freshwater spring."

While Muddanna's wife and son went to fetch water, the man said to Muddanna quietly, "Your troubles are only beginning. More is on the way."

"What troubles?" asked Muddanna in alarm.

"When you go home and tie up the bullocks, your wife will fall down dead. By the time you finish her funeral rites, your son will die. By the time you carry your son's body to the cemetery and come back after burying him, you'll find your two bullocks cold on the ground."

Muddanna said nothing. He just looked down at the earth under his feet.

When he came home, tied up his bullocks in the shed, and came into his hut, he found his wife dead. He took the body to the cemetery and buried her properly. Meanwhile, the son died in grief and despair at the death of his mother, who had fed him all his life, even begging for food for his sake. Muddanna carried him also to the cemetery and gave him a proper burial. He returned home thinking fondly of his two bullocks. But, when he looked for them, he found the bullock named Rama and the other one named Lakshmana lying dead near the back door, one on the left, the other on the right. He got them carried to a field and buried them with his own hands. Now he thought life was not worth living and went to the forest. He climbed a hill and threw himself down into a whirlpool. But nothing happened to him, not a hair was hurt, not even the point of a thorn touched him. He thought, "Ah, it looks as if I've a lot of *karma* to live through. I've got to suffer it till it's finished."

As he walked on, he saw a step-well with twelve steps under a guava tree that had plenty of fruit on its branches. Ugranarasimha, the Fierce Lord Who Was Half-Lion and Half-Man, had coveted the fruit of that tree, climbed on it, slipped, and fallen into the deep well. Similarly, a seven-foot tiger, a seven-headed snake, and even the Monkey God had climbed the tree for the fruit, slipped, and fallen into the well. Just as Muddanna was preparing to jump into it himself, the Fierce Lord called out to him in a piteous voice, "*Appa,* you look like a good man. Help me get out of this slippery well and I'll help you in time of need."

Muddanna said, "If you will give me the gift of death, I'll help you."

But the Fierce Lord said, "How can I kill someone like you and earn myself a stint in hell? Don't despair. Think of me whenever you need me; I'll appear and help you. Come now, get me out of here."

Muddanna helped him out and he vanished. The seven-foot tiger also begged him to help him out of the well, saying, "You want to die, don't you? Don't you know, I live by killing people like you? Help me out of here and I'll help you die."

Muddanna thought, "One can certainly trust a tiger to kill. The time to die is at last near. I've come to the end of my *karma*."

With all his might, he lifted the heavy seven-foot tiger out of the well. But the tiger, as he shook the water off his coat, had changed his mind.

"How can I kill someone who has saved my life? Think of me when you are in trouble; I'll appear and help you," he said and went on his way.

Thinking that at least the seven-headed snake would bite him and give him the death he longed for, he lifted out the snake and set him on dry ground. It too refused to bite him and asked him to think of it whenever he was in trouble. Then it too went on its way, leaving Muddanna where he was.

After a while, despairing of ever dying, he thought of visiting the tiger in his cave. The tiger wondered to himself what he could offer to one who had saved his life, and split his skull open. Out of it fell a large diamond. Muddanna picked it up, and went to visit the Fierce Lord, Ugranarasimha, who was so pleased to see his rescuer that he ordered him a grand dinner. He even sent his own son to the market to bring some fresh banana leaves for his guest's dinner. Muddanna had just given the boy the precious tiger-head diamond to look at; turning it over in his hand, the boy had come to the market. The princess of that city had just announced through the town crier that she would marry anyone who would bring her the jewel in the tiger's head. People had meanwhile reported seeing just such a jewel in the boy's hand. The palace guards went there with naked swords and took him at once to the princess. The boy confessed that the jewel was not his but Muddanna's. So they went after Muddanna, found him, and dragged him to the palace. He looked like an ordinary man, not at all like a hero. So they concluded he must have stolen it, and the princess ordered him thrown into jail.

Sitting on the floor of the jail, Muddanna remembered the seven-headed serpent, which appeared at once, making a hissing noise. It consoled Muddanna: "Look, don't be afraid. I'll go now and bite the queen. When the guards come with the news, tell them you know how to bring her back to life. Leave the rest to me."

It went at once to the queen's quarters and bit the queen. In no time, the news of the queen's sudden death by snakebite spread all over the city and made everyone shudder. Muddanna told his jailers, "I know how to bring her back to life. Try me."

They only mocked at him.

"You whoreson bastard, you're trying tricks on us. You think you'll get out of jail that way? Who can bring a dead woman to life?"

He said, "I can. Try me. Take me there in handcuffs and leg-irons and all. See what I can do."

"All right, let's see what you can do," they said, and dragged him to the queen's quarters, where her body lay. He remembered the seven-headed snake, who arrived at once and sucked the poison from the queen's wound. She sat up at once as if she had just woken up from a long sleep. The king thought this was truly a magician. He even thought that such a clever man would make a proper bridegroom for his daughter. But his daughter, the princess, had other ideas. She would marry him only on one condition.

"You did bring my mother back to life. But she and my father are now eighty years old. If, by your magic, you can make them young again, I'll happily marry you," she said.

Then Muddanna thought of the Monkey God, who leapt at once into his sight from nowhere. Muddanna said, "I have to go to the world of Brahma. Can you take me to him? I have to ask Him something."

The Monkey God sat him on his tail and made it grow and grow and grow till it reached all the way to the world of Brahma, and landed Muddanna there. He asked Brahma the Creator, "O Brahma, give me a fruit or something that will make people young."

Brahma smiled and said nothing. He took out a bunch of keys from his waist, gave it to a servant, and asked him to open the door of a room nearby. When the door opened, what did Muddanna see but his wife sitting there, combing her long hair! As soon as she saw him, she ran to him and fell at his feet, crying, "My husband, my husband." When Brahma asked his servants to open the door of another room, their son came out of it, crying, "O Father, I haven't seen you for so long!" When the door of the next room was opened, the two bullocks named Rama and Lakshmana were standing there, chewing their cuds. Nowhere could they find the fruit that would make men and women young again. Then Brahma the Creator asked Muddanna, "Tell me what you want: do you want the fruit that will make people young, or do you want your family, your *samsara*, back?"

Muddanna replied without any hesitation, "Lord, what are you saying? I don't want anything to do with that king, or that queen, or that princess, or that kingdom. The taste of the first morsel is best. I want my wife, my son, my bullocks. Let me take them home. Please."

Brahma sent them all home with him. All his troubles had come to an end as suddenly as they had begun and he lived happily thereafter.

42. Nagarani ("Serpent Queen")

A king had no children. He and his queen did everything possible, made vows and offerings, said hundreds of prayers, undertook pilgrimages, did anything anyone suggested. Finally, on someone's advice, the queen devoted herself to worshiping snake-stones. She circumambulated every snake-stone she saw on the roadside. She prayed ceaselessly. One day, while she circumambulated a snake-stone and offered milk to the image, a real cobra appeared and sipped the milk in the saucer.

"O Lord of Snakes, take pity on me," she pleaded.

The cobra said, "Yes, my daughter. I know what you want. You'll have a child. But you'll have to give the child to me, whether it is a son or daughter. Promise now."

She wanted to escape the brand of barrenness. She wanted no one to call her "Barren Queen" anymore. So she promised at once. She was soon big with child.

After a term of nine days and nine months, she gave birth to a girl. The little one was a beauty. The king and queen doted on her, couldn't take their eyes off her all day. In her joy, the queen forgot her promise to the Lord of Snakes. He was angry, came to her bedside one day and stung the queen, who foamed in her mouth and died in minutes. He didn't touch the king, because he hadn't given his word, but the cobra's anger smoldered.

The little girl grew up and became a young woman. One day the king and his daughter went for a walk to the flower garden outside town. There an old hag was feeding eggs to a baby snake. The sight disgusted the king. So he scolded the old hag, "You crone, what the hell are you doing?"

She flared at him and cursed him. "Look who's talking? You got a daughter by promising her to the Lord of Snakes. But you don't recognize him when you see him! You too will change into a snake!"

The princess was about to plead with her and say, "Please, please, granny! Wait a second!" But before she could utter a word, the hag had flourished a magic wand and thrown it at the king, who changed into a snake that instant and began to creep about. He hissed and circled round and round his daughter, unable to leave her. The princess was furious. She called the servants to arrest the old woman and take her to prison.

The old woman gave her a venomous look. "If anything happens to me, you too will become a snake like your father," she threatened.

The princess was in a panic now. She sank to her knees, shivered uncontrollably, and couldn't stop her stream of tears. The old woman's heart melted. She tried to console the young thing by saying, "Don't be afraid, nothing will happen to you." The princess fell at her feet and begged, "Give me back my father. Change him back into a man!"

The old woman said, "Princess, your mother got you by promising you to the cobra. But after you were born, she was so proud of your beauty, she forgot her promise and ignored him. That's why he killed your mother, and has now made your father like himself. But now, make a gold ring and put it around your father. When it slips off by itself he will become himself again. If anyone keeps that ring in their house, the house will not want for grain. Their cows will not get sick. Silver and gold will pour into their laps." So saying, she vanished.

The princess returned to the palace and got the goldsmiths to make a gold ring to fit the snake's body. The snake slithered away with the ring around it.

Some time after that, a farmer was returning home, tired after a day's work. He was thirsty. So he climbed down a well to drink water. There he saw that a huge cobra had left a gold ring on a rock, and was playing in the water. The farmer made no noise and tiptoed to the rock, picked up the ring, and ran with it. The cobra chased him. Hissing, he was at his heels till the farmer ran up a tree. As the cobra was about to go up the tree, an old hag appeared from nowhere. The cobra turned to her, became mild, and began to play with her. The farmer observed this change from the tree and spoke to the old woman.

"You're like my mother. At home we have no elders. Come and live with us. I'll look after you in your old age. Just send this cobra away, and come with me."

The old woman seemed pleased with the farmer's words. So she put a spell on the cobra, sent it away, and went with him.

The ring brought the farmer hoards of gold and silver. Even his rice fields had silver and gold pebbles. He became a millionaire. But he didn't suspect that the old witch too was after the gold ring, though she feigned indifference. One day, when the farmer was not home, she searched for it all over his house and found it. She grabbed it and left the house in a hurry. The farmer came home, searched for the old woman everywhere, but she was nowhere to be found.

The old woman slept in a midwife's house one night. When everyone was asleep, the glow of the ring filled the house with a strange light. The midwife, who got up in the middle of the night for something, saw the glowing ring and stole it at once. In the morning, the old woman looked for it in her clothes. It was missing. She screamed at the midwife. "You've taken my ring. Return it, or else!"

The midwife had hidden it in a grain bin. "I don't know what you are talking about. You can search for it, if you wish," said she.

The old woman looked for it everywhere, in corners, behind boxes, in cracks and in tiles, but she couldn't find it. She left the house downscast and baffled. As soon as she left, the midwife looked in her grain bin and found that all the grain had turned to pure gold. In her joy, she began to dance, forgetting even her slipping clothes.

Meanwhile, the cobra that had lost its ring came there, looking for it. When the midwife saw it, she shrieked in terror, dropped the ring, and ran out of the house half-naked. At once the cobra slipped into the ring and went creeping towards the palace.

It took a long time, a whole three months, to reach the palace. The time for the snake's molting was near. It hurried into the palace, crept straight to the princess's room, and began molting. As he shed his skin, the ring slipped out by itself. At once, the snake vanished and the king sat up in its place. The princess was ecstatic.

The king renamed his daughter Nagarani ("Queen of Snakes") and got her married to a suitable prince. As she treasured the snake's ring, she didn't lack for a thing all her life.

43. A Ne'er-do-well

A merchant and a ne'er-do-well (let's call him Bekabitti) lived in the same town. The merchant won his customers with slippery words and cheated them out of house and home. A miser, he never gave a penny to anyone. When people went to him for charity and contributions to renovate the temple, he would pretend he didn't understand what "contributions" meant. He would ask them for endless explanations of what and how and why, which tired out the visitors and drove them away. The ne'er-do-well, who was watching all this from the sidelines, wanted to teach the merchant a lesson.

He went to the merchant one day and said, "Sir, you know I'm

Bekabitti, the ne'er-do-well. I don't have anything to eat. I'd like to work for you."

The merchant thought he was getting him for free. So he said to Bekabitti, "If you're here today and gone tomorrow, it won't do for me. If you promise to work for me permanently, till I ask you to go, I'll give you a job. Otherwise, I'll give you nothing."

"That suits me very well. I'll work for you permanently. But if you throw me out, will you pay me a thousand rupees?"

"I throw you out? Never!" said the merchant, quite pleased. So they signed a contract accordingly.

Bekabitti moved in the next day and stayed with the merchant, according to the contract. In the morning, he asked the master, "What are my tasks? Tell me what to do."

The master said, "Look at this horse. Every morning, wet some horse gram and put it before him. Then take him to the tank for a wash. Bring him some grass. Then tie him up. That's about all for now."

"Is that all? That's easy," said Bekabitti.

He woke up next morning, wet some horse gram and put it in front of the horse, but at an arm's length. He waited a while and threw away the horse gram. Then he took the animal to the tank but never into the water. "Come, have a wash," he said to it, and waited. Then he cut a handful of grass and brought it to the horse, but never close enough for him to eat it. Then he threw it away.

After a few days of this treatment, the horse was famished and feeble. The poor beast could hardly walk. When the merchant came to the stable, the horse looked hardly alive, his eyes were half-dead. The merchant was furious.

"What's this, Bekabitti? Do you bring him any horse gram, or not?"

"Yes, master. I do. Twice a day."

"Do you wet the grain?"

"Yes, master. You can see for yourself."

Then he showed his master the heap of grain he had thrown together, after bringing it to the house every day. The master couldn't understand what the matter was.

"Why do you keep it here? Don't you make him eat?"

"No, master. I do only what you tell me. You asked me to wet the horse gram and place it before him. That's what I do. You never told me I should make him eat it."

The merchant struck his forehead several times in dismay.

"What about water for the horse?"

"I take him to the tank and bring him back."

"You don't make him drink?"

"No. Did you tell me to?"

"Now, do you bring him grass?"

"Surely, there is the grass, as much as a haystack."

The merchant was quite upset. Why did I ever get such a man for a servant? he thought. But if he sent him away, he'd have to pay him a penalty of a thousand rupees.

"Look here, Bekabitti," he said, after some thought. "From today on, make the horse eat the wetted grain. Make him drink the water. Make him eat the grass. Understand?"

Bekabitti did what he was told. The horse began to revive.

A few days later, the merchant had to visit his mother-in-law. He told Bekabitti to be ready for the journey in the morning. His wife was delighted that her husband was visiting her family. She made packets of curried rice and yogurt rice and snacks like *holigi* and *cakkali*. She packed them in a box and locked it. She gave Bekabitti a separate packet of rice and dish of roasted flour (*hurihittu*) and said, "Take these. These are for the road. Don't open that box. If you open it, scorpions will sting you, beware. If my mother gives anything for me, bring it back carefully."

The master and his servant left town at an auspicious moment. Bekabitti spilled his rice and the roasted flour all along the road while the merchant rode on in front of him. When they were halfway in their journey, they found a stream and a mango grove, where the merchant tied up the horse. He said to his servant, "Bekabitti, keep a couple of spoons of rice for me and you go ahead and eat. It will take me a while to bathe and say my prayers. Meanwhile, wash my dhoti and spread it on the bushes to dry."

When he went for his bathe in the stream, Bekabitti washed his master's dhoti, tore it into strips, and hung them all over the bushes. He ate all the rice, saving exactly two spoons of it for his master. He opened the box, ate all the *cakkali* and *holige* he could, threw away the rest, and put a couple of scorpions in the box. The merchant came back after his bath and prayers and asked Bekabitti to bring him a freshly washed dhoti to wear.

Bekabitti said, "Master, according to your orders I've spread your dhoti on the bushes. The pieces were not enough for all of the bushes, what I shall I do?"

The master looked at the fate of his dhoti and said, "*Ayyo!* Why did you do this? What shall I wear to my mother-in-law's house? Get me at least one of your own dhotis."

Bekabitti had deliberately brought a dirty dhoti, colored and streaked by Holi festivities. When the merchant found he had nothing else to wear, he wrapped it around his waist and looked like a striped tiger.

"All right, serve me some food."

"Master, I've saved two spoons of rice for you, just as you ordered. I ate the rest."

The merchant felt miserable. He scolded Bekabitti, using every bad word he knew. Then he said, "At least, get me the box!"

Bekabitti brought the box and put it before his master, who opened it and put his hand in it only to be stung by scorpions. Wild with pain, he cried, "Why the hell did you do this?"

"Sir, the mistress had said there were scorpions in the box. When I opened it, they weren't there. I thought she must have forgotten to put them in, so I put a couple of them in it. I didn't want my mistress's words to be false."

The merchant called him a bastard and other such names, and asked him to bring at least the *hurihittu*. Where was that to be found? Bekabitti told him, "The mistress had said, 'The rice and *hurihittu* are for the road.' So I scattered them carefully on the road as we came. It didn't last all the way. If you don't believe me, you can go back and see for yourself."

The merchant kicked his heels like a madman and cried in hunger and dismay. Then he pulled himself together and said, "Well, what's done is done. My mother-in-law lives in the next town. Go and tell her that I'm on my way. Then she will have cooked a dinner for me by the time I arrive."

Bekabitti went ahead and looked for her house. He found her sitting on a verandah and told her he was her son-in-law's servant. He had been sent ahead to give them the news of his arrival. The mother-in-law was delighted. She said, "Tell me how our son-in-law is."

"O, he is on his way. He must be just outside town by now. He's not very well these days and is on a strict diet. He has sent word to say that he'd visit you only if you give him what he wants. Otherwise he'll have to stay somewhere else."

"*Ayyo,* he's our family's only son-in-law. How can he go elsewhere? We'll give him whatever he wants. You'd better tell us everything he needs."

"Nothing much," said Bekabitti. "You must serve balls of flour, fry everything in bitter castor oil, and serve it with three hot green peppers. His drinking water must be boiling hot, with a lot of salt. He can sleep only in a small dark room on bare palmyra mats, surrounded by heaps of dry red chilies. All this is part of his regimen. That's what he has asked me to tell you."

The mother-in-law was alarmed. She wondered what strange and terrible diseases her son-in-law was suffering from. But she went in to make all the required arrangements. She didn't want anything to go wrong.

When the merchant arrived at his mother-in-law's, he was famished. She gave him water to wash his hands and feet with, and invited him to eat. He eagerly went to the kitchen, where he was lovingly served balls of flour, hot green peppers, and a tumbler full of boiling salt water. He could neither eat this nor leave it. What had come over his loving mother-in-law that she should serve him this kind of strange fare? Maybe they'd gone poor and bankrupt, he thought. Courtesy kept him from speaking out. He closed his eyes and swallowed the balls of flour. When he bit into the hot pepper, his mouth burned. So he drank the water that was all salt. His stomach was on fire. For courtesy's sake, he quickly asked his in-laws how they were and then came out of the kitchen. A bed was ready for him in a separate room to which he was led by his mother-in-law. The fire in his stomach and his bewilderment at what was happening was added to the reek of dry red chilies in the sacks all around his thorny palmyra bed. He was wretched and wondered why he had ever come to visit his in-laws.

Bekabitti enjoyed himself. He ate all the special dishes that had been originally made for a son-in-law. Then he latched his master's door from the outside and lay down nearby. In a little while, the merchant's stomach was rumbling in distress—he had diarrhea and had to go out. His need was urgent, but the door was latched. Though he called Bekabitti many times, there was no answer. He didn't want to be thought a nuisance. So, finally, he relieved himself in an empty gourd sitting in a corner and waited for morning. At dawn, Bekabitti unlatched the door. At once, the merchant ran out with the gourd to empty it outside the village before anyone saw him. Bekabitti woke up all the in-laws and said to them, "Your son-in-law is angry. He is leaving the house in a hurry. He asked me to tell you."

The whole household ran after him, crying, "Son-in-law, don't be made at us. Stop, stop, and talk to us."

In shame, the merchant ran faster and faster, trying to hide the gourd of shit he was carrying. The hunger of the previous day, loose bowels, a sleepless night with red chili sacks all around him—they all overwhelmed him. He could run no more. He threw the gourd to one side and sank to the ground in a dead faint.

His in-laws carried him home and nursed him. While they were busy, Bekabitti howled and wept in the street, crying, "My poor master! His own father-in-law and mother-in-law are trying to murder him! Help! Help!"

He went crying to the police, who came at once, arrested all of them, and took the merchant who was still in a swoon. There Bekabitti lodged a complaint.

"My master was running from the house with a gourd in his hand. His in-laws ran after him, caught him, and tried to kill him," he said.

A policeman ran out and brought back the gourd full of shit. By this time, the merchant was coming to. He hardly knew where he was or what had hit him. He stammered and asked what was happening. His mother-in-law told him everything. The police told him what Bekabitti had said to them.

At once, the merchant took out a thousand rupees from his satchel and gave them to Bekabitti, admitting defeat.

"Enough, enough!" he cried. "I've had enough of you. I'm defeated, done for!"

He folded his hands and saluted Bekabitti in a gesture of goodbye.

Bekabitti quit the merchant's service richer by a thousand rupees, and left him alone after that day.

44. Ninga on My Palm

A mother-in-law and a daughter-in-law were always at loggerheads with each other. They quarreled all day, and the son was sick of listening to their complaints. So he built a separate house for his mother and settled her in it.

Every day, he would give his mother some old blackened rice that his wife sent with him. The mother lost weight and grew thin. One day the son noticed it and asked, "What's happened to you? Don't you eat properly? Are you unhappy or what?"

He also said, "Maybe you need some buttermilk for your rice. Come to our house and take some."

One day the mother thought she would try and get some buttermilk from her son's house. She went there when he wasn't in. She was ashamed of begging from her son, but she was desperate for some buttermilk. When she asked for some, her daughter-in-law said, "You didn't want anything from us when you left. Now you want some buttermilk, do you? If you want it, you'll have to do as I say."

"Tell me what it is you want me to do. Let me at least hear it," said the mother-in-law.

The daughter-in-law told her, "You must take off your sari and everything you're wearing, and dance naked, chanting 'Ninga on my palm, look look at my shame!' Do you think you can do that?"

The mother-in-law cursed under her breath, "You wretch, why did you have to marry my son?" That day, the daughter-in-law relented and didn't insist on her condition. She gave her some buttermilk, greatly diluted with water.

The next day, the mother-in-law couldn't eat the plain rice. "Let's see if the wretch will give me some buttermilk," she muttered to herself, and went to her son's house. The daughter-in-law reminded her of what she had to do. "Isn't it enough to tell you once? Do I have to tell you every time you come here?" she asked.

The mother-in-law took off her sari, put it on her head, and danced naked, chanting, "Ninga on my palm, look look at my shame!" The daughter-in-law watched her with satisfaction and gave her some buttermilk.

When she went home, the mother-in-law was disgusted and couldn't touch the buttermilk. "She humiliates me and then she gives it to me. Who needs it?" she thought, and stayed home. In her misery, she grew even thinner.

Her son asked her the next time he saw her, "Why, what's the matter? Doesn't my wife give you any buttermilk?" She told him how she had to dance naked for it. He heard it all and simply said, "Come tomorrow. I'll be there."

When he went home, he asked his wife, "Don't you give my mother any buttermilk? She's getting thinner by the day."

"Why, of course, I give it to her whenever she comes here. Should I be delivering it to her house when she refuses to come here? What's she saying?" she asked.

"Just give it to her. She'll come here today," he said. But his mother didn't come all day. He had to go somewhere. He instructed his wife, "Even if I'm not here, give her the buttermilk."

Then he left through the front door and sneaked back through the side door, and hid himself in the *atta*. His mother arrived soon after, saying, "I couldn't come all day. Give me a drop of buttermilk."

"It's good you came now," said the daughter-in-law. "But you know what you must do."

The mother-in-law took off her clothes, made it into a bundle, put it on her head, and danced naked, chanting, "Ninga on my palm, look look at my shame!"

When she was gone, the son silently got down from the *atta*. He now knew why his mother looked so miserable and thin. Pretending to come in from the outside, he called his wife and said, "We must arrange a ceremony for our household gods." Then he went out and invited everyone he met. He sent a town crier around to nearby villages and letters to villages that were farther away. Then he went to his wife's parents' place to invite them personally for the occasion.

He told his parents-in-law, "Father-in-law, Mother-in-law, your daughter is deathly sick. If you want to see her before something happens to her, come soon. We've consulted priests and astrologers about her disease. No one could give us a remedy. Today we went to a guru, who asked us to undertake a vow. He said that you, her parents, must agree to come, naked as you were born, without a thread on your bodies. If you can do that and take part in a ceremony at our place tomorrow, we can have some hope for your daughter. Tomorrow, at two o'clock. Please."

Then he went home and decorated the doors of his house with festoons of mango leaves. He removed all the clothing in his house from his wife's reach and locked it up in his room.

The next day he gave all the guests a grand dinner and distributed betel leaves and nuts. He requested them all to sit down, saying, "Sit down for a while, if you please. I've a small speech to make."

His wife was unhappy throughout the dinner that her parents had not been invited to the ceremony. He consoled her by assuring her that they had been invited. "They will be here in a few minutes. Just be patient till two o'clock," he said.

Meanwhile, he had arranged for his mother to bathe, eat, and be comfortable. At two, his wife's mother came in stark naked, running anxiously into the house, crying out, "O my daughter, my daughter, what's happened to you?" Her father cried, "Tell us, what's happened to you?" He too was naked.

His daughter nearly died of shame. She beat her forehead, looked around for some cloth, any cloth, crying, "O god, if only I could lay my hands on a piece of cloth to cover them!"

As the assembled guests were wondering if her parents had gone mad, her husband began his speech.

"Listen. In our house, we were three once. My mother and my wife didn't get along. So I arranged for my mother to live in a separate house. She has been growing thinner by the day. All her life, she has been used to milk and buttermilk. So I had said to her, 'Come to our house and get some buttermilk. Don't eat the dry rice.' Whenever my mother came here to ask for a little buttermilk, my wife made her do shameful things. My mother had to strip herself naked, put her clothes on her head, and dance, chanting, 'Ninga on my palm, look look at my shame!' Only then would she get a little buttermilk to take home. To-day, I wanted to teach my wife a lesson. So I tricked her parents and asked them to come before you as they did."

Then he gave his wife the key to his room and said, "Go, open the door and bring your parents some clothes." She silently took the key and brought them clothes to cover their shame.

From that day on, the mother, the son, and his wife lived in peace in the same house.

45. Ogress Queen

Two brothers lived on a hill. They worked as carpenters. An ogress came to the hillside and began to eat cows and calves every day without their knowledge. "What's happening to the cows?" they wondered, and looked for the missing ones and couldn't find them anywhere. One day the ogress gobbled up the older brother. The younger one was scared by his brother's sudden disappearance and ran from the place, fearing for his life. The ogress at once took the form of a pretty woman in distress and followed him, crying aloud, "My husband, my husband! He's running away, leaving me alone!"

While he ran and she followed crying behind him, a king, who was out on a hunt, met them. He rebuked the man.

"Why are you running away from your wife? If you're such a coward, why did you marry her?"

"Your Highness, you don't know her. She's a man-eater, she has given me endless trouble," whined the poor man.

"Then let me take her off your hands. She's beautiful. I'll give you some money. Give her to me."

And the king gave him a thousand rupees and took the ogress back with him to his kingdom. He built a separate palace for her and lived with her exclusively, infatuated with her, ignoring his two wives.

Every night, when everyone was asleep, the ogress would wake up, go into town, devour cows and calves, and come back to her bed before dawn. People complained to the king and his officers of the mysterious way their cattle were disappearing. The king tightened security and appointed watchmen to guard every quarter of the town. Now the ogress found it hard to slip out at night and eat her fill. She began to starve eating ordinary food.

The king's youngest wife was pregnant. Her parents came to the palace to take her for the *kubusa,* or Blouse Ceremony. The ogress and the other queen wanted to go with her and take part in the ceremony. The king said, "Fine, why don't you?"

"I've got to take a blouse and a sari as presents. How can I go empty-handed?" asked the ogress.

The king sent her with saris and blouses. The young queen's parents arranged the ceremony according to the customs of their land. The ogress spoke in the middle of it all and asked them, "What, don't you have the custom of putting kohl in the young woman's eyes?"

They said, "No, we don't. Never heard of it."

She shook her head and insisted, "You must put kohl in her eyes. No *kubusa* ceremony is complete without it."

After the ceremony, she put poisoned kohl in the eyes of both queens. She smeared it in both the eyes of the pregnant younger queen and just in one eye of the other queen.

By the time they came home, the pregnant queen had lost both her eyes; the older queen had only one good eye. The ogress went to the king and mocked him: "You want to live with two blind women groping around? It's beneath your royal status. Send them away."

The gullible king banished them to the forest, where they survived on leaves and berries and travelers' leftovers.

The pregnant queen gave birth to a boy, under the trees. An old man, who like wandering in forests, happened upon them and asked them who they were. They told him. "Then come and live with me as my children," he said, and took them home.

The boy grew up there. The old man taught him everything he knew. When the boy went into town, the ogress queen knew at once that he was her stepson. She knew she had to get rid of him or else he would destroy her. So she lay down with a tight band round her head and groaned, "Headache. My head is splitting."

When the king asked her what the matter was, she said, "My head. My head."

"What shall we do to cure it? Shall I call the doctor?"

"No, that won't do. My mother lives in the Three-Headed Mountain. If someone goes there and brings headache pills from her, I'll live. Otherwise, this will kill me."

"Whom should I send?"

"Send anyone who's willing."

The king sent the town crier all over town with his tom-tom to announce a reward for anyone brave enough to bring the medicine from the mountain for the queen's headache. The boy heard it and said, "I'll go."

Though his mother warned him about the ogress queen's tricks and begged him not to go, he went to the king's palace for instruction. The ogress queen wrote a note for him to take to her mother: "This is my co-wife's son. Kill him." She put the sealed letter in his pocket and he set out on his journey.

He walked far and deep into the jungle. When he got tired, he lay down under a banyan tree and fell asleep. Just then, Siva and his wife Parvati were taking a walk. Parvati's eyes fell on the boy first and she brought Siva to see who he was. They saw the letter in his pocket, gently unsealed it, and read it. It said, "This is my co-wife's son. Kill him." They tore it up and wrote another, which said, "This is your daughter's son, your grandson. Love him and take care of him." They slipped the new letter in his pocket and woke him up.

"Where do you want to go?"

"I'm on my way to the Three-Headed Mountain."

"What for?"

"To get headache pills for our queen."

"Then take these three pebbles. Say, 'Cows and calves, Cows and calves, Cows and calves!' An angry demon will appear. Throw a pebble at him. He will lose half his anger. Throw another pebble. He will lose all his anger. Throw the third pebble and he'll carry you where you want to go."

Then they taught him the art of flying through the air.

He flew to the north and shouted, "Cows and calves! Cows and calves! Cows and calves!"

The angry demon appeared. The boy threw a pebble at him. The demon was now only half as angry. He threw another. The demon lost all his anger. When he threw the third pebble, the demon lifted him on his shoulder and whizzed to the Three-Headed Mountain.

The old ogress read the letter. She grumbled, "My daughter has no sense in her head. She has sent this lovely son of hers all alone, all the way! The idiot!"

And she hugged him and kissed him and gave him fruits and sweets. He enjoyed it all, but he was in a hurry.

"Granny, granny, my mother is dying. I must hurry. She'll die."

"O, don't be silly. Your mother cannot die like that. Her life is safe in this parrot here," the old woman said. She also showed him her ointments. Among them was one for blinding the eyes, another for restoring eyesight.

When he saw these, he seemed happier and promised he'd play there in the hills for a couple of days.

He waited around only till the old ogress went out to find food for herself. Then he picked up her two eye ointments, one for blindness, one for sight, and snatched up the parrot and left the mountain the way he had come.

He went straight to his own mother and put the ointment in her blind eyes. She began to see again. He also restored sight to the blind eye of his stepmother.

Just then, the king's servants came looking for him. He sent word: "Ask the king to come to this hut."

The king was furious at the young fellow's impertinence, and wanted to teach him a lesson. So he came on his royal elephant, his queen in the howdah beside him, a small army behind him. The boy amazed them by standing high in the sky. As he held out the parrot in his tightening hands, the ogress let out a blood-curdling cry, "*A y y a y y a y y a y y o o o !*" and she who had been beautiful all this while changed into a hairy, ugly, repulsive form. He broke the parrot's leg and threw the bird on the ground. The ogress fell from the elephant and writhed on the ground. He broke the parrot's neck, and the ogress lay twisted and dead on the ground.

The boy descended from the sky and told his father all the cruel mean things he, the king, had done to his mother. The king repented, burned his ogress queen on a bier of dry wood and cow dung cakes, and lived happily with his wives and his son.

46. An Old Couple

A king used to wander the streets of his city in disguise at night to find out the way his subjects lived and what they thought of his rule. Very late one night, he saw a light in a house. He was curious to know why the house was lit so late. So he went near, found a window open, and saw a very old couple, almost at death's door, making furious love. They were rapt in it. The king thought this was dreadful; he feared for his land. He even sat down with his head in his hands for a while. He couldn't think of anything else till dawn. He noted down the location of the house and went back to his palace.

Next morning, the king's servants knocked loudly on the old couple's door and summoned them to court. They were nonplussed till they heard why the king had sent for them. They were, after all, an experienced couple. The old man grabbed a handful of salt and tamarind and chilies; the old woman, a handful of ashes. They went to the palace. The king sat there utterly dejected. When they bowed to him, the king asked, "How are you two related?"

"We're husband and wife."

"Is that true?"

"Yes, it is true."

"All right. You're ancient. You've one foot in this world, the other foot in the grave. Still your desire for sex is strong. Whoever looks at you measures a grave. How come you're still at it? What is our land coming to?"

The old man and old woman looked at each other and smiled. In answer to the king's question, the old man poured his handful of salt and tamarind and chilies on the ground. The woman poured a handful of ashes. But they said nothing. The king was baffled. He scratched his face lengthwise. He scratched his face breadthwise. Then he seemed to count the hairs on his head. He didn't understand.

"What's this riddle? Tell me the answer," he said at last.

"O king, a man may be young, he may be old. As long as he eats salt and tamarind and chilies, as long as he has red blood, he would want sex," said the old man.

The woman added, "Till the body becomes ash, it will not give up sexual desire."

The king thought that this was true. He filled the laps of the old couple with gifts, but asked them not to forget to shut the windows the next time they were at it.

47. The Past Never Passes

A king was unmarried for a long time. He wanted to marry only the most beautiful woman of his kingdom. So he waited.

Once a beautiful gypsy woman came walking through the streets of his capital, telling fortunes. The king had never seen so much beauty in one person. The only thing that was wrong with her in the king's eyes was that she was slim, even thin. He thought, poor thing, she has lived a wandering beggar's life and she hasn't had enough food to eat. If she married him and lived in a palace, and got fed by the best cooks, she would fill out and flourish. Then there would be no one equal to her in beauty, not even in the world of gods, he thought.

He sent for her. Through his ministers, he proposed marriage to her, and married her in a splendid ceremony.

But the gypsy queen didn't put on weight and round out her angles as the king expected her to. Instead, she lost weight day by day and seemed to pine away. A month after the wedding, she was thin as a reed. In two months, she was thinner than a reed. The third month, everyone wondered if she would live. The king, in his anxiety, called in the doctors, who examined her and said there was nothing wrong with her. When he was making himself sick with worry, the minister said, "If you won't get angry with me, I'll tell you something that might help."

"What's that?"

"Her Majesty, if you'll remember, begged for food and ate leftovers till she came to the palace. So I suggest that you change her food. Don't serve her royal dinners. Leave food, the kind she likes, in various places in the palace, in cupboards and windowsills and ledges. Leave broken bread, rice, and fried vegetables. Let her find it on her own. She'll eat better and will flourish. She has to get used to a palace."

The king was willing to try anything, even this unusual remedy, for the queen's illness. Arrangements were made according to the minister's advice. The queen began to find a piece of bread in a hole, a handful of vegetables on a windowledge. So she ate piecemeal as she had always done. In a week, her body rounded out and seemed even to emit rays of light.

The king was happy and said, "The past—its smells are never lost, are they?"

48. A Peg and a Keg

A shepherd made a living by grazing other people's sheep. One day, on his way to the field, he saw something under a tree. It was a woman fast asleep on her back. The blowing wind had moved up her sari, and everything below her waist was visible. The shepherd went near her and looked closely. He thought there was a crack and a hole between her thighs.

"*Ayyayyo,*" he said, "Poor thing, she has a big hole there. Flies are swarming to it. What shall I do?" He looked around, found some clay, and began to fill up the hole with it. He dug up quite a bit of clay and tried to stop up the hole in the woman, who was still fast asleep.

While he was busy with this, a king who came there on a hunt saw him. "The fool! He's filling her up with clay. He doesn't know anything. But he would make a very good servant for my queen," he thought, and asked him, "What are you up to?"

The shepherd said, "Oh, this poor woman has a wound between her legs. Flies are swarming all over it. I didn't want them to lay eggs and make a nest there. So I'm patching it up with clay. That's all."

The king laughed and said, "Come with me. I'll look after you," and took him to his queen. He said to her, "Here, I've a new servant for you. He is innocent and knows nothing."

From that day, the shepherd did whatever the queen asked him to do. She used to get him to pour water for her bath, scrub her back, wipe her dry, and so on. One day, she sat down in the bathing house ready for a bath and asked the shepherd, "Come, why don't you also take off your clothes and join me? We'll bathe together." He obeyed, sat down naked opposite her, and they both poured warm water on themselves, scrubbed each other, and bathed. The queen looked at the shepherd's body again and again, and asked him, "What's that?"

He answered, "Oh, that, that's a peg."

The queen pointed between her own legs and asked, "Do you know what this is?"

He shook his head, meaning to say, "I don't."

She said, "That's a keg." Then she held his peg with her hand and said, "Come, put your peg into this keg." He obeyed and did so. From that day on, a new routine began. Every day they would undress in the bathhouse, put the peg in the keg, and then take baths.

After a while, the queen's attention was no longer on the king. He wondered why she had grown indifferent to him. What had happened?

He watched them both one day from behind a window in the bathhouse. The queen had taken off her clothes and was saying to the naked shepherd, "Come now, put the peg in the keg. We'll bathe afterwards." The king could not bear to see the sight. He walked right in and cut them both down with his scimitar, right there in the bathhouse.

49. The Pomegranate Queen

A certain *gowda* had two daughters. He had arranged a good marriage for his elder daughter, but he couldn't do that for the younger one. She was obstinate. She refused to marry any of the young men who were brought as possible bridegrooms. When she had thus refused many, many offers of marriage, the *gowda* could not take it any longer. He was an angry man and, one day, when his wife had gone to visit her elder daughter, he cut up his younger daughter into pieces and buried her in the backyard. Then he sent word to his wife that her daughter had suddenly taken ill and died, and that he had to bury her before she came home. The mother mourned for a long time.

But a pomegranate tree sprouted and grew in the place where the daughter's remains were buried. It grew tall and green, and it bore a single large flower that opened its petals only at night but at sunrise folded into a bud. The *gowda*'s younger daughter lived in it as the Pomegranate Queen; she played tunes on a *vina* every night. Every night the *gowda* and his wife would hear soft unearthly music, but they never found out where it came from.

Indra, the king of the gods who lived in the sky, had a son. One day, the young man was traveling through the heavens when he too heard lovely music wafted from the earth. He was astonished and wondered whether anyone on earth could play such beautiful music. It seemed to surpass the music of celestial minstrels (*gandharva*s). He traced the direction of the music and hovered over the pomegranate tree till he sighted the one large flower in it. He fell in a faint. When he came to, he saw the Pomegranate Queen playing the *vina* in the flower. Her beauty was more entrancing than the beauty of celestial (*apsara*) women. Indra's son fell in love with her at once. When she finished playing, she came out of the flower, and she too saw him and her heart began to beat fast. He asked her to marry him, and she said, without a moment's thought, that she would. But he said, "We'll have to wait a little. I'll go back to heaven and get my parents' permission," and sped back to his heavenly palace. And there, he went to his room and lay in his bed covered in blankets. His mother came to ask him to get up and eat his dinner, but he refused.

"Why, what's the matter?" she asked him.

He said, "I must get married."

She laughed and said, "Of course, we'll look for a bride at once. Now get up and eat."

He interrupted her. "No, no, that's not what I mean. I don't want you to look for a bride. I've already found one, in the earth-world."

"But you are not earth-born. Why do you need those mortals? They're not our kind. I'll get the most beautiful of *apsara* women for you. Just wait and see," said his mother.

But he was stubborn. "No, I want no woman from our world. No one is as beautiful in all three worlds as the Pomegranate Queen. And she plays better than any of our *gandharva* minstrels."

"If she is as good as you say, let me also go and see her," said she, and in no time mother and son arrived at the pomegranate tree in the *gowda*'s backyard. It was not dark yet. The sun had not set. So the pomegranate flower was not yet open. The mother asked impatiently, "Where is your Pomegranate Queen?"

"Wait, Mother, wait. Don't be in such a hurry. She is inside that flower. In a few moments it will open and you can see her," said Indra's son in a whisper.

She laughed at him. "My dear son, are you crazy or what? Do mortal women ever come out of flowers? Come, let's go home," she said.

He asked her to wait and watch, and told her that this pomegranate flower opened only at night and was shut all day. Even as they watched, the flower slowly opened and they began to hear the strains of *vina* music. His mother looked at her beauty and she too fell in a faint. The woman in the flower looked like a blaze of light. She shone like the sun and the moon together. She was indeed more beautiful than any *apsara* woman in heaven. The mother regained her senses very soon and said to her son, "You're absolutely right. I've never seen anyone as beauti-ful," and went to the Pomegranate Queen, talked to her, and took her with them into the sky-world, where the two were married in great style.

The pomegranate tree in the backyard now began to wither. One day it crumbled to the ground, a bundle of dry sticks. The *gowda*'s wife watched the flourishing tree suddenly dry up and die, and she couldn't understand why such things were happening. One day, while she was staring at the dry sticks, the Pomegranate Queen came down from heaven with her husband. As soon as she set foot in the yard, the dry sticks came to life, stood up straight, and sprouted green leaves. The *gowda*'s wife was amazed. She also noticed that the tree had again put out one large flower. In it, she saw her young daughter. She ran out, unable to contain her happiness, and asked her daughter, "O Daughter, are you here? Your father said you'd taken ill and died suddenly. That isn't true! You are alive!"

"No, what Father said was true. In his anger, he cut me to pieces and buried me here. I became this pomegranate tree and lived in this flower as the Pomegranate Queen all these months. But now I'm married to Indra's son and live with him in the heaven-world. When I left, this tree dried up. When I came back visiting to see how things were, it sprouted again and regained life."

Her mother said happily, "I'm glad you're happily married, wherever you are. All these days, your death was my only grief. I see now that you're well and happy. That's all I've ever asked for."

Then her daughter and son-in-law saluted her, received her blessings, and went back to their heaven-world. The *gowda*'s wife was peaceful and happy from that day on.

50. A Poor Man

A poor man lived a simple pious life, thinking of Lord Siva, working for daily wages, and caring for his wife and children. Yet he was miserably poor, and as he grew old he grew feeble. He needed money, but he couldn't bear to think of praying to God for money. Wouldn't God, who knows everything, know that his devotee is poor? If He wants to, He will give it all Himself, reasoned the poor man.

One day, Siva and Parvati were traveling through the world. Being father and mother to the world, they needed to know what was happening to whom. As they passed over the poor man's hut, Parvati said to Siva, "You know, don't you, that you have a great devotee here and that he is utterly poor? Aren't you going to do something for him?"

Siva said, "Yes, we must do something for him."

Right outside that village was the temple of their son, the elephant-faced god, Ganapati. They went to that temple and called on Ganapati.

"Ganapati, there's a fine man here in this place and he's very poor. We want you to give him five thousand rupees."

"That's all? That's easily done," said Ganapati.

"We want you to do it right away. Don't dillydally."

"No, I won't," said Ganapati, "But I can't give it to him today. I'll surely get the money to him tomorrow."

"Do that. Don't forget," said Siva and Parvati, and mounted their bull-vehicle and went their heavenly way.

A silk merchant was hiding in the temple, planning to steal the jewelry on the Ganapati idol. He overheard the conversation between the gods, and he changed his plans. He thought to himself, "Stolen jewelry is no good. It's hard to get rid of." Then he went straight to the poor man's hut and said, "I hear you're in need of money. Suppose I give you three thousand rupees today. Will you give me whatever money you get tomorrow?"

The poor fellow thought this was a strange bargain and said, "Yes," not knowing what to make of it. He told the merchant that he was expecting to get nothing the next day or any other day. The wily merchant knew better, and said, "That doesn't matter. Give me whatever you get tomorrow." Why should a poor man refuse such a good bargain when he was so desperately in need? The merchant gave him three thousand rupees on the spot.

Next day, the merchant went early in the morning to the poor man's hut, and sat outside waiting for Ganapati. He expected the elephant-faced god to arrive any hour and give the poor man his five thousand. But Ganapati didn't come that afternoon, didn't come that evening, and wasn't to be seen even at nightfall. The merchant was fretting and fuming, muttering that even gods don't keep their promises when it comes to money. By night, he was really angry. He went straight to Ganapati's temple. The door was shut. It was an old broken door. He kicked it and it fell open, but his foot got stuck in it. He tried to get his leg free, but he couldn't. He wriggled, he struggled, he jumped up and down, he pulled and pushed, but he couldn't work his leg loose. As he stood there fretting, Siva and Parvati stopped again at the temple on their way home and asked Ganapati, "Did you give the five thousand to the poor man?"

"O, yes. I've given him three thousand today. And I'll get him the other two thousand tonight," said Ganapati.

"Do that. That's very nice of you," said Siva and Parvati, and left.

The merchant, who was listening to all this, called Ganapati.

"O Ganapati, listen to me. Release me from this crack in the door, and I'll give you two thousand rupees."

Ganapati released his leg from the vice in the door and warned him, "Don't give it to me. Give it to the poor man. If you don't give it as promised, your legs will get stuck where you stand. Beware."

All that the merchant wanted was his leg back. He ran to the poor man's hut and gave him the two thousand rupees. That's how a poor man got five thousand.

51. The Princess of Seven Jasmines

A king had an only son. Once, for reasons they couldn't fathom, snakes increased in the kingdom and caused a lot of havoc. The young prince decided to look into the matter himself and fight the snakes. One day, after hunting and killing hundreds of snakes in the nearby forest, he rested under a tree and fell asleep. His servants were all around him. Just then, a great big snake, a seven-hooded snake, began to descend from the branches of the tree under which the prince was sleeping. The servants caught sight of it, drew their swords, and were about to cut it to pieces when the prince woke up and his eye fell on the seven-hooded snake above him. The snake looked at him, eye to eye, and there was a look of great pain in its eyes. The prince asked his servants to do nothing, but to step back. He addressed the snake directly.

"O king of snakes, what do you want?" he asked gently.

It replied in a human voice with human words. "*Appa*, for seven long years I've had a terrible headache. I haven't been able to attend to my duties as a king and I haven't been able to discipline my subjects. They are running amok and creating havoc wherever they go."

"Can we do something about your headache? What's the cure?"

The snake said, "If you go seven *yojanas* south of your kingdom, you'll come to a kingdom. The princess is an only daughter of the king there, and she is beautiful and delicate—she weighs only as much as seven blossoms of jasmine. She has never laughed, and when she does, three jasmine flowers will fall from her mouth. If you can bring the middle one of the three to me, and if I can smell its fragrance, my headache will vanish. Then, I promise you, I'll see to it your kingdom will never more be troubled by my snakes."

The prince said, "So it shall be," and set out that very day towards the southern regions. He sent word to his parents that he was going for such and such a job and asked them not to worry about him. As he traveled on, he came to a tank of clear water. He knelt by its bank to quench his thirst and his eye fell on a whole nest of ants that had fallen into the water. Even as they were struggling and drowning, he said, "Poor things!" and with his handkerchief he picked up the whole nest of ants and set them on dry ground. All of them survived. The king of ants was very pleased and grateful. He said to the prince, in the tiniest of voices, "You did us a good turn. We'll never forget it. If you ever need us, think of us, and we'll be there to help you."

"That's great," said the prince, and bade them goodbye.

As he moved on, he heard a fearful, strange cry in the forest. He went in search of its source, and soon found himself in front of an enormous giant body lying in the middle of the road. Apparently, some time ago, this giant *rakshasa* had eaten his fill, almost to bursting, and had fallen asleep, snoring with his mouth open, when a crow flying in the sky with a tamarind fruit had dropped a seed right into his wide-open mouth. The tamarind seed had taken root and grown into a huge tree while he was still fast asleep. By the time the prince arrived on the scene, the giant had woken up, but he couldn't get up or move his mouth even, pinned under the weight of the tree that had grown up there. He was making strange crying and gurgling noises. The compassionate prince cut down the tree, and the giant was able to pull off the roots and the rest of it from his mouth. The giant felt he was saved from a horrible death, and in his joy and gratitude he said to the prince, "If you ever need help in anything, just think of me."

The prince said, "That's good, I certainly will," and moved on. He soon reached the very kingdom the seven-hooded snake had spoken about. There he sent word to the king that such and such a prince from such and such a kingdom had come to visit him and that he had come specially to marry the princess who weighed no more than seven jasmines. The king summoned him to his presence and was very pleased with the looks and manner of the visiting prince. He said, "No one so far has had the courage to make this long journey and visit our kingdom. You look like someone special. But, if you really wish to marry my daughter, you'll have to succeed in three tasks I'll set."

"Tell me what they are," said the prince.

"We'll pour and mix together a hundred sacks of rice and a hundred sacks of black gram (*uddu*) and give the mixture to you. You must separate them by dawn."

The prince agreed to try, and the king's servants led him to a large room where a huge heap of rice and black gram lay all mixed together, and they left him there for the night. For a while he wondered what he could do, when he suddenly remembered the king of ants, who arrived with the speed of thought with his entire bustling entourage. Before the prince had told them what the task was, they had begun to work, and by morning they had separated the rice from the black gram and arranged them in two heaps. The king came to inspect the work of the prince in the morning, and said, "Bravo! That's a man after my heart. The next thing you have to do is to eat. We'll give you a hundred and one *pallas* of cooked rice and a hundred and one large measures of buttermilk. You'll have to mix them and eat all of it by morning."

As soon as they left him alone with the rice and the buttermilk, he thought of the giant, who arrived at once from nowhere, mixed the buttermilk and the rice, and ate it all up in just three mouthfuls.

When the king came to see him in the morning, he was astonished. "Terrific! You did that too. Now for the third task. Today our kingdom celebrates and worships Siva. There's a hill on the northern border and on it there's a big golden bell. You must go and ring that bell. It can be heard in all the seven kingdoms around here," said the king, and the prince replied, "Sure, I'm leaving for the hill of the golden bell this minute," and set out on his task.

When he got there and climbed the hill, he found a golden bell that was so large it looked like another hill on top of the first one. Ordinary mortals could not think of moving it. The prince thought again of the giant, who appeared at once and asked, "What's the matter? You called me again."

"You must help me one more time, giant. Just pick up this bell and ring it just once. Then you can go."

"Is that all?" said the giant, picking up the golden bell and ringing it gleefully with all his might, till the seven kingdoms all around rang and shook with the sound of it.

The prince returned and was received with honors by the happy king, who was delighted at finding such a valiant son-in-law. He arranged a festive wedding at once and gave his daughter in marriage to him, loaded the newlyweds with hundreds of gifts, and gave them a splendid send-off with long processions of horses and elephants and all that.

As the prince was coming home with his new bride, the princess who weighed no more than seven jasmines, they ran into acrobats who were showing monkey-tricks with their trained monkeys. The princess, who had never left the four walls of her palace and was innocent of all experience and had never laughed even once, asked the prince what they were doing.

"O that, that's a monkey show. Let's go see it," said the prince.

"What's a monkey?" she asked in her innocence.

"See it for yourself," said the prince, and took her by the hand and led her to the monkey show. She had never seen anything like it: monkeys that looked and acted like little men, somersaulted and walked and begged and played tricks on the audience. She began to laugh, and as she laughed, three divine jasmine flowers fell from her mouth. The prince picked up the middle one and put it safely in his pocket. On their way home, they stopped at the tree where he knew the seven-hooded serpent king would be waiting for him. As soon as the serpent king smelled the jasmine, his seven-year headache disappeared. He was very happy and, as a token of his appreciation, he gave the prince a snake-jewel and said, "If you should ever need me, look into this jewel and think of me. I'll help you overcome any obstacle."

The prince saluted the serpent king and took his leave. By the time he came back to his kingdom, snakes no longer infested it. They were all gone, as if by miracle. The king, his father, was delighted to hear of his son's many adventures, and he arranged another gorgeous wedding in his capital for his son and his bride, the princess who weighed no more than seven jasmines.

52. The Prince Who Married His Own Left Half

The king had a son. When the prince came of age, the king wished to get him married, but the young man didn't want to get married. He listened to no one's advice, not even to the elders'. The father became rather desperate and threatened to hang himself if the prince didn't get married. The son then said, "All right. Split my body in two and bury my left half in flowers. A woman will be born out of it. I'll marry her. I won't marry anyone else."

The king was terrified that his son would die during the operation of cutting him in half. He asked the prince, "Is there no other way, a simpler way?"

The prince said, "There's no other way. Other women are uncontrollable. It's hard to keep them in line."

The king finally agreed. An expert cleaved the prince's body into two halves and buried the left half in flowers. In a few days, a lovely woman came out of the flowers. The right half grew whole, and it was as if the prince had never been cut in half. The king got her married to his son according to the proper rites.

The prince had a wonderful palace built in a deserted place for his wife, and visited her there. The king also was very fond of his daughter-in-law. He too would visit her now and then and see that everything was right for her.

One day a wizard came to that place. On his way to some far-off country, he saw this wonderful palace in a deserted area and he started walking around it. The king's daughter-in-law, who was standing at her window, saw him and smiled at him.

The wizard took shelter in an old woman's house in the nearby village. The old woman used to make garlands for the king's daughter-in-law every day. The wizard made a fantastic garland one day, gave it to the old woman, and said, "Take this to the king's daughter-in-law and tell me what she says."

The old woman took the garland to the king's daughter-in-law, who unfurled it and got the message. Though she felt happy inside, she pretended to be angry; she pressed her hand in vermilion, slapped the old woman's cheek, and sent her home. The old woman came home weeping, and when she showed the man her cheek, he consoled her by saying, "Don't worry about it. It's nothing. She just wants to let me know that she is having her period."

A few days later, he made another garland for the palace and gave it to the old woman. This time, when she received the garland, the king's daughter-in-law dipped her hand in white lime and slapped the old woman's breasts. The old woman came home weeping. When the man saw the white marks, he said, "Don't worry. She wants to tell me that it's full-moon time."

In a few days, he sent the palace a third garland. This time the king's daughter-in-law dipped her hand in black ink and hit the old woman on her backside. She came home crying and told him what had happened. The man said, "You must read these things right, old woman. She wants me to go to the back of the palace on a dark new-moon night."

When he went there on the dark new-moon night, a rope was hanging from the back window of the palace. He gripped it and hauled himself up, and went in through a window. The king's daughter-in-law was waiting for him. She was happy and they made love. She said to him tenderly, "If you come like this in your natural shape, the guards at the gate will not let you in. So disguise yourself, and you can come here often."

The young man said, "That's easy," and used to visit her in the guise of a snake. He would enter the palace through the drainpipes. As soon as he came into her room he would change into a man, and they would make love. Many days passed in this way.

One day, when the prince came to see his wife, he saw a snake slithering out of the drainpipe. He at once called his servants and got it killed then and there. He asked them to throw the dead snake outside the palace, and went to his wife's chambers. When he said, "You know, I saw a snake coming into the house. Your luck was good. I saw it, got it killed and thrown outside," his wife howled and cried out, "*Ayyo!* What a terrible thing!" Then she fainted.

When she came to, after much first aid, she was grief-stricken inside that her lover had been caught and killed. But outwardly she pretended to be terrified of the snake and by her narrow escape. Before he left, the prince tried to comfort her by saying, "Why are you scared? The snake is really dead and gone."

From that day on, she was in mourning. She gave up food and sleep. One day a *dasayya,* a holy mendicant, came to her door asking for alms. She called him in and asked him a favor.

"Look here, *dasayya,* I'll give you a rupee. It seems there's a dead snake lying outside. Will you go check if it's there?"

He went out, checked and found it there, and came back to report that it was still there. She said to him, "Go take the dead snake to the cremation grounds, cremate it, and bring me the ashes. I'll give you two rupees for your trouble."

The *dasayya* agreed, took it to the cremation grounds, cremated it according to proper funeral rites, and brought her back the ashes. She gave him two rupees first, then added three more.

"Go now to a goldsmith and get a talisman," she ordered.

The *dasayya* went out again and came back with a talisman.

She placed her dead lover's ash in the talisman and tied it around her shoulder. Mourning her dead lover's death all day, she grew thinner. The prince heard about her emaciated state and thought, "My wife has some secret sorrow. I must go to her and console her. She's growing thinner each day."

He came to the palace and asked her why she looked so thin and sick. He talked to her in any number of ways. He asked her to tell him whatever was happening. But she didn't part her lips once. She didn't tell him a thing. He made her sit on his lap and used all the arts he knew, and persuaded her. Finally she said, "What else can I do? You've kept me here in a jail. I get to see your face here once on full-moon day and once on new-moon day. How can my heart be happy or content?"

The king's son felt very contrite when he heard about her sorrow.

"Then I'll stay here all the time, every day," he said, to console her.

That was not what she wanted. She said, "I'm going to tell you a riddle. If you answer it, I'll throw myself in the fire and die. If you can't answer it, you must throw yourself in the fire and die. If anyone asks afterwards why this happened, neither of us should tell them why. If you agree to these conditions, I'll tell you the riddle. Otherwise, let's quit."

The crazy prince agreed. He placed his hand in hers and gave her his word. Then she said,

"One for seeing,
Two for burning,
Three for wearing it on the shoulder—
A husband on the thigh,
A lover on the shoulder!
Tell me what it means."

The prince struggled and groaned for days to get the answer to the riddle. He could not, for the life of him, find any answer. So, according to his word, he fell into a fire and killed himself. His wife who was his own left half took another lover and lived happily.

53. The Rain King's Wife

A king's only daughter got bored with her studies one day and called her girlfriends for a picnic in the orchard. The palace kitchen made all the wonderful dishes they wanted to take, and they went to the orchard. They ate their dinner, which tasted like ambrosia. They even chewed their after-dinner betel leaf and betel nut like adults. The rain god thundered and sent down bolts of lightning. The princess looked up and said, "O Rain King, we're having our picnic right now. We've just had our dinner. Instead of now, couldn't you come at night?"

The rain stopped at once. So they also ate their evening meal in the orchard and went home.

The princess went to bed upstairs. That night the rain god removed a few tiles and let himself into her bedchamber. She woke up with a start and asked him, "*Ayyo,* who are you?"

He said, "*Arre,* didn't you say 'don't come now, come at night?' So I'm here."

"All right, I'm glad you did," she said. She made him tea, and warmed water for his bath. They had a nice long talk, at the end of which the rain god said, "You've treated me very well. What shall I give you in return?"

"I don't want anything."

"How come? You must ask for something you like."

"If you insist. You can bring me a nice silk blouse."

"That's easily done. I'll get you a blouse."

And the rain god went the way he had come.

On his way home, he bought a blouse for each of his two wives, Gangakka and Gaurakka, and a third one for the princess. He folded the third one and hid it in the pocket of his shirt, and gave Gangakka and Gaurakka their blouses. While one of his wives was serving him food, the other one rifled his pockets and found the third blouse. "To whom is he taking this?" she thought jealously, took it to the backyard, beat the blouse with leaves of poison ivy, and put it back in the pocket.

The rain god knew nothing about any of this. He tied a note to a crow's neck, tied the blouse piece to its talons, and sent it to the princess that night. The crow perched on her roof and cawed: "Ka! Ka!" She heard the cry of the crow and came out. She found a note in its beak, which she read, and accepted the blouse the crow had brought.

Next morning, when she put on the blouse after her morning bath, she began to itch all over. She went back to the bathhouse and bathed again. Baths didn't help. She was miserable. In disgust, she tore off the blouse from her chest and threw it on the garbage heap. Then she bathed in very cold water, and wore cool clothes and went to sleep.

The rain god came again.

"Why are you lying down?" he asked. "I'm here."

She didn't so much as stir. She said nothing, didn't say "Ha," didn't say "Hu," didn't so much as say "pickle," not a thing. He tried to talk to her and make her talk. He tried all his tricks. Then he got tired and angry. He said, "Look here, think carefully. If you do this to me, you'll wander like a beggar and eat other people's leftovers for food. Think about it."

She said not a word. She was furious.

"You won't talk to me, is that it? I'll come as an untouchable—if you lay eyes on me, that would be like talking to me. If you eat the fruit I bring, that would be talking to me. If I come as a donkey and piss, and you smell the stink, that would be like talking to me. You'll see."

He threatened. He raved and ranted. But she said nothing.

The trees dried up. The ponds went dry.

The rain god brought poverty to her parents. The drought in the kingdom forced them all to leave and wander through the land. They walked and walked in the hot sun. Their feet seemed to be on fire. On the road, there stood a large banyan tree. When they took shelter in its shade, their daughter refused the shade and stood in the horrid sun. Then they came to a melon patch. Huge ripe watermelons lay rolling all over the field. The father went over and brought one. They all ate from it, but she refused to touch it. Farther on, the rain god came as a Madiga (untouchable) cobbler and brought them three new pairs of sandals for their feet. "Why do you walk barefoot in the hot sun? Take these sandals," he offered. Her parents took them and put them on. She wouldn't touch them.

In the next village, there was a wise old woman. The princess's father and mother shared their troubles with her. She said, "Poverty may strike anyone. Please stay with me," and gave them room in her hut. They stayed there two days and on the third day found work in the fields.

They brought some millet. The mother said to her daughter, "Spread this grain on the ground and let it dry. I'll come back and grind it in the evening. Watch it." While she sat watching the grain dry, a donkey came and started eating. It even pissed on the grain. She did nothing. She didn't shoo it, beat it, or chase it away. The old woman of the house said, "What a lout you are! Sitting there, looking on when a donkey is eating and fouling your millet!" The disgusted old woman gathered the millet herself and took it inside.

Next day the rain god came to the door as a bangle-seller, crying, "Bangles, bangles!" She had no bangles on her wrist. She sat there without moving a muscle. The neighbor woman invited her: "Come here, *avva*. You don't have a bangle on your wrist. Come, wear some, here." But she didn't move. So the neighbor forced her to sit in front of the bangle-seller and went in to attend to her cooking. The princess and the bangle-seller were left alone. He was waiting for this moment. He grabbed her and vanished with her.

He arrived in another village at another poor old woman's house, asked her to cook for them and feed them for three or four days. She was delighted. "Surely," she said. "You are like a son. She is like a daughter-in-law." They stayed there. After four days, the old woman found the couple strange. She asked in some dismay, "What's the matter with you people? You look like husband and wife. You don't talk to each other. You don't say a thing to each other. What's the matter? I worry about you."

The rain god took her aside and confided in her. "Ask her why she is silent. Listen to whatever comes out of her lips. I'll be upstairs."

The old woman asked the princess that evening, "Why, what's happened between you that you are silent? Is there anything that you cannot tell me?"

"*Avva*, can I tell you anything without any fear?"

"Tell me everything without a fear." ·

"*Avva*, my girlfriends and I went to the orchard for a picnic. The sky was overcast, and rain darkened the sky. So I said, 'O Rain God, instead of coming now, couldn't you come tonight?' And he came to my room that night. He asked me what I wanted. I said, 'Get me a blouse.' He got one sewn, and sent it to me with a crow. I put it on. It gave me the most terrible itch. My body itched all day all over. He played a cruel trick on me. So I won't talk to him. I don't want to have anything to do with him."

He overheard the conversation. He came down, gave the old woman a thousand rupees, and took the young woman home. He called his wives, Gangakka and Gaurakka.

"Who touched the blouse in the pocket of my coat?" he roared.

"Not me, not me," they said.

"Tell me the truth. Who took it?"

"Not me! Not me! Ask Gaurakka," said one.

"Not me! Ask Gangakka," said the other.

They began to accuse each other. The truth came out in their quarrel.

"I don't want either of you in my house. What you did now you'll do again," said the rain god.

He had them tied to an elephant's legs and dragged through the streets.

Then he returned their wealth and pomp to his new love's parents, and they had a great wedding at their palace.

They are happy there, while we are sitting here.

54. Rich Man, Poor Man

The priest of the Monkey God temple was a poor man. He was very devoted to the god, worshiped the god every day, and kept the temple in order. But he was very poor. One day he thought of sewing up his torn shirt. But he had neither needle nor thread. So he sent his wife to the weaver's house to get a yard of thread. Then he went personally to the rich *gowda*'s house to borrow a needle. Before lending him the needle, the *gowda* said, "Look here, you may borrow our needle if you wish. But if you lose it, I'll take away your buffalo."

The poor man agreed and came home with the needle. Meanwhile, his wife had brought the thread. But the priest suddenly remembered it was time to offer worship to the god. So he said to his wife, "It's worship time. I've got to go. Take this needle," and threw her the needle before he left for the temple. She was careless and lost it. When she swept the floor, it went out with the garbage.

Next day, the *gowda* sent his servant to collect his needle. When he heard that the needle was lost and couldn't be found, the *gowda* drove the poor man's buffalo to his own house and tied it in his shed. But the buffalo was sickly and got sicker by the day. So the *gowda* ordered the buffalo to be driven to the untouchable colony, where they would kill it and skin it. The priest, when he heard this, came running to the *gowda*'s house, begging for the hide of the dead buffalo. The *gowda* told the untouchables that they could kill the buffalo and eat the meat, but they should give the hide to the poor priest. So, when they slaughtered the buffalo, they gave him the hide. He dried it and thought of selling it at the market.

He walked all day. He was tired, and it was evening. He found a great big tree in the woods and thought of resting there. He climbed it, put the buffalo hide on a branch, and fell asleep on another next to it.

Now, it so happened that a gang of robbers used to bring their day's ill-gotten loot there every evening and divide it up among themselves under that tree. That day, they had broken into a rich man's house and stolen a lot of gold, silver, and cash. Late that night, as they sat under the tree counting their day's plunder, a wind sprang up and shook the branches.

The violence of the wind dislodged the buffalo hide from the branch and it fell from branch to branch making a loud *dadal! dadal!* sound.

The robbers saw it coming down at them and fled in panic, calling out to each other, "It must be some ghost or goblin! Run, Bhimya! Run, Kariya! Yamanya, don't leave me behind!"

Their noisy exit woke up the priest, who came down the tree, found to his delight a great treasure lying before him, waiting for him to gather it—which he did, scooping up every last coin and jewel. When he came home and wanted to measure his good fortune, he went again to the *gowda* to get a rice measure. The *gowda* was suspicious and gave him the measuring vessel with a little beeswax stuck to its bottom. The priest didn't notice it. He measured all his gold and silver and returned the vessel. A silver coin had stuck to the wax. The *gowda* looked at it and asked the man, "Hey, where did you get these coins?"

The priest replied, "I sold my buffalo hide in the market and they gave me a lot of money."

The *gowda* said to himself, "If a single sickly buffalo's hide can fetch so much money, how much more will my cattle fetch? Our house is full of cattle and I will be even richer than I am now." So thinking, he sent all his cattle to the untouchable colony and asked them to slaughter them all and bring him the hides. Dreaming of big money, he carted the hides from market to market. Who would give him big money for them? He hardly got a couple of hundred rupees for all the hides.

A few weeks later, the priest, no longer poor now, went to the *gowda* and asked him, "*Gowda-re,* give me the coconut shells you've thrown in your backyard." And he burned them, collected the ash in a large bag, loaded it on a bullock, and took to the road.

He crossed two or three towns and decided to camp in a Bullock God's temple outside the fourth town. At that time, another man, a merchant, came to the same temple to rest for the night. He was carrying a bagful of pearls and diamonds. When they fell into a friendly conversation, the merchant asked him, "What do you trade in?"

"O, mostly gold dust," answered the priest casually.

Then they went to sleep. When the priest was fast asleep, the merchant planned to exchange his bag for the priest's and leave town. So he sneaked out in the middle of the night, took the priest's bag from his bullock, placed his own on it, and left. He didn't even check the contents of the bag he took. In the morning, the priest found that the bag looked different and heavier. He opened it and was delighted by the pearls and diamonds in it.

Again he went to the *gowda*'s to borrow the rice measure. Again, the *gowda* stuck a piece of beeswax on it and gave it to him. The priest measured his pearls and diamonds, and this time a pearl and a diamond stuck to its bottom. The *gowda* looked at them, and asked him in astonishment, "Where did you get them?"

"I sold a bag of ashes," said the priest.

The *gowda* was furious. He screamed, "You took the coconut shells from my backyard and got the ashes, didn't you? I'll burn your house and get my ashes!"

And he ordered his men to burn down the priest's house and gather the ash in bags. When he took the ash to the market, nobody would buy it. At the end of the day, a potter bought the ash for a quarter of a rupee.

On his way back, the frustrated *gowda* badly needed a cup of tea. He went to the tea shop, drank his tea, and looked for the quarter to pay for it, but he had lost it somewhere in his anxiety over the ashes. He almost got beaten with shoes over the price of a cup of tea.

Meanwhile, the merchant who had stolen the priest's bag of ash fared no better. He had taken it into his town market and poured it out, bragging that it was all gold dust. When mere ash poured out of the bag and flew into everyone's eyes, people beat him up with their shoes.

The *gowda* was now angry. He decided to throw the priest into the river. He and all his people shut up the priest in a trunk and took it to the riverbank. Just as they were getting ready to throw it into the water, two beautiful deer appeared. The party got excited and everyone wanted to hunt them. While the hunt was on, the trunk with the priest in it sat on the riverbank unattended.

A shepherd driving a herd of three hundred sheep happened to come that way. His eye fell on the trunk. When he opened it, he found the priest crouching in it.

"Why are you lying in a box like that?" he asked.

The priest said, "They're taking me to my wedding."

"Really?" said the shepherd, who had never found a woman to marry him.

"If that's so, take all my sheep and let me take your place. I want so much to get married. I'll be so grateful."

The priest began to feign reluctance.

"What do you think? Don't I want to get married?" he protested.

But after making the shepherd beg and cry and insist, the priest climbed out of the box with his help, got him to sign the sheep over to him, and put the shepherd in the box, asking him to make no sound. Then he drove the herd of three hundred sheep to some distance.

The *gowda* and his party hurried back after a futile hunt and threw the trunk into the river without a thought. A little while later, lo and behold, there was the priest happily coming towards them, making driving noises like "*chigaa! chigaa!*" at a herd of three hundred fat sheep. They were astonished, and the *gowda* asked him where he had gotten the sheep and how he had gotten out of the trunk at the bottom of the river. He said, "O *gowda-re*, how can I tell you how wonderful it was? I am grateful to you. But you dropped me in shallow water. So I got only three hundred sheep. If you had thrown me in deeper waters, and in a trunk that had heavier stones, I'd have brought back many more sheep. I would be even more grateful to you if you would throw me into the river again. Will you please?"

The *gowda* laughed at him. "Are you crazy? Don't you think we want sheep too? We'll also bring some back from the river. You throw us into the river. If you don't show us the right place, we'll kill you," he said.

Then the priest asked them to get some trunks. They brought ten or fifteen. The whole party was in a hurry and got into them, urging him to weigh them down with big rocks. The priest put locks on them and got them thrown into the river, one by one, slowly, and with great satisfaction.

Then he came back to the village and began to live in a mansion as big as the *gowda*'s own. Soon he became the *gowda* himself and began to rule the village.

He is there and we are here.

55. A Sage's Word

A king had a grown-up daughter. He was trying to get her married, so he showed her the pictures of many princes. But she didn't care for any of them. Finally, she said one day: "Don't worry, father. I'll go find a bridegroom for myself." So she went, with a retinue of servants.

She went far. She reached a forest in the heat of day. As she was by now dying of thirst, she sent off her people in all directions in search of water. No one could find any river or well or tank anywhere.

A cook's son was part of the retinue. He too went looking for water. At some distance, he saw a big hill. A glittering stream was flowing from its side. As he came to the foot of the hill, he saw a *rishi* (a sage) muttering and chanting under a tree. He was also pouring water from one hand to another. The boy approached him and asked, "What are you doing, old man?"

"Nothing much," he answered. "I've mastered a magic spell. When the water in this hand joins the water in this other hand, people who don't want to get married get married. Like the joining of water to water."

"Then, can I ask you something?"

"Go ahead. Ask."

"Our princess is out on the road searching for a suitable bridegroom. Please find her one."

"Look, how about getting you to marry her?"

"Old man, don't talk like that. She's a princess. I'm a cook's son."

"Young fellow, see what a *rishi* can do. Tell me your name."

"Karreppa" ("Black fellow").

"What's the princess's name?"

"Shakuntala."

"Good. Here, Karreppa and Shakuntala are a couple now," he said, pouring the water of one hand into another.

The cook's son was bewildered. He filled his pitcher with water and went back. The princess was dying of thirst. When he gave her water, she drank lots of it. It tasted sweet, divine. Happy in her satisfaction, she asked, "Who are you?"

"I'm your cook's son, madam."

"Where did you find this water?"

"Some distance from here. I walked till I came to a big hill. A stream flows on that hillside. There I saw an old man. He was pouring water from one hand to another. I asked the old man what he was doing. He said, 'Some people refuse to marry anyone. By adding this hand's water to that, I can get them to marry.' Then I said, 'Old man, our princess is one such. Where is a bridegroom for her?' 'Right here,' he said. He then poured the water from one hand to another, and said that you and I will marry."

The princess was furious. "This lad is talking nonsense without any respect for rank," she said, and called her servants.

"Hang him up from that tree and give him lashes till he is blue," she ordered. They did as they were told and left him there. He hung there, black and blue, groaning till night fell.

That region had a king. He had no children. He used to pray to Goddess Kali every day for a child. That night, the goddess appeared in his dream and told him, "Tomorrow at dawn, go hunting in the forest. You'll hear sounds of crying. You'll find a boy there. Do not inquire into his religion, his birth, or his family. Pick him up and make him your son."

Accordingly, the king went hunting in the forest. He looked everywhere, keeping his ears open for human sounds. He heard groans. When he went near, he found a young man of sixteen or twenty hanging from a tree, his hands and feet tied with ropes. His body was all bloody. The king brought him down gently, got him untied, and took him home. For six months, they gave him every kind of attention. The young man thrived on it. The king got him tutors and educated him. In five or six years, he made him his heir.

Meanwhile the princess wandered through many lands and came home without a husband. Her father was disappointed. He talked to her in great sorrow: "What's the matter with you, my girl? All your girlfriends are mothers of four and five children. If the king's daughter is like this, what will ordinary people do? I have to listen to a barrage of bad words from my people. Just make up your mind, and marry someone. Please."

That sounded right to her this time. She even felt her hair was beginning to show signs of gray. So she told him decisively, "All right then. Get me pictures. I'll choose one picture and name the man. You can arrange the wedding then."

The king, her father, at once got busy and brought her hundreds of princes' pictures, as before. She looked and looked, put aside hundreds, and chose one of them. He was none other than the cook's son, who had newly become a prince, given to a king by the goddess. As soon as her eyes fell on the picture, the sage's power had begun to work on her. She couldn't take her eyes off the picture. She accepted him.

The king, her father, wrote letters, made journeys, ordered all sorts of arrangements, and they had a gala wedding. According to custom, the bridegroom's party took the bride to their place. There, when the couple were alone in the bedchamber, the princess wanted to touch her husband's feet. He stopped her. He said, "Wait. I've something to say."

"What is it?" she asked.

He answered, "I became a prince by your good deeds."

He told her about the day he was hung up by the tree and was beaten, and how his luck had turned that day, how it had led to this happy wedding. They talked for a long time and were delighted with each other.

56. The Serpent Lover

A young woman, let's call her Kamakshi, was married to a husband who was no good. He went after a concubine. She was patient—she thought that the man would mend his ways and return to her tomorrow, if not today. But he got more and more deeply infatuated with his harlot and took to staying with her night and day. His wife thought, "This is God's will, it's His game," and held her tongue. Two or three years passed.

One day, an old woman who lived next door talked to her. "What is this, my dear? How can you take it, when your husband never talks to you and lies in the pigsty of a harlot's house? We must do something about it. I'll give you some love medicine. Mix it with his food and serve it to him. Then your man will be your slave. He'll live at your feet, do whatever you wish. Just watch."

The despairing young wife thought, "Why not?"

She brought home the old woman's potion and mixed it with sweet porridge. But, to her horror, the porridge turned blood-red. She said to herself, "This stuff, whatever it is, instead of making him love me, may make my husband crazy. It may even kill him. Let him be happy with anyone he wants. If he is alive, by God's grace, he'll come back to me some day." And she poured the blood-red porridge into a snake hole behind her house.

It so happened that there was a snake in that hole, and it drank up the sweet porridge. The love potion acted on it and the snake fell madly in love with her. That night, it took the shape of her husband and knocked on her door. Her husband, as usual, was out. She was startled by the knock. Who could it be? Should she let the person in? When she peeped through the chink in the door, there was a man outside who looked exactly like her husband. When she talked to him, he talked exactly like her husband. He had the same voice and manner. She took him in without asking too many questions and he made her very happy that night. He came to her night after night, and in a few days she was pregnant.

When the snake came to know of it, he wanted to tell her the truth. He said, "Kamakshi, who do you think I am? Your husband? No, I'm the king of snakes. I fell in love with you and came to you in his shape."

Then he shed her husband's form and became a five-headed serpent. She was terrified and shut her eyes. He changed back into her husband's form again.

"You know now I'm the king of snakes. I live in that snake hole behind your house. I drank your porridge, and I don't know what you put in it, but I fell in love with you. I couldn't help coming to see you and making love to you. You're pregnant now, but there's no need to panic about it. I'll see to it that everything goes well. Your husband will come back to you and live happily with you. I'll also arrange for that harlot of his to come and be your servant," he said, and went back to his hole in the ground as a snake.

The place buzzed with the news of the woman's pregnancy, and the errant husband heard about it too. He flew into a rage. "How could she do this to me?" he screamed. He went straight to his father-in-law and protested, "Father-in-law, I haven't slept in the same bed with your daughter for three years now. She has taken a lover, the whore. How else did she get pregnant?"

The father-in-law summoned his daughter and asked her, "Your husband is saying these slanderous things. What do you say?"

She replied, "He has never been good to me. But I've done nothing wrong."

Her father wasn't convinced.

That night she talked to the king of snakes, who said, "Ha, that's very good. Don't you worry about it. Tomorrow the king's court will be in session. Go there bravely, and say, "The child in my womb is my husband's, no one else's.' If they don't believe you, say then, 'I'll prove it to you by taking the test of truth. In the Siva temple, there is a king cobra. I'll hold it in my hand and prove to you the truth of what I say. If I'm false, I'll die.' "

Next day, the raja's court assembled. The raja said to the husband, who was there with his complaint, "Tell us what your suspicions are. The elders can clear the doubts."

The husband got up and said, "Elders, I have not slept in the same bed with my wife for three years now. How did she get pregnant? You tell me what you think."

She rose and expressed utter surprise. "O Elders, if my husband is not with me in this, where can I go for witnesses? He comes to me every night. That's how I got pregnant. If you don't believe me, I'll go handle the cobra in Siva's temple. If I've done any wrong, may it bite me and kill me."

The elders agreed to the chastity test.

The whole court adjourned to the Siva temple. There was an awe-some five-headed snake coiled round the Siva-linga. Kamakshi concentrated all her mind and senses, and prayed aloud so that everyone could hear, "O Lord, the child in my womb is my husband's. All other men are like brothers to me. If what I say is false, may you sting me to death."

Then she put out her hand and took the cobra, who was none other than her lover, the king of snakes. He hung around her neck like a garland, opened his hoods, and swayed gently. The onlookers were awestruck. They said, "*Che, che,* there has never been such a chaste wife. There never will be another better than her," and saluted Kamakshi. They were ready to worship her as a paragon of wives, a *pativrata.* The husband was bewildered and felt like a fool.

Nine months passed. She gave birth to a divine-looking son. He glowed and was beautiful. Her husband forgot all his doubts when he saw his son. He took to playing with the child every day for a long time after dinner. The concubine became anxious about his coming later and later each day, and so asked a maid to investigate the matter. The maid reported, "He has a lovely son. Your man plays with him a lot after dinner. That's why he comes late."

The concubine too wanted to see the child. Through a discreet maid she sent a message to Kamakshi that she would love to see the child of the man they both loved. Would she kindly send him with her maid for a short time?

Kamakshi, coached by her serpent king, said she would send the child on one condition.

"I've put a lot of jewelry on my son. I'll weigh him when I send him to you, and I'll weigh him again when he is returned. If anything is missing, that concubine will have to become my servant and haul pitchers of water to my house."

The confident concubine agreed and said, "Who wants her jewelry? She can weigh him all she wants." Before Kamakshi sent the child, she took him to the king and weighed the child with all his ornaments in the king's presence. The concubine was very taken with the child, took him home, played with him for half an hour, and sent him back carefully without tampering with any of his ornaments.

On his return, Kamakshi and her maids weighed the child again in front of the king. The king of snakes had done his bit meanwhile. Several ornaments were missing and the weight came up short. The king at once summoned the astonished concubine and ordered her to haul water to Kamakshi's house.

Her husband gave up the concubine's company, favored his wife in all things, and was supremely happy with her. In the happiness of regaining her husband, Kamakshi forgot the king of snakes. She was wholly absorbed in her husband and son now.

One night, the king of snakes came to see how Kamakshi was doing. He saw her lying next to her husband and child, fast asleep, contentment written on her face. He couldn't bear this change. In a fit of jealous rage, he twisted himself into Kamakshi's loose tresses, which hung down from the edge of the cot, and hanged himself with them. In the morning, on waking, she felt that her hair was heavy. Wondering what was wrong with it, she shook it, and the dead snake fell to the floor. She was grief-stricken.

Her husband asked, "Why do you weep over the carcass of a snake? How did a snake get into our bedroom anyway?"

She replied, "This is no ordinary snake. I had made offerings to him so that I might get my lost husband back. It's because of him you're with me now. He's like a father to my son. As you know, a snake is like a brahmin, twice-born. Therefore, we should have proper funeral rites done for this good snake, and our son should do it."

The husband agreed, and the son performed all the proper funeral rites, as a son should for a father. Kamakshi felt she had repaid her debt and lived happily with her husband and her son.

57. A Shepherd's Pilgrimage

A brahmin once started out on a pilgrimage to Kashi. A shepherd who was grazing his sheep on the mound asked him, "*Swami*, where are you going?"

"I'll go where I want to. You stay with your sheep," said the brahmin.

"O brahmin sir, please tell me where you are going," begged the shepherd.

The brahmin replied, "I'm going to Kashi."

"If you're going to Kashi, I'll come with you," said the shepherd.

"What will you do with the sheep?"

"O, nothing. They'll graze their fill and then they'll go home. People there will look after them. Let me go with you."

"All right, you can come with me," said the brahmin.

So they walked towards Kashi together. After a little while, the shepherd asked, "*Swami*, where is Kashi?"

"You'll see it, you'll see it. Don't be in such a stupid hurry."

"*Ayyo*, then show it to me. Where is it?"

"Don't behave like an impatient demon. Just come with me. You are a shepherd. You won't be able to see the goddess of the Ganges anyway."

"You said you'll show me Kashi. Where is it?" asked the shepherd.

"It's not too far. Come and see the bank of the Ganges," said the brahmin, showing him the holy river.

"Then where is Kashi?"

"Here, you idiot, right in front of you. This is Kashi. And this is the River Ganges. And don't you talk to me now. I have to take my bath," said the brahmin.

"*Ayyo*, why are you doing this to me? I was grazing my sheep and you said you would show me Kashi. Here you show me this river, this water. You are a phony brahmin. Do we have to come this far to see a bit of water? Don't we have water in our village tank?" scolded the shepherd.

The goddess Ganges heard this and found it terribly amusing. Everyone was overawed by her river, the Ganges, holiest of rivers. Here was someone who wasn't even impressed by it. So she laughed aloud, and came straight up out of the river. She held him by the chin affectionately, asked him to open his mouth and show her his tongue. When he put out his tongue, she called him a poor dear fool and wrote magic letters on his tongue and blessed him: "May you understand the language of all eighteen million beings. And you'll be crowned king in three days. But if you tell anyone about this, may your head break into a thousand pieces!" And then she vanished.

The brahmin meanwhile dipped and dipped in the holy water of the Ganges and didn't get even one glimpse of the goddess. But the idiot shepherd had understood everything in a flash, in that one moment. He left the brahmin behind and walked on by himself. He listened to the birds and understood what they said. He listened to the ants and understood what the ants said.

He soon walked into a city where the reigning king had just died. According to custom, they had sent out the royal elephant with a garland. While the people of the city stood in the streets anxiously waiting for the elephant to pick the next king and garland him, it wandered towards the shepherd, who was standing there watching the fun, threw the garland round his neck, picked him up, and placed him on its back.

The people cheered and led him to the palace to crown him king. They even found a princess for him and asked him to rule the kingdom.

One day, he asked his queen to play *pachisi* on the terrace. As the two of them sat down to play and started rolling the dice, a line of ants was forming close to where they sat. The ant at the head of the line saw the couple playing dice, and turned around. The whole line scattered at once and began to move away. The ant-in-chief asked the one in front why the line was moving away. It replied, "O, look, the king is sitting there. I felt a bit shy."

The chief ant replied, "Why do you have to be shy? Let's march right in front of him. What can he do to us?"

The king heard it all. He understood every word of it and burst out laughing. The queen asked him why. He said evasively, "Because I'm going to win and you're going to lose."

She said, "I know that's not why you laughed. Tell me the truth."

He said, "Well, I could tell you. But if I did, my head would split into a thousand pieces."

"Even if your head should split into a thousand pieces, you should tell me. Yes, you must," said the queen, pouting.

"Do I really have to tell you? Don't you want me to stay alive?"

"Live or die, but you must tell me why you laughed the way you did."

"Then I'd rather die. Make arrangements for the funeral. Order seven cartloads of sandalwood for the cremation fire," said the king. And at once she ordered seven cartloads of sandalwood and made a fire in a pit.

Before he threw himself in the fire he thought he should circumambulate his capital city. As he walked through the city in a ritual procession, his eyes fell on a he-goat and a she-goat grazing on an old fort wall. The he-goat said, "Get me those leaves that have fallen there. I can't reach them."

The she-goat replied, "I can't. It's too close to the edge. I may fall and die."

The he-goat said, "If you die, I won't become a widower. I'll get another she-goat. I'm not like the foolish king of this country who is ready to fall into the fire because he can't tell his wife what's on his mind. Why can't he throw her into the fire and get himself another queen?"

The king stopped there for a minute and heard what the he-goat had said. He turned to his wife and asked her, "Do you really want to hear why I laughed?"

"Yes, what else?" she said.

"If I tell you, I'll die!"

"Then die if you must. Tell me first and then die," said she.

By this time they had come to the pit of fire. When they reached the edge, instead of jumping into it himself, he seized her and threw her into the blazing fire. Then he got himself another queen and lived for a long time.

58. Sister Crow and Sister Sparrow

The crow and the sparrow were once great friends. When they went on a picnic one day, they were caught in a rainstorm. The crow had a house made of cow dung, the sparrow a house of stone. When the rain began to pitter-patter, the sparrow quickly finished her meal and flew home. The crow thought she could wait a little longer. She was too lazy to fly. She sat on a lame donkey stropping its beak for quite a while, and when she went home she was quite wet. Her house made of cow dung had all melted away. She thought she might as well go the sparrow's house and spend the night there. The sparrow was snug and warm in her stone house, all her doors secure and bolted shut. The crow knocked on the bolted door and said:

Sister Sparrow, Sister Sparrow,
I'll die in the cold,
I'll die in the rain,
if you don't open the door,
if you don't open the door!

The sparrow said, "Wait a minute. I'm feeding my children."
After a while, the crow knocked again and said,

Sister Sparrow, Sister Sparrow,
I'll die in the cold,
I'll die in the rain,
if you don't open the door,
if you don't open the door!

"Wait, wait," said the sparrow. "I'm feeding my husband."
The crow waited in the rain some more, knocked again and said,

Sister Sparrow, Sister Sparrow,
I'll die in the cold,

I'll die in the rain,
if you don't open the door,
if you don't open the door!

"Wait, wait, I'm making beds for my husband and my children," said
the sparrow from inside.

The poor crow waited some more in the rain, and cried,

Sister Sparrow, Sister Sparrow,
I'll die in the cold,
I'll die in the rain,
if you don't open the door,
if you don't open the door!

At last the sparrow opened the door, but saying impatiently, "You're
always in a hurry, aren't you?"

The crow was wet and shivering. The sparrow asked her after a while,
"Sister Crow, where would you like to sleep? Will you sleep on the
chickpea sack or the lentil sack?"

"O, I'll be happy to sleep on the chickpeas."

"All right then, there it is."

As the crow was still shivering with the cold, she asked for a little
warm stove. And as she was hungry, she also asked for a piece of betel
nut to chew on, and then sat warmly on the chickpea sack.

When everyone was asleep, shouldn't the crow be quiet? No, she
couldn't do that. She took the chickpeas out of the sack one by one,
put them on the stove, warmed them, and began to crunch on them
noisily. Whenever the sparrow asked, "What's that noise?" the crow
would answer, "Nothing really, Sister Sparrow, I'm just chewing on the
betel nut you gave me."

The *katum-katum* sound of crunching chickpeas was heard all night.
And by morning, the crow had eaten more than her fill, and couldn't
hold her bowels. She shat copiously and filled the now-empty chickpea
sack. After she had done so, she knew at once she couldn't stay there
any longer. She knew she would be scolded and perhaps even beaten
when found out. So, as soon as the door was opened early in the morning, she flew out in a hurry, with a flurry of wings. Sister Sparrow was
taken aback and said to no one in particular, "What's the matter with
Sister Crow? She didn't even stay for a cup of tea. She left without even
saying goodbye."

Then she made some tea and drank it with her family, when the
children began to pester her.

"*Amma,* it's cold. Warm us some chickpeas."

And they went to the chickpea sack, put their hands in, and screamed, "*A y y a y y o o!*"

"What's the matter, children?"

"Auntie Crow has dirtied the whole sack!" cried the sparrow's children.

The sparrow was quite angry now. She called her children together and told them to watch for the crow when they were playing outside. "If you see her, call her. Tell her, 'Mummy is making sweet sweet porridge. She wants you to come in and have some.' "

Sure enough, when the children were at play, the crow did fly above them. They at once called out to her, "Auntie Crow, Auntie Crow, Mummy is looking for you. She's made sweet sweet porridge and she wants you to come in and have some."

The crow came in happily, crowing as she entered, "Sister Sparrow, I hear you've cooked some sweet porridge. It's always delicious."

"O yes, do come in. I'd asked the children to invite you."

The sparrow meanwhile had heated a tile till it was very hot and had kept it ready in a corner. When the crow asked her, "Where shall I sit?" she said at once, "There, on that tile!"

As soon as the crow sat down, she was burned all over, and she flew out cawing loudly in pain. The sparrow mocked her: "Sister Crow, Sister Crow, you're the perfect guest. You stay in our house, you eat our chickpeas, and you leave us a sack of your shit!"

The sparrow children jumped up and down in sheer joy at their mother's act of revenge. The crow never came that way again. The sparrow washed everything clean and gave her children fresh chickpeas.

59. Siva Plays Double

A *saukar* (rich man) was very vain. Riches go to rich people's heads. He even thought that he was equal to Lord Siva. So he had the town crier announce through the village that he should be worshiped in all the temples instead of Siva and that special songs of praise should be sung about him. His servants beat up anyone who disobeyed his orders. He was a terror. The terrified townsmen stopped worshiping Siva. They gave up wearing holy ash on their brows. They repeated the *saukar*'s name as if it were Siva's and told prayer beads.

Siva, of course, came to know about this scandal. He decided to teach the rich man a lesson and came to the town one morning in the guise of a holy man. He roamed the streets loudly reciting praises of Siva. This was strictly against the *saukar*'s orders. So his servants beat up this holy man and softened him up. They didn't listen to his cries and arguments. The *saukar* shouted, "*Badmash!* You talk of Siva? What has he done? I'm the one who pays the workers in this town, I give them grain. Think of me, not Siva."

The holy man went back to the temple yard where he slept, his body bruised and blackened.

Then the *saukar* had to go out. He called his wife and said, "I have to inspect work in the fields. I may be late, don't wait up for me. Let everyone eat."

Hardly had he left his house and turned the corner when Siva took on his appearance and arrived there. As an exact look-alike, he had the *saukar*'s face, manner, and voice. He went into the house and called the servants.

"Look here, Rama, Bhima," he warned them. "I've just heard that some wily magicians have come into town. They may come here in my shape and deceive you. These robbers are planning to deceive us and take our property. So, be careful. Throw out anyone who looks like me. If they make trouble, let me know."

The servants sat at the door, ready with cudgels. He went in and said to his wife, "I've a bad headache. So I came home." Then he bathed for a long time and ate dinner and talked to her.

By this time it was noon. The real *saukar*, tired after a morning's supervision and work in the fields, came home. His servants, Rama and Bhima, sat at his gate with cudgels. They didn't even get up. When they laid eyes on him, they were startled. But they didn't give him a chance. They caught him, cudgeled him, and mocked him: "Ah, you think you'll hoodwink us by dressing like our master. You scoundrel, take this, and this, and this!"

The *saukar* was nonplussed. He began scolding them as usual: "Bastards, you've begun to get drunk even at noon. Don't you recognize me?"

They didn't. They only boxed his ears. Then he thought it might be better to return by evening when they might have sobered up. He was hungry and sore. When he came back in the evening, he received the same treatment. He got angry at first, then pleaded, then begged. It was all in vain.

Just then he heard Siva's voice from inside, sounding exactly like his own. The servants responded, "Master, someone is here, pretending to be you!"

Orders came from within the house. "What are you waiting for? Beat him and send him about his business!"

So they did. He was sore and tender in every limb, he had bruises all over, and blood flowed from his head as his own servants ran him out of town. "God, what did I do? Why are they doing this to me? Some pretender must have taken my place," he thought. "I will take the case to the elders tomorrow," he decided, as he slept on the hard unpaved stones of the temple yard.

Next morning, he went to the village elder's house even before the old man was fully awake. He presented his case, pleaded with the elder, asked the village council to save him. The elder recognized him, listened to his story, and then sent a messenger to the *saukar*'s house. But he and his fellow-elders were baffled by the news that there was another *saukar* there who looked exactly like this one. The elder decided to get to the bottom of this mystery and called the townspeople to the temple. When summoned, Siva came to see them, looking and acting exactly like the *saukar*. The unhappy *saukar* was already there. The people looked at both of them: this one was like that one, that one was like this one. Doubles, twins. No one could tell who was the real *saukar*. Baffled, they were at their wits' end when an experienced old man suggested a test. "The real master of the house would know all the details of the house. Let's ask them," he suggested. So they asked, "How many cows are there in the shed? How many sheep? How much money is in the money box?"

When the elder asked these questions, both the *saukars* gave him the same answers. Eighteen cows, thirty sheep. Finally he asked, "How much cash do you have in the money box?"

The real *saukar* said, "About five thousand."

Siva said, "Five thousand five hundred fifty-five rupees, two annas."

Here at last was a difference. So they sent messengers and had the money box brought to the temple. The elder counted the money in everyone's presence and it was exactly five thousand five hundred fifty-five rupees and two annas, not a rupee more, not an anna less, exactly as Siva had said.

So they thought that the real *saukar* was the false one and gave him a hundred lashes till he felt ripe and tender all over. Chased out of town by little boys, he staggered to the Siva temple outside the ramparts. He thought of God then.

"O Siva, save me," he cried. "Why is this happening to me?"

When you're down, you think of God, don't you?

The Lord, sitting at home, heard him crying. "At last, he thought of me," he said, and came into the temple at once, in the guise of the holy man. He asked innocently, "Why are you crying?"

"*Swami*, what shall I do? I know now what I did wrong. Two days ago, you came to my door and I asked my servants to beat you. Today someone who looks like me has taken my place. I've no place to go. I took the case to court and that other fellow won it. What shall I do?"

"Go home now. It's all God's sport. You were a rich man because God gave you riches. If He doesn't give, where will you be? Worship Him. Go home now and you'll find everything as it was before," said Siva, and healed all his bruises.

When he came home, they looked after him and served him and, to his surprise, asked no questions. They only wondered why he looked strangely subdued. He became a devotee of Siva.

60. The Sparrow Who Wouldn't Die

A rich *gowda* and his men were sowing peas. As they were sowing, a sparrow fluttered down from a *jali* bush and started eating the peas. As she was eating the peas, the peasant caught the sparrow, tied her legs, and hung her up on the bush. As she was hanging there, he asked, "Are you dead, Sparrow dear?" When he asked her that, she answered,

> Not dead, not dead!
> I've eaten the rich *gowda*'s peas,
> Now I'm swinging on a swing!

When she answered thus, he picked her up and threw her into boiling water. Throwing her into the boiling water, he asked her, "Are you dead, Sparrow dear!" When he asked her that, she answered,

> Not dead, not dead!
> I ate the *gowda*'s peas,
> I swung on his swing,
> Now I'm bathing in his warm water!

When she answered thus, he put her in the flour mill and ground her to powder. Having ground her to powder, he asked her, "Did you die now, Sparrow dear?" When he asked her that, she answered,

I didn't die, I didn't die!
I ate the *gowda*'s peas,
I swung on his swing,
I bathed in his water,
Now I sleep in his turning mill!

When she answered thus, he took out the flour in the mill and made
it into batter, cooked it into a savory (*jhanaka*) paste, and ate it all up.
Having eaten the *jhanaka*, he went out at dawn to shit. As he squatted
down, out flew the sparrow from his asshole. And as she flew, she said
to him,

"*Gowda, Gowda,* see how I tricked you!"

She is there and we are here.
Sleep now, my grandson, sleep now.

61. A Sparrow With a Single Pea

A sparrow flew all over the village and brought back a
single pea. As she was about to eat it, sitting on a fence, the pea slipped
from her beak and fell to the ground. The sparrow flew down and
started searching for it when a thorn pricked her forehead. Blood
flowed from the wound and the sparrow said, "Look, look, my vermilion mark!"

Next day, the wound festered and there was pus. The sparrow said,
"Look, look, sandalpaste on my brow!"

In another day, there were maggots in her brow.

"Look, look," said the sparrow, "My little ones!"

Next day, as she died, the sparrow said, "Look how I sleep!"

62. Tales for a Princess

A king had an only daughter. When she turned sixteen,
he was anxious to see her married. He called her one day and said,
"Daughter, I've decided to find you a husband."

She had obviously thought about it. She said, "I want to find my
own husband, father. Build me a seven-storeyed house."

"Surely, I'll build you one. But how will that help? If you sit in a seven-storey mansion, will that produce a bridegroom?"

"I'll marry the man who can make me speak to him three times. Build the house for me and hang a necklace on the first gate. Get a live black king cobra for the second gate, a bear for the third, and a tiger for the fourth."

The bewildered king ordered the seven-storey palace built, and arranged for the necklace, the cobra, the bear, and the tiger at the four gates. He sent the town crier with his tom-tom around his kingdom announcing his daughter's wishes: anyone who can make her speak three times will win her hand in marriage.

Scores of candidates came into town, but they hadn't reckoned with live black cobras and bears and tigers. They could hardly go anywhere near the palace.

One day, two friends, both handsome men, were passing through the city and happened to walk outside the by-now notorious palace. The princess saw them from her window and liked their looks. So she sent them a note in her own hand. The note said:

No one in the world has succeeded so far, but one of you may. Frankly, I'm sick of waiting. Why doesn't one of you try?

The friends read it, looked at each other, and laughed out loud. As they laughed, they also heard the laughter of the maids who had brought the note. The two friends stopped laughing and asked them, "Why do you laugh?"

"O, no reason."

"Come now, you must tell us. We are strangers here, and we'll tell no one. We promise."

The maids liked them. They said, "The king mustn't know. If he learns that we've talked to you, he'll chop off our heads."

"We won't tell him. We don't even know him. Tell us."

The girls giggled some more and said, "We planned this seven-storey palace and helped build it. We know all about it. On the first gate hangs a beautiful necklace. It will scintillate in the sun and it will distract you. Don't stand there gaping at it. Go to the next gate and give an egg to the black cobra. He'll love it, and you can slip through. At the third gate, give the bear some honey. At the fourth, feed the tiger a piece of meat. When they eat these, they'll let you pass. You can get all these things in the shops nearby."

The two friends lost no time in buying an egg, some honey, and a piece of meat for the animals guarding the gates. When they came to the gate, one of them was fascinated by the necklace and stood there lost in admiration while his friend moved on. He fed the egg to the snake, the honey to the bear, the meat to the tiger, and soon stood before the princess. Now, how should he talk to her and make her talk to him? He thought for a minute and began a story.

"A king had a daughter ready for marriage. So he chose a young man and said, 'I'd like to give my daughter to you.' But the elder brother of the princess had given his word to one of his friends. He had also said, 'I'll give my sister in marriage to you.' Without telling each other, they had even arranged marriages for the girl. The father had said, 'It'll be on Monday.' The brother too had said, 'Monday.' When Monday came, the two bridegrooms and their parties arrived, all dressed up, from two different directions. The bride was so embarrassed by this confusion that she jumped into a well. One of the bridegrooms was so affected that he too jumped into the well to join the bride. The other bridegroom was so affected that he left the place and went on a long pilgrimage. Now, I can't tell for the life of me, who is the right husband for her. Could it be the man who went on a pilgrimage? Or the man who joined her in the well?"

The clever princess, who had held her tongue so far, couldn't help breaking her silence, and answered pertly, "Of course, the man who jumped into the well with her! Not that fellow who ran away."

"Ah, that seems right," said the man, and began another story.

"Three friends set out on a journey to a distant city. They went to the pier to catch a boat, but they were too late. It had just left. So they decided to sleep there till morning. The place was infested with robbers, and these men were carrying a lot of money. So they agreed that they should take turns and one person should stay awake; each would keep watch for four hours. The first man, who was a carpenter, found a piece of wood and carved a female figure to while away his time. Four hours went by and it was time for the next man to keep watch. He was a painter, so he colored and painted the doll. At the next watch, the third man, a goldsmith, put jewelry on the doll's body. Now, if it came to life, whose wife should the doll be? The carpenter's? The painter's? The goldsmith's? I've never been able to decide."

The young man didn't have long to wait. The princess spoke up and told him, "You must be dumb. How can she be anyone's except the goldsmith's?"

"Ah, that seems right," said the man, and immediately began his third story.

"In a certain town, a brahmin lived with his daughter, who went to the village school. There, a teacher used to beat her every day, even though she did nothing wrong and was actually very good at her class work. She asked him one day, 'I do all my lessons right and on time. Why do you beat me?'

"The teacher, who was a bit of a lecher, said, 'Promise me one thing and I won't beat you anymore. When you get married, promise that you'll come to me first before you go to your husband's bed.'

"The girl, tired of being thrashed every day for nothing at all, agreed. Maybe she was very young, and didn't know what she was really promising. Anyway, the thrashing stopped from that day on. The girl grew up, came of age, and got married. On her wedding night, as she came to her husband's bed, she said to him, 'I must do something first. I promised my teacher that I would go to him first on my wedding night.'

"The husband said, 'You must go then. A promise is a promise.'

" 'I'll be back soon,' she said and left, taking with her a bit of gold as a gift for her old teacher. On the way, in the darkness of the night, four robbers waylaid her.

" 'Give us all that jewelry on your body and that gold piece, or else we'll kill you,' they said.

"But she was not scared. She replied, 'Brothers, I'm going somewhere to keep an old promise. After I've done that, I'll come here on my way back. Then you can have all the jewelry I'm wearing. You can trust me.'

"And they trusted her and let her go. Before long, a tiger stopped her.

" 'I'm very hungry,' it growled. 'I'm going to eat you.'

"She said to the tiger, 'Can you wait a little? I've got to go see my old teacher. I promised him I would. Just let me go now and I'll come back. You can eat me then. I promise.'

"The tiger too couldn't help trusting her and so he let her go. She walked and walked for a long time and arrived at her teacher's house. She knocked on his door, and when he opened it he was astonished to see her, his old pupil, tired but pretty, and all decked out in her bridal dress and jewelry. He asked her, 'What's the matter? Why did you come here in the dead of night?'

"She answered, 'I gave you my word that I would come and see you on my wedding night. So I came.'

"The old schoolmaster said, 'How silly of you! I must have been teasing you when you were a little girl. I'm surprised you took it seriously, after all these years. You are an innocent, a very rare one.'

"And he took her in, gave her fruit and sweets to eat, and blessed her. She nibbled on a sweet, but she was in a hurry to go back.

" 'Now that this is done, I should go back. There are people waiting for me.'

" 'In the middle of the night? Rest here and go in the morning,' he urged.

" 'No, I must go now,' she insisted.

"Then he offered to send a servant with her. But she refused all such escort, though the schoolmaster, his wife, and children (who were all up by now) showed much concern. She bade them all a quick goodbye, asked them not to worry on her account, and hurried back. The girl's goodness and merit (*punya*) meanwhile had brought the poor starved tiger a run of luck. Soon after she left, he had found a fat he-buffalo and was happily finishing off a great meal when the girl appeared.

" 'You can eat me now,' she said.

"The tiger said, softly, 'You are my sister. You are my mother. Because of your *punya*, I got this fine meal, this juicy buffalo. I can eat this for days. Go now, with my blessings.'

"Farther on, she met the four robbers and offered them all her jewelry and the gold that the teacher didn't want to accept. But she had brought them good luck too—a great big cart loaded with cash and silver had come their way soon after she had left. They were just sitting down to divide the loot among themselves.

"They said, 'Sister, because of your *punya* we are rich now. We will give you a dowry and take you home.'

" 'No, I don't want any of that,' she said, and hurried home to her husband.

"Now, I'm quite lost," said the storyteller. "I can't, for the life of me, decide who did the greater deed. Was it the husband who let her go to another man on his wedding night? The teacher who didn't take advantage of her? Or the robbers who trusted her? Or the tiger who put aside his animal hunger and took her at her word? I can't tell."

The princess didn't even let him finish, and spoke: "Of course, the robbers' letting her go wasn't much. The tiger letting her go was a bit better, but not so great. But the husband letting her go was the greatest thing."

Before she had even finished speaking, she realized she had already spoken three times to the young man—but she wasn't unhappy about it. She happily told her father, "*Appa*, here at last is my husband!"

The king, who was waiting for this moment, ordered huge colorful canopies to be put up all over the city, asked the town crier to announce at once the gala event in every street and lane, got every nook and corner washed and decorated, and arranged a fabulous wedding. The bride and groom were happy and so was everyone else.

63. The Talking Bed

A *gowda* had seven sons. He had got six of them married. The seventh son had not liked any of the girls who were offered in marriage to him. Finally he found one to his liking in a neighboring village. Her father had five sons and a daughter. The young man said he would marry only on the condition that his father-in-law would feed him rice and ghee for twelve years. The father-in-law agreed and the wedding took place. The young man didn't bring his wife home but went instead to his in-laws and stayed with them. All through the first year they served him rice and ghee, a full measure of cooked rice and a full measure of ghee. He would eat it all up and go back to bed. He didn't do a spot of work. His five brothers-in-law and their wives grumbled and complained. When they couldn't take it any longer, the five brothers-in-law asked their father for their share of the ancestral property, and the old man divided up all he had and gave them their shares.

Meanwhile, the young man never even spoke to his wife. He just ate his meals and went to bed. His father- and mother-in-law fed him and served him faithfully and tired themselves out. Their property melted away and disappeared day by day. They began to grind cheap *ragi* in their grinding stone, and ate it while feeding their son-in-law rice and ghee according to their promise. Eleven years passed this way. On the first day of the twelfth year, the young man talked to his wife:

"Eleven years have passed. Ask your people to cut the coral (*hali-vana*) tree in the backyard and fill my room with the timber."

They did so.

Next day, he asked his wife to bring him a chisel and a hammer and leave them in his room. She did so.

He ate his midday meal and started working on the wood. He

worked all day and all night, for months. He carved a bedstead in a style no one had ever imagined. It took him a whole year to finish it. Then he told his wife, "Ask four men to come here tomorrow." The old father-in-law brought four strong men the next day. When they came, the young man asked them to lift the bedstead on their backs, and led them to the city of Mysore, where he asked them to place it on a high mound. The whole city came to see it. Two eyes were not enough to look at it. People said, "This bedstead is magnificent. Only a rajah can sleep on it." "We must get this as a present for our rajah," they said to each other. When they asked the man the price, he said, "The bedstead will tell you. Ask it." They wondered how a piece of furniture could speak. More crowds came to see the wonder. They asked the men to carry it to the palace yard.

The bedstead had four places where they could light lamps, four dolls carved on the four legs, and on all four sides there were statuettes of men and dogs. They brought it to the palace. The queen offered it worship. It was evening. The rajah announced through the town crier's drum, "The king will ascend the bedstead."

After a feast, he had the bedstead carried to his room and he lay on it alone. As he finished a nap, the smallest of the carved dolls said, "Brother, I'll go and see the sights of Mysore city."

The rajah had told his minister to stand guard with his naked sword, and he had come to the palace that night with his sword unsheathed. Meanwhile, the minister's wife had a holy mendicant (*gosavi*) for a lover. When she heard the town crier's announcement, she had sent word to her *gosavi:* "If the rajah is going to ascend his new bed, everybody will be at the palace watching the spectacle. Let's go off by ourselves." He had said, "Let's do that." She went to his place with a bundle of food and all her gold and saris, ready to elope. But the *gosavi* said to her, "Meeting like this is no good. Wherever we go, your husband will come after us. You must kill him and bring me his head."

She went home, cooked some rice on the stove, and went herself to the palace to fetch her husband home to eat his dinner. She insisted that he should come home at once. He came home, ate his dinner, and went to sleep. She cut off his head and placed it on a golden platter and covered it in a flower-patterned piece of cloth. But when she went back to the *gosavi* to tell him she had done what he had asked her to do, he scolded her, "You whore, today you cut off your husband's head because I asked you to. Tomorrow, someone else will ask you to cut off my head and you will do that too. How can anyone trust you?" He threw her out. She ran home in despair, joined the head to her husband's body, and began to cry bitterly over her folly.

The doll saw all this and came back to the palace and said, "Brother, I saw everything. This rajah is a sinner. Spit on him." It told the other dolls the whole story. The rajah now knew that his minister had died and why.

After a little while, another doll went out. The chieftain and the priest of that town used to offer a human sacrifice every year to Kali, the Black Goddess, in her temple. They always chose a young boy for the purpose, and this year too they had captured a young boy. The boy groaned and cried. The doll went up to him and talked to him. "I'm an orphan and they are going to sacrifice me," the boy cried. The doll released him and asked him to tie it up in his place. The boy did as he was told and escaped. The worshipers came to the temple, offered ritual worship to the goddess, and one of them lifted his sword to cut the sacrificial victim to pieces before the goddess. The doll pulled out the slab of stone on which it was lying and ran away, making a big noise. In the confusion, the uplifted sword slipped and fell on the neck of the goddess's image and beheaded it, to everyone's horror. Chaos followed and the worshipers began to blame each other and quarrel among themselves. "What shall we tell the maharajah if he inquires into what happened?" they asked each other anxiously as they scattered and went home.

The doll went back to the palace and told its brothers the whole story and said, "This fellow is no rajah. Men are being sacrificed in his kingdom. Spit on him," it said.

After a little while, the third doll went out. The rajah's consort had a brahmin lover. As the rajah was sleeping that night alone in his new bed, she sat alone at her window. The brahmin lover came to her room and opened the door. The doll watched them sitting and eating together. The doll wrapped himself in a piece of cloth like the brahmin's servant and said, "Master, Mistress, I'm hungry, give me something." The queen gave him *cakli, vade,* and other snacks. The doll brought them out and hid them all under a rock outside the palace.

Then the fourth doll went out to see what was happening in town. It wandered through the marketplace and went to the Kali temple. Under the image of the goddess was buried a crate of gold. Four townsmen were digging under the image to get at the gold. The doll went to a corner and crowed like a rooster. They didn't know what it was, were scared by the noise, and ran away. The doll came back to the bedstead and told the other dolls, "What sort of a king is this one? He has given his wife to a lover. Besides, his subjects are digging under the very image of the goddess. Spit on him."

The rajah heard everything and lay there terror-stricken, making not a sound.

Next morning, he came out of the bedroom and held court. He invited everyone to attend. He called the priest of the temple and asked him what was happening in the temple. The priest was too scared to open his mouth. "Don't be scared. Tell me the truth," ordered the king. The priest confessed, "We were offering a young boy as a sacrifice to the goddess when the boy escaped, the stone came loose, and in the confusion the sword fell on the image and beheaded it."

Then the rajah called for the minister and soon found he had really died. He summoned the minister's wife, who told him lies: "He ate something that didn't agree with him, and he died vomiting horribly." When he called his queen to his presence and asked her about her lover, she said, "I'm innocent. I've never stepped out of my room and I love no one but you." When the rajah asked his servants to search under the rock outside the palace, they found the *cakli* and the *vade* she had given the doll. The queen was struck dumb. He punished the chieftain, the priest, the minister's wife, and his own—he had them quartered and hung up on the city gates. Then he got the treasure from under the goddess's image and gave it all to the man who had made the bedstead.

The man who made the bedstead took the treasure home to his wife, made a lovely swing for his father- and mother-in-law, who had faithfully cared for him for twelve years, and made them swing happily on it. Then everyone was happy.

64. A Thief, a Ram, a Bear, and a Horse

A thief had a wife who suited him very well, and the two of them lived by cheating others in various ways. Once, he set out on his usual rounds and bought a ram from a goatherd. As he drove it before him on his way to the next village, it was evening and it also began to rain. He ran and took shelter in the verandah of a house. It continued to rain. So he thought he would dry his clothes and sleep the night there, and go about his business in the morning. He took off his clothes, wrung them dry, and hung them out. Then he tied the ram to a pillar at his feet and slept with almost no clothes on his body. In the small hours of the night, the man of the house came out to answer a call of nature and saw this man lying on his verandah fast asleep, with no blanket or cover, almost naked. He shook him awake and asked who he was and why he was lying in the cold with nothing warm around him. "Aren't you cold?" he asked, with concern.

The thief said, "I come from such and such a village. I don't feel the cold, even if I wear no clothes. That ram at my feet eats up all the cold around me."

The man of the house was astonished. "I've an old mother in my house. She is always cold and complains night and day in this season. The warmest woolen blankets are not warm enough for her. She gives me no peace and we get no sleep. Why don't you sell me your ram that eats up the cold?" he offered.

"*Che, che!* This ram is a rare creature. I'll never be able to get another like it. How can I part with it?"

"Whatever the cost, I'll pay it. You must give it to me. I want my mother's last days to be comfortable, warm, and happy," urged the man. After much hesitation, the thief said at last, "After talking to you, I feel your mother and my mother are really the same. All right, I'll give it to you. But if I part with it, I'll have to buy another like it. I don't even know where to look for one. This one cost me five hundred rupees."

The man of the house didn't want to wait a minute longer lest the stranger should change his mind. He went into the house and hurried out with five hundred rupees. The thief took the money, led the ram into the house to the old woman's bedside, where he tied it to her bedpost at her feet, and left before it even dawned.

That night, the man of the house slept the sleep of the contented man. Early in the morning, his old mother felt terribly cold, and began to make noises like "Ha!" and "Hu!" The ram, tied to her bedpost, thought that another ram was in the room, making battle noises. He, too, spoiled for a fight and butted the old woman thrice. The old woman died on the spot and made no further noise. Till morning, the son heard no more Ha!'s and Hu!'s. The sun rose and was two yards high, but the old mother was silent. "Aha, the ram has eaten up all the cold in her room. So she's at last sleeping happily," thought everyone in the household. But she didn't even get up for mealtimes. When they went in to wake her up, they found her gone to the land of Siva. They could see that the ram had butted the old woman with its horns and killed her. The man of the house blamed himself for her death. "I got her killed for nothing," he said, and hit his forehead in remorse as he moved her body to the burial ground. Then he vowed revenge against the thief who had made a fool of him.

The thief was hurrying with the money to the next village when he found himself in a forest. As he made his way through a narrow path, a bear jumped on him from somewhere and attacked him. He wrestled with the bear's forepaws and tried to get out of its deadly bear hug. The bear was scared too and dropped dung. The silver rupees in the thief's pocket also fell to the ground. In the struggle, the rupees were mixed with the dung. Neither the bear nor the thief could let go of each other's grip. Right then, a soldier came riding his horse that way and saw the man and the bear in hand-to-hand combat. He also saw bear dung with silver rupees in it. He was quite amazed by the sight. So he dismounted and came up to them, asking, "What are you doing with that bear?"

"O, nothing," gasped the thief. "This pet bear of mine drops dung full of rupees. So I'm making him do it. Yesterday, he dropped a thousand rupees. Today, for some reason, he's dropped only five hundred. So I'm forcing him to drop some more."

The soldier's mind raced at the thought of rupees. What's the point of making war and courting death? If he had only one such pet bear, he could live like a king, he thought, captured by a fantasy. So he said to the thief, "Just give me that pet bear and I'll bless you all my life." All this while the thief was struggling with the bear.

"*Che, che,* how can I give away such a precious animal? I get money everytime it takes a crap. Give it away? Just forget about it! Impossible!" said the thief.

"O, don't say that. I've three thousand rupees on me. I also have this horse. Take both and give me your bear," begged the soldier. After many such pleas, the thief reluctantly agreed.

"All right, give me the money here. Come behind the bear like this and hold him. He will drop another five hundred any minute. After he has done that, you can take him home. Look after him carefully, like your own son," said the thief.

The soldier gave him the money, gave him the horse, and stood behind the bear holding it. The thief released himself from the bear's grip, mounted the horse, and rode away. How long can a man hold a bear? Soon the soldier's grip weakened, the bear slipped loose, scratched his face and mauled him, and ran away. It dawned on the soldier that he had been cheated. He, too, vowed vengeance, decided that he would get his three thousand back somehow, and went in search of the scoundrel.

By the time the thief reached the next village on his horse it was night. He thought it would be a good idea to rest that night there and go back to his hometown the next day. But he had three thousand on him and needed to be safe somewhere. He looked around and found the house of a harlot. She was the king's own harlot. He went to her and asked for shelter. He offered her twenty, even thirty, rupees for a place to sleep in. She agreed and gave him a place on the verandah. He tied up his horse and went to sleep. But he woke up before dawn, removed the horse dung the animal had dropped in the night, and arranged three or four heaps of rupees under the horse. Then he went back to bed. When the harlot came there in the morning to wake him up, she saw the horse and noticed the heaps of rupees near the horse's hind legs.

"Look, rupees! Rupees! How did they get here? . . . Who cares how they got here? Let me get them before he wakes up," she said to herself, and put her hand to the dung, when the thief sat up. He said, "Lady, that dung is mine, not yours. Don't touch it."

That wasn't just dung. There was money in it.

"What did you say?" she asked, not believing her own eyes and ears.

"O, really nothing. My horse drops ten thousand rupees a day with its dung. It's morning now, isn't it? It should have dropped at least a thousand," he said casually.

She went back and counted. There were a thousand rupees. She began to fancy the horse. If it gives ten thousand a day, how much does it add up to in a month? How much can even a king give? If only she had this one horse, she could live without depending on any king, she thought, and said, "You look like a good man. Why don't you give me that horse?"

"*Che, che,* what will I do if I give you that horse? I can't get another one like that for a hundred thousand."

"All right then, I'll give you a hundred thousand and buy it from you," said the harlot. He didn't agree. He made it clear he wouldn't part with it for love or money. At last, she threatened to tell the king, who would certainly like to have such a horse himself and would seize it by force. The thief feigned great fear at the mention of the king and said weakly, "All right, give me at least a hundred thousand. I'll leave my horse and go. What else can I do?"

She at once got busy, pawned all the jewelry the king had given her, raised a hundred thousand, and gave it to the thief. He tied the horse to a tree in her yard and left the place. The horse dropped ordinary horse dung all day till evening, as was its wont. The harlot began to suspect something was wrong but decided to wait till the next day. The horse dropped ordinary dung as usual. She now knew she had been cheated, felt quite ill, and took to bed.

That very evening, the man who had bought the ram from the thief and the soldier who had bought the bear arrived at her house looking for the scoundrel. They stayed there and the harlot overheard them talking about how they had been cheated. So she joined them and told them her story. Next morning, all three went in search of the con man.

Meanwhile, the thief went home directly after he took the harlot's hundred thousand. He knew they would come after him. So he called his wife and instructed her thus: "Tomorrow, I want you to dress up as Lakshmi, the goddess of wealth, and wait in the attic. When I call you, just come down, and leave a trail of rupees behind you as you walk."

Next day, he arranged a huge banquet and invited the whole town. Hundreds of guests arrived, and they were fed in long rows. The man who had bought the ram, the soldier who had bought the bear, and the harlot who had bought the horse—all three of them also arrived at his doorstep, looking for him. The thief courteously offered seats to them as to everyone else. They planned to wait till all the guests had left and then corner him.

After a while, the thief brought out a round grinding stone, placed it under the attic, and began to offer it worship, chanting various spells in a loud voice. The guests crowded around him to watch what he was doing. After chanting for a long time, he looked up at the attic, and begged, "O Mother, Lakshmi, Goddess, come down, come down!" His wife, as arranged beforehand, descended from the attic dressed as the goddess and began to pour down a stream of rupees from the lap of her sari. The thief said, "Enough, enough! Please!" and begged her to stop. She stopped and vanished into the attic. The three victims watched all this with their mouths open, their hearts filled with fresh greed. They now wanted the round grinding stone for themselves. As soon as all the guests left the house, the three caught hold of him and said, "You have deceived us and made fools of us. Unless you do as we tell you now, we'll take our case to the king."

"What do you want?" he asked.

"Give us that grinding stone and we'll forgive you," they said in one voice.

The thief refused point-blank at first, but soon softened a bit, and finally his wife persuaded him to yield to their demands. Unwillingly, he parted with the grinding stone. They carried it out, and even before they reached the town's outskirts they had begun to quarrel about who should have it first. Some people say they came to blows and even killed each other. The thief, of course, lived happily with his wife.

65. Three Blouses

A certain simple-minded brahmin was married early, before he had finished his education. He learned all he could in his village, went to the nearby villages to learn more, and finally went to Benares to learn all he could. His education never came to an end. After many years, however, he returned home to live with his wife. His wife, meanwhile, had become a grown woman and gone astray. Being experienced, she did not lack for lovers. But she had one obstacle: a crazy husband sitting all day on the porch of her house, with his nose in his books. Unless she found a way of getting rid of him, she couldn't easily do what she most wanted to do. So, one day, she thought up a ruse. She gave him an old torn blouse of hers and asked him to sell it and get her a new one. After all, he was a simpleton, a brahmin bookworm. He took the blouse and went around town with it, asking people to buy it. People only laughed at him. No one would give him a new blouse.

Next day, he went to another village. He hawked through the streets wherever he saw women: "Who will take this blouse and give me a new one? Anyone, anyone?" The women laughed at him and went their way. He roamed through fourteen villages this way and went to a big town like Belgaum, hawking his blouse at the Saturday fairs. The townsmen teased him, but he wasn't discouraged. Finally, three women who had come to the fair wanted to teach him a thing or two and have some fun as well. They came up to him and said, "We'll get you a new blouse. Come with us."

One of them took him aside, wrapped him in one of the saris she had just bought, and took him home. She told her husband, "The seamstress is here. I'll have to give her my measurements for my blouse. I'll be back." While her husband waited outside, she took the brahmin into her bedroom and made love to him. Then she gave him a new blouse and sent him away, asking him to come back the next day.

She then went to see her two friends and bragged about what she had just done. One of them said, "Is that all? That's nothing to brag about. Wait and see what I do."

The next day, the second woman took the simple brahmin to her house. This time he was not even disguised. She hid him under her bed that night. When her husband fell asleep next to her, she leaned against him. He was fast asleep and began to snore. Then she silently made a sign to the brahmin under her bed to join her. She slept with him right there in her bed and, when they were done, sent him away soon after with a new blouse.

When she bragged next day to her two friends about what she had done, the third woman pooh-poohed her, saying, "What's so great about that? Wait till you see what I do."

That evening, the third woman took the brahmin secretly to her house and hid him under a flowering sky-jasmine (*mugilamallige*) tree in her backyard. After their night meal, she suggested to her husband that it would be nice to sleep outdoors in the moonlight. She spread her bedroll under the *mugilamallige* tree, took her husband by the hand, and said, seductively, "Have you ever climbed this tree and seen the fun? It's quite something."

"No, I haven't. What will I see from the tree?"

"Go up and see for yourself. You'll see a vision: as if a man and a woman are doing it right here. They become one and then become two. I've seen that myself," she said.

The foolish husband said, "Really? Is that so? Let me see," and climbed up the tree all the way to the top branch. As he was busy climbing, she brought out her brahmin from his hiding place and made love to him under the tree. The husband in the tree looked at what they were doing, felt dizzy, couldn't believe his eyes. In a kind of panic, he started clambering down. She had meanwhile pressed a blouse into the brahmin's hand and asked him to make himself scarce, which he did.

The husband climbed down, reached the ground, and said, "Let's get into the house. This tree is bewitched by some demon or something. Let's get out of here." She quickly rolled up the bed and went in with him.

The next day, all three met the brahmin and told him, "Your wife is no different from us. She has sent you out with an old blouse just to get you out of her way."

When he came home with her old torn blouse and three brand-new blouses in his hand, his wife knew at once what had happened. She also knew that he now knew all her secrets. She gave up her lovers, and he was more wary of her ways. They made each other happy.

66. Three Magic Objects

Three brothers lived in utter poverty. One day, it got so bad that they couldn't find anything to eat. So they sat in a row on the riverbank, their heads in their hands, three pictures of utter despair. God took pity on them, appeared to them, and asked why they were so miserable. They told him that they were poor and hungry. God gave each of them a gift: he gave one a gun, another a cap, and the third a wheel. "Make use of these and try to make a living," he said, before he vanished.

The brother with the gun and the one with the wheel found ways of making a living. But the brother with the cap didn't know what to do with it. An idea occurred to him. Why not marry the king's daughter?

So he put on his cap and found to his surprise that it made him invisible. He went to the palace and made love to all the servantmaids. When they wondered who or what this was that gave them so much pleasure, he suddenly took off his cap and made himself visible. Just as he was showing off, the king's men caught him, snatched the cap from him, beat him up, and threw him out. He came crying to his brother who had the gun. The brother gave him his gun. Then he sneaked back into the palace with it and started pointing it at the servants, but they ganged up on him, overpowered him, took his gun away from him, and threw him out again.

This time he went to the second brother, who gave him his magic wheel. He disguised himself as a bangle-seller and came to the palace sitting on his wheel. Hawking his wares, he shouted, "Bangles, bangles, does any one want the world's very best bangles?"

The queen and her attendants called him in and tried the bangles on, very pleased with their colors and shapes. The princess too wanted them. So she came to the cart and climbed into it. As he slipped the bangles on her wrist, he said to his magic wheel, "Take us home!" and the wheel at once flew into the sky. The princess was quiet till they were halfway there and then she said to him, "I'm very thirsty. Could we stop somewhere?" He thought that she would run away if he let her go anywhere. So he himself climbed down the wheel and went to fetch water. But she was very clever. As soon as he turned his back, she said to the wheel, "Take me home!" and it took her back to her palace. As he came back with the water, both wheel and princess were gone. He felt helpless. He broke down and cried.

A holy man who was passing by asked him what the matter was. The man told him his story and said, "I cry because I've nothing in the world. I've lost my brothers' gun and wheel and my own magic cap. I've nowhere to go."

The holy man asked the poor fellow to stay with him in his banana grove. After a few days, he began to trust the stranger. One day, the holy man called out to him and said, "You can eat the fruit of all these trees except one," pointing to one particular tree.

He was quite good for a few days and did as he was told. But one day he stood under the forbidden tree and thought, "Why did he say I shouldn't eat the fruit of this tree?" and plucked a banana and ate it. It was delicious, but as soon as he had finished eating it, horns grew on his head. Terrified, he ran to the holy man, who screamed, "You didn't listen to me! You ate the fruit! That's what happens to people who eat from that tree!"

But soon he relented. He went into the yard, brought back some herbs, and poured their juice into his guest's ear. At once, the horns dropped off. Now the young man knew how to get rid of the horns.

At the first opportunity, he plucked a basketful of the bananas from the forbidden tree, made his way back to the palace, and sold them all. The fruit looked lovely and everyone bought some. After he had sold them, he quickly slipped away and went home. Now everyone who ate the fruit had horns growing on their heads—men, women, and children. They had now only one thought, one worry: how to get rid of the horns.

The king had to cancel all engagements because he couldn't appear in public with his horns. A few days later, the young man went around hawking, "Antidote for horns, antidote for horns!"

Everyone in the palace flocked to him. The king hurriedly called him to his presence and begged of him, "We'll give you anything. Get rid of my horns."

The young man said, "Give me back my gun, my wheel, and my cap. And give me your daughter in marriage."

The king ordered all the magic objects to be returned to him at once. The young man poured the juice of the holy man's herbs into everyone's ears and the horns clattered to the floor. There was a gala wedding and he came home with his bride to his brothers in the aerial cart built around his wheel. He became a rich man and lived with his wife a happy life.

67. Three Sisters Named Death, Birth, and Dream

In a little town like this one, there lived a poor, poor boy. Call him Racha, if you need a name. Racha had no father, no mother, no kith and kin whatever. He was utterly alone. He made a living by going every day to the forest, cutting wood, and selling bundles of it in town.

The town had its annual fair. All the boys of his age put on new shirts, wore new turbans, and strutted about like cocks-of-the-walk. Racha was too poor to buy anything new or old. He felt sorry for himself. He walked far out of the town, sat on the bank of the river, and cried into his knees, remembering his father and mother. He cried and cried till he dropped off to sleep.

When he woke up at sunset, he saw golden fish playing in the water. Fascinated, he gazed at them. "How marvelous!" he exclaimed. "If I could catch just one of those golden fish and sell it, I would never be poor again," he thought, and stalked around to catch one. When one of the fish leaped out of the water, he dived into the river with both eyes open. Just as he was losing breath and trying to surface, someone pulled him down, far down. He was suddenly in front of a door. He pushed it open. There was no one inside. Whoever it was that had dragged him down wasn't anywhere around. Cautiously, he tiptoed in. A great fabulous palace. Great big sofas and chairs with pillows. Tables and soft downy beds. Wondering where he was, he sank into one of the beds and fell asleep at once.

When he opened his eyes, the house was lit with electric lamps of many colors. Three beautiful women came towards him, each more beautiful than the next. They pointed at him and each said, "He is mine," "He's mine," "He's mine." After much haggling, they agreed that he should be husband to all three by turns. It wasn't difficult for him to agree. He soon found that they were three sisters. The eldest was Sister Death, the youngest was Sister Birth, and the middle one was Sister Dream.

He also saw three large locked rooms in the palace. The first one had a golden lock on its door, the second one a silver lock, and the third an iron lock.

He was to spend each night with a different sister. At dawn all three would vanish. But before they vanished, they took care to warn him: "Don't even look into these three rooms. The rest is yours." And they would leave the keys with him before they left. He kept his word, and many days passed.

Being alone all day began to bore him. One day, unable to bear the boredom, he opened the door with the golden lock. Inside it, there stood a heavenly golden elephant, an elephant with seven golden trunks. It even spoke like a human being.

"Brother Rachanna, I'm glad you came. Climb onto my back. Let's roam through three worlds, all in three minutes. Come," it said.

He said "Okay," and clambered onto the elephant's back. In three minutes it sped through three worlds and returned to the palace room.

That night, when the three sisters named Death, Birth, and Dream came home, they found elephant tracks, and asked him, "Why did you do this?" He told them the truth. They liked his truthfulness and told him not to open the doors of the other two rooms.

Next day, when they were gone, his curiosity got the better of him. He opened the second door with the silver lock. There stood a silver stallion. It too spoke like a human being and invited him to ride on his back—which Racha did. It too showed him sights of the three worlds in three minutes and returned him to the palace.

That night again, the three beautiful sisters found tracks—this time, the hoof prints of a horse. They asked him, "Why did you do this?" He told them the truth. They liked his truthfulness but warned him strictly never, never to open the third room. Never, they said, whatever happens.

But on the third day, his curiosity was unbearable. "I've seen two. Why not the third? Let's see what happens," he said to himself, and opened the door with the iron lock on it. In there stood a mule. It too spoke to him like a human being, inviting him to ride on its back. As soon as he climbed onto it, it flew to his hometown, a place like this town, threw him down, gave him a kick with his back leg, and left him there.

Racha longed for his beautiful wives. "Why didn't I listen to them?" he cried in despair. He dived into the river over and over and searched for the magic palace door.

Such is man's life.

68. The Three-Thousand-Rupee Sari

A young man lived with his wife and mother. The wife was very beautiful. For some time, the man was quite a good husband and even followed her about, quite infatuated with her beauty. But he changed towards her. His fancy began to roam, he went after a harlot in town and neglected his wife.

Now, every day the daughter-in-law would go about her household chores as usual, cooking and cleaning till the sun went down. When it was time for the father-in-law and mother-in-law to go to bed, she would ask her mother-in-law, "Where shall I sleep today?" What could the mother-in-law say? One day she said, "Sleep anywhere. Sleep on the verandah." Another day, she asked her to sleep in the kitchen. The next day, it was the attic. Very soon, the daughter-in-law had slept in every possible part of the house. Still she kept asking her mother-in-law every night, "Tell me, where shall I sleep tonight?"

One day, the older woman lost her patience. She screamed, "I've had enough of this. My son has gone astray, and you bother me every night like this. Go sleep in the cremation grounds! Who cares? I'm sick of you."

The obedient daughter-in-law took her at her word. And when her in-laws fell asleep, she tucked her bedroll under her arm and went straight to the cremation grounds outside town and slept there. She too was sick of things. She gave up asking her mother-in-law and took to sleeping every night in the cremation grounds.

"Cremations grounds, says my mother-in-law. And cremation grounds it will be," she muttered to herself. She went there every night, and returned home in the morning to begin the chores of the house.

Now, a *sadhu*, a holy man, used to live there in an old well in the center of the cremation grounds. One day, he asked himself, "What's this female smell here, in this place of death? Which desperate woman could have come to this frightful place?"

And he clambered out of the well onto level ground and looked around. He saw the daughter-in-law curled on the ground, and asked her what she was doing there. She told him how her husband had left her for a harlot in town and how her mother-in-law had asked her to sleep in the cremation grounds. "If that's the way it is, do sleep here," he said. Soon they began seeing a lot of each other, this *sadhu* and this daughter-in-law. They became lovers.

Meanwhile, one day, the husband went to the market to buy a sari for his harlot woman. Being a poor man, he bought a sari for ten rupees. But the *sadhu* had also come there to buy a sari for his beloved. He had asked her, "Tell me what kind of sari you fancy. I'd like to buy you one."

The woman had said, "I want a sari that costs a thousand rupees for the warp, a thousand for the woof, and another thousand for the border. That's the only kind I want."

He had said, "Consider it done."

The *sadhu* had a bundle of money set aside from years of begging. He now took all of it in a little glass jar and went to the sari shop. They had a sari that really cost only a thousand rupees. When the shopkeepers heard him mention three thousand, they were delighted. They could make a profit of a whole two thousand. So they showed him the thousand-rupee sari and said it cost three thousand. He counted out the money he had and they let him take the sari. When he took it in his hand, the weave was so fine he could fold it and fit it neatly into the glass jar he had brought the money in. While the *sadhu* was buying this expensive sari, what was the husband doing but gaping in wonder and saying to himself, "Look, here I am buying a cheap ten-rupee sari for my woman. And this *sadhu* in rags bought one for three thousand. For whom is he buying this? What kind of woman could she be who would wear a three-thousand-rupee sari? I must look into this."

Somehow, a faint suspicion also crossed his mind: "I've been neglecting my wife and going into the back streets. My wife is a beauty. What could she be doing right now?"

So that night he didn't visit his concubine but slept at home. He pretended to be sleepy just when it was time for his wife to go to the cremation grounds. She was bothered. She was restless. It was time for her tryst, and she had even asked for a sari. But here was her husband asking her to do this and that and make his bed for the night, all of which she did—surprised though she was by his unwonted behavior. He lay down on the bed she had made and soon pretended to fall asleep. He even snored quite noisily.

She was taken in. She waited a while and, when she felt sure he was really fast asleep, she went out with a small copper water pot (as if she were answering a call of nature in the fields).

She arrived at the cremation grounds, copper pot in hand. She didn't know that as soon as she had left home, her husband had quickly gotten up, wrapped himself in a blanket from head to foot, and followed. At the cremation grounds, she climbed down into the low well where the *sadhu* lived. The husband hid himself and watched. His wife and her lover did whatever they usually did together. Then she put on the three-thousand-rupee sari he had brought for her. After a few moments, she suddenly said, "What am I going to do with this sari? How can I take it home or wear it anywhere except in the cremation grounds?"

And she quickly took it off, held it to the flame of the lamp that was burning close by, and burned the entire three-thousand-rupee sari to a heap of ashes. She dipped a finger in the ash and wore a dot of ash as a mark on her forehead. Then she left.

Her husband quickly hurried home before her and lay down in bed as if he had been asleep all this time. She came home soon after and she too went to bed.

At dawn he woke up and asked her for a pot of water for his morning's ablutions. In the field, as he answered his calls of nature, he saw in the bushes around him some big round ball-like flowers (*cendu huvu*), some as big as his hand. He plucked a few. When he came home, she dutifully gave him water to wash his hands with. He asked her to bring a lighted lamp for him. When she brought it, he proceeded to burn the fresh-petaled ball-like flowers in the flame. As she watched him, her woman's heart couldn't bear to see a flower being burned mercilessly. So she protested: "What are you doing? They are such lovely round flowers. We could make garlands, offer them to the gods, or wear them in our hair. Would anyone burn flowers like this?"

He replied at once, "*Che, che!* These are just plain wildflowers. They cost nothing, not a penny. I just plucked them from the bushes in the fields. I know people who don't mind burning whole saris worth three thousand rupees, and just wear a bit of the ash on their foreheads. Compared to that, what's so great about burning this worthless flower?"

She was cut to the quick. She at once understood what he meant. "This husband of mine knows all about me. I can't live anymore," she thought. She waited impatiently for the night. That night too the husband slept at home, though the wretch didn't so much as touch her or utter her name. As soon as she was sure he was fast sleep, she quietly got up. She unbound her long hair and strangled herself with it without a sound.

Her mother-in-law missed her early in the morning. Every day, the daughter-in-law was the first to wake up and begin household work at the crack of dawn. When she didn't stir as usual, the mother-in-law began to be anxious. Her fool of a son had gone astray and taken to prostitutes; did he kill his wife or something? When she didn't find her daughter-in-law anywhere in the house, she stood at her son's door and screamed at him: "Where is she? Did you kill her, did you strangle her with your dirty hands?"

He was wakened by this noise. He got up and opened the door. His mother rushed in and saw the daughter-in-law dead in a corner, her long hair noosed round her neck. She began to beat her breast and cry, "You killed her, you killed her! Why did you do it?"

He tried to calm her down and say to her, "Don't make such a rumpus. I didn't kill her. I haven't touched her."

But his mother was distraught. She wouldn't listen to anything he said. She called neighbors and relatives to help her bring the dead woman out of the house and prepare the body for a proper cremation. As they carried the body to the burning grounds, the husband walked in front and the mother-in-law walked behind, crying all the way, saying, "I have only one son and he's no good. And I had one gem of a daughter-in-law. O Siva, look what's happened."

They placed the body on a bier of firewood, and the husband touched it with a torch of fire. The body began to burn. The smell of burning flesh brought out the *sadhu* from his well. He came to the bier and saw the face of the dead woman now burning. He stood there and stared till the fire took hold, and he suddenly let out a shriek.

"O my doll, my beauty, even in death how beautifully you burn!" With these words, he threw himself into the leaping flames.

The husband was stricken in his heart when he saw the strange *sadhu* leap into the fire. "This man was with her for some three days, and he has now leaped into the fire after her. What about me? I married her in a public place; she was my wife for so long. And I'm still alive," he thought, and threw himself into the fire.

The old mother-in-law was beside herself with grief and shock. She said, "What am I doing here? My daughter-in-law is dead. My son is dead. I too must go. What is there at home to return to?" And, before anyone could stop her, she too fell in and perished in the fire of her daughter-in-law's bier.

Thus four people died in one fire, and it smoked for a long time.

69. Thug and Master-Thug

In a certain town lived two rival thieves, called Thug and Master-Thug. Thug was a strong man, a wrestler. Master-Thug was very clever. Thug couldn't bear the fact that the other fellow, thin as a reed, should be known as Master-Thug. One blow and this fellow would reel seven reels and fall to the floor—but he has this title!

Once they both went to a town like Belgaum to rob houses. Master-Thug broke into a rich man's house and stole ten thousand rupees. On the way, he met Thug, who knew right away by the looks of his pockets that the other thief had a lot of money. So Thug decided to rob Master-Thug. He stuck to him like a leech and engaged him in casual conversation. Night fell and they both went to a public hostel, found a place to sleep, and spread their blankets for the night. Master-Thug soon fell asleep. Thug got up silently and searched the sleeping man's pockets, his bag, and even his bedclothes. But he couldn't find a trace of the ten thousand rupees. Disappointed, he too fell asleep, wondering where the other man could have hidden it. But when he woke up in the morning, Master-Thug was up already, his pockets bulging obviously with the money. Again, they talked of this and that, and resumed their journey.

It was evening again and they found a hostel in another town, found a place to spread their blankets, and went to bed. Master-Thug, as before, was the first to fall asleep. Thug kept awake and deftly, silently, searched his rival's belongings for the money. He didn't find any trace of it. He even searched the corners and cracks of the room. He didn't find it. He slid his hand into the rafters and poked in the bushes outside. The money wasn't anywhere to be found. He too fell asleep, quite nonplussed.

Next morning, Master-Thug employed two muscular men as his bodyguards and started out with them. Thug joined them. When they reached the outskirts of their hometown, Thug stopped and asked his rival, "Where did you keep your money the last two nights? I'm curious."

"Ah," said Master-Thug with a laugh. "That's where the art of thuggery lies. I know why you have been following me. So, every night, I hid the money right under *your* bed. How would you find it by looking into my clothes, my pillow, my bed?"

Thug saluted him and said, "No wonder you're called Master-Thug," and went home.

70. Tree Trunk for a Boat

A boatman made a living by ferrying passengers across a river. Once he ferried a group from one bank to the other. He waited for passengers for the return trip, but no one turned up. After a long wait, he got into his boat and was paddling back alone when he ran into a flood that came at him from upstream. Before he could say "Ha!" both banks overflowed. He could not hold the boat to its course. The current carried the boat with it. He managed to save his life by jumping off and swimming to the bank. So he lost his boat to the flood, and from that day on he had no way of feeding his family. Being an active man, he planned on making another boat and went to the forest looking for a big tree with a large trunk.

Though he looked for a long time, he could not find a trunk that was suitable for a boat. Some were thin, some had knots. He searched all day and all evening till night fell and it was dark. Clouds gathered, and it looked like rain. He walked towards home with long strides, but it got darker and he was caught in a big rain. He couldn't see his way. He got drenched. Wet and hungry, having eaten nothing since morning, he stepped suspiciously through the underbrush till at last he saw a light in a house. He walked towards it.

It was a hut. He knocked on the door. A wrinkled old man opened the door. The boatman said, "Grandpa, I came to the forest looking for a tree to make a boat with. It got dark and I got caught in the rain. Can I stay the night and go home in the morning?"

The old man nodded. "Come in. We dying men don't carry our houses on our backs. Do come in and stay."

He went in. The old man had an old woman with him. There was nothing else in the hut. They didn't seem to have cows or calves, dogs or children. The boatman was a bit surprised. "These two stay alone in this forest. It takes guts," he thought. His stomach was drumming for food. The old couple didn't offer him any. "Why not ask?" he thought, and asked, "Grandpa, would you have a piece of bread? I'm very hungry."

The old man said, "Just sleep for a while. We'll wake you up when food is ready."

So the boatman lay down. But, with hunger drumming in his belly, how could he sleep? A few minutes later, he heard movements. Then he saw the old man open the lid of a box, take a leather cap from it, put it on his head, and say, "Go, go!" At once, the old man disappeared. The old woman was right behind him and put on another leather cap. She too said, "Go, go!" and she too disappeared. The boatman's mouth went dry. "Is this real, or is it a dream?" he asked himself and pinched himself. He sat up, baffled. Then, slowly recovering from his astonishment, he got up and went close to the box. He saw two more leather caps in it. He put one on and said, "Go, go." There was a swishing noise and he felt he was flying through the air. Before he could blink, he had descended and arrived in the kitchen of a king's palace. All the dishes for a grand dinner were ready in large vessels. The cooks and servants had gone out of the kitchen after cooking and washing up. Suddenly, in the middle of it all, he saw the old man and old woman he had seen in the hut. They were gobbling up whatever they fancied and stuffing the gold plates and dishes into their satchels. When they saw the boatman enter, they hurriedly put on their caps and said, "Back to the hut, back!" And they were gone in a trice. The boatman said to himself, "Ha, now I know why they don't cook at home!" and began to eat the food prepared for the king's dinner. He feasted on the king's meat and swilled the king's wine, many cups of it, till he got drunk. He forgot his leather cap and lay happily besotted on the floor, his legs stretched wide.

When it was the king's dinnertime, the cooks and servants came in and saw the mess in the kitchen. The dishes were half-eaten, spilled on the floor, plates were missing, pots were empty. The boatman lay in a corner. They hauled him up and thrashed him. The blows woke him from his drunken stupor. They tied him up and took him to the king.

"Your Majesty, here, we've caught him. This is the fellow who has been stealing gold and silver and food from the kitchen these many nights," they said.

The king was furious. "You scoundrel, you son of a whore!" he screamed. "Tie him to a tree and set fire to him. Cremate him alive!" he ordered.

The servants walked him to a huge dried-up tree and tied him to its trunk. They piled firewood all around him. The boatman looked around and a thought occurred to him: "If I had only found this tree trunk earlier, all this wouldn't have happened. What shall I do now?"

Before they lit the fire, they asked him the customary question, "What's your last wish?"

The boatman's allotted life span wasn't yet at an end, obviously. He suddenly remembered the leather cap.

"Masters, masters, I left my leather cap in the palace kitchen. My last wish is just to wear it. I'd like to die in it. Please."

A lackey ran in and brought him the cap. Before he put it on his head, he said to them, "Light your fires!" They lit the firewood and he put on the cap and said, "Back home, back home!" He vanished into the air at once. Everyone there cried out in one voice, "Magic, what magic!"

The boatman descended outside his own hut with the tree tied to his back. The tree was upright, the ropes were intact. His wife ran out, untied the knots, and released him, and asked, "What's all this?"

He said, "Nothing much. You remember we needed a proper tree trunk for our boat. God himself tied me to this tree and sent me here."

He carved a beautiful strong boat out of the tree trunk and lived happily with his wife, plying his boat as before.

71. The Turtle Prince

In a certain kingdom, the king had no children for many years. Neither did the minister. So they went to consult sages and holy men. They all said that couples will get children if they worship Siva. Accordingly, they both worshiped Siva with great devotion, and, sure enough, their wives became pregnant. Then the king and the minister said to each other: "If we both have boys, let them always be together as king and minister. If one of us has a boy and the other a girl, the girl should be given in marriage to the boy." They agreed happily; each put his palm in the other's and exchanged promises.

Nine months later, the queen gave birth to a baby turtle. The minister's wife gave birth to a lovely girl. The king was at first disgusted. But then, as the saying goes, even if you beget a bandicoot you'll learn to love it. So the king and queen loved the turtle as if it were a son. The minister and his wife had no trouble doting on their lovely daughter.

As the turtle prince and the minister's daughter grew up, the king began to worry. He confided in the queen, reminded her of the exchange of promises between him and the minister. The queen said, "That is all very well. If our child had been a boy, a human being, your agreement would have worked fine. Now this one is a turtle. How can you go ask for a bride?"

But the turtle, who was listening to their conversation, lying in another bed, suddenly spoke up and said, "Why are you worried? Am I not your son? Father, go and ask. Let's see what the minister says."

They were astonished to hear the turtle speak in a man's voice, for he had never spoken a word before that moment. They were also delighted that they had a language in common with their abnormal son. The king even thought that this turtle was no ordinary turtle but must really be some enchanted prince under a curse to wear a turtle's form. How else would he be able to speak now like a man? Thinking such thoughts, he went to the minister's house in a palanquin, and said, "Dear friend, we should arrange the wedding between your daughter and my son, just as we agreed years ago."

While the minister was hesitating to reply, and looking for the right thing to say, his daughter spoke: "Father, why do you want to break your word for my sake? Whoever he is, prince or pauper, angel or animal, I'll marry anyone who'll bring me the celestial *parijata* flower."

The king went home and reported to the turtle what the minister's daughter said. The turtle said, "Father, don't give it a second thought. Take me to the sea and leave me in the water. I'll take care of the rest."

So they sat him in a palanquin and took him to the seashore.

The turtle swam happily in his element and went to the Udaya mountain. There he did penance and prayed to the Sun God. The Sun was pleased with his penances and appeared to him in all his dazzling splendor.

"My son, you were really a prince in your previous life. But you were arrogant and once threw a turtle on a sage out of sheer mischief. So he put a curse on you that you should be born as a turtle. Then you came to your senses. You humbly begged him to relent and take back his curse. He took pity on you and said, 'When you go to the Udaya mountain and please the Sun God, you'll shed the turtle form and become a prince again. Be patient till then.' Your moment has come," said the Sun God, blessed him, and vanished.

The turtle disappeared, too, and in his place stood a glowing prince. He saluted the Sun gratefully and started his quest for the *parijata* flower.

On his way he met a sage who practiced penance for only one minute each day. The prince greeted him respectfully and asked, "Master, where will I find the celestial *parijata?*"

"I don't know, my boy. Go on for a mile or so. My guru lives there. Ask him."

He walked the distance of a mile, and met a sage who practiced penance for only two minutes each day. He greeted the two-minute sage and asked him, "Master, where can I find the celestial *parijata* flower?"

"I don't really know. If you walk another mile or so, you'll find my guru. Ask him."

When, after walking a mile, he found a sage who practiced penance for three minutes each day, he asked the same question.

"Where, master, can I find the celestial flower, *parijata?*"

The sage looked at him and thought, "If anybody can bring it, this young man can." So he answered his question. "Look here, to the north of here, there's a temple of the elephant-faced god. Beyond it, there's a lake. Celestial women come to the lake every day to bathe in it. When they take off their saris and enter the water, you should go and steal a sari, any sari, and run away with it. Don't ever look back. If you do, you'll die like other princes before you. Run to the temple of the elephant-faced god and take refuge in it. You'll find the *parijata* flower."

The prince went to the lake and waited for the celestial women. As soon as they came, they took off their saris and entered the water. He grabbed a sari, ran without looking back till he reached the temple, and locked himself in it. One of the women came after him. She stopped before the locked temple door, and pleaded, "Please, O prince, return my sari. I beg of you with folded hands."

After she had assured him that he would come to no harm, he opened the door and gave the naked celestial her sari, which she quickly wrapped around herself. Then he came out and they met, and she liked the prince. When she heard what he was after, she promised to bring him the *parijata* flowers he wanted, and went back to her world, the world of the gods.

By midnight, she returned to the temple, gave him the celestial flowers and slept with him. Early next morning, before she left, she gave him a flute and told him she would appear whenever he played on it.

On his return journey, the three-minute sage asked him, "Prince, did you get what you wanted?"

"Yes, master, by your blessings."

"Did you meet the celestial woman?"

"Certainly. I'll show you, if you wait a minute," said the prince, and played on his flute. At once, she appeared. Even the sage gaped at her beauty.

The three-minute sage said, "Prince, listen. I've a yogic wand that will beat up anyone you want it to. All you have to say is, 'Get so-and-so,' and it will get him. You're of the warrior caste, you'll find it handy. Take it and give me the flute."

The prince exchanged the flute for the wand, and, after walking a few steps, turned around and shouted orders to the wand, "Get that sage and bring back the flute!"

The yogic wand beat the sage till he was black and blue. He couldn't bear it anymore. So he returned the flute and sat down dejected like a monkey.

The prince walked a mile with the wand, the flute, and the *parijata*. The two-minute sage also fell for the beauty of the prince's celestial companion and offered to exchange a sack he had for the prince's flute. The sack was no ordinary sack; it could give the owner whatever he wished. The prince took the magic sack, pretended to walk away, and ordered his yogic wand to get the wily sage. The wand punished the sage and brought back the flute. The old man sat downcast, his body in pain and his mind filled with dismay.

The prince moved on with the flute, the sack, the wand, and the *parijata* flower. The one-minute sage was also infatuated with the celestial beauty when the prince showed her off, and offered him his sandals for his flute. Those sandals too were no ordinary sandals—they could carry you wherever you wished to go. The prince made the exchange, pretended to take a few steps, and gave orders to the yogic wand, which beat up the sage and recovered the flute. This sage too sat there, helpless and mad.

The prince reached the palace secretly that night with all his precious objects, and hid them away. Then he prayed to the Sun, became a turtle again, and took only the *parijata* flowers to his parents. He fell at their feet and said, "I've brought the flowers from heaven. You must arrange the marriage."

The minister too heard about it. The turtle went to his house and gave his daughter the flowers. What could the minister do? Without another word, willy-nilly he had to arrange the wedding between the turtle and his daughter. As the minister had two younger daughters, he arranged their weddings as well, with two other princes. He housed all the sons-in-law in his own mansion. The minister's younger daughters went happily to bed with their husbands. But how could the minister's eldest daughter, betrothed before birth to a turtle, how could she do anything with a turtle? "This is my lot," she said to herself, and slept quietly next to the turtle.

The sisters and their husbands laughed at the eldest sister and called her a turtle's darling! They wanted to mock her further and so the two men decided to go hunting. The turtle also wanted to go. His wife, the minister's daughter, pleaded with him not to go, but he was adamant. After an argument, she went to her father and said, "Father, your eldest son-in-law wants to go hunting. Give him a chariot too."

Everyone in the household heard her and laughed aloud and clapped their hands. They found him a lame nag for a horse and a blunt sword for a weapon. She had to bear the insults silently. The turtle consoled his wife and went with the others on the hunt. The servants had to lift him and make him perch on the saddle. But, as soon as he was alone, he changed into a prince and went into the forest, galloping ahead of everyone.

The other two sons-in-law saw two huge tigers in the forest. Before they could hide, the tigers sighted them and roared, and the two princes ran for their lives. The soldiers were in one place, the chariots in another, and the young men in still another place. It was chaos.

"Who needs to hunt?" said one to the other. "Let's go back and tell them we didn't find any game today."

The other said, "How can we do that? We made fun of that turtle. It would be better if we took something to show."

Yet both of them were cowards. One more roar, and they both fled the forest. On their way home, they saw the turtle. They were astonished by what they saw. He had killed both tigers, spread the dead animals next to him, and was resting under a tree, chewing betel nut and betel leaves. They went up to him, and he offered them some betel leaves and nuts. They asked him to do them a favor.

"Give us these tigers. We'll give you whatever you ask."

"Then give me the left half of your mustaches."

They thought this was easy. What'd be lost if they gave a part of their mustaches? Handsome men will be handsome anyway, whether they grow a mustache or shave it off or keep only a half of one. If we take these tigers from the hunt, we'll get rewards, maybe even a part of the kingdom. Mustaches, like grass, will grow in no time. So they gave him half their mustaches.

The people of the capital welcomed them and took them with their dead tigers to the palace in a procession. The princes hastily made up stories about why they had half a mustache each. Whatever rich princes do is beautiful, isn't it?

The turtle prince was there too, limping behind the procession with his lame horse. No one talked to him. Street urchins followed him all the way to the palace, taunting and teasing him.

That night, the minister's first daughter went to bed very sad that her life had become a laughingstock. Next to her was a sorry-looking turtle, fast asleep.

When she fell asleep, the turtle, who wasn't asleep at all, changed into a prince, undressed her, and caressed her all over. Then he changed back into the turtle. When she woke up in the morning, her clothes were disheveled. Who could have come into the bedroom? She looked at the turtle. It lay like a piece of stone. She decided to find out what had really happened that night, and said nothing to anyone. Then she went to bed early the next night and pretended to be fast asleep. The turtle waited for a while and changed into the prince and came towards her. She caught hold of his outstretched hand and sat up. She knew now that her husband was no turtle but a glowing prince. She fell at his feet and begged him, "My lord, you must give up this disguise at once."

He said, "Wait till tomorrow. Ask everyone to come to court. We'll show them some fun."

Next day, the court was full. Everyone was there—the three sons-in-law, the three daughters, the king, the minister, their wives. The two younger sons-in-law came to the court, strutting and showing off their tigers. Everyone applauded. Suddenly, the turtle interrupted them and asked in a commanding human voice what had happened to their mustaches. They babbled. At that moment, the turtle shed his shell and became a prince before everyone's eyes. A light glowed from his body. He took the mustaches of the sons-in-law from his pocket and told the assembly the true story. The sons-in-law slunk away in shame. The king made the turtle prince his heir, placed a crown on his head, and lived happily.

72. A Wager

A king had an only son. Every day the king would finish his morning bath and devotions, have something to eat, then saddle his horse, go on his rounds in the city, come home by noon, and call his son to eat the midday meal with him. He had taught his son every kind of art that a prince should know. One day, after the usual rounds on his horse, he came home, had a wash, sat down for his midday meal, and called his son to join him. But that morning the son had thought: "My father takes his horse out every day. When am I going to do the same? Let me take my horse out today, ride twenty-five miles, and return by the time he finishes his meal. Let me surprise him."

So he untied his horse, sat on it, spurred it, and whipped it lightly. The horse galloped so fast it was like flying in the air. It didn't even leave a whiff of dust behind it. In no time, he came to a new village. As he cantered through the streets, the prince saw the local rich man's daughter sweeping their dooryard. She was utterly beautiful and he stopped in front of her to pose her a riddle:

O *Idiga* man's daughter, tell me, of all sesames
  which is the smallest sesame?

She replied at once:

Of all the flowers, tell me now,
  what's the price of jasmine?

The prince flew into a rage. He said to her, "O *Idiga* man's daughter, you don't know who you're talking to. You talked back to me. So I'll marry you and shut you up in my basement. If I don't, I wouldn't be my father's son."

She countered at once, "O king's son, I'll marry you then, and I'll get your own son to tie you up to the post in the marketplace. If I don't, my breast is no breast but a nut of the *ekke* tree."

The prince rode back to his palace home, tied up his horse, and went to his room, and lay there face down on his bed. The king came out and looked at the horse, which was foaming at the mouth, panting after a long hard ride. He asked the grooms, "Who has been riding this horse?" They answered, "No one else but the prince, sire." So he went to his son's room and found him lying face down on his bed. "Come, eat with me," he said. The son wanted no food. The king asked, "What's wrong? Did I do something?" The son said, "No, father, not you," and told him how he had taken a ride into the next town and how the *Idiga* girl had insulted him, bandied wager for wager.

"So," he said, "I must marry her and teach her a lesson. I want you to get her here and arrange my marriage."

The father tried to reason with him. "That's no good reason to marry anyone. Furthermore, they are of the *Idiga* caste, and we are *Kshatriyas*. We are different kinds of people with different customs."

But the prince wouldn't listen. He would touch no food till they agreed to his wishes. The king finally yielded to his son's stubbornness, and said he would try. Then he asked the groom to saddle his horse, and rode into the next town and talked to the *Idiga* girl's father. The *Idiga* gentleman was quite overcome with awe when his servants announced that the reigning king himself had come to visit him. He went into a panic. The king quelled his fears and said, "Please don't be afraid. You've done nothing wrong. We would like to make a marriage alliance with your family. My son likes your daughter."

The *Idiga*s were delighted. The marriage was arranged. The wedding was to take place three or four months later. The prince, meanwhile, ordered an underground basement house to be built three miles out of town and got it furnished and ready for his bride.

Four months later, the marriage took place. When it was time for the bride to go to her father-in-law's place, she called her father aside and told him, with tears in her eyes, "*Appa*, you must now forget any hopes you may have for your daughter's future. It's finished."

"What are you talking about?" asked the father. "You have a whole kingdom at your feet. You're a prince's wife, the future queen. He's not lame, he's not blind. He looks wonderful. What's wrong? Why are you crying?"

"*Appa*, this prince came here a few months ago. And he said to me,

> O rich man's daughter, of all sesames
>   which is the smallest sesame?

I replied,

> O great king's son, of all the flowers,
>   what is the price of jasmine?

He thought I was talking back to him and mocking him. He made a vow at once that he would marry me and shut me up in a basement. So I too made a wager that I would marry him, beget a son by him, and get his own son to tie him to the post in the marketplace. That's why he's married me now. I've heard he's got a basement house all ready for me. It looks as if he'll win his wager. How do I win mine?"

Then the father said, "Daughter, if you'd told me all this, we would never have agreed to this marriage."

"Now it's done. A wager is a wager. Promise to help me and I'll tell you what to do," said the daughter. She had her own plans.

When the father promised her his help, she asked him to dig and build a secret passage, a tunnel, between the basement house and his own mansion. Then she left for the palace.

The prince didn't even look at her. He sent her to the basement house and shut her up in it. Then he went to another country in search of a new bride, married again, and lived with his new wife quite happily.

Meanwhile, the father finished making a secret passage between his daughter's basement house and his own. When he visited her, she said to him, "Father, I've got to win my wager. So I want you to find me an expert teacher of acrobatics and several women acrobats, in fact, a whole troupe. Will you bring them here as soon as you can?"

He found the teacher and the troupe for her in no time and brought them secretly through the tunnel into the basement house. The teacher was an experienced old man. She gave him a high seat and said to him, "Grandfather, tell me all the different kinds of dances and acrobatic feats you know."

"I know any number of things, not only acrobatics, but the arts of magic, black and white, that can call up demons and spirits, and I've the ash that can put people to sleep."

"O yes?" said the young woman, and proceeded to take lessons from him every day, and learned all his arts. Then she came out one dark night with her father to the field outside her husband's palace and pitched an acrobats' tent there. Next morning, the town crier was engaged to make announcements through the town that there would be a fantastic new show outside the palace. The prince too came to watch the show. More than anything, he was dazzled by the *saukar*'s daughter and her incredible skill in dance and acrobatic feats. He was stricken by her beauty. He sent for the old acrobat, and asked him who the lovely acrobat was. The old man told him she was his own daughter. The prince told him, "I would like to visit her tonight."

The old man was disgusted by this proposition and told the *saukar*'s daughter about it. "*Amma*, the king's son has cast his eyes on you. What shall I do?"

He was quite nonplussed when he heard her say, "That's all right. Ask him to come tonight."

Well, that night, the prince dined and wined happily, and came to the tent with many costly gifts. The *saukar*'s daughter came down from her cot and asked him to sit on it.

"My lord, what's your wish?" she asked, as if she didn't know.

He replied, "I like you a lot. Can't take my mind off you, ever since I saw you dance this evening."

So they bathed and ate together, and gave each other much pleasure.

"I've never seen anyone so beautiful and artful as you. Ask what you want and I'll give it to you," said the prince, sated with pleasure.

"O, I want very little," she said. "Give me the ring on your finger, as a memento."

"Take it," he said, and gave it to her, promising to visit her again the next night. And he spent the next night with her, and gave her the necklace he was wearing. On the third night, she took from him the dagger at his waist.

The next day, the acrobats left the palace outskirts. She went back to her father's house with the old acrobat and his troupe, gave them money and many gifts, and returned to her underground basement house. She was happy to see that she was pregnant. Nine months and nine days later, she gave birth to a baby boy. As he grew up, she taught him all the arts she had learned from the old man. He grew up to be a very clever, a very accomplished young man. One day, mother and son were having their dinner and chatting, when the mother asked him, "I've a wager and I can't win it without you. Will you promise to win it for me?"

"Of course," said the son, thinking that nothing could be more precious than one's mother. "Tell me what it is, and I'll do it."

"Listen carefully, my son. Before you were born, I was sweeping our dooryard. The king's son came riding and asked me out of the blue,

'O *saukar*'s daughter, tell me: of all the sesames,
    which is the smallest sesame?'

"And I replied,

'O king's son, of all the flowers
    what's the price of jasmine?'

"And he was furious. He made a vow at once, and said to me, 'You talked back to me. So I'll marry you and shut you up in a basement. If I don't, I'm not my father's son.'

"I countered at once with a wager, 'If I don't marry you, and get your own son to tie you up to the post in the marketplace, my breast is not a breast but an *ekke* nut!'

"Then that prince did marry me and shut me up here in this basement house. That prince, your father, has fulfilled his vow. I have to fulfill mine. And it depends on you, my son."

"If my father never came here, how did I come about?" asked the son, all eyes and ears by now. Then she told him about the acrobats and the three nights she spent with the prince.

Then she showed him the tunnel. The young man hastened to his grandfather's mansion through the tunnel and asked him for an old shirt, some old half-pants, and a dirty blanket. The grandfather, who knew something was afoot, arranged to get them. The young man wore them and went towards his father's city. About a mile away from the palace, he saw a hut and approached it. The old woman of the hut inquired, "Where do you come from? Who are you? Have you eaten or would you like something to eat?"

He answered "I don't have a home to call my own. I wander here and there in search of work and wages."

She said, "I too am alone. I've nobody to call my own. Stay here with me. I live by selling milk and buttermilk."

He accepted her invitation, and stayed with her, grazing her cows all day. He made friends with other young cowherd boys, played village games with them, and learned the ways of the bazaar nearby. One day they were roaming the streets and came to the palace. He said, playing the innocent, "Look, what a beautiful and strange-looking house!"

His friends enlightened him and gave him the gossip.

"O that, that is the palace. The king's story is quite something. He married a woman from the village and has shut her up in a basement house. After shutting up his first wife, he went and married a second wife. They say he is quite happy with the new one and has several children. Up there in the third storey is their bedroom. In the middle of it stands a golden cot with silver legs on which they sleep. They have servantmaids at their beck and call all hours of the day to bring them their slightest wish and to give them baths and massages." And so on, they told him everything they had heard, adding spice and salt to it.

That evening, he tied up the cows in the shed, waited for the night, and went to the palace. Deftly, he threw the ash that makes people fall asleep into the eyes of the guards, and they sank down in sleep in the very places they stood. He entered the palace bedroom and, sure enough, the king and queen were sleeping on the legendary bedspread on a golden cot with silver legs. He removed the silver legs one by one, replacing them with banana trunks cut to the right lengths; he removed, with the lightest of fingers, every piece of jewelry the queen was wearing from all over her body; then he came out on silent feet, as he had gone in. He hid the jewelry in a hole behind the hut and went to bed.

The king and his queen stirred in their sleep. The banana trunks on which the cot was precariously perched slipped from under them, and they rolled to the ground, shocked awake. When they lit the lamps, they found to their amazement that all the jewelry was gone. Even the silver legs of the cot were gone. They shouted for all the servants and the guards, but no one knew a thing. The king punished them all. He called the bailiff and gave orders that the thief be caught at once. Whoever it was, he seemed to be no ordinary thief. He seemed well-versed in all the black arts.

Next day, when the young man was driving his herd of cows, he met the bailiff making his rounds in broad daylight. He asked him, "Bailiff sir, you seem to have started work early today. What's the matter?"

The bailiff replied, "Go your ways. Some clever thief has robbed the king's bedroom, and the king is punishing us all. We have to catch him right away or else we will lose our heads. Don't ask too many questions. Just go about your business."

The young man said he could perhaps help in bringing the thief to justice. The bailiff said, "If only my son-in-law were here! He would have caught this thief in two minutes!"

"Isn't he in town? Where did he go, sir bailiff? Can I go get him?" said the young man, showing concern.

"O, how can you? He left town the day after he married my daughter. His skin was the color of oil, a bit on the brown side. He always wore white clothes. He was about your height and weight. . . ." The bailiff went on to give him a full description of his absent son-in-law.

The young man listened to everything carefully, made sympathetic noises to the bailiff, and drove the cows home early that day. He warned the old woman, "Grandma, there are robbers in town. They've even robbed the king's palace. You'd better be careful. Bolt all doors before you sleep. I'll sleep in the shed with the cows and guard them."

But he didn't sleep there that night. He dressed himself up as the bailiff's son-in-law and went to the city gates, where the bailiff was keeping watch in the dark. He addressed him as father-in-law, and said, "Father-in-law, why are you sitting here alone like this?"

The bailiff was taken aback but was also happy to see his absent relative.

"I was just talking about you to someone today. Where have you been all these days? The king got robbed yesterday, so he has put me on day-and-night duty at the city gates."

"That's what I heard and so I hurried back," said the young man.

"That's my boy! I'm so glad you're back. You can help us catch this thief. But first go home and see your wife. She would be so pleased," said the bailiff.

The young man took his leave and went to the bailiff's house and said to the bailiff's wife: "Mother-in-law, I'm employed in the south, far away. The weather there has completely changed my skin color and looks, as you can see. I thought I should come home, be with my wife for a couple of days, and go back. I'll soon arrange to take her there."

She and her daughter welcomed him and gave him a fine dinner. Then he joined the daughter in bed, slept with her, and left quietly before dawn.

When, next day, the king asked the bailiff, "Did you catch the thief?" all he could say was, "Master, what shall I say? Yesterday he came in the guise of my long-lost son-in-law, slept with my daughter, and disappeared. He is no ordinary thief, believe me."

The king agreed. "He does look like a superthief. I'll make the rounds myself tonight and catch him," he said, and sent out warnings to the entire city through the town crier.

The young cowherd came home early again and warned the old woman, "It looks as if the king himself will make the rounds of the city today and try to catch the thief. You'd better be careful lest the thief come into this house. Check the doors before you sleep."

Then he went out and bought puffed rice, peanuts, fried *bondas,* and other snacks, as well as cigarettes and matches. By midnight, he had built a little booth and set up shop on a street corner. He kept it open, with a little oil lamp flickering all night, and sat at the till. The king came there on his rounds and asked him, "What are you doing, keeping a snack shop open at this midnight hour? Who'll come and buy from you at this time?"

The young man winked and said, "O, there are always night people. Every night ten men come from this side and ten from that. Trade is quite brisk at this time."

The king thought that it must be the thieves who came at night to the shop for a bite to eat, and said, "Look here, I have to catch a thief in that gang. I'm no other than the king. I've decided to catch him myself."

The young man pretended to be all agog, and whispered to him respectfully, "*Swami,* master, of course, of course. I'll be at your service. Anything you say. But those fellows have come and gone already tonight. If only I'd known. . . . But tomorrow I'll arrange to catch them, bind them up, and deliver them to you. I promise."

Next day, he drove the cows to pasture as usual, returned as usual, and warned the old woman again, "Robbers are rampant in town. Double-lock the doors before you sleep. I'll sleep in the shed."

Then he went to a laundryman, gave him a costly jewel, and bought from him a large bundle of dirty linen. He also picked up a large burlap bag and some rope. He went to the tank, disguised as a laundryman, and started washing the clothes. The king came there late that night on his rounds, his face hooded in a cloak. He asked the fake laundryman, "What are you doing at this hour washing clothes?"

The man replied, "O sir, I'm the same fellow who runs the booth at night. Now I have to wash these clothes. These belong to the robbers. They want the dry ones right away. They'll come here to change into disguises and they will give me more clothes."

The king was all fired up and said, "Then I'll wait here and catch him."

"I'll help you, sir. But then, if you stand here like that, strong and tall, they will see you and vanish. You must hide in this bundle of clothes and make no noise," said the young rogue, smothering the king in the dirty linen and tying a bed sheet all around him, making a firm knot at the top.

At the crack of dawn, people began to come towards the tank for water. He called them all and said, pointing to the bundle of clothes, "Here, this is the thief. Take him in this bundle and tie it up to the post in the marketplace. Don't listen to anything he says. He's much too clever for all of us, as you know."

The people carried the bundle, with the king screaming and shouting inside, and tied it up to the post. By the time they got there, the young man was already sitting there, dressed like a lord, in a high chair, twirling his mustache. He had meanwhile sent for the king's old father. When he arrived, he asked the people to untie the bundle.

"At long last. Let's see the face of this superthief. Untie it," he ordered. Out of the bundle scrambled a bewildered and disheveled king. When he looked at his captor, he was amazed, for the young man looked like himself. His second queen also hurried to the place and saw the two of them, look-alikes—her husband tied to a post in the marketplace, and a young man standing stylishly in front of him with a whip in his hand. King and thief, thief and king, handy-dandy, it was hard to tell who was which. Only their ages gave them away.

Then the young man addressed the crowd and told them that he was really the prisoner's son. He also sent for his mother in the basement house. She hurried to the marketplace and quickly asked the servants to untie the king. She told the assembly about her wager, why and how she was married, and how her son now had helped her win the wager. She showed them the dagger, the necklace, and the signet ring that had once belonged to the king. They went with her to inspect the underground tunnel her father had built for her. Then the king said, "You are truly my first wife. Queen, you've won your wager."

Then he called his son to his side and embraced him. Everyone, needless to say, was happy.

73. What the Milk Bird Said

In those days, snakes, bears, tigers, and such other wild animals could talk, just like you and me. One day the village chieftain's daughter, who was very pregnant, went to get kindling in the woods. A milk bird was singing:

Come, father's daughter, father's wife, ji ji!
Come this way, come, father's daughter-in-law and son's own wife, ji ji!

She gathered dry twigs and branches, but she was troubled by the song. "Why is the milk bird singing such a weird song? O mother!" she grumbled to herself. By noon, she had filled her basket with kindling. She could not lift it and set it on her head all by herself. She looked around for someone who might help. The hot sun was merciless, and under her feet the earth was as hot as a sheet of metal. She wilted in the heat, and stood there restless, finding everything unbearable. Just then, a cobra came that way. She said to the cobra, "Brother Cobra, come help me with this basket."

The cobra said, "If I help, what will I get?"

"What can I give you? I'm going to have a baby. If I get a son, I'll name him after you. If I get a daughter, I'll marry her to you," she said.

The cobra said, "That's a deal," and lifted the basket onto her head and watched her carry it home.

Seven months passed, eight months passed. When it was nine months and nine days, she gave birth to a daughter. That bitch, Goddess Setivi, came and wrote her future and fortune on the baby's forehead, as she does on every newborn baby's. Just when Setivi was leaving, the mother of the newborn woke up and saw her, quickly grabbed the end of the goddess's sari, and stopped her.

"What did you write on my baby's forehead?" she asked.

"I've written what the milk bird said. I've written that she'll marry her own son," said Setivi, before she slipped through the door.

"If what you write is true, may you become a widow, you bitch!" cursed the mother. (That's why the goddess is a widow.)

Three months passed, and the cobra came hissing to the village gate and lay across it. People tried to scare it and chase it away, but it didn't move. It didn't let anyone go into the village or come out. The elders sat in council. They decided someone had made a vow and promised something. That must be why the Cobra God lay full-length across their gate. They announced through the town crier that whoever had made a vow should fulfill it.

The village chieftain's daughter knew at once why the cobra had come. He was asking her to make good her word. So she got up and dressed her baby daughter in new clothes, put a new bonnet on the little one's head, painted eye-black in her little eyes, and gave her the breast. Then she took the baby in a basket, placed it before the cobra, saluted him, and came away. The cobra spread its hood and carried the baby into the woods.

Years later, the chieftain's daughter bore a son. He grew up and started playing *cinni-dandu* with a chip and a stick. One day he sent a chip flying and hit a girl who was carrying a pitcher of water home. In her anger, the girl scolded him: "We all know what makes you so bad, you rascal. A snake took your sister. What do you expect?"

He came straight home and pestered his mother to tell him what had happened to his sister. She hesitated at first and then told him, "Yes, that's true, that's what happened." And she told him the entire story. "If that's what happened, I'll go and get her back," he said, and would not wait even a day. He didn't listen to his mother's pleadings and arguments. He left with a small bundle of food.

He went and went and went, far into the thick of the woods, through the thorny jungle. He tired himself out and fell asleep under a banyan tree. When he woke up, he smelled something, looked around, and saw a wisp of smoke rising from the banyan's upper branches. "What kind of smoke is this?" he asked himself and climbed the tree.

In its top branches, among the leaves, there was a house. The door was shut. He knocked on it. "Anyone inside? I'm thirsty, can you open the door and give me some water?" he shouted. A woman opened the door. Her eyes and nose and expression were all just like his mother's. He told her who he was, named his mother's name and family. She suddenly realized who he was and cried out "Brother!" She threw her arms around him and she wept. She told him her entire life's story, how the cobra had brought her up, taught her everything, and finally married her.

"Sister, let's go home!" he said.

"O, no! How can we escape my husband? He is a terror. If he even sees you he'll kill you," she said.

But he told her what to do. So she hid him carefully and boiled milk on the stove. The cobra came home and hissed, "Some new smell, something new!" Suddenly he recognized the smell. "O the milk!" he cried, and eagerly drank the sweet-smelling scalding milk, which he couldn't resist, and died on the spot.

Then brother and sister made their way towards their village. The sister was fully pregnant. On the way, she had to give birth. She laid one egg after another every few steps. Her brother followed her, broke the eggs one by one, and smeared them on the stones. He crushed and crunched scores of them. But one little egg rolled into a crack in the ground and he couldn't reach it however hard he tried. He and his sister thought, "What can a little egg do? It will die in the heat." And they moved on. They were hardly within earshot of their village when the egg in the crack hatched into a baby snake. It crawled out and moved fast. It soon overtook them and waylaid them.

"I won't let her go. You'd better go home alone. Or else I'll bite you," it said to the brother, raising its hood.

Not knowing what to do, he left his sister behind and went on alone. The baby snake forced her to return to the banyan tree, married her, and they lived for a long time in the house in the tree.

74. Who Is the Greatest?

Once there were two kings. One of them had seven sons and the other had seven daughters. Though they were in different kingdoms and didn't know each other, they both decided it was time to get their offspring married. The king who had sons called his servants, gave them seven pictures of his seven sons, and asked them to search for proper well-born brides for each of them. The king who had seven daughters also called his servants, gave them pictures of his seven daughters, and sent them forth with orders to find suitable royal bridegrooms for them.

The servants of both kings wandered through the land in search of proper mates for their princes and princesses. Word traveled from one ear to another, and everyone in the land heard about this search.

In a village lived a *gowda* who also heard about it, and he decided to invite both parties to his place. With him as a mediator, the parties met, exchanged each other's pictures, and found that the matches were perfect. They went back to their respective kings, who were overjoyed to hear the good news. The whole capital set about making grand preparations for the sevenfold wedding. But, when they got together soon after for the marriage negotiations, the *gowda* was also present. He said to them, "Don't arrange the wedding ceremony in this house or in that one. Arrange it in my village. We would be delighted to make the arrangements. Please let us."

The kings accepted his invitation and finished the betrothal ceremonies that day.

Each king brought seven cartloads of people and things for the wedding to the *gowda*'s village. When they asked the *gowda*, he asked his men, "Where shall we hold the wedding?"

Then he answered his own question. "Go to my fields. Get a *magi* gourd that is neither at the top nor at the bottom of the creeper but in the middle. Pluck it and bring it here."

His men went to the fields and brought him the gourd. He made a hole in it and put all fourteen cartloads of people and their things in the gourd and said, "Go ahead and have the wedding in here."

The *gowda*'s daughter had gone to the well to get a pitcher of water and came back to her father's house. She felt the need to make water. She went near the *magi* gourd, which was lying outside. She didn't know what was in it. She made water all around it. The force of that flood carried the gourd far away and finally to the sea. A fish in the sea gobbled it up in no time. Then a hovering sea crane swooped down, caught the fish, and swallowed it. A fisherman caught the bird with his net and took it to the farmers' market on Friday.

Now an old woman in another village called her daughter, gave her four or five rupees, and said, "Go to the farmers' market and buy me a chicken or a goose. With the rest of the money, buy some groceries. Don't dillydally. Come back soon."

On her way to the market, the old woman's daughter met the fisherman. She bought the sea crane from him, tied it round her waist, went to the market, bought some things there, and hurried home.

Her mother asked her, "Did you bring the bird?"

"Yes, I did. A nice sea crane," she said, and loosened the cloth around her lap, but there was no crane. It had vanished. A louse in her sari had swallowed the sea crane. Her mother thought she was telling lies and got into a rage. So she pulled out a stick and gave her daughter a good beating. The daughter couldn't bear it, and she began to menstruate. The mother, disgusted, called the washerman and gave him the daughter's soiled clothes to launder.

The washerman took them to the river and began to soak them and beat them on the stone. Then the louse split open and out came the sea crane. The astonished washerman took out the bird, pulled off the feathers, and cut it with a knife. In its crop, he found a fish, and inside the fish he found a gourd, which seemed to be hollow. He thought that the hollow gourd could be used as a lamp and so he placed it on top of a pole outside his house. There was a big wind soon after, and the gourd was blown down. It fell and broke. At about this time, inside the gourd, the wedding of the seven princes and the seven princesses was finishing up. They, their clan, and all their guests came out one by one and began to find their way home.

Now, tell me: Which is the biggest of them all? Is it the gourd that can hold fourteen cartloads, or is it the *gowda*'s daughter, who sent the gourd rushing to the sea by making water on it? Or is it the fish that gobbled up the gourd? Is it the sea crane that swallowed that fish that had gobbled up the gourd? Is the louse that devoured the sea crane bigger than all these, or is it the girl who tied the crane in the sari round her waist? Who is bigger? Is the washerman who bundled it all up and took it to the river the greatest of these?

ANSWER: It's quite possible that the *gowda* knew how to grow a gourd as big as that one. It's also possible that his daughter sent it rushing to the sea with the water she made. A fish could have eaten it, a crane could have eaten the fish, and certainly a fisherman could have caught the crane. But the old woman's daughter who had a louse that ate the crane that ate the fish that swallowed the gourd that had fourteen cartloads of men and things in it, that girl is the greatest. But what about the washerman who took her sari to the river with all these in it? That's nothing unusual. Washermen lug to the river bigger bundles of clothes than that.

75. Why the Sky Went Up

Once upon a time, the sky and the sun were quite close to the earth. The sun's heat was unbearable. People died of sunstroke. One day an old farmer who had just shaved off all his hair went to work in the fields. The sun's heat was so fierce that his shaven head cracked in two, and he died at once.

His daughter was pounding rice in the yard. The long pestle that she used for pounding went higher and higher as she gathered speed. Finally, it struck the sky and rebounded back on her head. She too died of a cracked skull.

Her mother was grief-stricken that her husband had died in the fields and her daughter at home. So she cursed the sky.

"You bastard sky, you bastard sun, why don't you go up and give us some space?"

The sun and the sky heard the curse and began to move upwards. At about that time, a washerman was moving his load of laundry to the river on the back of a donkey. The poor animal was tottering under the heavy load and couldn't walk straight. So he gave it a couple of kicks, when it dropped the load of dirty clothes and began to run. In a panic, he shouted, "Ho, ho, stop! Stop!"

The sky and the sun thought that someone was asking them to stop going up any further. So they stopped where they are now. If that washerman had not cried "Ho, ho, stop!" at that time, the sky and the sun would have gone up and up, and they would have gone so high we would have had no sunshine or rainfall, and we wouldn't have been able to live at all. So we must really remember that washerman with gratitude.

76. The Worship of a Household God

An old woman and a young girl were pulling out weeds and grass in a field when a twig from a *togari* plant pricked the girl's ass. She leaped up at once and screamed, "*Ayyo appa, ayyo amma!*" The old woman panicked, thinking that some snake might have bitten the girl.

"What, what happened?" she asked in fear.

"This wretched twig pricked me. It pricked me so hard that I've blood there and it hurts bad."

"*Ayyo,* you fool. I was afraid a snake or something had bitten you. You cry now for a twig. What will you do when your husband's prick is thrust in there? You'll cry loud enough for the whole town to hear, I'm sure."

These words stuck in the young girl's mind.

She got married. On the first night, the family left her and her bridegroom alone in the bedroom. She talked and laughed for a while, but whenever the husband came near her she slipped away from his grasp. She wouldn't let him touch her. She was running from corner to corner as he came close. He tried all sorts of tricks, but she never gave him her body. The whole night passed this way, and the husband left in the morning.

He came back and tried again the next day and the next and the next. But she never let him get anywhere near her. He began to worry about it. Then he thought it might get better if he took her to his house. But she just wouldn't lie next to him anywhere. He felt dejected. He couldn't eat or sleep properly. Whatever he did, his thoughts circled around his wife's refusal to sleep with him. He was full of suspicions about her as well.

When he stood in the field thinking these thoughts, a shepherd came there driving his herd. He saw this fellow standing there dazed, and asked, "What are you so full of thoughts for? A newly married man like you should be laughing all day, giving friends *bidis* and betel leaves. You've barely been married for three days. Your head is already between your legs. What's wrong?"

He felt too shy to tell the shepherd his problem. He stuttered about this and that. The shepherd finally got it out of him.

"My wife is very nice, she laughs and talks to me. But she runs away when I try to lie down with her. She is scared or something. I don't understand it. What shall I do?"

The shepherd laughed and said, "O, is that all? Don't worry too much about it. I'll tell you what to do." Then he whispered something in his ear and said, "Do as I tell you. She'll hang around your neck all day and she'll hate to be away from you even for a minute."

The man came home, ate his meal, and said to his wife, "Tomorrow we shall celebrate the festival of our household god. We fast till midday, wipe and clean the whole house, and then offer worship to our god. Nothing should be polluted. You understand?" Then he went to sleep on the verandah.

She woke up early the next morning, washed and wiped the floors, bathed herself, and also helped her husband to bathe. Then she cooked a festive meal and offered it to the god's image on a banana leaf, as was the custom. Just then the man said, "That's not the way we do it. You must take your clothes off." And he took off all his own clothes. Naked, they both lit incense and prostrated themselves before the god. Then he asked her to bring some butter. When she brought it, he asked her to put some on her vagina. When she did that, he saluted the god again and stood in front of her.

"Just keep looking at me," he said.

As she stared at him, her eyes traveled below his waist. She said, "Look, look, that thing of yours is nodding like a chameleon!"

He said, pointing to her, "It wants to eat that butter down there. That's why it's nodding its head, saying 'I want it, I want it.' "

"Go ahead, feed it," she said.

Then he came close and fed it the butter in her vagina. She said, "Go on, let him eat as much as he wants. Give him more, some more." The husband fed it all the way.

From that day on, she didn't remember the twig that pricked her once or the old woman's words. She thought only of the festival of the household god. She began to urge her husband every day, "Let's make offerings to the household god. Let's do it again." Then she would put butter on herself and urge her husband, "Come, feed your thing, feed it more butter." That's all she cared about.

77. A Story to End All Stories

A certain king was enormously learned. He knew all the arts. Once, on a whim, he sent word through his provinces that he would give a reward of a thousand rupees to anyone who could tire him out with a story; if he ever got bored and stopped saying "Hmm, hmm" to the story, he would admit defeat and pay up.

Learned pundits came to his court from over a hundred places, told him story after story till *they* got tired and sick. He continued to say "Hmm, hmm" every sentence of their telling. He never tired of it.

Finally a pundit came from the north. He told the clever king many long and involved stories. The king enjoyed them all and never once showed any sign of fatigue. The pundit exhausted himself and felt defeated. His face fell. One day, as he was walking away from the palace, utterly dejected, he met an old friend who asked him, "Why do you look so depressed?"

The pundit was happy to see him and unburdened himself of the whole story. The friend said, "Is that all? Cheer up. Take me with you tomorrow and I'll defeat him."

In spite of all the pundit's protests, the friend went with him to see the king, who gave him permission to begin a new story, and so he began one.

"Once upon a time, in a certain town, there lived a king. Near the town was a big pond. On its bank was a huge banyan tree. Right under it, a farmer had stored all his *ragi* grain in several *kanaja*s (grain containers) after harvesting and threshing the *ragi*. Thousands of sparrows lived in the banyan tree. Every sparrow would eat a grain, take a small drink of water in the pond, and fly back to perch on the tree. There were twenty enormous *kanaja*s filled with grain. Each day, a sparrow would fly down, eat a grain, take a small drink of water, and fly back to the tree. Then the next sparrow would fly down, eat a grain, take a small drink of water, and fly back to the tree," and so on.

And he went on like this for hours. The king began to get tired of saying "Hmm, hmm, hmm" to every sentence of the story. Every day, after the morning bath and food, they would gather for the story, which never seemed to end.

Again the storyteller resumed: "The grains of *ragi* were not exhausted. The sparrows continued to eat. One of them would eat a grain, drink the water, and go back to the tree. Then the next one would eat a grain, take a drink . . . ," and so on.

The king was disgusted. "*Thu*, this fellow is repeating himself over and over. How can I keep on saying 'Hmm, hmm' to him?" he wondered wearily. Finally he asked the storyteller, "For days you've been telling me the story. Tell me, by now, how many *kanaja*s of grain got empty?"

"*Ayyo*, my lord, in all that I've told you these many days, not even one quarter of a *kanaja* was eaten by the sparrows. There's so much more left for the sparrows to eat and for me to tell. So one of them ate a grain, drank the water, and went back to the tree. And then the next one . . . ," and so on.

The king's heart sank. For days, he had hardly been able to attend to any of his household or state affairs. "When will all the twenty *kanajas* get over? *Ayyo, ayyo,* how many more days will it take? How long,

O lord!" he cried within himself. He was afraid he would be stuck with saying "Hmm, hmm" for months. So he said to the storyteller, "You win. You're a great storyteller. With your story, you've brought me the biggest headache of my life. You've achieved something that none of the great pundits could achieve with their beautiful stories. You're greater than all."

Then he gave the man his reward of a thousand rupees and was happy to see the pair of them go.

As soon as they were outside, the two friends skipped with joy that they had taught a foolish king a lesson. "We've done it," they said. "Never more will he trouble a learned man or a storyteller."

A Flowering Tree
A Woman's Tale

[Note: AKR wrote this essay to be presented as a lecture in 1991 at a conference on language and gender at the University of Minnesota. In this unrevised paper, we have left the oral style intact. Our intention was to indicate the type of in-depth analysis that each of the tales in this volume richly deserves but that unfortunately AKR did not live to complete. —Eds.]

In this short paper, I shall present a story about a woman, told by women in the Kannada-speaking areas of south India, hoping that you will hear even through my translation the voice of the woman teller; then offer a reading of it for discussion; and suggest, in passing, certain characteristics of the genre of women-centered tales.

Indian folktales told around the house usually have animals, men, women, and couples as central characters. There may be other second-ary characters like supernatural beings, both divine and demonic, but they are not the focus of domestic oral tales. If the tales are comic, they invert and parody the values of the serious ones. In them kings, tigers, and demons, even gods and goddesses can be figures of fun and act as morons, as they do not in the serious ones. King and clown change places. Thus the folktales of a culture have a number of contrast-ing genres that are in dialogue with each other. Each kind of tale has special characteristics, its own "chronotope," if one wishes to invoke Bakhtin.

For instance, animal tales tend to be political: about how the power-less, the small, and the cunning sidestep or outwit the powerful. It is not surprising therefore that the *Pañcatantra,* a book of tales meant to educate princes on the ways of the world, should consist mostly of animal tales. Where men are the protagonists, especially in tales of quest, women are secondary: they are usually part of the prize, along with half a kingdom; sometimes they help the hero in his quest for the magic flower or do his derring-do (get the milk of a tigress or whatever) and slay the ogre, thereby qualifying him to marry her and receive his half of the kingdom. These stories end in marriage—for they speak of the emancipation of the hero from the parental yoke and the setting up of a new family, as he comes into his own.

In women-centered tales, by contrast, the heroine is either already married or she is married early in the tale, and then the woman's troubles begin. In a tale called "The Crab Prince" or "The Fish Prince" (*edikumāra, mīnakumāra*), the young woman is often sold or married to a wild, murderous animal bridegroom, and the rest of the story tells you how she made him human, handsome, and gentle. In another, she marries a man fated to die soon, as Savitri does in the classic tale, and vies with Yama, the God of Death, tricking him into giving her husband a long life, among other things. In "The Dead Prince and the Talking Doll" tale (No. 12), he's already dead, astrologers having predicted that he would lie as a dead man till a good woman served him for twelve years (or pulled out the thousands of needles from his body), after which he comes to life.

In such tales, not only is the pattern of the tale different (not easily accommodated by Propp's schemes, which work well for male-centered tales), but the same symbols that occur elsewhere may take on different meanings. For instance, a snake in a male-centered tale is usually something to be killed, a rival phallus, if you will. In women-centered tales, that is, where women are the protagonists and also usually the tellers, snakes are lovers, husbands, uncles, donors, and helpers[1]. Thus, the meaning of the elements, the interpretation of the symbolism, depends on what kind of tale it is: a snake in an animal tale, in a male-centered tale, and in a women-centered tale is not the same animal. Symbols, far from being universal, do not even mean the same thing as you move from genre to genre. So the gender of the genre, if one may speak of such—and surely the gender of the teller, the listener, and the interpreter—becomes important in interpretation. A woman's culturally constructed life-forms, her meaning-universe, is different from a man's

---

1. See A. K. Ramanujan 1991b; and Sudhir Kakar 1989.

in such tales. This simple-minded essay is meant to further the exploration of this universe of women's discourse.[2]

Other kinds of women's tales counter various constructs and stereotypes (held by both men and women), like the passive female victim, conceptions of karma, or even chastity. As I've spoken of these elsewhere, I'd like to talk today of a tale that speaks of a woman's creativity, her agency, and of the way it is bound up with her capacity for speech. The rest of this paper will speak in some detail of one story, "A Flowering Tree" (No. 19), collected in several versions in Karnataka over the past twenty years by me and fellow-folklorists. [AKR's translation of the tale here is omitted.]

One could say many things about this story. For instance, one of its themes resonates with our present concerns with ecology and conservation. Each time the heroine becomes a tree, she begs the person who is with her to treat it/her gently, not to pluck anything more than the flowers. Indeed, we were told by our mothers when we were children not to point to growing plants in the garden with our sharp fingernails, but only with our knuckles; our fingernails might scratch the growing ends. Poems like the following in classical Tamil speak of the sisterhood between a woman and a tree:

What Her Girl Friend Said

to him (on her behalf) when he came by daylight

Playing with friends one time
we pressed a ripe seed
into the white sand
and forgot about it
till it sprouted

and when we nursed it tenderly
pouring sweet milk with melted butter,
Mother said,

2. This essay is part of a series which may be called Women's Tales: They Tell a Different Story. See Ramanujan 1982a, 1982b, 1989, 1991b, 1993. As suggested in these papers, different kinds of women's materials are relevant in constructing proverbs and riddles used by women, women saints' lives and poems, tales and *vratakathas* told by women in women-only contexts, wedding songs, retellings of myths and epics by women, and so on. Folktales are a part of this "female tradition" yet to be explored and seen as a whole vis-à-vis other parts of the culture. The folktale universe itself (both men's and women's tales) is in a dialogic relation to the more official mythologies of the culture.

"It qualifies
as a sister to you, and it's much better
than you,"
praising this laurel tree.

So
we're embarrassed
to laugh with you here

> O man of the seashore
> with glittering waters
> where white conch shells,
>   their spirals turning right,
> sound like the soft music
> of bards at a feast.

Yet, if you wish,
there's plenty of shade
elsewhere.

Anon., Naṟṟiṇai 172 [Ramanujan,
Poems of Love and War (1985), p. 33.]

Or the Virasaiva poem that connects the gentle treatment of plants
with other kinds of love, by Dasareswara, a saint who wouldn't even
pluck flowers for his god but only pick up the ones that had dropped
to the ground by themselves:

Knowing one's lowliness
in every word;

the spray of insects in the air
in every gesture of the hand;

things living, things moving
come sprung from the earth
under every footfall;

and when holding a plant
or joining it to another
or in the letting it go

> to be all mercy
> to be light
> as a dusting brush
> of peacock feathers:

such moving, such awareness
is love that makes us one

with the Lord
Dasarēśwara.

Dasarēśwara [Ramanujan,
Speaking of Śiva (1973), pp. 54–55]

When a woman is beautiful, they say in Kannada, "One must wash one's hands to touch her" (*kai tolakondu muttabeku*).

There is also the suggestion that a tree is vulnerable to careless handling like a woman. A tree that has come to flower or fruit will not be cut down; it is treated as a mother, a woman who has given birth. Thus the metaphoric connections between a tree and a woman are many and varied in the culture. A relevant one here is that the words for "flowering" and "menstruation" are the same in languages like Sanskrit and Tamil. In Sanskrit, a menstruating woman is called a *puspavati*, "a woman in flower," and in Tamil, *pūttal* ("flowering") means "menstruation." Menstruation itself is a form and a metaphor for a woman's special creativity. Thus a woman's biological and other kinds of creativity are symbolized by flowering. In this tale, as in a dream, the metaphor is literalized and extended. The heroine literally becomes a tree, producing flowers without number over and over again, as the occasion requires. It is her special gift, which she doesn't wish to squander or even display.

She makes her secret known to her sister first only because they have no money, because she wishes to save her mother from some of the rigors of poverty. After that, her gift becomes known to others and she has to display it at their bidding.

As described in the tale, of the five times she becomes a tree, she does it voluntarily only the first and the last times. The second time, her mother orders her to show her how she has earned her money, because she suspects her of selling her body. Then the prince eavesdrops on one of these transformations and wants to have such a woman for himself. Once he gets her, he compels her to become a tree in his bedchamber on his wedding night, and on every night thereafter. It becomes almost a sexual ritual, a display of her spectacular talent to turn him on, so that they can sleep together on the flowers from her body. Even before she gets used to it, thanks to the flowers that pile up outside her bedroom window, her young adolescent sister-in-law becomes curious, puts her eye to a chink in their door, and wants to show her off to her companions. She uses her clout as an in-law (and her mother's) to coerce her to go with her alone to the orchard; she and her pubescent teenage girlfriends tease her ("Will you do it only for your lovers?"), play on the sexual nature of her talent, and force her to become a tree. And, despite her abject requests not to hurt her, they ravage the tree; when she is returned to her human state, she too is left ravaged, mutilated. It is a progressive series of violations till she finally ends up being a "thing."

In a way, people have begun to treat her as a thing, asking her "to make a spectacle of herself" by displaying her secret gift. One might say that even the first time she herself becomes a tree to sell her flowers she makes of herself a commodity. The fifth and last time she becomes a tree she has to wait for the right person and the safe occasion, another bedchamber, in an older, married sister-in-law's household, with a husband who has missed her and searched for her and thereby changed.

These five occasions seem pointedly to ask the question: when is a woman safe in such a society? She is safe with her own sister,[3] maybe with her mother, but not quite with a newly wedded husband who cares more for a display of her talent than for her safety, and most certainly not with her teenage sister-in-law or her mother-in-law. She is safe only with a married sister-in-law (who is probably not threatened or envious) and, lastly, with a husband who, through an experience of loss, has matured enough to care for her as a person.

As I said earlier, she is most vulnerable when she is a tree. She can neither speak nor move. She is most open to injury when she is most attractive, when she is exercising her gift of flowering. Each time she

---

3. In women's tales, the true antagonist as well as the helper for a woman is another woman, just as in the men's tales the hero battles always with an older male, a father-figure, often with brothers. Stepmothers, stepsisters, mothers-in-law, sisters-in-law, rival women who usurp the heroine's place abound in these tales. In the tale of "The Lamp-stand Woman" (No. 36), even Fate is Mother Fate. (In a man's tale, Outwitting Fate, Fate is Brahma, a male.) Men in women's tales are usually wimps, under the thumbs of their mothers or other wives; mostly they are absent. Sometimes they are even dead, waiting to be revived by their wives' ministrations. Mother-in-law tales in south India have no fathers-in-law. The wife and the mother share a single male figure (who is both son and husband); the older and younger woman are rivals for power over him. In other tales, where the central figure is an active heroine, she may battle with a man, usually a husband—sometimes she has to rescue him from his scrapes, often from bondage to another woman. In a tale called "A Wager" (No. 72, an Indian oral tale, found also in the eleventh-century *Kathāsaritsāgara;* it is also the story of Shakespeare's *All's Well That Ends Well,* which he gets from Italian novella writers, who probably got it from India), she talks back or outriddles an arrogant spoiled prince, who vows that he will punish her for outtalking him. In a number of tales with active heroines, as in The Peasant's Clever Daughter, she answers every riddle that the king poses, and wins by outwitting his plans to seduce her; she has the full power of speech and uses it to her and her family's, often to the whole kingdom's, advantage.

becomes a tree, she begs the one who is pouring the water to be careful not to hurt her. Yet, paradoxically, when she is mutilated, she cannot be healed directly. She can be made whole only by becoming the tree again, becoming vulnerable again, and trusting her husband to graft and heal her broken branches.

The recurrent unit of the story is "girl becoming tree becoming girl." This is also the whole story; the recurrent unit encapsulates the career of this woman in the story. What are the differences between a woman and a tree? A woman can speak, can move, can be an agent in her own behalf in ways that a tree cannot. Yet symbolically speaking, the tree isolates and gives form to her capacity to put forth flowers and fragrance from within, a gift in which she could glory, as well as to the vulnerability that goes with it. It expresses a young woman's desire to flower sexually, and otherwise, as well as the dread of being ravaged that the very gift brings with it. In telling such a tale, older women could be reliving these early, complex, and ambivalent feelings towards their own bodies—and projecting them for younger female listeners.[4] If boys are part of the audience, as they often are, the male could imaginatively participate in them, which might change his sensitiveness towards women.

The repetition of the unit, girl becomes tree becomes girl, marks the divisions of the story, gives it its narrative time, the chronos of the "chronotope." In a typical male-centered story, it is marked by the adventures of the prince, his failures and final success, often measured in threes. The spaces in the women-centered story are marked by alternations of interior and exterior (the *akam* and *puram* of classical Tamil poetics), by alternations of domestic and public space in which the action takes place. In this story, the five instances of the transformations move from her own yard to the prince's bedchamber, then to the orchard, where it is most dangerous, and back to a second bedchamber. Indeed one of the oppositions between a woman and a tree is that the former is an interior (*akam*) being, living both indoors and having an interior space, a heart, all of which are meant by the South Dravidian term *akam*, while the latter lives outdoors, in public space (*puram*). It is one of the ironies of this story that she is forced to become a tree in the wrong space, in the bedchamber. And when she becomes a tree in the orchard, the greatest harm comes to her. These emphasize the special symbolic charge of the tree: it's not any old tree, but a phase in a human career; its past and future are human and female, capable of

---

4. I am indebted to a discussion with Sudhir Kakar for this formulation.

living both within and without. Such is the time-space, the chronotope, of this woman's tale. Other women's tales also play with this balance and alternation between interiors and exteriors.

In the orchard, with the wild pubescent girls, she becomes a tree, full of fears that are all too real, and she is unable to return to her whole human female being: she becomes a "thing," something that has the face of a woman but the helplessness of the tree. She is neither woman nor tree but both, betwixt and between. The "thing" cannot move by itself and does not speak. She lives in the servants' quarters, both within and without. It is only when she speaks to a "significant other," her husband in this tale, and tells him her story that she is able to return to her original female body. She waits for recognition by him. She waits to tell her story in its entirety and give him instructions on how to heal her: pour water on her, and, when she becomes a tree, to lovingly put back the broken leaves and branches in their place, and pour the water on them—and she will be whole again. This is also the time when she voluntarily and for her own good undergoes the transformation. She has recovered her agency.

I would suggest that agency in these women's tales is connected with their being able to tell their own story and with its being heard.[5] After the first time, every time she protests that she doesn't wish to become a tree she is not heard; she is forced to do so against her will. Many women's tales end with this kind of self-story being told and being heard. Very often, as in the story of "The Dead Prince and the Talking Doll" (No. 12), it is told in the next room to a lamp or a talking doll, which says Hmm Hmm! as a human listener would when he hears a story. And the husband overhears it and learns the truth about his wife. It moves her from being a silent or unheard woman to a speaking person with a story to tell. Indeed, the whole tale tells the story of how this woman acquires a story through experience, mostly suffering; till then she has had no story to tell. In some tales, as in "The Lampstand Woman" (No. 36), this is explicit: she is usually a princess whose life is a blank at the beginning; she marries and her troubles begin. She be-

---

5. In other tales there are other ways of being an agent in her own behalf: for instance, in tales of abandoned wives who have to travel, often to rescue their own dastardly husbands, they travel in male disguise—as women writers like George Eliot and Charlotte Brontë often wrote under male pseudonyms. In some tales, they are not safe with their brothers or fathers who have incestuous designs on them, though the folktale universe, as it explores many different emotions and attitudes to the same situation, also presents protective brothers, though rarely protective fathers.

comes a servant, usually in her own sister-in-law's house, is accused of stealing a child's necklace, and is punished. Her head is shaved and a lamp is placed on a cow dung patty and slapped on her shaved head. She becomes a living lampstand and has to light the path of visitors. But she hardly speaks till her suffering reaches its nadir, and her husband from whom she is separated arrives, and she has to light his path to his bed. He doesn't recognize her, asks for a story; she tells her own story, and as the story proceeds it dawns on the husband that he is in the presence of his own wife, who is now a Lampstand Woman, to whom all these horrible things have happened unbeknownst to him. When the whole story is recapitulated in her own voice, he recognizes her, and the tale ends in reunion.

One may add that speech not only means agency for the woman but also sexuality. In many Kannada tales, the phrase for sexual intimacy between a woman and a man is "they talked to each other." In a tale about a husband who is not sleeping with his wife, the forlorn wife is asked by a caring old woman, "Isn't your husband talking to you?" When she hears he is not, she proceeds to find ways of making the husband first talk to the wife even angrily: she asks the young woman to put pebbles in his yogurt or rice, or to pack salt into his curry so that he will get angry with her and they can have words. At the end of "The Dead Prince" story, the prince and the young woman are found "talking to each other all night."

Since writing the above regarding the transformation of the "dumb" woman to a speaking person, and the relation of speech to a woman's agency, I came across Ruth Bottigheimer's pages on speech in the Grimms' household tales, especially in their "Cinderella" (Bottigheimer 1987:ch. 6). She points out how speech is an indication of power. Many recent sociolinguistic works have been concerned with the question of who speaks when, for discourse is a form of domination, and speech use is "an index of social values and the distribution of power within a society" (Bottigheimer 1987:51. For an extensive bibliography on the subject, see Thorne, Kramarae, and Henley 1983).

In English, one speaks of "having a voice, having a say"; in German, *mundig* (from the word for "mouth") means legal majority, legal personhood. The poor do not have it; they are silent. Women, like children, should be seen, not heard. The good woman has a soft low voice and says little: Cordelia in *King Lear* is praised for it. Eve's sin begins with her speaking to Satan. "Since the early days of the Church, women had been barred from speaking in the house of god, as well as preaching, teaching, or speaking in public," says Judith Brown in her *Immodest Acts, The Life of a Lesbian Nun in Renaissance Italy* (Brown 1986:59–60). There are many jokes about garrulous women: women, generally speaking, are generally speaking.

In the folktales that Wilhelm Grimm rewrote in his later editions, as a male rewriting women's tales, he gives women little direct speech; he also substitutes *sagen* ("said") for *sprechen* ("spoke"), as the latter is more forthright. *Sprechen* emphasizes the act of speaking, and *sagen* the content of an utterance (Bottigheimer 1987:55). In W. Grimm's last version of "Cinderella" (1857), Cinderella, the good girl, speaks only once in direct speech; the bad women, the stepsisters and the step-mother, five and seven times; the prince in authority has eight direct speeches, and the ineffectual father only three—and two of them are mere thoughts. However, this feature may be different in different cultures: in Danish variants, where women have greater freedom and power, Cinderella is not gagged as in the German ones. It would be interesting to ask similar questions in the Indian context, especially of tales that are told by both men and women. It would also be important to see how men like myself interpret these tales and what biases they bring to them. That's one of the reasons for presenting this paper to this audience.

The fact that women have either been silent or written for the drawer, as Emily Dickinson did, or written under male disguises and pseudonyms is related to this taboo on women's speech. The many women writers and artists in all three worlds directly address such taboos, both gross and subtle, that still exist across many cultures.

Notes on the Tales

[It was clearly the intention of A. K. Ramanujan (hereafter AKR) to provide complete notes for each and every folktale included in this collection. Unfortunately, he did not live long enough to finish that task. We decided to include the two dozen or so sketches of such notes and to leave them unedited (except for obvious misspellings and incomplete references to sources) with the full awareness that they would have been revised and amplified by AKR. Note that when AKR places "Ind." after a tale type number (e.g., 455 Ind.), he is suggesting that the tale in question is an Indic variant of the Aarne-Thompson (hereafter AT) tale type; see also AKR's incomplete notes on tellers and collectors, which are printed here as an appendix. We have added tale type and motif identifications wherever AKR had not provided them or where we believe another identification is possible. All such editorial additions are contained in brackets. In those instances where we could find no tale type identifier, we have noted "No known tale type" (NKTT). This does not mean that the tale in question is not a bona fide tale type but only that it is not to be found in the standard tale type indices:

Aarne, Antti, and Stith Thompson. *The Types of the Folktale*. 2nd revision. FF Communications No. 184. Helsinki: Academia Scientiarum Fennica, 1961.

Bødker, Laurits. *Indian Animal Tales: A Preliminary Survey*. FF Communications 170. Helsinki: Academia Scientiarum Fennica, 1957.

Jason, Heda. *Types of Indic Oral Tales Supplement*. FF Communications No. 242. Helsinki: Academia Scientiarum Fennica, 1989.

Thompson, Stith, and Warren E. Roberts. *Types of Indic Oral Tales: India, Pakistan, and Ceylon*. FF Communications 180. Helsinki: Academia Scientiarum Fennica, 1960.

For tales not to be found in the above standard reference sources, we consulted the relevant motif indices:

Thompson, Stith. *Motif-Index of Folk-Literature*. 6 vols. Bloomington: Indiana University Press, 1955–1958.
Thompson, Stith, and Jonas Balys. *The Oral Tales of India*. Indiana University Publications Folklore Series No. 10. Bloomington: Indiana University Press, 1958.

The fact that more than a third of this rich Kannada corpus of traditional folktales is not identifiable by tale type number suggests that the task of tale-typing Indic folktales is by no means yet complete. When a revision of the Aarne-Thompson index is undertaken, we trust that all the tales contained in this anthology will be included.—Eds.]

1. A Story and a Song

TYPES AND MOTIFS

We need a special name and index number for stories about stories like this one. I would suggest a new set of motifs under Q 390, Punishment for not telling stories. The tale types could be listed under a new division added at the end of the international index as 2500, Stories About Stories. They may have to be cross-listed under numbers like 516, as such metastories enlist or combine with other types. For instance, in another Kannada tale, four stories that a man keeps to himself seek to revenge themselves by throwing down a boulder, breaking a branch over his head, becoming fishhooks in his food, and a snake in his bedchamber. A friend who hears them talk while he is asleep saves the man from these perils, exactly as in AT 516, Faithful John.

COMMENTARY

For obvious reasons I have placed this story about the perils of not telling the stories you know at the beginning of the book. This story is a story about why stories should be told. They are told because they cry out to be told. If they are not, they rankle and take revenge. Here the story and the song transform themselves into material objects. For futher comments on this genre, see Ramanujan 1989.

In this worldview nothing is ever lost, only transformed. Untold stories and unsung songs become shoes and coats, and take revenge against the niggardly nontellers. Material and nonmaterial things are all made of one substance, according to a familiar Hindu point of view; some are *sthula*, "gross," others are *suksma*, "subtle." Nothing is truly destroyed—things are displaced, converted, transformed, according to a belief in the "conservation of matter."

The flames of lamps don't get extinguished at night: when they are put out, they simply move from home to temple, and return to the wicks when the lamps are lit again next evening. Such a belief is part of a more extensive folklore about lamps. The flame is personified as Jyotiyamma (Sanskrit *jyoti*, "flame, light" + Kannada *amma*, "mother, lady"), the lamp as mother and goddess. Today, some people worship even the electric light switches with turmeric and vermilion. In a family household, lamps must be lit at sunset and should not be extinguished by blowing on them (it's like spitting on them); one speaks euphemistically of "filling a lamp" (*dīpa tumbu*), not of "putting out a lamp." One should remember and fold one's hands worshipfully to one's gods, especially to Lakshmi, the goddess of good fortune, as a lamp is lit— for she comes in at that auspicious hour by the front door and will leave by the back door if it is open. So every evening, at lamp-lighting time, the front door is kept open and the back door shut. Anytime one wishes fervently for something or when one hears good news, one lights a floor lamp for the family gods. Weddings, temple services, all kinds of auspicious rituals have lamps as part of them. Lamps are lit at inaugural ceremonies, dramatic or dance performances, arrayed in rows in the month of Kartika (corresponding to November/December) and Sravana (July/August). Divali or Dipavali is an annual festival of lamps. Great temples have special calendrical festivals in which hundreds are lit. In every temple, as well as in the gods' room in a house, shrine lamps must burn ceaselessly. If a lamp goes out suddenly, it's an ill omen. Thus lamps and flames are symbols of life, wealth, family happiness. The belief that they never truly go out, only move out temporarily, is part of a wishful need for their unremitting auspicious presence.

[No known tale type (henceforth abbreviated NKTT), but it appears to be Motif N 454.2, King overhears conversations of lamps (India only, henceforth abbreviated IO).]

2.   Acacia Trees

TYPES AND MOTIFS

Tale type AT 722 Ind. We need a new number for tales like "Acacia Trees," an incest tale. I would suggest 722 Ind., Brother Wishes to Marry Sister, or 451B Ind., because it expresses an extreme or pathological form of the brother-sister bond.

Tale types AT 450–455 are tales about brothers and sisters, mostly expressing love for each other, sister seeking and rescuing brothers (or vice versa) who are in danger or under a spell, transformed into monkeys, cows, or birds. Aarne-Thompson classifies such incest tales under AT 722, which begins with a brother wanting to marry his sister, who flees from him, and lists them only for Russian. Thompson-Roberts (1960) does not report them at all for India. We have many examples of Type AT 722 in Kannada and other Indian languages.

VARIANTS

In other Kannada tellings, a) the brother and sister fall into a pond and are transformed into fish. Later, a thorn tree grows out of the bones of the brother-fish, and a fruit tree from the bones of the sister-fish; b) when the sister jumps into the water, the moon takes her away into his moon-world, marries her, and gives her children.

COMMENTS

Among the many brother-sister relations detailed by Kannada tales, we have chosen only three: incest, brotherly/sisterly love, sibling rivalry. "Acacia Trees" is the most explicit treatment of a brother's incestuous wish for his sister. In "Hanchi," the "Kannada Cinderella" story, the heroine is forced to flee when her brother falls in love with her. The motif of the young woman fleeing from a father's or brother's incest appears often in these tales. See Aarne-Thompson on 510B for European examples. [See Ramanujan 1983.]

In many Indian communities, brothers take ritual pledges to love and protect their sisters. These pledges emphasize a woman's social and economic need for protection by a male in her natal family when she has no way of protecting herself. The ritual pledge protects the woman from the brother's own desires as well. The traditional enmity between the husband's sister and his wife may be traced to this pledge and to the lifelong bond between brother and sister that is threatened by the alien woman who marries the brother.

[Motif R 224, Girl flees to escape incestuous brother + AT 780, The Singing Bone.]

3. The Adventures of a Disobedient Prince

TYPES AND MOTIFS

Type AT 923, Love Like Salt + AT 413, Marriage by Stealing Clothing + AT 465A, The Man Persecuted Because of his Beautiful Wife + AT 554, The Grateful Animals.

As indicated above, this complex romantic tale has several sections, which often occur as independent segments or tales:

(1) The hero is banished by his father, who wishes to hear praise of himself. This action propels the hero out of his home into the wide world. This is a variant of 923, Love Like Salt, better known in the West for its use in the King Lear story. Characteristically, in this Indian tale, not daughters but sons are questioned and tested by the old father. In the traditional Indian familial pattern, the sons stay in the paternal home, while daughters are expected to leave, become part of another family, love (and obey) the men they marry. A Kannada proverb says, *kotta hennu kulakke horage*, "A daughter given away [in marriage] is outside the family." Note how the Japanese adaptation of Lear in the film *Ran* also changed the daughters into sons. Yet 923B, The Princess Who Was Responsible for Her Own Fortune, in which an unmarried daughter defies her father, marries a poor, weird, or diseased man and makes him rich through her wit, is also told widely in India.

(2) Marriage by stealing clothing (413 Ind.): The hero meets an old woman (Motif N 825) who asks him not to go in a certain direction, but he does (Z 211) and sees celestial maidens bathing. He steals the sari of one of the bathing women (H 1335) and runs, but he looks back and is turned to stone. The old woman restores him (Z 121.3) and he succeeds a second time. The celestial woman lives with him as his wife as long as he keeps her sari, which is stitched into his thigh. This sequence of events occurs in many classic Indian collections of novellas like the Sanskrit *Daśakumāracarita* or the Tamil *Madanakāmarājan*.

(3) The king covets the hero's wife (AT 465A) and, on the advice of wicked counselors, assigns him dangerous tasks, which he performs with the aid of his celestial wife or wives. Each quest takes him to a different world (the subterranean world of serpents, the undersea world, etc.); in each, he marries another celestial princess. The final task sends the hero to get news of the king's ancestors. On his wife's advice, he jumps into a crater of fire, enters the netherworld, is helped by the

god of fire, and returns radiant with the daughter of the Fire God as his bride. He persuades the king and his wicked counselors to likewise enter the fire so that they too can visit heaven. They plunge to their deaths.

(4) He is reconciled to his father, who is by now impoverished (like Lear). He entrusts his mother with the safekeeping of the celestial's sari, but she naively lets the celestial wives take it, which at once allows them to fly back to heaven, leaving him destitute. This action starts the hero on his last set of adventures. He goes to heaven in quest of his wives. Indra, the king of heaven, imposes four tasks on him (AT 577), which he accomplishes and thereby wins his four wives legitimately, with Indra's blessing. He accomplishes these through grateful animals (AT 554)—ants, a crocodile, a bee, and a bharani bug, all of whom he has helped in his previous journeys. Sections of this tale, like the last one, are told both in Asia and in Europe, retold in famous collections like the *Kathāsaritsāgara* and the Arabian Nights, as well as in European collections like the Grimms' in German and Afanas'ev's in Russian. The story is known to Indonesia, central Africa, and the French in Missouri.

COMMENTS

This type of tale carries a paradigm, a scenario, for the initiation of a young man: he is banished from the parental home, meets up with an old woman or man who serves as a mentor, sees celestial women naked, and brings one of them home by stealing what covers her naked beauty; he then fights against a father/king who covets his wives and who sets him tasks, sends him on dangerous quests to different realms (like earth, air, fire, and water), where he marries the princess of each; finally, he loses his wife, whom he had originally won by deception, and has to win her again by legitimate accomplishments, by doing tasks set by his bride's father—another father-figure who is loath to let his daughters go. He accomplishes them with the help of animals whom he has helped earlier, creatures that represent different realms, like earth, air, and water in this tale. His last task is that of distinguishing his true spouse from among illusory look-alikes. A mere redescription of these motifs suggests that they could be read in psychological terms as steps in a novice's progress towards mastery and adult selfhood: conflict with different kinds of father-figures, enlisting the help of various feminine figures, winning through kindness the support of the animal world. The very last scene of the story completes the drama when he demonstrates to his own father his married bliss with his four wives (from four realms), thereby realizing his original wish to rival and surpass his father, for which he had been banished in the first place.

The aesthetic intricacy and finish, the smooth progression from task to task, and the rounding out of the frame tale (father banishes son, son rescues father, finally son proves himself to father, the last scene fulfilling the very first) are very much a part of the hero's reaching maturity. An accomplished tale embodies the accomplished hero; the aesthetic form enacts the ethos.

[Motif H 508.1, King propounds questions to his sons to determine successor + AT 413, Marriage by Stealing Clothing; AT 465, The Man Persecuted Because of his Beautiful Wife; AT 554, The Grateful Animals.]

4. Bride for a Dead Man

[AT 934B, The Youth to Die on his Wedding Day (but cf. Thompson and Roberts, *Types of Indic Oral Tales*, type 336, The Bridegroom and the Picture of the Tiger; and Jason, *Supplement,* type 934B-*A, Escape from Death. Cf. also Motif E 121.1, Resuscitation by a god.) This tale includes elements of both the Markandeya story and the Savitri story, which are told widely in India.]

5. A Brother, a Sister, and a Snake

[AT 450A, The Brother Transformed to a Snake.]

6. A Buffalo Without Bones

[AT 653B, The Suitors Restore the Maiden to Life (IO).]

7. Cannibal Sister

TYPES AND MOTIFS

Type AT 315A, The Cannibal Sister, is a special Indian variant of Type AT 315, The Faithless Sister. In other Indian variants, the cannibal is a father/king, an older sister (fought by the younger), or a sister-in-law. In each case, the psychological nuance would be different: for instance, the cannibal father would express fear of an all-devouring father, but a cannibal sister-in-law would indicate suspicion of and rivalry with a female outsider who usurps one's brother.

COMMENTS

In this tale, an aspect of brother/sister relations is explored—the reverse of the loving ones, as in AT 450 or 450A (see No. 5, A Brother, a Sister, and a Snake), where brother and sister save and protect one another. Here the younger sibling, the newcomer to the family, is seen as a predator, a destroyer of the very family she is born into, and therefore fit only to be destroyed. As in all such cases, projection of the older child's own murderous feelings is never absent. Furthermore, the tale explores the fear of the evil child, the "bad seed" (a favorite motif of horror movies), or of the psychotic or grasping relative who devours and savages an entire extended family—which depends for its existence on the limits placed on any one person's use of others' attention and resources. Such tales also more than hint at the fear and hatred of the strange new child who supplants the older child in the affection of the parents. The tale, of course, is told from the point of view of the triumphant savior, the older child, the survivor.

8.   Chain Tale

TYPES AND MOTIFS

Type AT 2045A. See the note on the next chain tale, which is a full-blown example.

COMMENTS

Our first chain tale is an ancient one, first recorded in the *Kathāsaritsāgara* (eleventh century). It is a satire on world-renouncers, who begin by trying to reject sex, property, and desire in order to get out of the wheel of ordinary human life (*samsara*). But they get caught up by one tiny desire, which leads to another, which leads to still another desire, starting an endless series. They are caught in the wheel, and they are householders again. It all hangs by a G-string, a loincloth, one repression. One isn't sure whether it's a real mouse outside or the mouse within the loincloth that gnaws at it.

[For another published version of this tale, see Narayan 1989:114–115.]

9. Another Chain Tale: What an Ant Can Do

COMMENTS

Chain tales, cumulative tales, and formula tales are closely related genres. Their audience tends to be small children under five, who love the games of repetition and the linguistic play characteristic of their stage of development. Cumulative tales (like "The House That Jack Built" in English) are designed like a game. As Thompson (1946, p. 230) says, "since the accumulating repetitions must be recited exactly, . . . many of these tales maintain their form unchanged over long periods . . . and in very diverse environments. . . . A simple phrase or clause is repeated over and over again, always with new additions, working up to a long final routine containing the entire sequence." This final sentence is in the nature of a formula, often in verse—so such tales are often called "formula tales." Chain tales are cumulative tales with a stricter narrative logic: every additional episode is dependent on the previous one. Many of them are centered on animal actors, usually small animals—ants, parrots, monkeys—and their ingenuity or folly. Told as they are to small children, stories about the cleverness of a helpless little thing like an ant and its final victory over larger arrogant animals are appealing.

Such tales are usually structured towards a bilateral symmetry: the first part is a series of rejections, in this tale by frog, snake, snake charmer, rat, cat, dog, stick, and boy. Once the ant stings the boy and he agrees to do the ant's bidding, the series unfolds in reverse order until the ant's original desire (to save its young baby) is accomplished. If the first part is A> B> C> D . . . the second is . . . D> C> B> A.

[NKTT, but cf. AT 2034E, The Bird Seeks a Mason to Free Its Young (IO).]

10. The Clever Daughter-in-law

TYPES AND MOTIFS

Type AT 1535 Ind., Mothers-in-law and Daughters-in-law. Many of the incidents of Type 1535, The Rich and The Poor

Peasant, are transposed to mother-in-law and daughter-in-law stories in south India. The clever daughter-in-law is persecuted; often the mother-in-law even tries to murder her (S 51.1), but the young woman survives all and finally triumphs. In some tales, the daughter-in-law tricks the mother-in-law into taking her place in the sack that will be thrown into the river (Motif K 842) or, as in this tale, comes back from the forest with the robbers' loot (AT 1653) and terrifies the mother-in-law into submission.

COMMENTS

In the present tale, two other independent tales are woven in: AT 956B, The Clever Maiden at Home Alone Kills the Robber(s), where she bites off his tongue, and a tale about a clever woman who subdues the god(dess). In the latter comic tale, told all over south India, the persecuted daughter-in-law takes a favorite dish to the Monkey God's (or Goddess's) temple, which is usually outside the village and often deserted, eats it all with relish while the god(dess) looks on longingly and puts his hand on his mouth or nose as a gesture of astonishment. The change in posture of the god's stone image causes a commotion, and the daughter-in-law undertakes (for a reward) to set it right. She either threatens to beat the god (or goddess) with a broomstick or, worse still, threatens to fart in his face. As she proceeds to make good her threat, the god sets himself right.

Such mother-in-law/daughter-in-law tales seem to be endemic to India, though they use motifs and episodes from well-known types with a new twist. These tales come in two forms depicting different power relations: 1) where the mother-in-law is powerful and cruel, and 2) where the daughter-in-law is cruel (Motif S 54) and tortures the older woman, as in "Ninga on My Palm" [No. 44 in this volume].

To my knowledge, in no mother-in-law tale do we find a father-in-law alive or a strong son. (See what happens in the rare instance when a strong son is present, as in "Ninga on My Palm"). The tales presuppose a rivalry between the women for the favor of a single male figure on whom they are dependent. Traditionally, all women were supposed to be dependent on one male or another. Manu, the ancient lawgiver, decrees in a notorious sentence: "A woman is not qualified for independence. In childhood, she should be dependent on a father, in marriage on a husband, in old age on a son." Where only one male (the son) is present in the household, the scene is set for rivalry between mother and wife.

Atte, the Kannada word for mother-in-law, also means "father's sister, aunt," indicating that the two are often the same in Dravidian kinship systems: a woman can marry her *atte's,* father's sister's, son. Such a situation makes for greater continuity and intimacy between the mother's house of one's childhood and the mother-in-law's. In north Indian households (with Indo-Aryan kinship systems), where such marriage alliances are not preferred, the discontinuity is great and daughters-in-law are initally aliens. Yet, in both the north and the south, family politics, women's dependency, and the gathering of power in the hands of aging mothers, especially mothers with sons, make the mother-in-law/daughter-in-law situation one of rivalry, bitterness, and violence. The news in contemporary Indian newspapers regarding bride burnings and the persecution of daughters-in-law, as well as the thousands of nostalgic folk songs sung by women about their mother's houses (*tavarumane*), are witness to this pattern.

Many of the European tales about cruel stepmothers tend to appear in India as mother-in-law tales. There are no stepfather tales in Hindu India, as widows are traditionally forbidden to marry again.

The deficiency of our present tale type indices is clearly seen in the absence of all references to mother-in-law tales, a widespread Indian genre. Many of the tales need to be reclassified in Indian terms.

[Motif S 51.1, Cruel mother-in-law plans death of daughter-in-law (IO) + AT 1653, The Robbers under the Tree. See AKR's notes on this tale in Ramanujan 1991a:328.]

11. A Couple of Misers

TYPES AND MOTIFS

AT 750A, The Wishes. Told from Finland to Indonesia, this popular tale exemplifies the saying "When God wishes to punish, he answers one's prayers." In Europe, the god-figure is represented by Christ and/or Peter.

COMMENTS

The limited number of wishes is crucial to the point of the story—two to make mistakes with, a third wish to undo them. The third wish returns the greedy characters to where they were at the outset, chastened by the terrifying experience of their wishes coming true. This kind of tale is another warning against greed, and against trying to change your station or the status quo. The best-known European variant is, of course, Midas and the Golden Touch.

[Cf. AT 775, Midas' Short-sighted Wish]

12.   The Dead Prince and the Talking Doll

TYPES AND MOTIFS

AT 437, The Supplanted Bride (The Needle Prince). Another story like No. 4, in which a faithful wife is fated to marry a dead man but restores him to life. In Europe it is often called The Needle Prince because she "finds a seemingly dead prince whose body is covered with pins or needles and begins to remove them. When she has finally removed all but a few, she leaves the side of the prince for a moment, or falls asleep. A servant girl, etc., takes her place, removes the last few needles, and marries the restored prince. The mistake is afterwards explained" (Thompson and Roberts, p. 64). In one Indo-Iranian telling, she has to fan the corpse for seven years, but she is supplanted at the last moment.

The story is often combined with the special Indian Lear-type of AT 923B, The Princess Who Was Responsible for Her Own Fortune (Motif H 592), reported in twenty-five Indian versions.

COMMENTS

The central motif of the virtuous woman being supplanted, after she has devoted years to a husband, by a rival, a low-class false bride, is well known in European tellings as well as in Indian ones. These stories dramatize the deep fear of the competing vigor, sensuality, and guile of a lower class, as imagined by other classes. It also dramatizes the psychological split between the Black and White Bride (AT 403), two alternating aspects of the female seen from the point of view of the marrying male. The Indian tale emphasizes both the magical life-giving capacity of a devoted wife and the loneliness of a new bride in an eerie household, locked up within fourteen doors with a dead husband, as compared to the comforts of a full-scale extended family. As in other such women-centred stories, the denouement and the reversal of fortunes are effected by the recounting of the entire story.

[AT 437, The Supplanted Bride + AT 870, The Princess Confined in the Mound.]

13.   A Dog's Daughters

[NKTT, but cf. Motif T 511.1.4, Conception from eating mango (IO); Motif B 491.1, Helpful serpents; Motif Q 2, Kind and unkind.]

14.   A Dog's Story

[AT 303, The Twins or Blood-Brothers; includes Motif K 2111, Potiphar's Wife, and Motif D 765.1.2, Disenchantment by removal of enchanting pin (thorn); cf. also AT 449, The Tsar's Dog.]

15.   Dolls

TYPES AND MOTIFS

Type AT 1373.

COMMENTS

This type seems to me to represent the growth of conscience in a person who has none. This growth is accomplished by planting three dolls who speak up when the wife in No. 15 is about to do something wrong. They objectify her own conscience, or superego, if you will, when she greedily sets about eating the best parts of the fish. Such tales seem to express an understanding of the phenomenon of "projection," in which a rejected inner voice or impulse is attributed to an external object or person.

[NKTT, but cf. Motif W 125.2, Gluttonous wife eats all the meal while cooking it (IO).]

16.   Double Double

[NKTT, but cf. Motif J 2072, Short-sighted wish.]

17.   Dumma and Dummi

TYPES AND MOTIFS:

AT 1149 Ind., Ogre (or Tiger) Frightened by Children. A whole group of tales (AT 1145–1154) concerns itself with the ogre (or wild animal) frightened or overawed by a woman, a barber, or a child.

COMMENTS:

This tale about little people scaring off a big tiger is a tale told to very small children. Eating too much and breaking wind in a big way, even exploding a pumpkin with the fart, especially appeals to the scatological fancies of small children. As Martha Wolfenstein points out in her 1954 book, *Children's Humor,* children of five or six love to make (and hear) jokes about peeing, shitting, farting, etc. See also No. 60, "The Sparrow Who Wouldn't Die," and No. 58, "Sister Crow and Sister Sparrow."

[NKTT, but cf. Motif F 451.3.13.3, Dwarf breaks wind so hard he capsizes canoes, and K 1727, Tiger frightened at hearing unknown wind (IO).]

18. Dwarfs

Gulak gulak, owk owk are onomatopoetic words that are supposed to imitate the sounds made by pods rattling, dogs barking, etc. English-speaking dogs go bow-wow and Kannada dogs go *owk owk*. [For one of the early inventories of such sounds, see Antti Aarne, *Variantenverzeichnis der Finnischen Deutungen von Tierstimmen und Anderen Naturlauten* (1912), Hamina: Suomalaisen Tiedakatemian Kustantama.]

TYPES AND MOTIFS

AT 1211, The Peasant (Woman) Thinks the Cow Chewing Her Cud is Mimicking Her. Told in many languages—Finnish, Irish, Russian, Greek, Turkish, and in different regional languages of India—this tale of a dwarf's rage at being called insulting names has several Kannada variants: e.g., a man with thick lips is touchy about being called *Tutiya* ("Lippy" or "Lip-man"), hears the word in a dog's bark and kicks the dog to death. A plant grows in its burial place. He hears pods rattle and say, "*Tutiya, Tutiya!*" So he cuts them down and makes soup with them. The soup boils, making "*Tutiya, Tutiya*" noises. So he pours it into the river, which also calls him "*Tutiya, Tutiya,*" so he attacks it and finally drowns in the river. In another tale, a fool kicks goats and cows because he thinks they mimic him when they chew their cuds.

COMMENTS

In this tale on the phenomenon of paranoid projection, it is significant that it begins with the dwarf's wife calling him a midget first. Then he hears it everywhere. He cannot bury or silence the word, the shaming voice—it comes alive, transferred from wife to plant to buffalo to dog to babbling river. It is originally a toddler tale. Toddlers are just beginning to make the distinction between self and nonself. The tale plays on the confusion between the two, between human, animal, and inanimate objects, and between human words and nonhuman cries and noises. Kids laugh a great deal at the fool for not making the distinction that's beginning to seem so obvious to them. Such tales also reinforce the distinction.

[NKTT, but it is a cumulative tale involving a chain with interdependent members (Motif Z 40).]

19.   A Flowering Tree

TYPES AND MOTIFS

Various tale types seem to be enmeshed in the fabric of this moving tale; the latter part is a version of Type AT 706, The Maiden Without Hands. She becomes the wife of a king, loses hands and feet, is driven forth, gets hands and feet back, and is finally restored to her husband. This tale is seamlessly joined to the first part, which centers on the heroine's ability to become a flowering tree (Motif D 215) in order to provide flowers. While other tales (see Type AT 408, "The Pomegranate Queen," No. 49) feature a tree becoming a girl, this one reverses the usual motif.

[AT 467, The Quest for the Wonderful Flower (IO). See also AKR's comments in Ramanujan 1991a:333; and especially his extended discussion of this tale included in this book.]

20.   Flute of Joy, Flute of Sorrow

TYPES AND MOTIFS

Type AT 534 Ind. Other versions have wild buffaloes or a bull instead of a cow. In one, the hero pours milk into a snake hole; the grateful snake blesses him with a golden body. The flutes are stolen by a parrot or an old woman instead of by a crow.

This story is told all over India (twenty-four versions recorded so far) and has not been reported for other parts of the world. Its first part has an affinity with 510B, which makes it a kind of male Cinderella tale, with a cruel stepmother and protective godmothers. Cows are explicitly maternal figures in Hindu India, and are worshiped as *gomata*, "Cow Mothers." The golden hair motif (T 11.4.1) is as in Egyptian mythology.

COMMENTS

In folktales of this kind, the mother (and father) figures are split into two characters, one good, one evil. Here the "bad breast," the stepmother who feeds him leftovers and sets her husband the task of killing him, is contrasted with "the good breast" of the seven cows that give him milk and protection.

The motif of the flutes of joy and of sorrow (B 501.1) has a surprising development here. The hero, being left only with the flute of joy, can express and communicate no sorrow. All his feelings come out sounding happy on the flute of joy. It reminds one of the passage in Kierkegaard on the way the artist is fated to turn suffering into notes of music.

[AT 534, The Youth Who Tends the Buffalo Herd (IO).]

21. Fools

TYPES AND MOTIFS

Type AT 1210, The Cow Is Taken to the Roof to Graze. Type AT 1245, Sunlight Carried in a Bag into a Windowless House.

Hundreds of numskull stories (Types AT 1200–1349) are told all over India, as elsewhere. Sometimes they are organized into a series, as in the present tale or as in AT 1332, Which Is the Greatest Fool, or they are strung elaborately into whole fooltowns, as in the British tales of the men of Gotham or the Danish tales of the fools of Molbo. The best-known of these in southern India are the adventures of Paramartha Guru and His Disciples, first told in written form by Father Beschi, an Italian Jesuit who lived in Tamilnadu and wrote in Tamil in the eighteenth century. One is not sure whether he reported these from Europe or heard them locally. Yet they have certainly become part of the Tamil, Telugu, and Kannada oral traditions. [For a translation of Costantino

G. Beschi's collection, see Benjamin Babington, *The Adventures of the Gooroo Paramartan* (London: J. M. Richardson, 1822).]

Numskull tales, as in Europe, are very old, told and retold in the earliest collections like the *Jātakas* and the *Pañcatantra*. Large numbers of them punctuate the longer romances in the *Ocean of Story*.

COMMENTS

Numskull tales are often the opposite of riddles, with which they share a preoccupation with the play of logical operations and the defiance of what one would call common sense. A riddle begins with a question that seems illogical and sorts out the logic in the answer: e.g., Question: A white house without a window or a door. What is it? Answer: An egg. Numskulls begin with a logical practical question and end with a foolish illogical answer: e.g., Q: How shall we bring light into a dark house? A: In baskets. As we can see in the above example, the numskull takes a phrase like "bring light" literally.

Both riddles and numskull tales play at crossing a culture's categories (that seem logical and self-evident within a specific culture): e.g., animate/inanimate, natural/man-made (as in the above riddle about the egg being likened to a house), literal/metaphoric, material/immaterial, etc. For instance, in the present tale, sunlight is treated as a material object that can be carried from one place to another.

Riddles frequently depend on metaphors; numskull tales, on undoing the metaphors. The latter literalize metaphors. "Guard the door," says a man to the fool. The fool pulls out the door and guards it [AT 1009, Guarding the Store-room Door]. They undo the ambiguity of idioms in a language. "This rice is for the road," says the woman to the fool, who casts the rice along the way on the road. The shock, the surprises, and the fun of these tales are in the lively play across these categories.

For other uses of literalization, see No. 43, "A Ne'er-do-well," in which a con man plays the literal fool. Literalization is a much wider device: it can be used by canny jesters to make a point. Tenali Rama once offends his royal master, and the king angrily asks the jester never to show his face, so the jester walks about with a pot over his head. (For an insightful discussion of this theme, see David Shulman 1985). It can be a creative device in myth, magic, ritual, and folk medicine: to soften a lover's heart, a woman might chew a hard nut; love is supposed to be blind, so the love god is pictured as blind. In all these cases, language is primary and other forms are modeled on it. [The frame story might be related to AT 1384, The Husband Hunts Three Persons as Stupid as his Wife.]

22. A Jackal King

[NKTT, but cf. Motif J 512.13, Jackal accidentally made king but joins other jackals in howling at night. Killed (IO).]

23. For Love of Kadabu

TYPES AND MOTIFS

Type AT 1687, The Forgotten Word AT + 1351, The Silence Wager. Told widely both in India (fifteen versions recorded so far) and elsewhere, literally from China to Peru, this tale has been well studied. See Brown 1922; Clouston 1887, vol. 2:23–25.

24. A Girl in a Picture

[NKTT, but cf. Motif F 420.7.1, Visit to Water-goddess's underwater home; and Motif T 11.2, Love through sight of picture.]

25. The Glass Pillar

[NKTT, but cf. Motif Q 241, Adultery punished; Motif Q 414.0.3, Burning as punishment for adultery; and Motif K 2285, Villain disguised as ascetic nun.]

26. A Golden Sparrow

[NKTT, but cf. Motif B 103.2.1, Treasure-laying bird; Motif Q 272, Avarice punished; and Motif J 2415, Foolish imitation of lucky man.]

27. The Greatest Thing

TYPES AND MOTIFS

Type AT 2031B, The Most Powerful Idol. In the Judaic and Islamic traditions, this story is known as "Abraham Learns to Worship God," in which Abraham first worships a star at nightfall, then the moon which obscures the star, then the sun, and finally gives up idolatry.

COMMENTS

Another cumulative tale with a human actor, which satirizes human desire—here the desire to search for the greatest thing to worship. Such tales tend to have a circular, self-defeating structure. This one ends up unexpectedly with a man worshiping his own belly.

The classic tale of this kind in India is The Man Who Seeks the Greatest Being as a Husband for his Daughter, Type AT 2031C, told all over India, and told in our earliest collections—the *Jātakas,* the *Pañcatantra,* and the *Kathāsaritsāgara.* It goes like this: A sage catches a mouse, which changes into a girl. He treats her as his daughter and wants to marry her to the greatest being in the world. He begins with the sun, then goes to the cloud that covers the sun, the wind that moves the cloud, the mountain that stops the wind, and finally to a mouse that digs holes in the mountain. He changes his daughter back to a mouse and marries her to a mouse, thereby returning everything to the status quo. Such tales are arguments for the status quo, against someone wishing to live beyond the station to which he was born, and are so used in conversation.

28. Hanchi

TYPES AND MOTIFS

AT 510B, Cap O'Rushes + AT 896, Lecherous Holy Man and the Maiden in the Box.

COMMENTS

It is not surprising that in this Indian variant of a Cinderella tale the heroine is identified by the food she makes, not by a slipper. Hindus are intensely conscious of what to eat and when and of the moral and psychological consequences of eating certain foods (e.g., cow's flesh). Rules enjoin and forbid various kinds of food transactions: eating and fasting, the giving and the taking of food as a marker of caste and status. Food is classified according to principles like the three qualities (*gunas*)—Goodness, Passion, Darkness (*sattva, rajas, tamas*)—and according to medical or folk taxonomies of hot and cold.

Sex, elsewhere considered the primary source of symbolism, yields place to food. Intercourse is described in terms of eating and feeding. The Sanskrit word for sexual and other pleasure or enjoyment is *bhoga*, from the root *bhuj*, "to eat."

[For further discussion, see Ramanujan 1982a; also Ramanujan, 1956b. AT 510B, The Dress of Gold, of Silver, and of Stars.]

29.   The Horse Gram Man

[NKTT, but cf. Motif K 1317.7, Woman mistakes passer-by for lover. Substitution in the dark; Motif K 1311, Seduction by masking as woman's husband; and Motif N 275, Criminal confesses because he thinks himself accused.]

30.   Hucca

TYPES AND MOTIFS

Type AT 1643 Ind., Fools Who Sell Objects to Find Treasure + AT 1600, The Fool as Murderer. Another numskull tale, pan-Indian, which combines two tales in a series. In the first, the fool's naiveté allows him unexpectedly to come into a fortune. In the second, his clever brothers discredit him by a trick. Similar tales are told about foolish wives who cannot keep secrets, as in AT 1381, The Talkative Wife and the Discovered Treasure.

COMMENTS

In this genre, a person (the fool) confounds the human and the nonhuman, treats the bull as a baby and undertakes to bargain with a tree. In another genre of tales, say the *märchen* tales of magic, it would be perfectly proper to do so. In No. 20, "Flute of Joy, Flute of Sorrow," seven cows suckle and protect a boy. In No. 51, "The Princess of Seven Jasmines," a snake has a migraine and asks the hero to go in quest of a remedy. Obviously, the genre determines what is common sense and what is not. What is folly in one genre is magic in another. The willing suspension of disbelief is called forth by some genres and dispelled by others. In one, the same motif makes you laugh; in another, it thrills you. Genres specialize in certain aesthetic effects and emotions.

[AT 1643, The Broken Image + AT 1600, The Fool as Murderer.]

31. The Husband's Shadow

[AT 1419H, Woman Warns Lover of Husband by Singing Song.]

32. In the Kingdom of Foolishness

TYPES AND MOTIFS

Type AT 1534A, The Innocent Man Chosen to Fit the Stake (Noose). Reported twenty-one times so far only from India, this tale usually has three parts: 1) the holy man and his disciple; 2) the collapsed wall; 3) the man chosen to fit the stake. The second section is often told as a separate tale (AT 2031A). This popular tale, describing a topsy-turvy land, with its biting political satire and lethal ironies, has inspired plays in many Indian languages and given rise to proverbs like the following Urdu-Hindi one:

andher nagarī caupaṭ rājā
ṭake ser bhājī ṭake ser khājā

A city of misrule, a ruinous king:
a penny (for) a *ser* of vegetables,
   a penny (for) a *ser* of sweets.

(A *ser* is a measure.) In Kannada, the proverbial phrase *duddige pan-ceru*, "five measures (of anything) for a penny," derives from this story.

COMMENTS

The logic of this story, like the logic of many other num-skull tales and fooltowns, comments on values revered in the culture. Here the folktale takes on the well-known Hindu logic of ethical responsibility in theories of *karma* (action and consequence). One is reminded of stories like the one in the *Mahābhārata* ("Anusasana Parva") in which a snake bites an old woman's son to death. A hunter catches the serpent and wants to punish it, but the wise mother asks him not to put it to death, as that would not bring her son back to life. An argument ensues, at the end of which the snake speaks up: "O foolish hunter, I didn't bite this child out of anger or choice. I was sent by Death on this errand. If there is any sin in this, it is his." The hunter is not convinced. The serpent philosophizes: "The potter's wheel, rod, and other things are not independent causes for the pot. They are causes working in union. So one must doubt any simple relationship of cause and effect." And so on. Death then appears and argues, "O serpent, I was guided by Time to send you on this errand. I'm like a cloud tossed by the wind. All creatures in heaven and earth are influenced by time. Why do you blame me?" The hunter, still angry, shouts, "Then both you and the serpent are to blame. I shall kill you both." Then Time (*kāla*) arrives and says, "Neither the serpent nor Death is guilty, nor am I. We are only the immediate exciting causes of this death. O hunter, the past karma of this child is the true cause of this death. Neither the snake nor Death, neither you nor the mother, is the cause. The child's death is the result of its own karma." Bhishma, lying on his deathbed of arrows on the battlefield, tells this story to Yudhishtira, who is grief-stricken and guilt-ridden over his part in the deadly war. The present folktale uses the same logic (of passing the buck) and reduces it to absurdity—one more commentary on a classical position.

33. In Search of a Dream

TYPES AND MOTIFS

Type AT 550, Search for the Golden Bird, is known to the tellers of *The Thousand and One Nights* and is told in both the Middle East and Europe. It has been collected in many regions of India (twenty-seven known variants).

COMMENTS

In the present telling, a special emphasis is placed on the dream. The story is explicitly about a search for a dream—the quest is not for a magic bird or a princess (though we have them too) but to make a night's dream come true by day. So the usual dreamlike folktale motifs of transformation (princesses into tree, fruit, bird, and twig) are literally shown to be components of a dream. The king's dream, on the other hand, has shown him something real but not yet actual. The dreamer dreams of what's already real somewhere else, which is why it can be searched for and made present. Meanwhile two sets of sisters (the two old women and the five princesses) are reunited. The usual motifs of the dim-witted elder brother(s) betraying the younger and usurping the bride, quite common in other tellings of AT 550, are absent here because the emphasis is on making a dream actual, not on sibling rivalry.

The youngest brother naturally wins princesses and a kingdom, pursuing another dream, that is, a young man's dream. The old king's caprice turns out to be a test of his son's ability to make an impossible dream come true, a wise test for leadership. Such a tale begins in caprice and ends in wisdom. Beheading the princesses to transform them is a dramatic lesson: every dream has its price. Daring, an appropriate use of violence, and a trust in the ultimate return to normalcy are part of a hero's equipment.

[For a Santali telling of AT 550, see Ramanujan 1991a:181–186.]

34. King and Peasant

[NKTT, but cf. Motif P 411.1.1, Peasant and his wife in hut near castle as contrasts to king and queen.]

35. Kutlavva

TYPES AND MOTIFS

Type AT 1540, The Student from Paradise (or Paris), popular in Renaissance collections, an oral tale related from England to Indonesia. According to Antti Aarne, who studied 300 versions of it, European versions usually play on the words "Paris" and "paradise": a student says he is from Paris, and a bereaved wife hears it as Paradise. Then she sends money and gifts to her dead husband through the student from Paradise. Kaarle Krohn thought that the story (without the Paris/Paradise pun) originated in India (see Thompson 1946:169).

36. The Lampstand Woman

TYPES AND MOTIFS

Type AT 930, The Prophecy. In the Aarne-Thompson index, types 930–945 are tales of fate. Other tales of fate, prophecy, etc. in this collection are "Muddanna" (No. 41), "What the Milk Bird Said" (No. 73), "The Mother Who Married Her Own Son" (No. 40),

and "A Sage's Word" (No. 55). Mother Fate = *vidhiyamma*. Fate is
female in these folktales.

[NKTT, but cf. Motif M 302.2, Man's fate written on his skull; Motif H 11.1, Recognition by telling life history. See also AKR's comments
in Ramanujan 1991b.]

37.   The Magician and His Disciple

TYPES AND MOTIFS

Type AT 325, The Magician and his Pupil. Well-known
in many parts of India and also throughout Europe, this tale was used
as a test case in a nineteenth-century controversy over the Indian origin
of European folktales. Theodor Benfey, in the Prolegomena to his
Pantschatantra (1859), used it to illustrate the way in which tales from
India are taken over into Mongolian literature and through this inter-
mediary carried to Europe. Some fifty years later, his disciple, Emman-
uel Cosquin, used the same tale to dispute the Mongolian connection
and to confirm the Indian origin of the tales. "Among the most popular
of oral stories" in Europe (Thompson 1946:69), it is told in the six-
teenth century by Straparola, appears in collections of the Near East
and southern Siberia, and is told in the Dutch East Indies, the Philip-
pines, and North Africa, and was brought to Missouri by the French
and to Massachusetts by Portuguese-speaking Cape Verde Island Ne-
groes (see Thompson, ibid, for details). The plot is remarkably constant
in all these tellings. Minor variations occur in the Transformation Flight
(Motif D 671), in which the hero transforms himself into objects, animals, or other persons to deceive the pursuer. In some tellings, we have
an Obstacle Flight (D 672), in which the fleeing hero throws behind
him magic objects that become obstacles in the pursuer's path (e.g.,
comb becomes forest, pebble becomes hill).

COMMENTS

In India this tale of rivalry between an older and a
younger man throws light on Indian "Oedipal patterns." As I've written elsewhere, the Indian Oedipus-figure is pursued, exiled, or otherwise overwhelmed by the father-figure. Unlike the Greek (and European) Oedipus, he almost never kills his father, but submits to him. But
the overt rivalry between the generations is most often seen in guru/
disciple stories. Guru and disciple are traditionally equated with father

and son. The classic, and classical, case is that of Vasista and Visvamitra in the *Mahābhārata,* which also involves the Brahmin/Kshatriya rivalry and hierarchy (see Ramanujan 1983). It is characteristic, I think, of Indian folklore patterns that in this tale the disciple/son vanquishes and almost (but not quite) kills the guru/father. In the classical instances (e.g., Vasista and Visvamitra), the younger man never wins. In the folk-tale, he does win, but the rivalry stops short of parricide (guru-cide). In European tellings, the disciple (as cat, etc.) bites off the head of his master (as a rooster). The above is a simplified discussion of a complex issue.

The motif D 622.1, animal by day, man by night, in which a woman or a man takes into her/his bedroom a bird in a cage or an animal that turns into a human being at night, is a common motif. See Tale No. 71, "The Turtle Prince."

38. A Minister's Word

[NKTT, but cf. Motif C 495.2.2.1, "Yes"—"No"—"Very Well" (IO). For another telling of this tale, see Narayan 1989:22–25.]

39. Monkey Business

[AT 2037A*, Series of Trick Exchanges: razor-pot-bride-drum by tricky fox (IO).]

40. The Mother Who Married Her Own Son

[AT 931, Oedipus. See also Ramanujan 1983.]

41. Muddanna

[AT 160, Grateful Animals, Ungrateful Man. Cf. Bødker, type 1120.]

42. Nagarani ("Serpent Queen")

[NKTT, but cf. Motif S 215, Child promised to animal; Motif Q 266, Punishment for breaking promise; Motif D 191, Transformation: man to serpent (snake); and Motif D 1076, Magic Ring.]

43. A Ne'er-do-well

[AT 1000, Bargain Not to Become Angry.]

44. Ninga on My Palm

[NKTT, but cf. Motif P 262.1, Bad relations between mother-in-law and daughter-in-law; and Motif S 54, Cruel daughter-in-law.]

45. Ogress Queen

[AT 462, The Outcast Queens and the Ogress Queen (IO). See Ramanujan 1991a: 73–79 for a Kashmiri version of this tale.]

46. An Old Couple

[NKTT, but cf. Motif C 110, Tabu: sexual intercourse; and Motif P 15.1.1, Disguised king taught courtesy by peasant.]

47. The Past Never Passes

[NKTT, but cf. Motif D 551, Transformation by eating.]

48. A Peg and a Keg

[AT 1545B, The Boy Who Knew Nothing of Women.]

49. The Pomegranate Queen

[AT 780A, The Cannibalistic Brothers (IO).]

50. A Poor Man

[NKTT. Cf. Motif K 233, Trickster escapes without paying.]

51. The Princess of Seven Jasmines

[AT 554, The Grateful Animals.]

52. The Prince Who Married His Own Left Half

[NKTT, but cf. Motif F 525.2, Man splits in two parts; Motif H 607.3, Princess declares her love through sign language; not understood; Motif H 611.2, Sign message sent by girl to enamored prince: interpreted by prince's friend; and Motif H 541.1, Riddle propounded on pain of death. See also AKR's comments in Ramanujan 1991a.]

53. The Rain King's Wife

[NKTT, but cf. Motif D 2143.1.0.1, Rain caused to fall in certain place by rain god (IO); and Motif K 2222, Treacherous co-wife.]

54. Rich Man, Poor Man

[AT 1535, The Rich and the Poor Peasant; AT 1653, The Robbers under the Tree.]

55. A Sage's Word

[AT 930A, The Predestined Wife.]

56. The Serpent Lover

[AT 433C, The Serpent Husband and the Jealous Girl (IO). See also AKR's comments in Ramanujan 1991b.]

57. A Shepherd's Pilgrimage

[AT 670, The Animal Languages.]

58. Sister Crow and Sister Sparrow

[AT 123, The Wolf and the Kids.]

59. Siva Plays Double

[AT 757, The King's Haughtiness Punished.]

60. The Sparrow Who Wouldn't Die

[AT 2041, The Bird Indifferent to Pain.]

61.   A Sparrow With a Single Pea

[NKTT, but possibly a fragmentary or abridged version of AT 2034D, Bird's Pea gets stuck in socket of Mill-handle (IO).]

62.   Tales for a Princess

[AT 945, Luck and Intelligence.]

63.   The Talking Bed

[AT 622, The Talking Bed-Legs (IO).]

64.   A Thief, a Ram, a Bear, and a Horse

[AT 1539, Cleverness and Gullibility.]

65.   Three Blouses

[Motif K 1545, Wives wager as to who can best fool her husband; and AT 1423, The Enchanted Pear Tree.]

66.   Three Magic Objects

[AT 566, The Magic Objects and the Wonderful Fruits.]

67.   Three Sisters Named Death, Birth, and Dream

[NKTT, but cf. Motif B 102.4, Golden Fish; Motif C 611, Forbidden Chamber, or Motif C 611.1, Forbidden Door; and Motif C 952, Immediate return to other world because of broken tabu.]

68.   The Three-Thousand-Rupee Sari

[NKTT, but cf. Motif C 735.2.5, Tabu: sleeping in cemetery; Motif H 1355.2, Quest for beautiful saree for the queen; and Motif T 249.1, Adulterous wife convicted, commits suicide.]

69.   Thug and Master-Thug

[NKTT, but cf. AT 1525, The Master Thief.]

70. Tree Trunk for a Boat

[NKTT, but cf. Motif F 841.1.11, Boat made of tree trunk; and Motif D 1067.2, Magic cap.]

71. The Turtle Prince

[Cf. AT 433B, King Lindorm; AT 465A, The Quest for the Unknown; and AT 569, The Knapsack, the Hat, and the Horn. For a study of this tale, see Blackburn 1995.]

72. A Wager

[Cf. AT 870, The Princess Confined in the Mound; and AT 1525G, The Thief Assumes Disguises.]

73. What the Milk Bird Said

[NKTT, but cf. Motif S 215, Child promised to animal; Motif B 604.1, Marriage to snake; R 111.1.5, Rescue of woman from snake-husband; and I 412, Mother-son incest.]

74. Who Is the Greatest?

[NKTT, but cf. Motif Z 33.4.1, Louse and Crow make covenant of friendship (IO).]

75. Why the Sky Went Up

[NKTT, but cf. L 351.1, Sun is cursed by man for its burning rays (IO); and A 625.2.2, Why the sky receded upward (it was struck by a woman's pestle) (IO).]

76. The Worship of a Household God

[NKTT, but cf. Motif J 1744, Ignorance of marriage relations; and K 1315.7, Seduction by posing as teacher or instructor.]

77. A Story to End All Stories

[AT 2301A, Making the King Lose Patience.]

Glossary

[Note: Kinship terms may refer to any person of the appropriate gender and age.]

akka	older sister/woman
amma	mother
anna	(older) brother
appa	father
arre	"What!" "Hey!"
atta	attic
avva	mother, woman (respectful)
ayyo	a cry of distress, pain, surprise, anxiety, etc.
badmash	used to scold men or boys (borrowed from Hindi/Urdu)
bava	holy man
bhappare	can mean either "Well done!" or "Terrible!"
Brahma	Hindu god, especially of creation
burning ghat	cremation ground on a riverbank
che, che	expression of rejection or disapproval (cf. "No, no" or "tsk, tsk")
dasayya	wandering holy man
dhoti	man's sarong-like lower garment
duddu	generic term for money, coins
garuda	bird, upon which the god Visnu rides
gosavi	wandering holy man
gowda	village headman (+ re = honorific)
Idiga:	low caste, toddy-tappers
Indra	king of the gods, god of rain and clouds

Kashi	holy city of Benares
Kshatriya	warrior caste
lakh	100,000
Lakshmana	epic hero, brother of Rama
Lakshmi	goddess of wealth, wife of Visnu
naga	snake
ninga	a variant of *linga*, the phallic image of Siva
palla	unit of measurement
Parvati	goddess, wife of Siva
pativrata	a faithful wife
punya	religious merit
ragi	a kind of grain
rakshasa	malevolent being, enemy of good, "demon"
Rama	epic hero
rangoli	geometric designs made on the ground with powder; part of a woman's housekeeping
rishi	a sage, holy man
sadhu	wandering holy man
samsara	cycle of birth and death; worldly life
sanyasi	wandering holy man
saukar	rich man
Savitri	mythological exemplar of the devoted wife
Siva	Hindu god
swami	holy man, god, master
tapas	religious austerities
vina	musical instrument
yojana	unit of measurement (cf. league)

Bibliography

Beck, B. E. F.
  1986.   Social dyads in Indic folktales. In Stuart Blackburn and
           A. K.Ramanujan, eds., *Another Harmony: New Essays on the
           Folklore of India,* pp. 76–102. Berkeley: University of California
           Press.
Beck, B. E. F., et al., eds.
  1987.   *Folktales of India.* Chicago: University of Chicago Press.
Benfey, Theodor.
  1859.   *Pantschatantra Fünf Bücher indischer Fabeln, Märchen und
           Erzählungen.* 2 vols. Leipzig: F. A. Brockhaus.
Beschi, Fr. C. G.
  1822.   *Paramārtta Kuruviṇ Katai: The Adventures of the Gooroo
           Paramartan.* Trans. Benjamin Guy Babington. London: J. M.
           Richardson.
Blackburn, Stuart.
  1995.   Coming out of his shell: Animal-husband tales from India. In
           David Shulman, ed., *Syllables of Sky: Studies in South Indian
           Civilization,* pp. 43–75. New Delhi: Oxford University Press.
Blackburn, Stuart, and A. K. Ramanujan, eds.
  1986.   *Another Harmony: New Essays on the Folklore of India.* Berkeley:
           University of California Press.
Bottigheimer, Ruth B.
  1987.   *Grimms' Bad Girls and Bold Boys: The Moral and Social Vision of
           the Tales.* New Haven: Yale University Press.
Brown, Judith R.
  1986.   *Immodest Acts: The Life of a Lesbian Nun in Renaissance Italy.*
           New York: Oxford University Press.
Brown, William Norman.
  1919.   The *Pañcatantra* in modern Indian folklore. *Journal of the
           American Oriental Society* 39:1–54.

Brown, William Norman.
    1922.   The silence wager stories: Their origin and their diffusion.
             American Journal of Philology 43:289–317.
Clouston, William Alexander.
    1887.   *Popular Tales and Fictions: Their Migrations and
             Transformations.* 2 vols. Edinburgh: Blackwood.
Dorson, Richard M.
    1986.   *The British Folklorists: A History.* Chicago: University of Chicago
             Press.
Goswami, Praphulladatta.
    1960.   *Ballads and Tales of Assam: A Story of the Folklore of Assam.*
             Gauhati (India): Department of Publication.
Islam, Mazharul.
    1982.   *A History of Folktale Collections in India, Bangladesh and
             Pakistan.* rev. ed. Calcutta: Panchali Prakasan.
Kakar, Sudhir.
    1989.   *Intimate Relations: Exploring Indian Sexuality.* New Delhi:
             Viking.
Kirkland, Edwin Capers.
    1966.   *A Bibliography of South Asian Folklore.* Indiana University
             Publications, Folklore Series no. 21. Bloomington: Indiana
             University Press.
Narayan, Kirin.
    1989.   *Storytellers, Saints and Scoundrels: Folk Narrative in Hindu
             Religious Teaching.* Philadelphia: University of Pennsylvania
             Press.
Ramanujan, A. K.
    1956a.   The clay mother-in-law. *Southern Folklore Quarterly* 20:130–135.

    ———.
    1956b.   Some folktales from India. *Southern Folklore Quarterly* 20:154–
             163.

    ———.
    1973.   *Speaking of Siva.* Harmondsworth, UK: Penguin.

    ———.
    1982a.   Hanchi: A Kannada Cinderella. In *Cinderella: A Folklore
             Casebook,* ed. Alan Dundes, pp. 259–275. New York: Garland.

    ———.
    1982b.   On women saints. In John Stratton Hawley and Donna Marie
             Wulff, eds. *The Divine Consort: Rādhā and the Goddesses of India,*
             pp. 316–324. Berkeley: Graduate Theological Union.

    ———.
    1983.   The Indian Oedipus. In *Oedipus: A Folklore Casebook,* ed. Lowell
             Edmunds and Alan Dundes, pp. 234–262. New York: Garland.

    ———.
    1985.   *Poems of Love and War.* New York: Columbia University Press.

    ———.
    1987.   Foreword. In B. E. F. Beck et al., eds., *Folktales of India.*
             Chicago: University of Chicago Press.

————.
1989.   Telling tales. *Daedalus* 118.4:239–261.

————.
1990.   *Who Needs Folklore? The Relevance of Oral Traditions to South Asian Studies.* South Asia Occasional Paper Series no. 1. Honolulu: University of Hawaii, Center for South Asia Studies.

————.
1991a.   *Folktales from India: A Selection of Oral Tales from Twenty-Two Languages.* New York: Pantheon.

————.
1991b.   Toward a counter-system: Women's tales. In *Gender, Genre, and Power in South Asian Expressive Systems,* ed. A. Appadurai, F. Korom, and M. Mills, pp. 33–55. Philadelphia: University of Pennsylvania Press.

————.
1993.   On folk mythologies and folk puranas. In Wendy Doniger, ed., *Purāṇa Perennis: Reciprocity and Transformation in Hindu and Jaina Texts,* pp. 101–120. Albany: State University of New York Press.

————.
Forthcoming. *A. K. Ramanujan: Collected Essays,* ed. Vinay Dwarwadker. New Delhi: Oxford University Press.

Sandhya Reddy, K. R.
1992.   Folktales. In Krishnamurthy Hanur, ed., *Encyclopaedia of the Folk Culture of Karnataka, Vol I: Introductory Articles,* pp. 255–263. Madras: Institute of Asian Studies.

Shulman, David.
1985.   *King and Clown in South Indian Myth and Poetry.* Princeton, N.J.: Princeton University Press.

Thompson, Stith.
1946.   *The Folktale.* New York: The Dryden Press.

Thorne, Barrie, C. Kramarae, and N. Henley, eds.
1983.   *Language, Gender, and Society.* Rowley, Mass.: Newbury House.

Troger, Ralph.
1966.   *A Comparative Study of a Bengali Folktale: Underworld Helpers. An Analysis of the Bengali Folktale Type: The Pursuit of Cotton, A-T 480.* Translated from the German by Herman Mode. Calcutta: Indian Publications.

Wolfenstein, Martha.
1954.   *Children's Humor: A Psychological Analysis.* Glencoe, Ill.: Free Press.

List of Tellers and Collectors

[Note: When known or inferred from the name, the gender of the teller has been indicated as m. or f. —Eds.]

Title	Teller	Collector
1. A Story and a Song	No data	Simpi Linganna. *Uttara Karnātakada Janapada Kathegaḷu*, 1972. New Delhi: Sahitya Akademi
2. Acacia Trees	Siddalingamma, f., 45, Viraśaiva caste; Krishnarajanagar, 1972	K. Y. Sivakumar 1972:37–40
3. The Adventures of a Obedient Prince	Kurubagatti; Kittur, 1956	B. T. Patil
4. Bride for a Dead Man	Chennavva Marihala, f.; Shahapur, 1968	A. K. R.
5. A Brother, a Sister, and a Snake	Chennavva Marihala, f.; Shahapur, 1968	A. K. R.
6. A Buffalo Without Bones	Chitradurga district (?)	Krishnamurthy Ms.
7. Cannibal Sister	No data	No data
8. Chain Tale	Shankara Mungarawadi, m.; Gokak, 1968	A. K. R.

263

Title	Teller	Collector
9. Another Chain Tale: What an Ant Can Do	No data	No data
10. The Clever Daughter-in-law	No data	H. J. Lakkappa Gowda. *Janapada Kathavali,* 1971. Bangalore: Karnataka Co-Op Publishing
11. A Couple of Misers	No data	Kambar Ms.
12. The Dead Prince and the Talking Doll	No data	No data
13. A Dog's Daughters	No data	No data
14. A Dog's Story	Uliveppa, m., 32, Domba caste; Dharwar	Kambar Ms.
15. Dolls	Ragau, *Karnataka Janapada Kathegalu;* Mysore, 1969	A. K. R. (?)
16. Double Double	No data	No data
17. Dumma and Dummi	Belgaum, 1956	Kurbetti Ms.
18. Dwarfs	Belgaum, 1956 (?)	Kurbetti Ms.
19. A Flowering Tree	Siddamma, f.; Tumkur	Dhavalasri, in *Janapada Kathamrta,* vol. 3 (1968), pp. 32–42
20. Flute of Joy, Flute of Sorrow	M. B. Kurbetti; Belgaum, 1956	Kurbetti Ms.
21. Fools	Belgaum Ms.	A. K. R. (?)
22. A Jackal King	No data	No data
23. For Love of Kadabu	Primary school teachers; Belgaum, 1956	A. K. R. (?)
24. A Girl in a Picture	Shankara Mangarawadi, m.; Gokak (Kambar Ms.), 1968	A. K. R.
25. The Glass Pillar	No data	A. K. R. (?)
26. A Golden Sparrow	Sushilabai G. Kulkarni, f.; Dharwar	A. K. R.; Kambar Ms.

Title	Teller	Collector
27. The Greatest Thing	No data	A. K. R.; Kurbetti Ms.
28. Hanchi	Chennamma, f., 65, Viraśaiva caste; Kittur, 1955	A. K. R.
29. The Horse Gram Man	No data	No data
30. Hucca	Ellappa Kambara, m.; Ghodageri, 1968	A. K. R.; Kambar Ms.
31. The Husband's Shadow	No data	No data
32. In the Kingdom of Foolishness	No data	No data
33. In Search of a Dream	No data	A. K. R.; Kambar Ms.
34. King and Peasant	No data	No data
35. Kutlavva	No data	A. K. R.; Kambar Ms.
36. The Lampstand Woman	No data	D. Lingayya. *Padineḷalu*, 1971, pp. 16–20. Sidlaghatta: Kannada Kala Sangha
37. The Magician and His Disciple	Arera Balappa, m.; Akkatangerahala, 1968	A. K. R.; Kambar Ms.
38. A Minister's Word	S. Shankar Nagarshetti, m.; Kittur, 1955	A. K. R. (?)
39. Monkey Business	S. T. Desai; Dharwar	A. K. R.; Kambar Ms.
40. The Mother Who Married Her Own Son	No data	No data
41. Muddanna	No data	A. K. R.; Krishnamurthy Ms.
42. Nagarani ("Serpent Queen")	No data	No data
43. A Ne'er-do-well	No data	A. K. R.; Kambar Ms.
44. Ninga on My Palm	No data	No data

Title	*Teller*	*Collector*
45. Ogress Queen	Smt. Gowravva, f.; Dharwar, 1968	A. K. R.; Kambar Ms.
46. An Old Couple	No data	No data
47. The Past Never Passes	No data	No data
48. A Peg and a Keg	No data	No data
49. The Pomegranate Queen	No data	No data
50. A Poor Man	Basavani Kabadigi, 38, Lingayat caste; Sivapura	A. K. R.; Kambar Ms.
51. The Princess of Seven Jasmines	No data	A. K. R.; Kambar Ms.
52. The Prince who Married His Own Left Half	Ellappa Kambara, m.; Ghodageri	Taped by C. Kambar
53. The Rain King's Wife	Ms. Shanta, f.; Dharwar, 1968	A. K. R.; Kambar Ms.
54. Rich Man, Poor Man	No data	A. K. R.; Belgaum Ms.
55. A Sage's Word	Chennappa Walikara, m.; Raichur, 1968	A. K. R.; Kambar Ms.
56. The Serpent Lover	Mrs. Bagavva Sidramappa, f.; Badigera Akkatangerahala	A. K. R. (?)
57. A Shepherd's Pilgrimage	No data	No data
58. Sister Crow and Sister Sparrow	No data	No data
59. Siva Plays Double	Chennanna Walikara, m.; Raichur	A. K. R.; Kambar Ms.
60. The Sparrow Who Wouldn't Die	No data	A. K. R. (?); Kurbetti Ms.
61. A Sparrow With a Single Pea	No data	No data
62. Tales for a Princess	R. S. Naik, m., from his grandmother in Kumta, 1956	Naik or AKR?

Title	Teller	Collector
63. The Talking Bed	No data	C. Murthy's Ms.
64. A Thief, a Ram, a Bear, and a Horse	Ms. Sushilabai Kulkarni, f.; Dharwar	A. K. R.; Kambar Ms.
65. Three Blouses	No data	No data
66. Three Magic Objects	No data	A. K. R.; Belgaum Ms.
67. Three Sisters Named Death, Birth, and Dream	No data	A. K. R.; Kambar Ms.
68. The Three-Thousand-Rupee Sari	Chennavva Maryala, f.; Shapura, 1963	A. K. R.
69. Thug and Master-Thug	No data	A. K. R.; Kambar Ms.
70. Tree Trunk for a Boat	No data	No data
71. The Turtle Prince	No data	A. K. R.; Kambar Ms.
72. A Wager	No data	A. K. R.; Krishnamurthy Ms.
73. What the Milk Bird Said	Smt. Bhagirathi Sidramappa, f.; Badigera Akkatangerahala	A. K. R. (?)
74. Who Is the Greatest?	Sivajirao, m., 55, Budubudike caste	K. Narayana, C. I. I. L.
75. Why the Sky Went Up	No data	A. K. R.; Belgaum Ms.
76. The Worship of a Household God	No data	No data
77. A Story to End All Stories	Lakkajji, 60, Viraśaiva caste; Nelhsara, Shivamogga Dt.	B. Nelhsara, in *Dakṣina Karnatakada Janapada Kathegaḷu*, 1979, p. 246. New Delhi: Sahitya Akademi

List of Tale Types

[Note: Tale type numbers refer to the standard index: Antti Aarne and Stith Thompson, *The Types of the Folktale: A Classification and Bibliography*, 2nd Revision, FF Communications No. 184 (Helsinki: Academia Scientiarum Fennica, 1961). The list is designed to assist comparative folklorists who may wish to discover whether this volume does or does not contain a version of a particular folktale being investigated. IO is our abbreviation for India Only, meaning that the tale in question is reported only in India. For a fuller discussion of the tale type identification numbers on this list, see the "Notes on the Tales" section. —Eds.]

AT 123	tale 58
AT 160	tale 41
AT 303	tale 14
AT 315A	tale 7
AT 325	tale 37
AT 413 + AT 465 + AT 554	tale 3
AT 433B (?)	tale 71
AT 433C	tale 56
AT 437 + AT 870	tale 12
AT 450A	tale 5
AT 462 (IO)	tale 45
AT 467 (IO)	tale 19
AT 510B	tale 28

Text:	Maple-Vail Manufacturing Group
Display:	Maple-Vail Manufacturing Group
Composition:	10/13 Galliard
Printing and binding:	Galliard